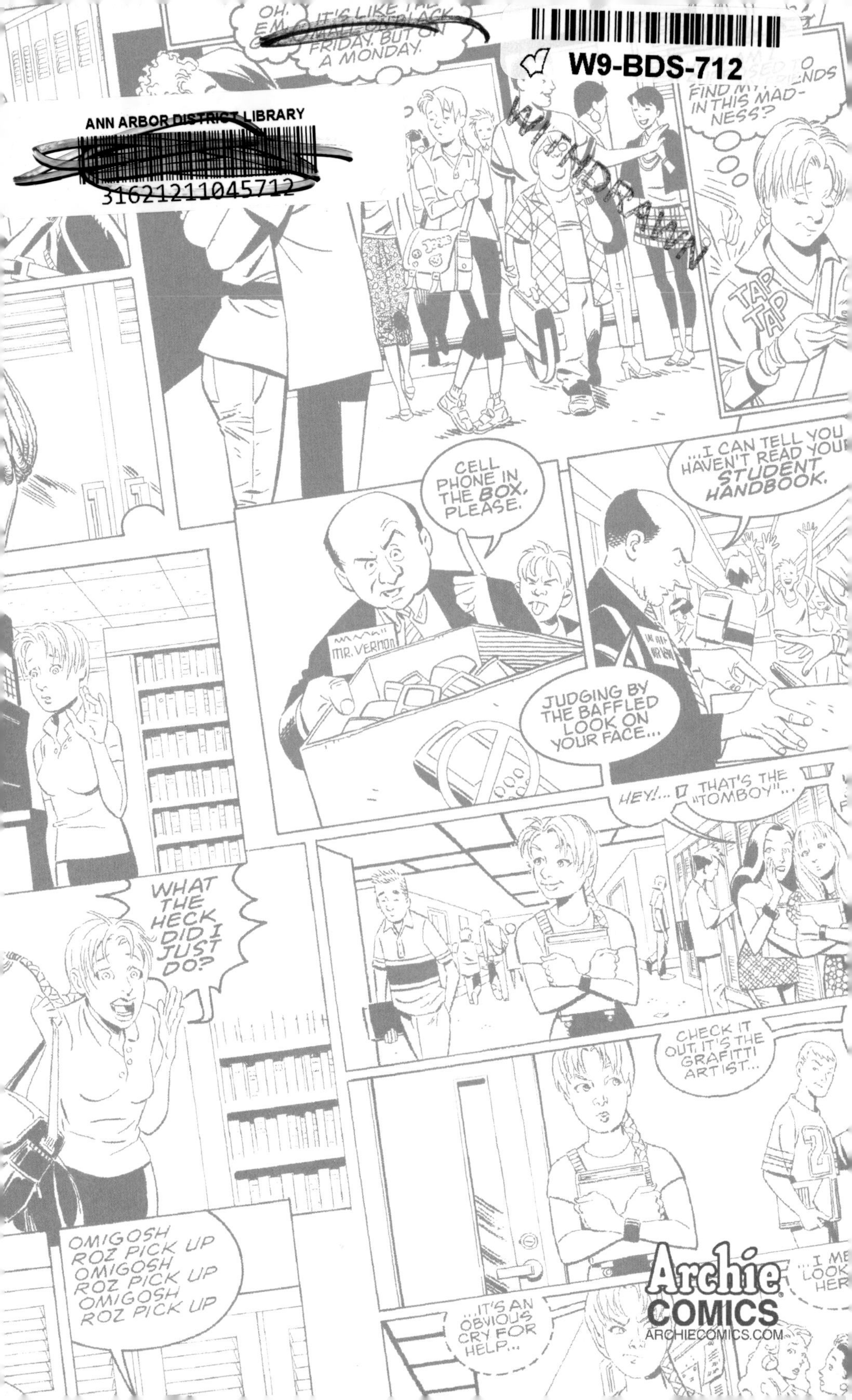
FRIDAY, BUT ON A MONDAY.
IN THIS MAD- NESS?
TAP TAP
CELL PHONE IN THE BOX, PLEASE.
MR. VERNON
...I CAN TELL YOU HAVEN'T READ YOUR STUDENT HANDBOOK.
JUDGING BY THE BAFFLED LOOK ON YOUR FACE...
HEY!... THAT'S THE "TOMBOY"...
WHAT THE HECK DID I JUST DO?
CHECK IT OUT, IT'S THE GRAFITTI ARTIST...
OMIGOSH ROZ PICK UP OMIGOSH ROZ PICK UP OMIGOSH ROZ PICK UP
...IT'S AN OBVIOUS CRY FOR HELP...
Archie COMICS
ARCHIECOMICS.COM

ARCHIE® COMICS PRESENTS

JINX ™

Jinx.
Published by Archie Comics Publications, Inc.
325 Fayette Ave, Mamaroneck, NY
10543-2318 Copyright © 2012
by Archie Comics Publications, Inc.

everything
changes in
high school!♥

LITTLE JINX GROWS UP

Written by J. Torres

Pencils by Rick Burchett

Inks by Terry Austin

Colors by Mark McNabb

Additional Colors by Jason Jensen

Letters by John Workman

Publisher/Co-CEO Jon Goldwater
Co-CEO Nancy Silberkleit
President Mike Pellerito

Co-President/Editor-in-Chief Victor Gorelick
Director of Circulation Bill Horan
Executive Director of Publishing & Operations Harold Buchholz
Executive Director of Publicity & Marketing Alex Segura
Edited and Designed by Suzannah Rowntree
Production Manager Stephen Oswald
Editorial Assistant Duncan McLachlan
Proofreader Jamie Lee Rotante

Torres, J., Jinx. Little Jinx grows up / written by J. Torres ; pencils by Rick Burchett ; inks by Terry Austin ; colors by Mark McNabb ; letters by John Workman
p. : chiefly col. ill. ; cm.
Summary: For most of her life Li'l Jinx has been a bit of a tomboy and life was easy to understand. Now that she's in high school, a 'more mature' Jinx Holliday is discovering that growing up is a lot more complicated. Jinx deals with the stuff that we all encounter when we reach high school.
Interest age group: 010-014.
ISBN: 978-1-936975-00-6 (hard cover) ISBN: 978-1-879794-91-7 (trade paper)
1. High school girls--United States--Comic books, strips, etc. 2. High school girls--United States--Conduct of life--Comic books, strips, etc. 3. Teenage girls--United States--Comic books, strips, etc. 4. Graphic novels. 5. Young adult fiction, American.
I. Burchett, Rick II. Austin, Terry III. McNabb, Mark IV. Workman, John V. Title. VI. Title: Li'l Jinx grows up VII. Title: Little Jinx grows up VIII. Title: Archie comics presents Jinx
PN6727.T67 J56 2012   813/.6 [Fic]

CONTENTS

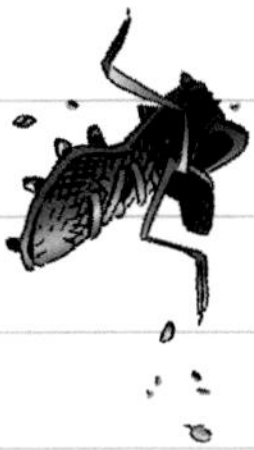

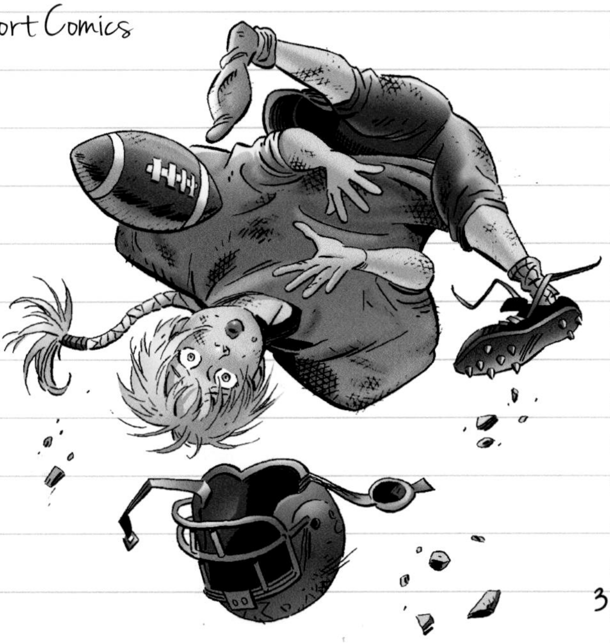

cast of jinx

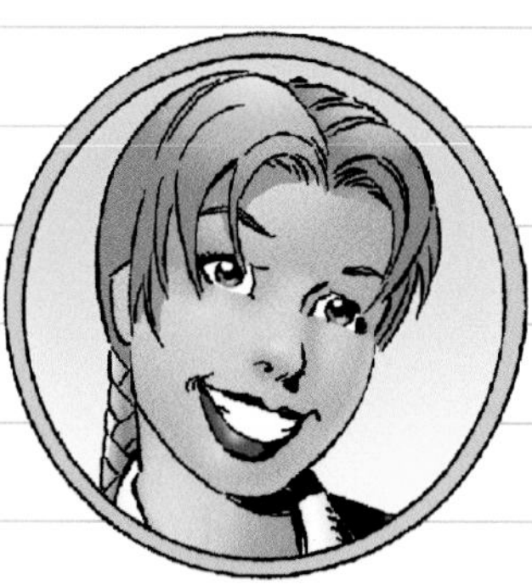

JINX
your hero

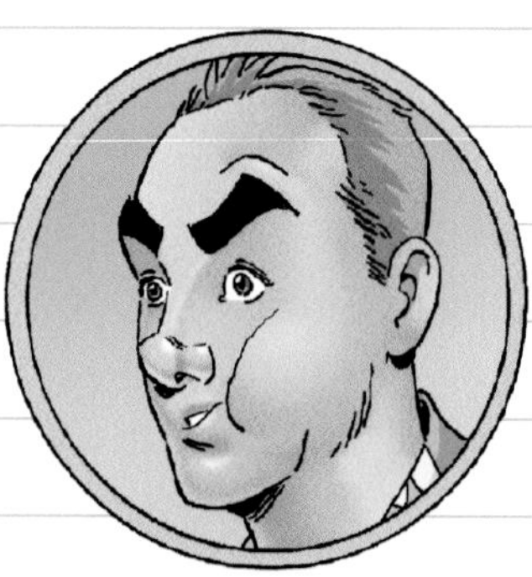

HAP
her father

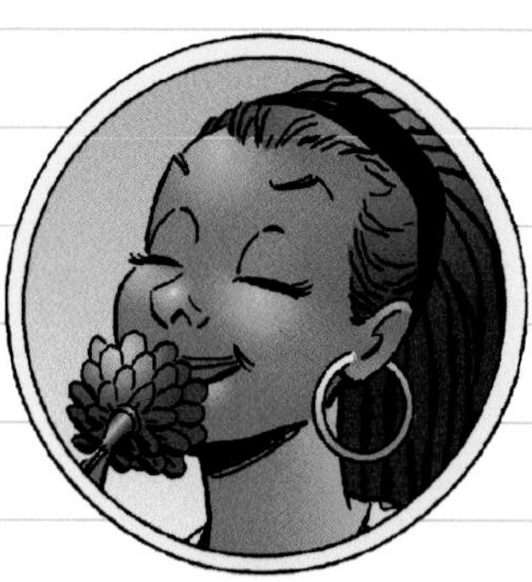

ROZ
friend, optimist

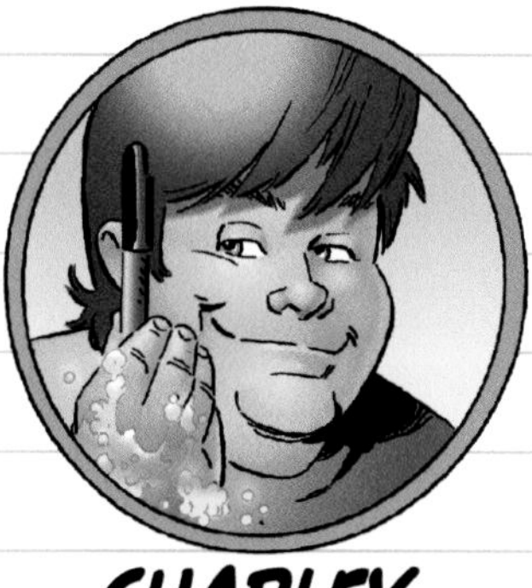

CHARLEY
frenemy, rival

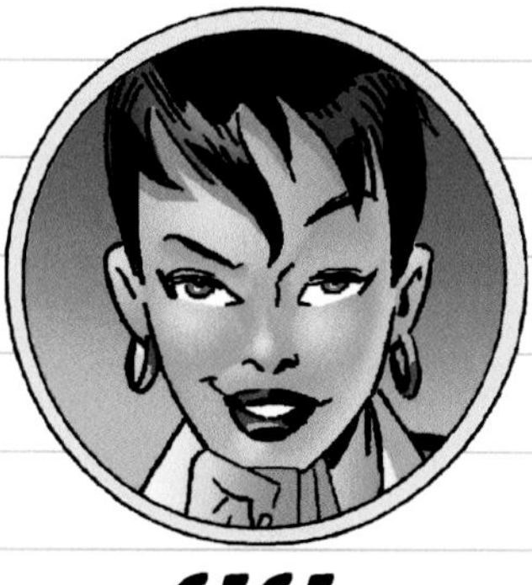

GIGI
frenemy, glam queen

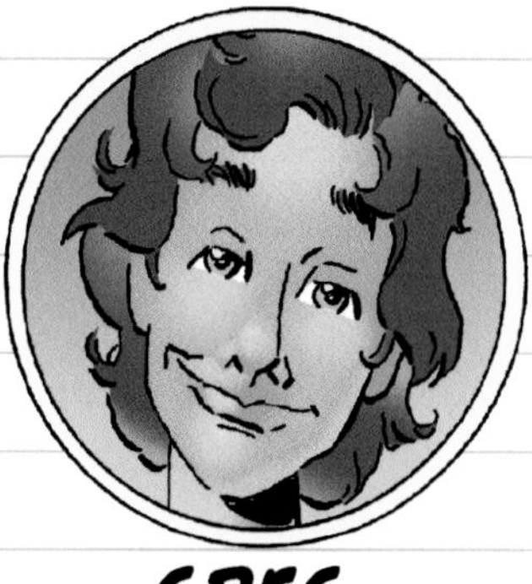

GREG
friend, skater

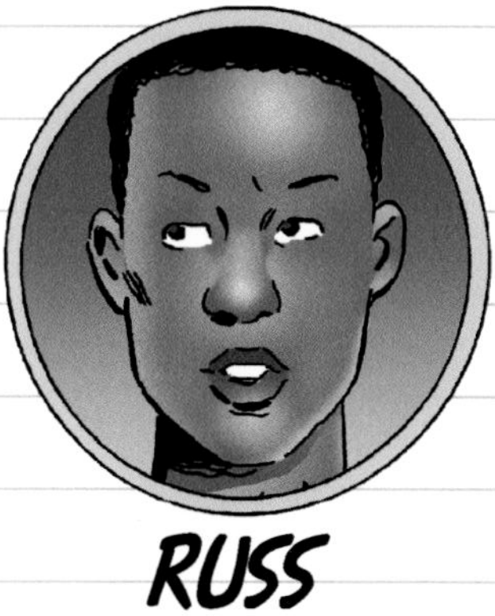

RUSS
friend, jock

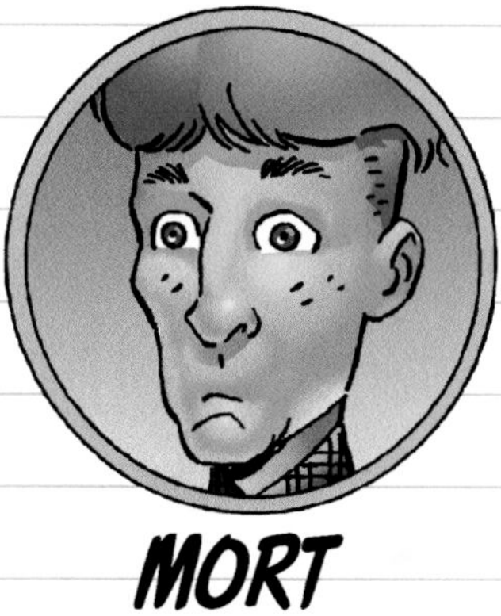

MORT
friend, pessimist

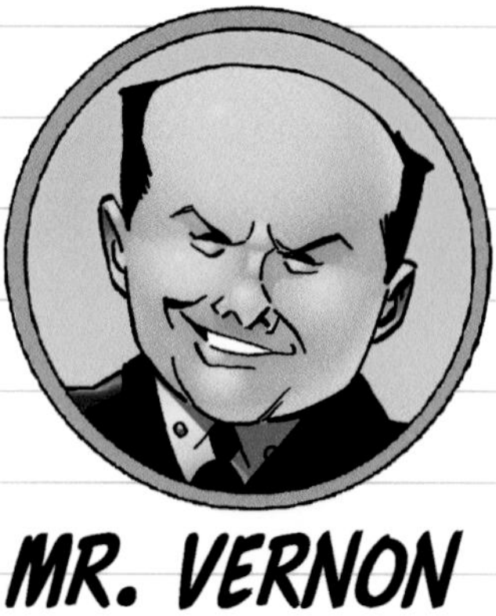

MR. VERNON
h.s. principal

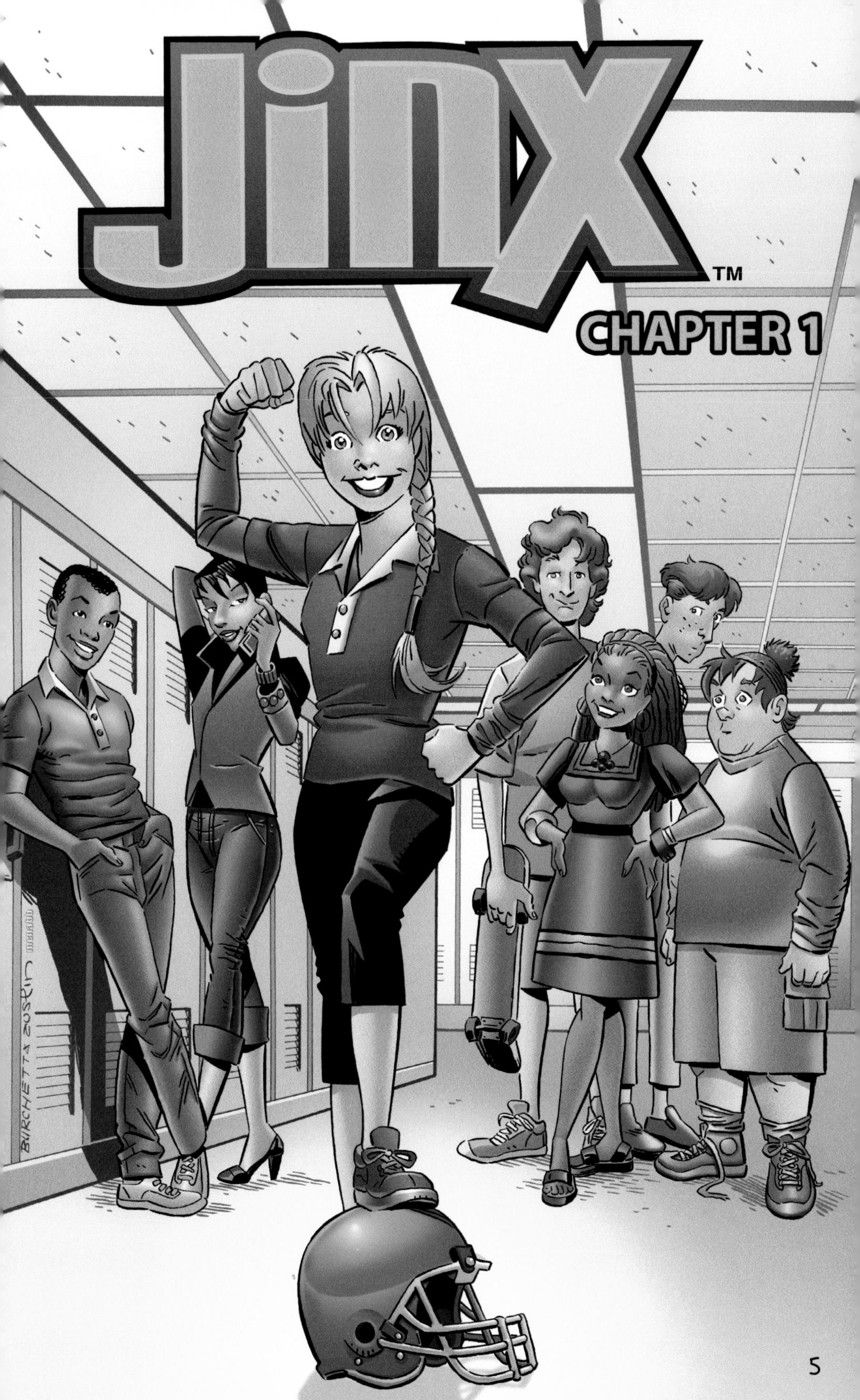
JiNX™
CHAPTER 1

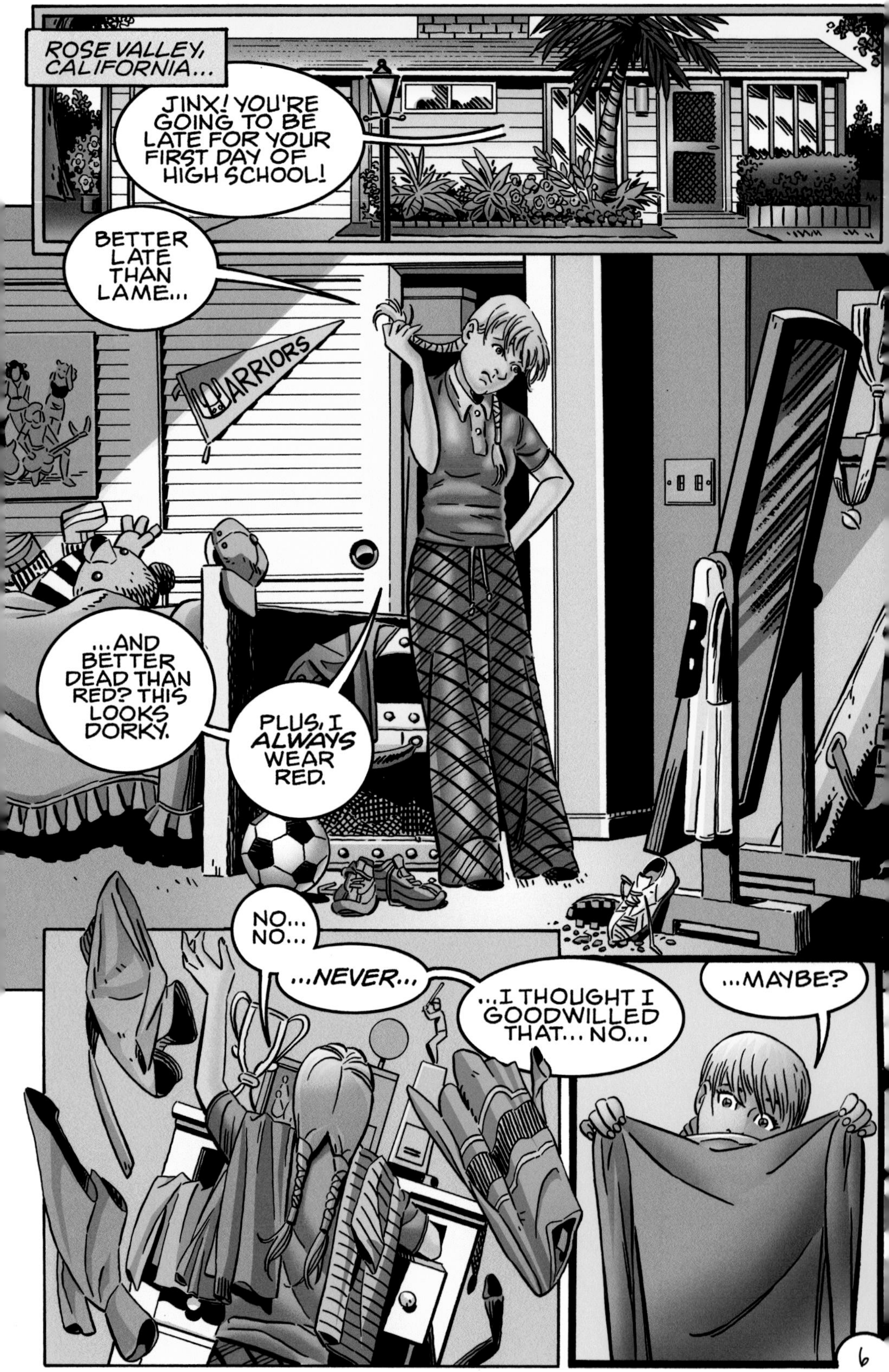
ROSE VALLEY, CALIFORNIA...
JINX! YOU'RE GOING TO BE LATE FOR YOUR FIRST DAY OF HIGH SCHOOL!
BETTER LATE THAN LAME...
WARRIORS
...AND BETTER DEAD THAN RED? THIS LOOKS DORKY.
PLUS, I ALWAYS WEAR RED.
NO... NO...
...NEVER...
...I THOUGHT I GOODWILLED THAT... NO...
...MAYBE?

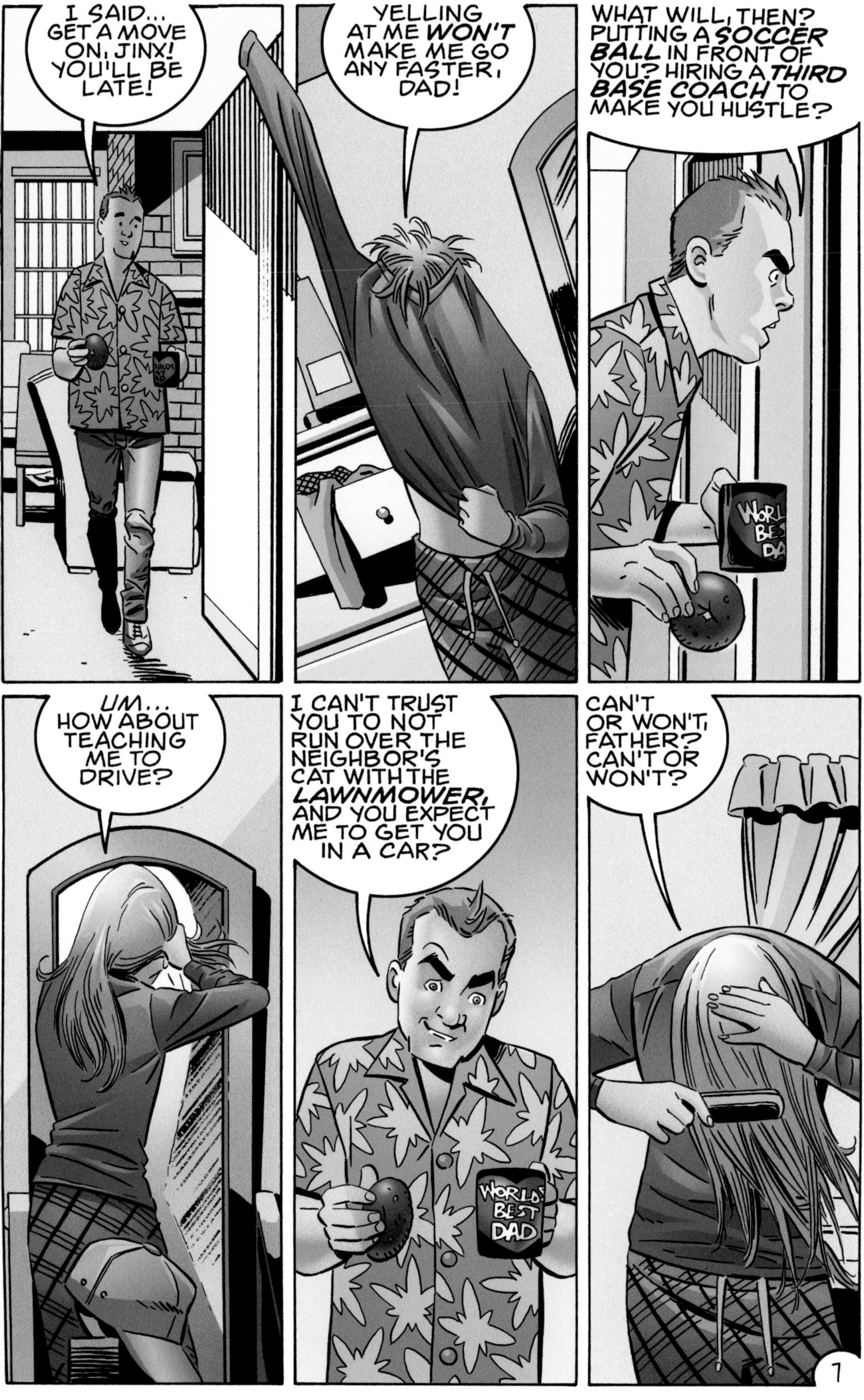
I SAID... GET A MOVE ON, JINX! YOU'LL BE LATE!
YELLING AT ME WON'T MAKE ME GO ANY FASTER, DAD!
WHAT WILL, THEN? PUTTING A SOCCER BALL IN FRONT OF YOU? HIRING A THIRD BASE COACH TO MAKE YOU HUSTLE?
WORLD'S BEST DAD
UM... HOW ABOUT TEACHING ME TO DRIVE?
I CAN'T TRUST YOU TO NOT RUN OVER THE NEIGHBOR'S CAT WITH THE LAWNMOWER, AND YOU EXPECT ME TO GET YOU IN A CAR?
WORLD'S BEST DAD
CAN'T OR WON'T, FATHER? CAN'T OR WON'T?

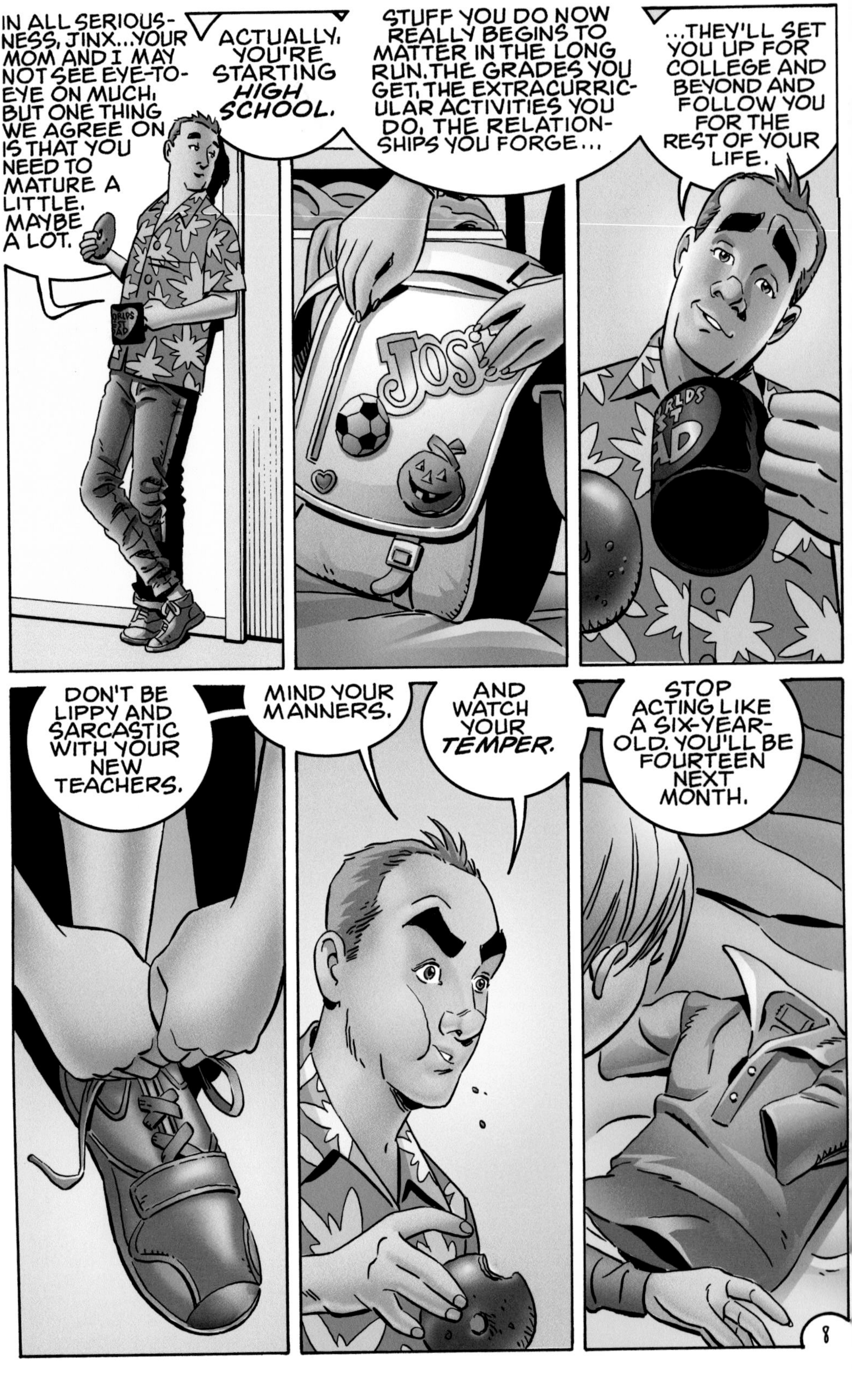
IN ALL SERIOUSNESS, JINX...YOUR MOM AND I MAY NOT SEE EYE-TO-EYE ON MUCH, BUT ONE THING WE AGREE ON IS THAT YOU NEED TO MATURE A LITTLE. MAYBE A LOT.
ACTUALLY, YOU'RE STARTING HIGH SCHOOL.
STUFF YOU DO NOW REALLY BEGINS TO MATTER IN THE LONG RUN. THE GRADES YOU GET, THE EXTRACURRICULAR ACTIVITIES YOU DO, THE RELATIONSHIPS YOU FORGE...
...THEY'LL SET YOU UP FOR COLLEGE AND BEYOND AND FOLLOW YOU FOR THE REST OF YOUR LIFE.
JOS
DON'T BE LIPPY AND SARCASTIC WITH YOUR NEW TEACHERS.
MIND YOUR MANNERS.
AND WATCH YOUR TEMPER.
STOP ACTING LIKE A SIX-YEAR-OLD. YOU'LL BE FOURTEEN NEXT MONTH.

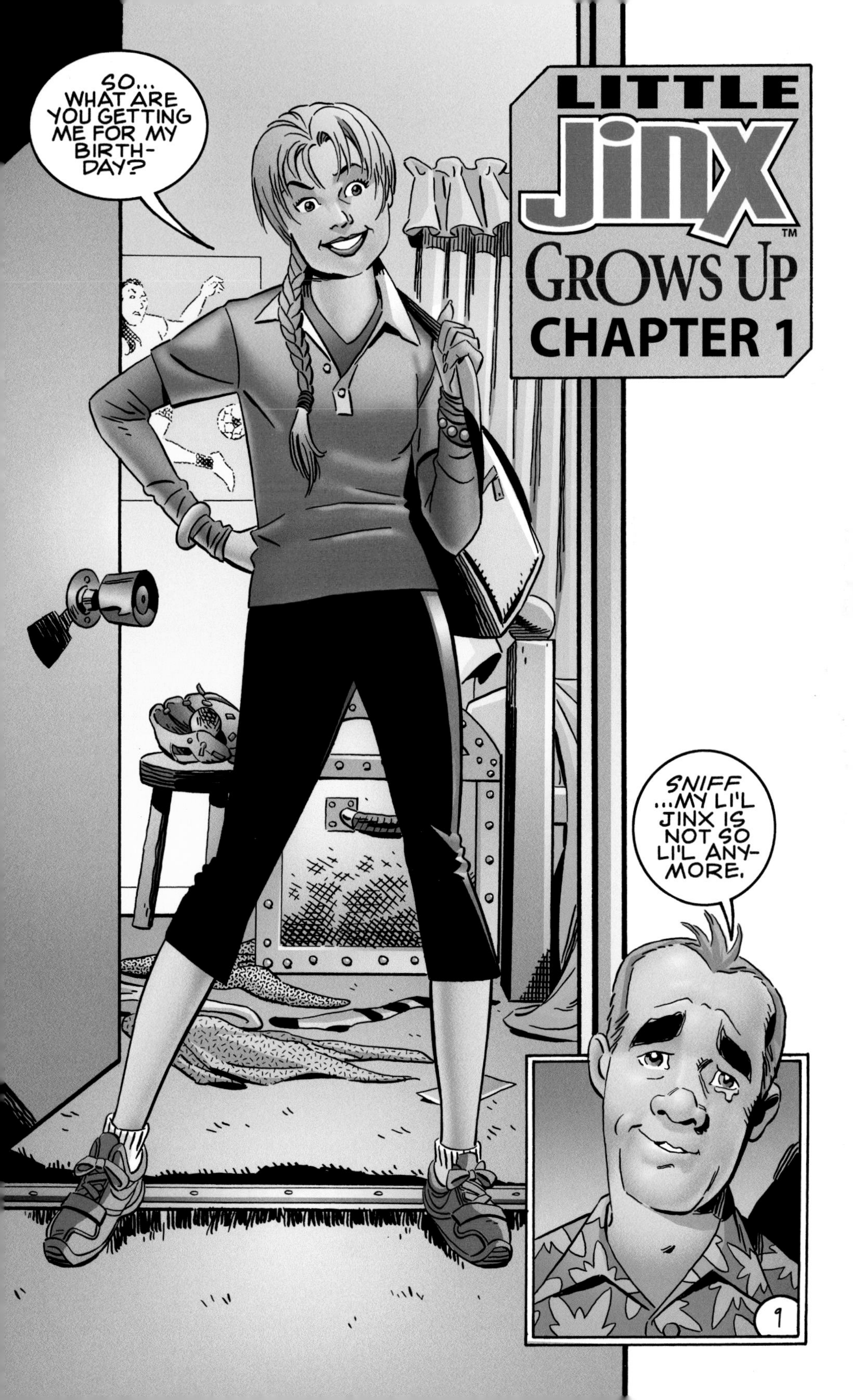
SO... WHAT ARE YOU GETTING ME FOR MY BIRTH-DAY?
LITTLE JINX™ GROWS UP
CHAPTER 1
SNIFF ...MY LI'L JINX IS NOT SO LI'L ANY-MORE.

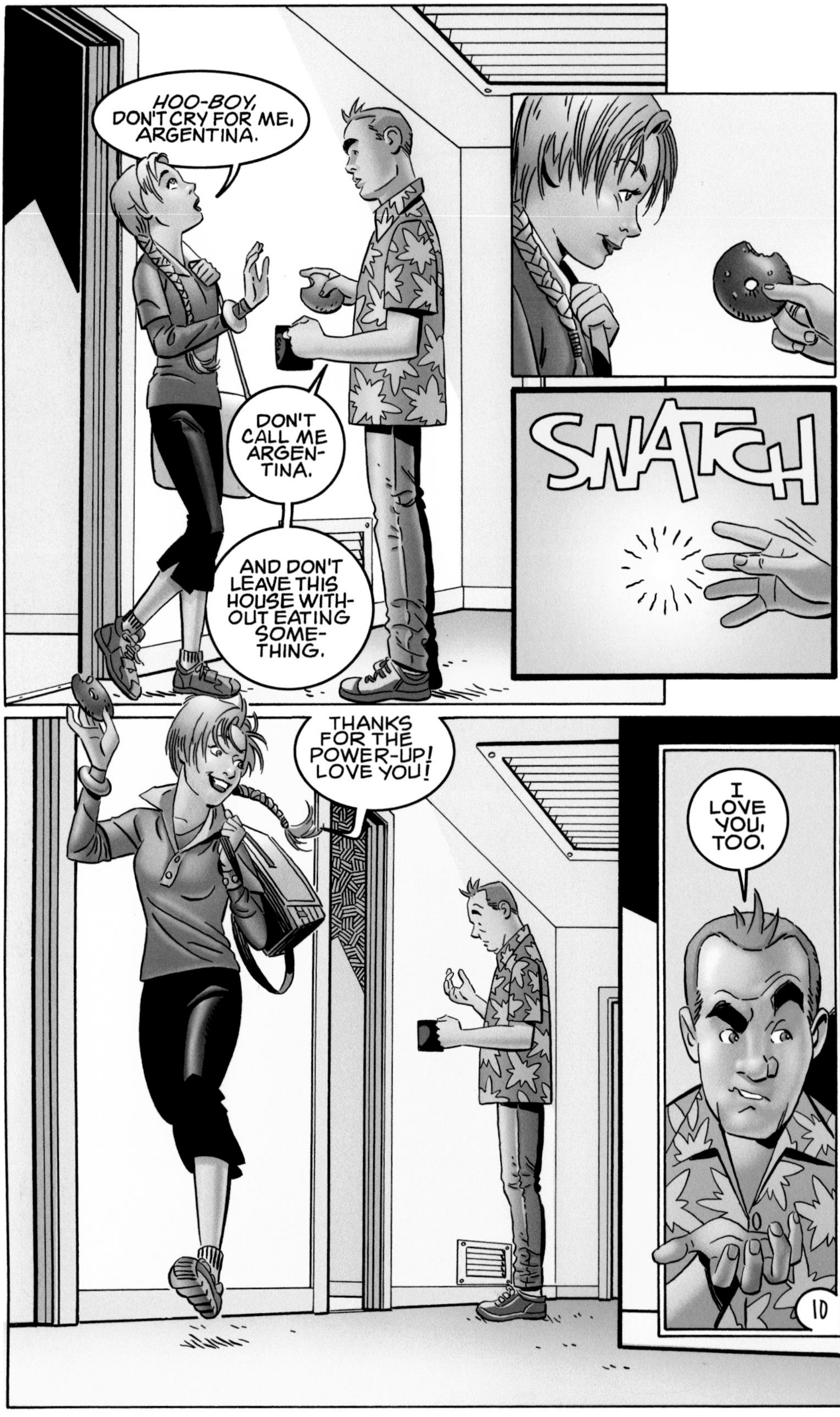
HOO-BOY, DON'T CRY FOR ME, ARGENTINA.
DON'T CALL ME ARGEN-TINA.
AND DON'T LEAVE THIS HOUSE WITH-OUT EATING SOME-THING.
SNATCH
THANKS FOR THE POWER-UP! LOVE YOU!
I LOVE YOU, TOO.

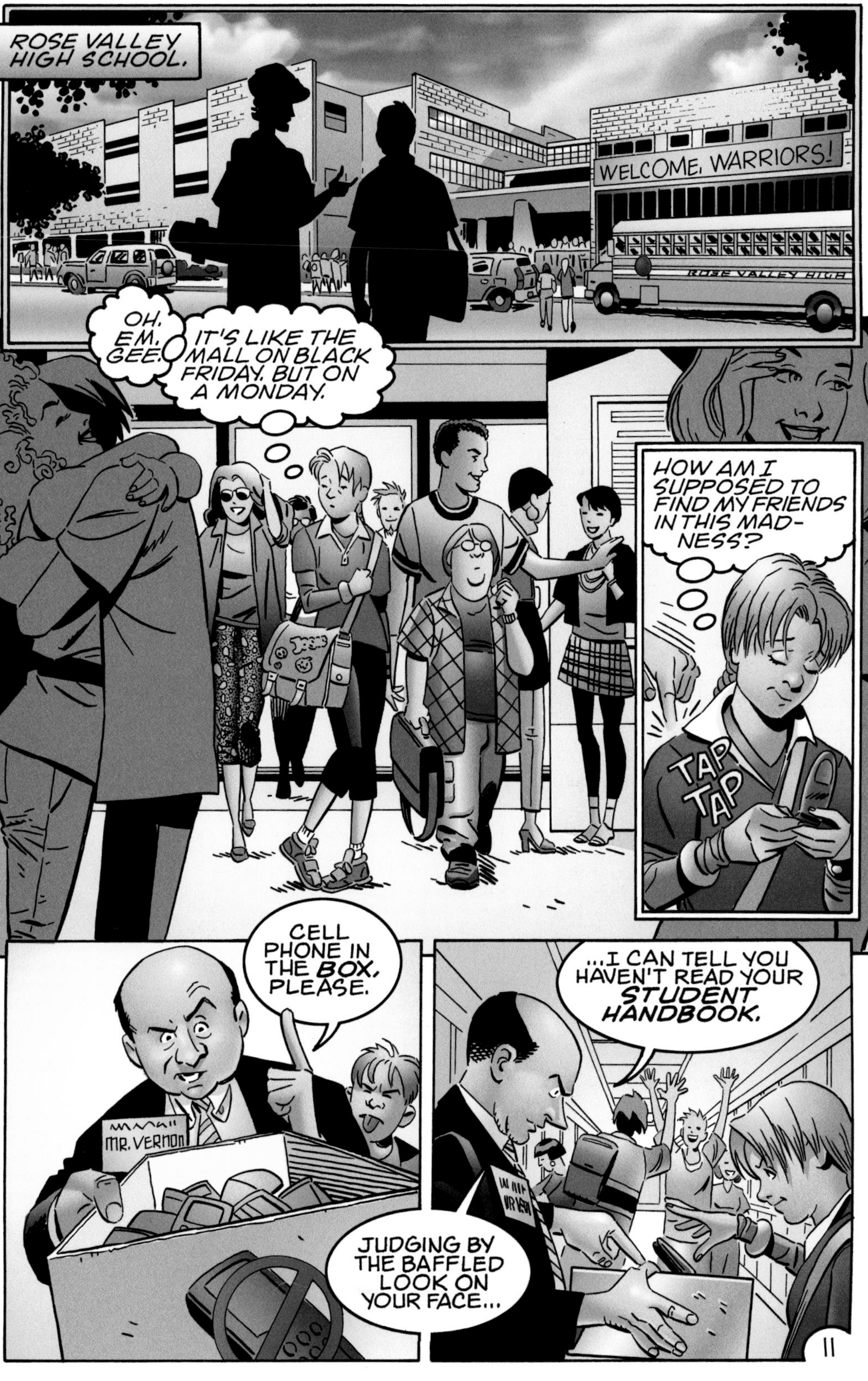
ROSE VALLEY HIGH SCHOOL.
WELCOME, WARRIORS!
ROSE VALLEY HIGH
OH, EM, GEE.
IT'S LIKE THE MALL ON BLACK FRIDAY. BUT ON A MONDAY.
HOW AM I SUPPOSED TO FIND MY FRIENDS IN THIS MADNESS?
TAP TAP
CELL PHONE IN THE BOX, PLEASE.
MR. VERNON
JUDGING BY THE BAFFLED LOOK ON YOUR FACE...
...I CAN TELL YOU HAVEN'T READ YOUR STUDENT HANDBOOK.

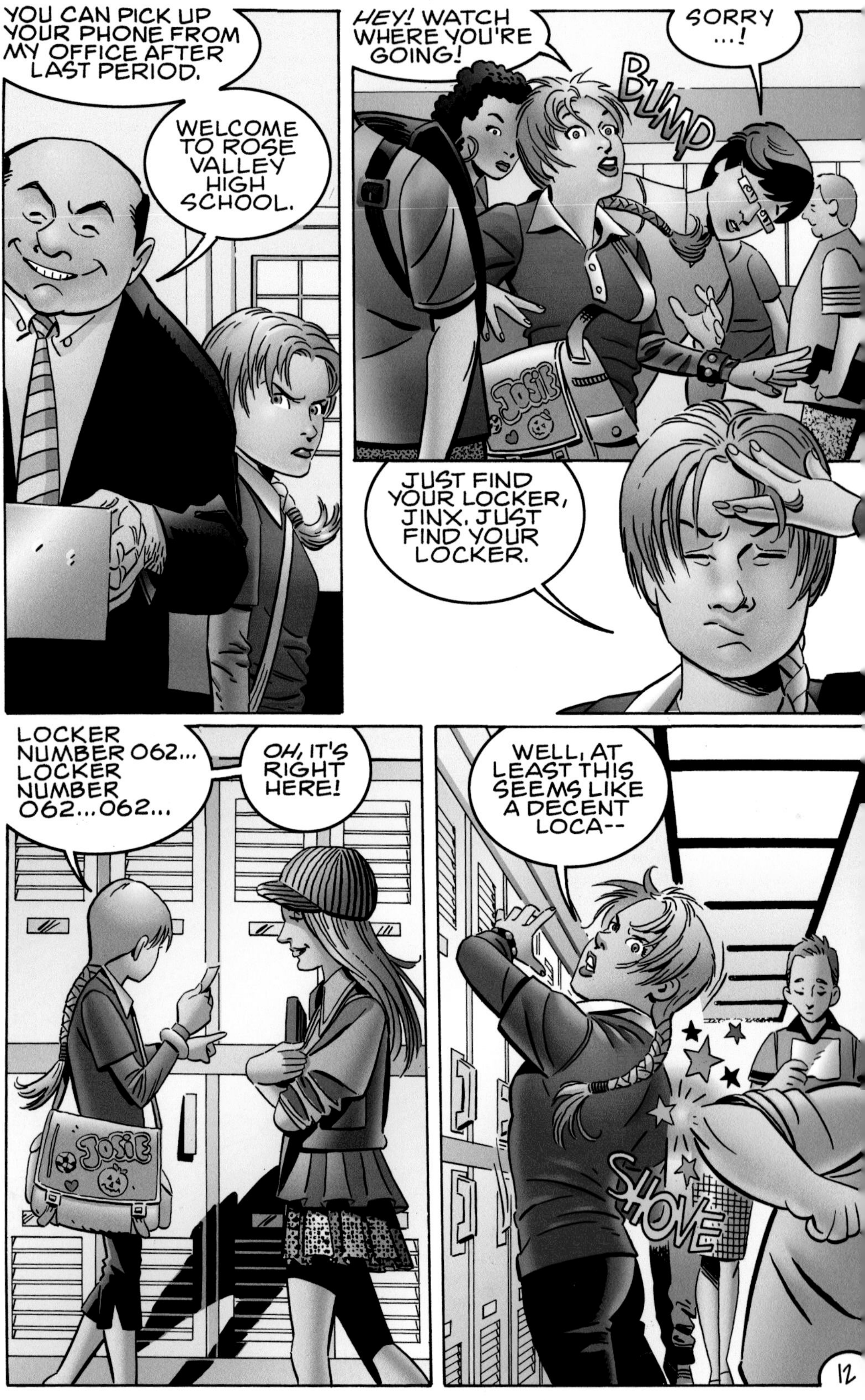
YOU CAN PICK UP YOUR PHONE FROM MY OFFICE AFTER LAST PERIOD.
WELCOME TO ROSE VALLEY HIGH SCHOOL.
HEY! WATCH WHERE YOU'RE GOING!
SORRY ...!
BUMP
JUST FIND YOUR LOCKER, JINX. JUST FIND YOUR LOCKER.
JOSIE
LOCKER NUMBER 062... LOCKER NUMBER 062...062...
OH, IT'S RIGHT HERE!
JOSIE
WELL, AT LEAST THIS SEEMS LIKE A DECENT LOCA--
SHOVE

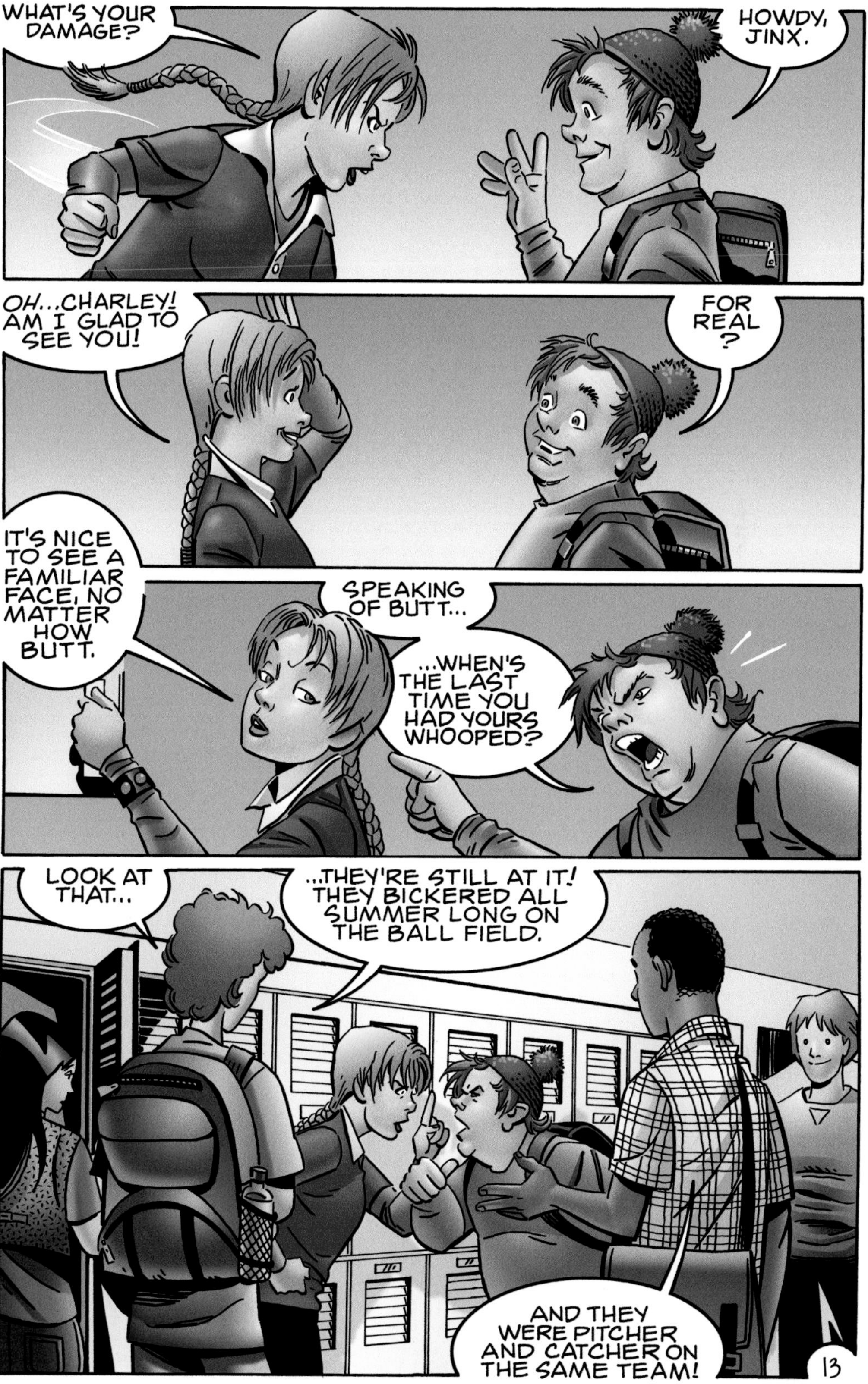
WHAT'S YOUR DAMAGE?
HOWDY, JINX.
OH...CHARLEY! AM I GLAD TO SEE YOU!
FOR REAL ?
IT'S NICE TO SEE A FAMILIAR FACE, NO MATTER HOW BUTT.
SPEAKING OF BUTT...
...WHEN'S THE LAST TIME YOU HAD YOURS WHOOPED?
LOOK AT THAT...
...THEY'RE STILL AT IT! THEY BICKERED ALL SUMMER LONG ON THE BALL FIELD.
AND THEY WERE PITCHER AND CATCHER ON THE SAME TEAM!

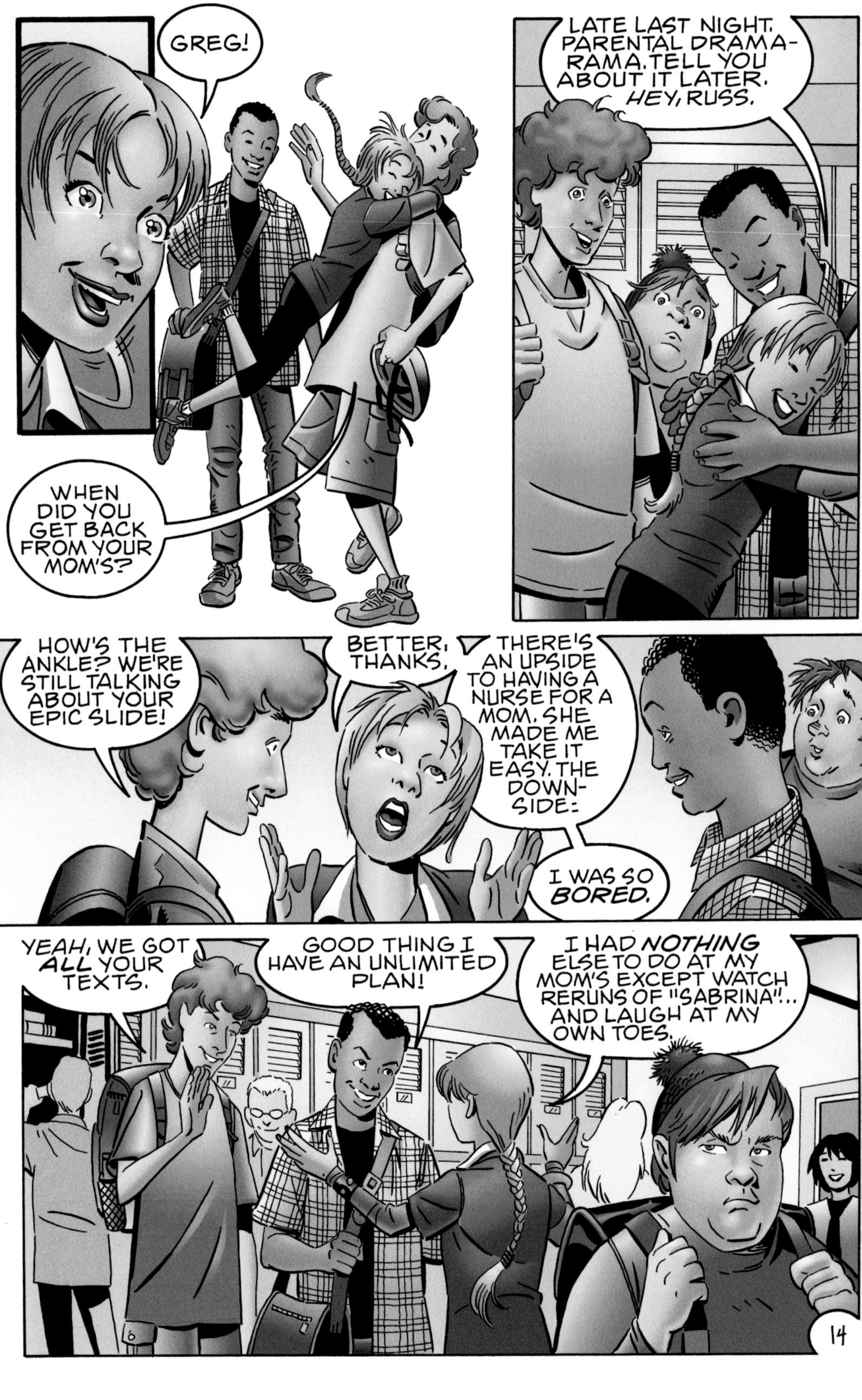
GREG!
WHEN DID YOU GET BACK FROM YOUR MOM'S?
LATE LAST NIGHT. PARENTAL DRAMA-RAMA. TELL YOU ABOUT IT LATER. HEY, RUSS.
HOW'S THE ANKLE? WE'RE STILL TALKING ABOUT YOUR EPIC SLIDE!
BETTER, THANKS.
THERE'S AN UPSIDE TO HAVING A NURSE FOR A MOM. SHE MADE ME TAKE IT EASY. THE DOWN-SIDE:
I WAS SO BORED.
YEAH, WE GOT ALL YOUR TEXTS.
GOOD THING I HAVE AN UNLIMITED PLAN!
I HAD NOTHING ELSE TO DO AT MY MOM'S EXCEPT WATCH RERUNS OF "SABRINA"... AND LAUGH AT MY OWN TOES.

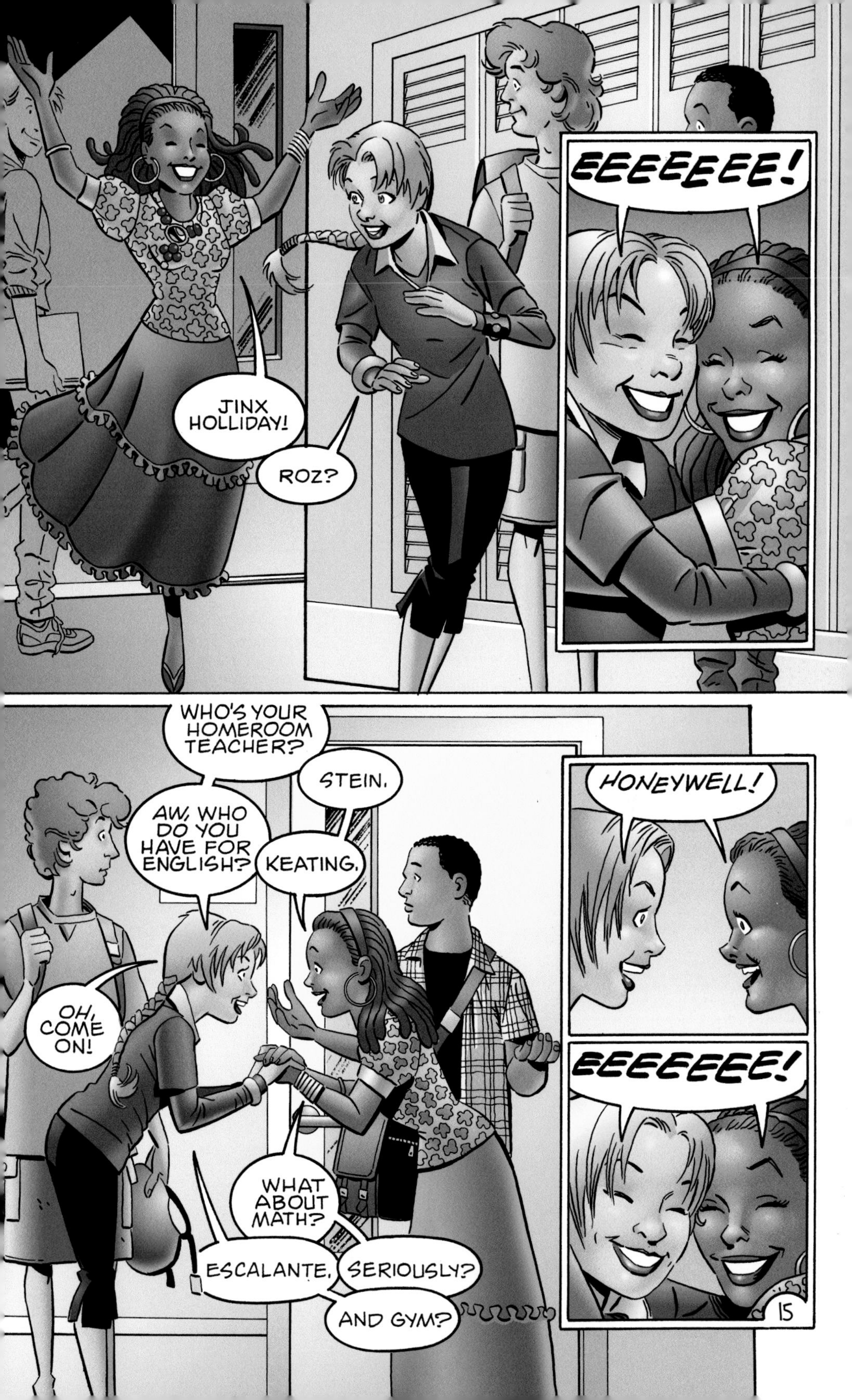
JINX HOLLIDAY!
ROZ?
EEEEEEE!
WHO'S YOUR HOMEROOM TEACHER?
STEIN.
AW, WHO DO YOU HAVE FOR ENGLISH?
KEATING.
HONEYWELL!
EEEEEEE!
OH, COME ON!
WHAT ABOUT MATH?
ESCALANTE.
SERIOUSLY?
AND GYM?

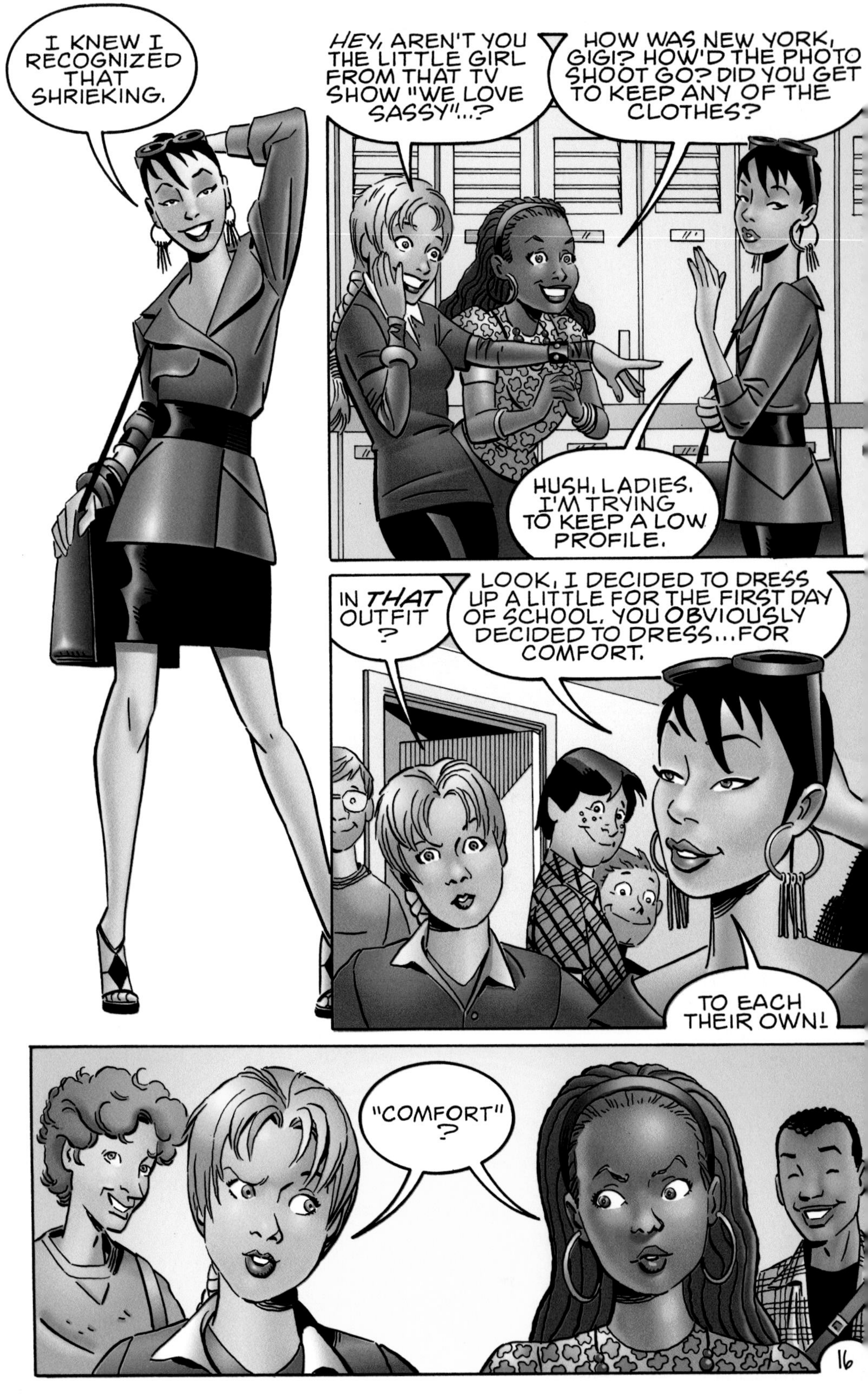
I KNEW I RECOGNIZED THAT SHRIEKING.
HEY, AREN'T YOU THE LITTLE GIRL FROM THAT TV SHOW "WE LOVE SASSY"...?
HOW WAS NEW YORK, GIGI? HOW'D THE PHOTO SHOOT GO? DID YOU GET TO KEEP ANY OF THE CLOTHES?
HUSH, LADIES. I'M TRYING TO KEEP A LOW PROFILE.
IN THAT OUTFIT?
LOOK, I DECIDED TO DRESS UP A LITTLE FOR THE FIRST DAY OF SCHOOL. YOU OBVIOUSLY DECIDED TO DRESS...FOR COMFORT.
TO EACH THEIR OWN!
"COMFORT"?

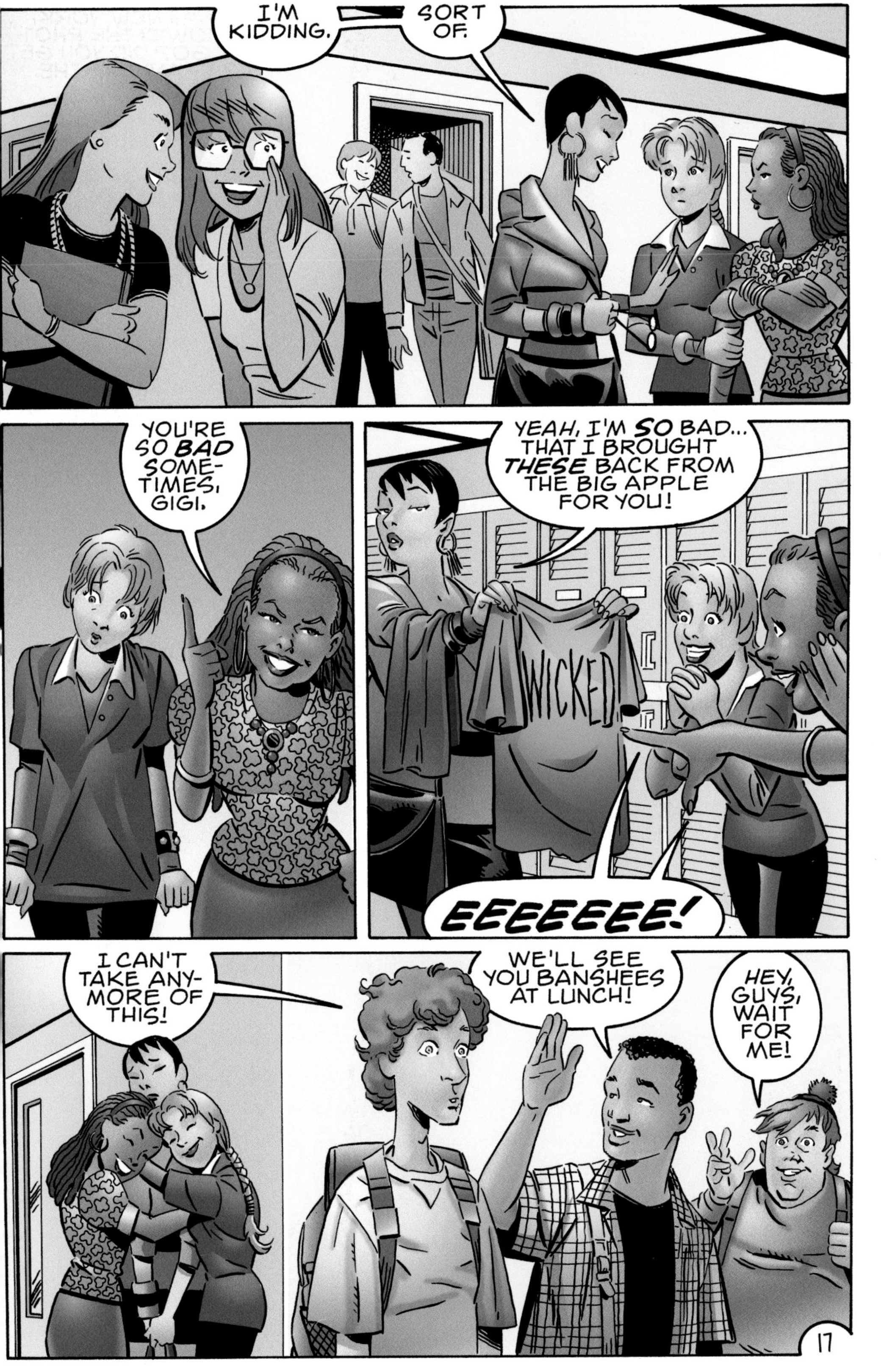
I'M KIDDING.
SORT OF.
YOU'RE SO BAD SOME-TIMES, GIGI.
YEAH, I'M SO BAD... THAT I BROUGHT THESE BACK FROM THE BIG APPLE FOR YOU!
WICKED
EEEEEEE!
I CAN'T TAKE ANY-MORE OF THIS!
WE'LL SEE YOU BANSHEES AT LUNCH!
HEY, GUYS, WAIT FOR ME!

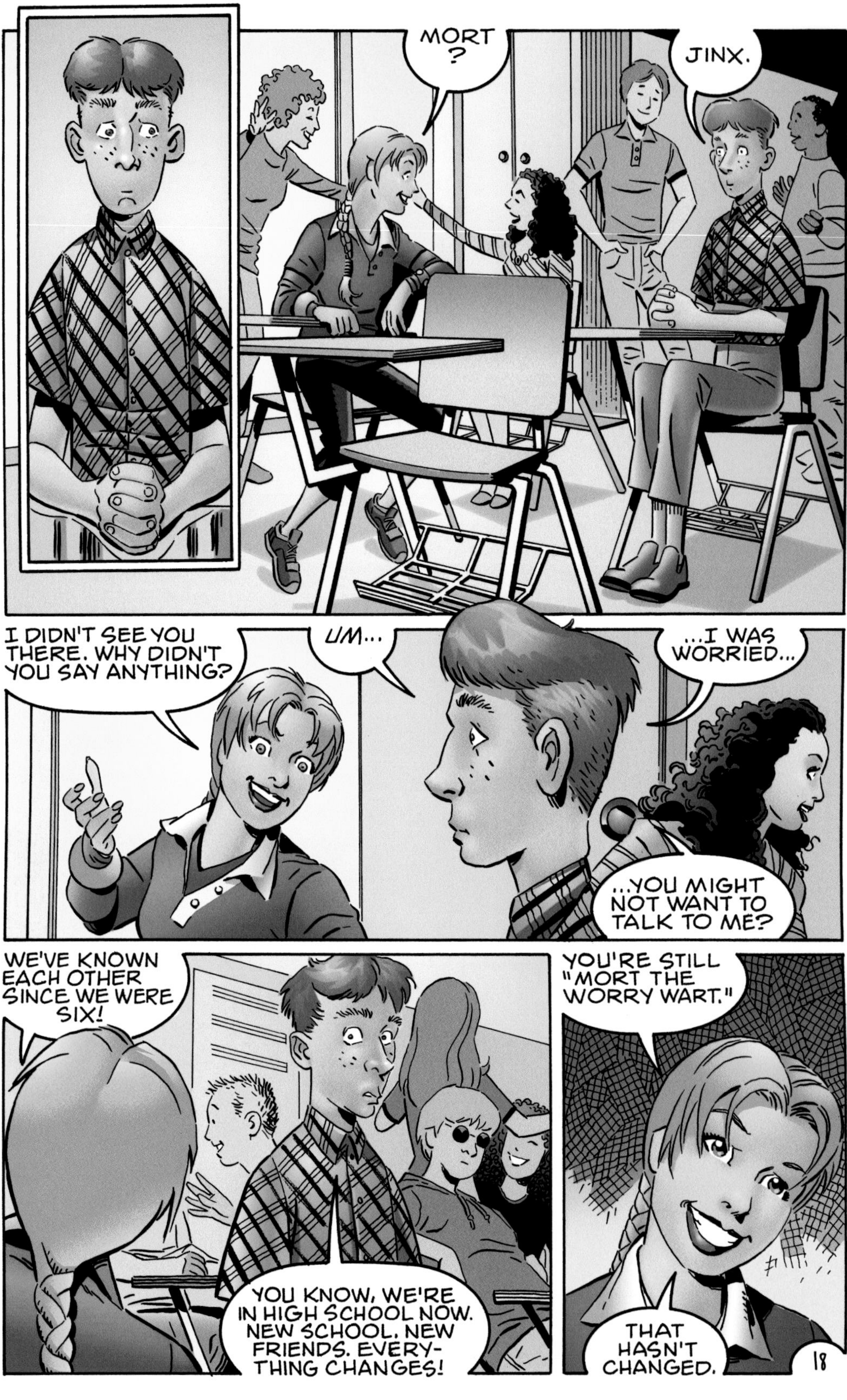
MORT?
JINX.
I DIDN'T SEE YOU THERE. WHY DIDN'T YOU SAY ANYTHING?
UM...
...I WAS WORRIED...
...YOU MIGHT NOT WANT TO TALK TO ME?
WE'VE KNOWN EACH OTHER SINCE WE WERE SIX!
YOU KNOW, WE'RE IN HIGH SCHOOL NOW. NEW SCHOOL, NEW FRIENDS. EVERY-THING CHANGES!
YOU'RE STILL "MORT THE WORRY WART."
THAT HASN'T CHANGED.

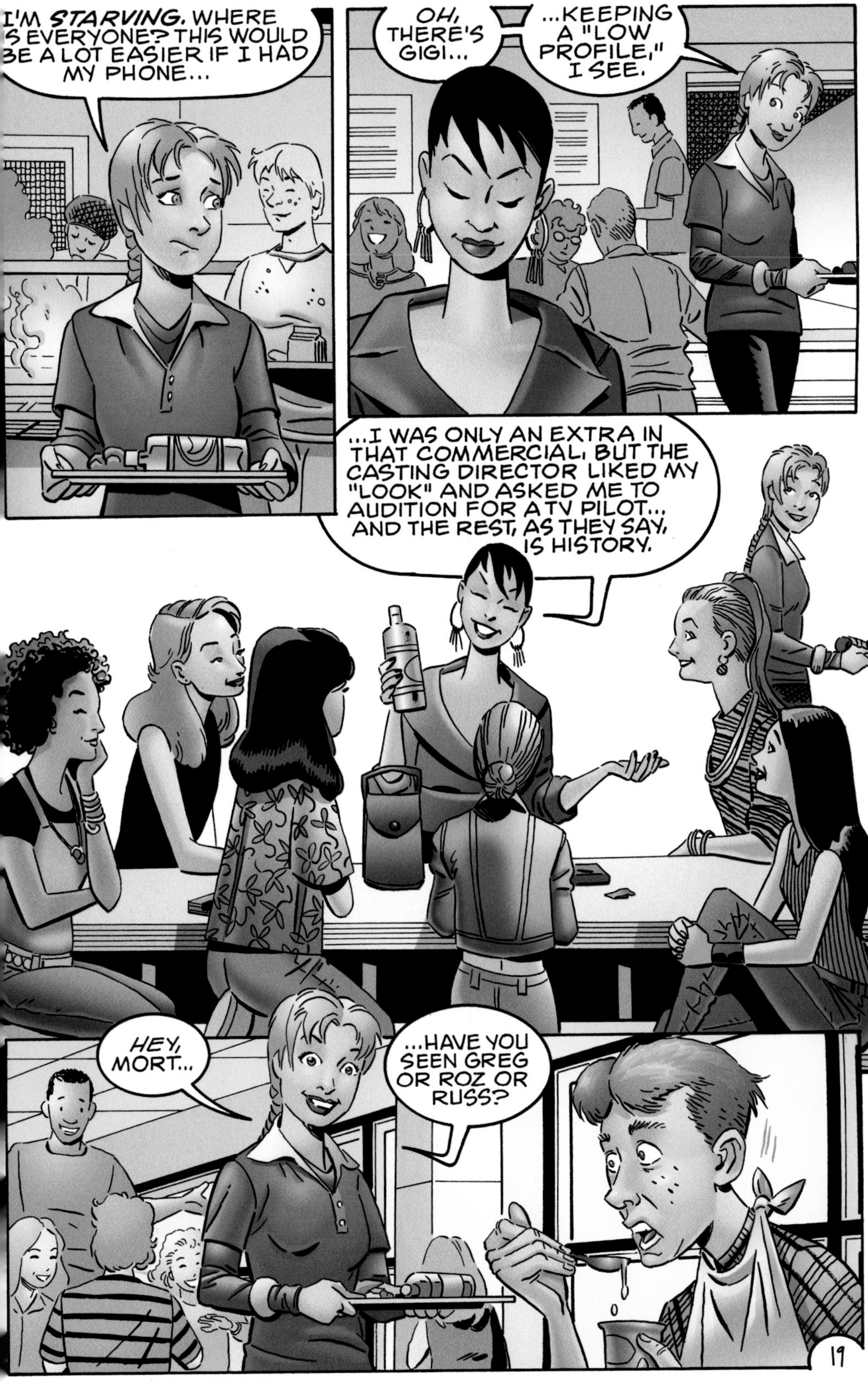
I'M STARVING. WHERE 'S EVERYONE? THIS WOULD BE A LOT EASIER IF I HAD MY PHONE...
OH, THERE'S GIGI...
...KEEPING A "LOW PROFILE," I SEE.
...I WAS ONLY AN EXTRA IN THAT COMMERCIAL, BUT THE CASTING DIRECTOR LIKED MY "LOOK" AND ASKED ME TO AUDITION FOR A TV PILOT... AND THE REST, AS THEY SAY, IS HISTORY.
HEY, MORT...
...HAVE YOU SEEN GREG OR ROZ OR RUSS?

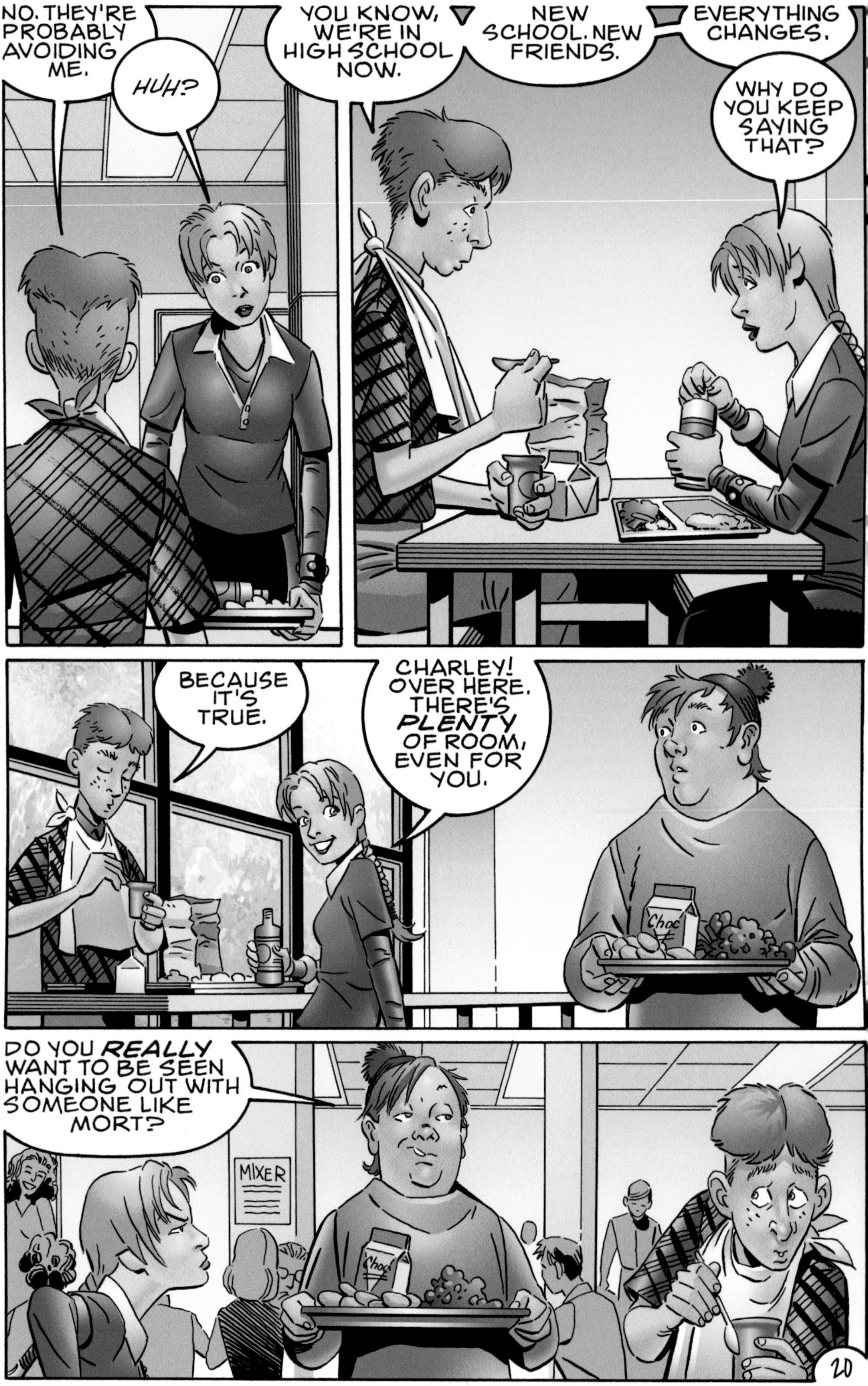
NO. THEY'RE PROBABLY AVOIDING ME.
HUH?
YOU KNOW, WE'RE IN HIGH SCHOOL NOW.
NEW SCHOOL. NEW FRIENDS.
EVERYTHING CHANGES.
WHY DO YOU KEEP SAYING THAT?
BECAUSE IT'S TRUE.
CHARLEY! OVER HERE. THERE'S *PLENTY* OF ROOM, EVEN FOR YOU.
Choc
DO YOU *REALLY* WANT TO BE SEEN HANGING OUT WITH SOMEONE LIKE MORT?
MIXER
Choc

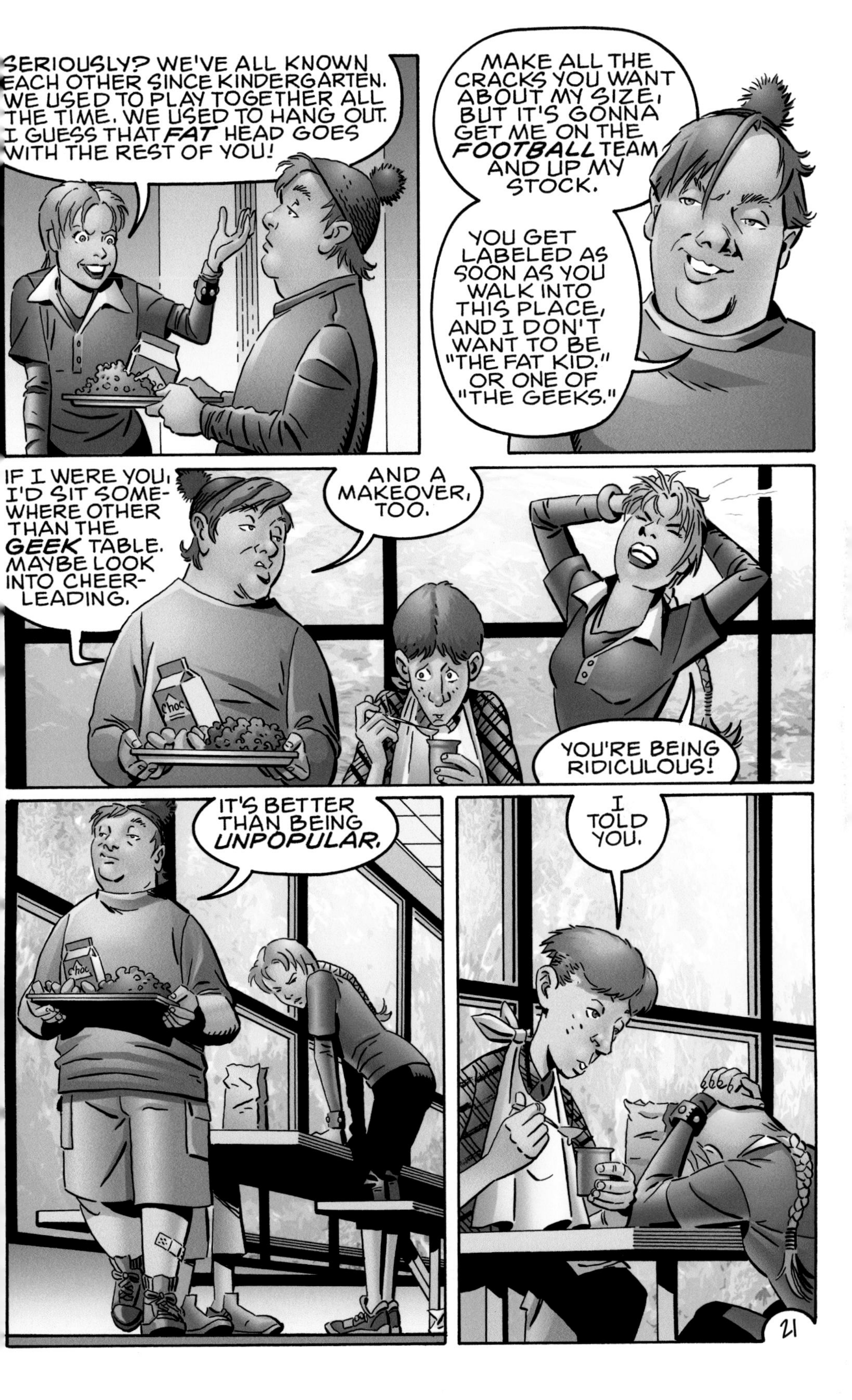
SERIOUSLY? WE'VE ALL KNOWN EACH OTHER SINCE KINDERGARTEN. WE USED TO PLAY TOGETHER ALL THE TIME. WE USED TO HANG OUT. I GUESS THAT FAT HEAD GOES WITH THE REST OF YOU!
MAKE ALL THE CRACKS YOU WANT ABOUT MY SIZE, BUT IT'S GONNA GET ME ON THE FOOTBALL TEAM AND UP MY STOCK.
YOU GET LABELED AS SOON AS YOU WALK INTO THIS PLACE, AND I DON'T WANT TO BE "THE FAT KID." OR ONE OF "THE GEEKS."
IF I WERE YOU, I'D SIT SOMEWHERE OTHER THAN THE GEEK TABLE. MAYBE LOOK INTO CHEERLEADING.
AND A MAKEOVER, TOO.
YOU'RE BEING RIDICULOUS!
IT'S BETTER THAN BEING UNPOPULAR.
I TOLD YOU.

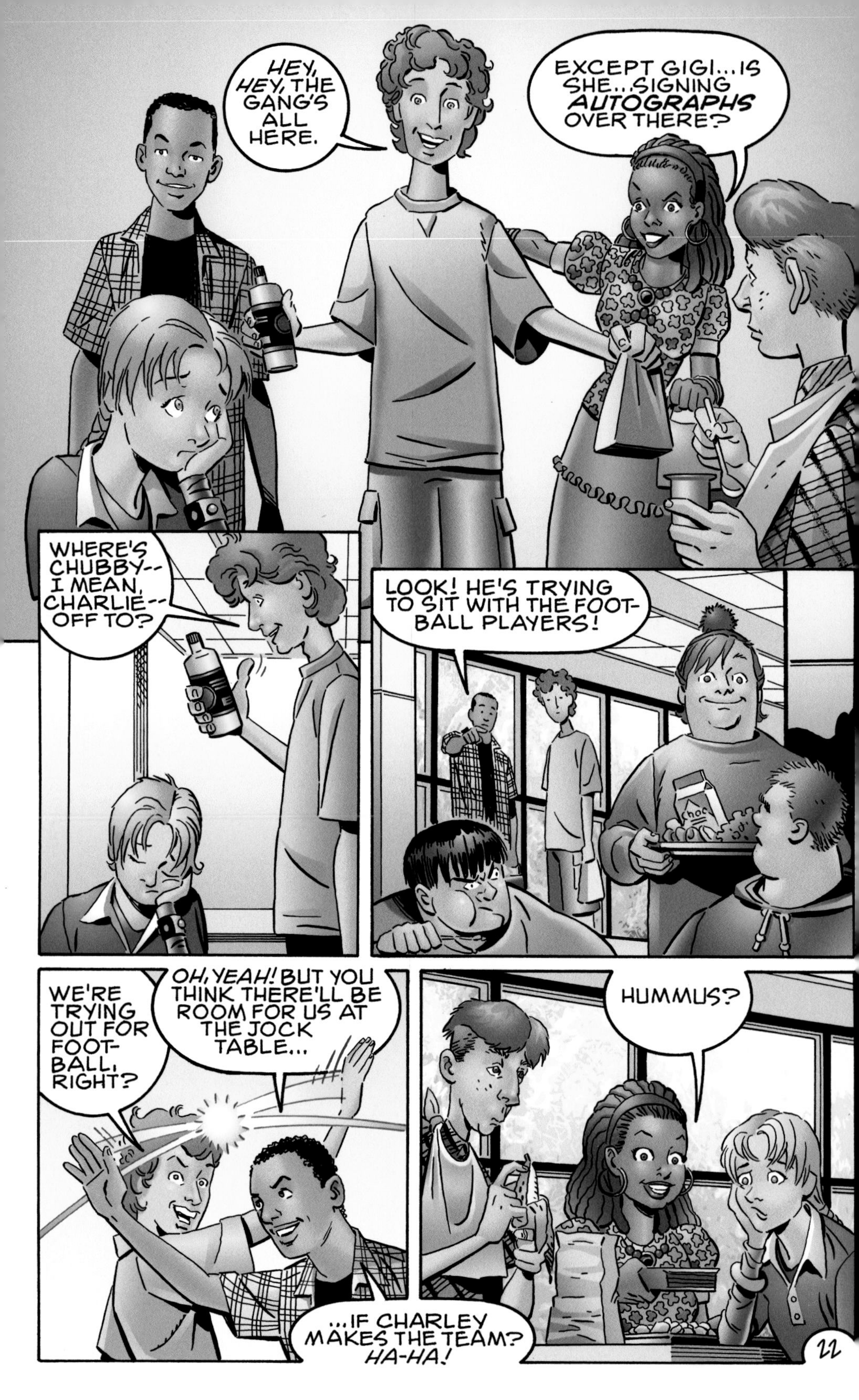
HEY, HEY, THE GANG'S ALL HERE.
EXCEPT GIGI...IS SHE...SIGNING AUTOGRAPHS OVER THERE?
WHERE'S CHUBBY-- I MEAN, CHARLIE-- OFF TO?
LOOK! HE'S TRYING TO SIT WITH THE FOOTBALL PLAYERS!
WE'RE TRYING OUT FOR FOOTBALL, RIGHT?
OH, YEAH! BUT YOU THINK THERE'LL BE ROOM FOR US AT THE JOCK TABLE...
...IF CHARLEY MAKES THE TEAM? HA-HA!
HUMMUS?
CHOC

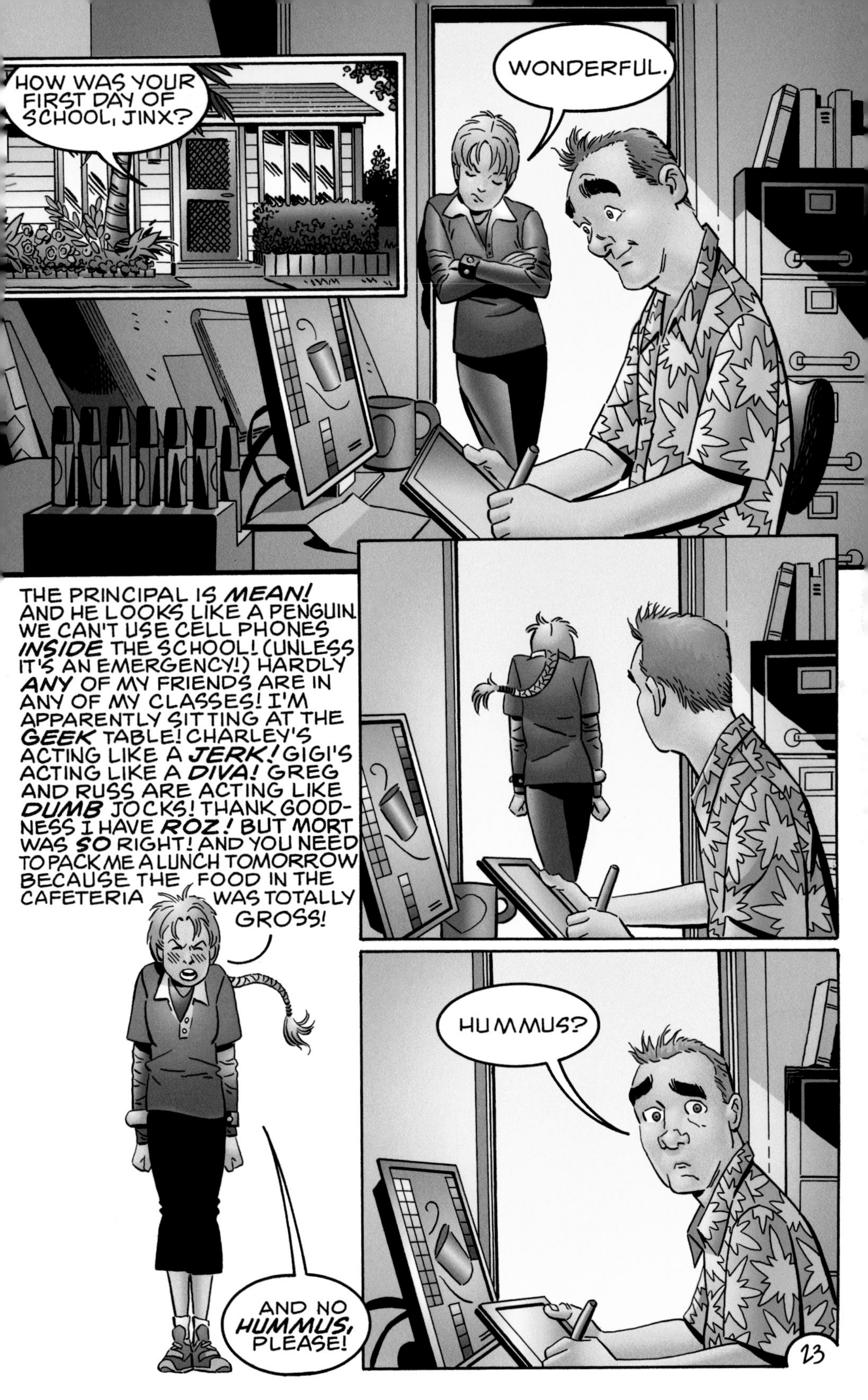
HOW WAS YOUR FIRST DAY OF SCHOOL, JINX?
WONDERFUL.
THE PRINCIPAL IS *MEAN!* AND HE LOOKS LIKE A PENGUIN. WE CAN'T USE CELL PHONES *INSIDE* THE SCHOOL! (UNLESS IT'S AN EMERGENCY!) HARDLY *ANY* OF MY FRIENDS ARE IN ANY OF MY CLASSES! I'M APPARENTLY SITTING AT THE *GEEK* TABLE! CHARLEY'S ACTING LIKE A *JERK!* GIGI'S ACTING LIKE A *DIVA!* GREG AND RUSS ARE ACTING LIKE *DUMB* JOCKS! THANK GOODNESS I HAVE *ROZ!* BUT MORT WAS *SO* RIGHT! AND YOU NEED TO PACK ME A LUNCH TOMORROW BECAUSE THE FOOD IN THE CAFETERIA WAS TOTALLY GROSS!
HUMMUS?
AND NO *HUMMUS,* PLEASE!

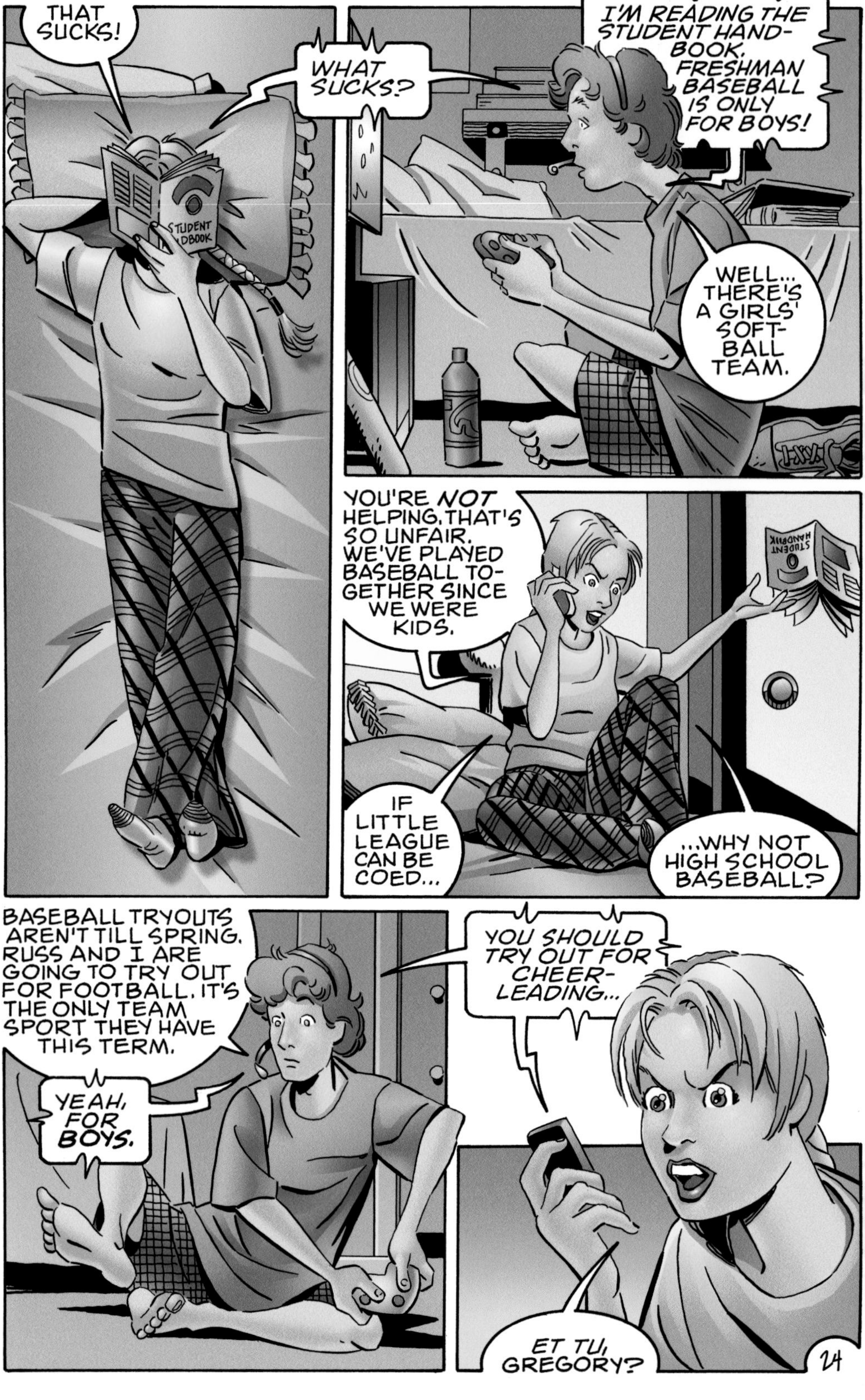
THAT SUCKS!
WHAT SUCKS?
I'M READING THE STUDENT HAND-BOOK. FRESHMAN BASEBALL IS ONLY FOR BOYS!
STUDENT HANDBOOK
WELL... THERE'S A GIRLS' SOFT-BALL TEAM.
YOU'RE NOT HELPING. THAT'S SO UNFAIR. WE'VE PLAYED BASEBALL TO-GETHER SINCE WE WERE KIDS.
IF LITTLE LEAGUE CAN BE COED...
...WHY NOT HIGH SCHOOL BASEBALL?
BASEBALL TRYOUTS AREN'T TILL SPRING. RUSS AND I ARE GOING TO TRY OUT FOR FOOTBALL. IT'S THE ONLY TEAM SPORT THEY HAVE THIS TERM.
YEAH, FOR BOYS.
YOU SHOULD TRY OUT FOR CHEER-LEADING...
ET TU, GREGORY?

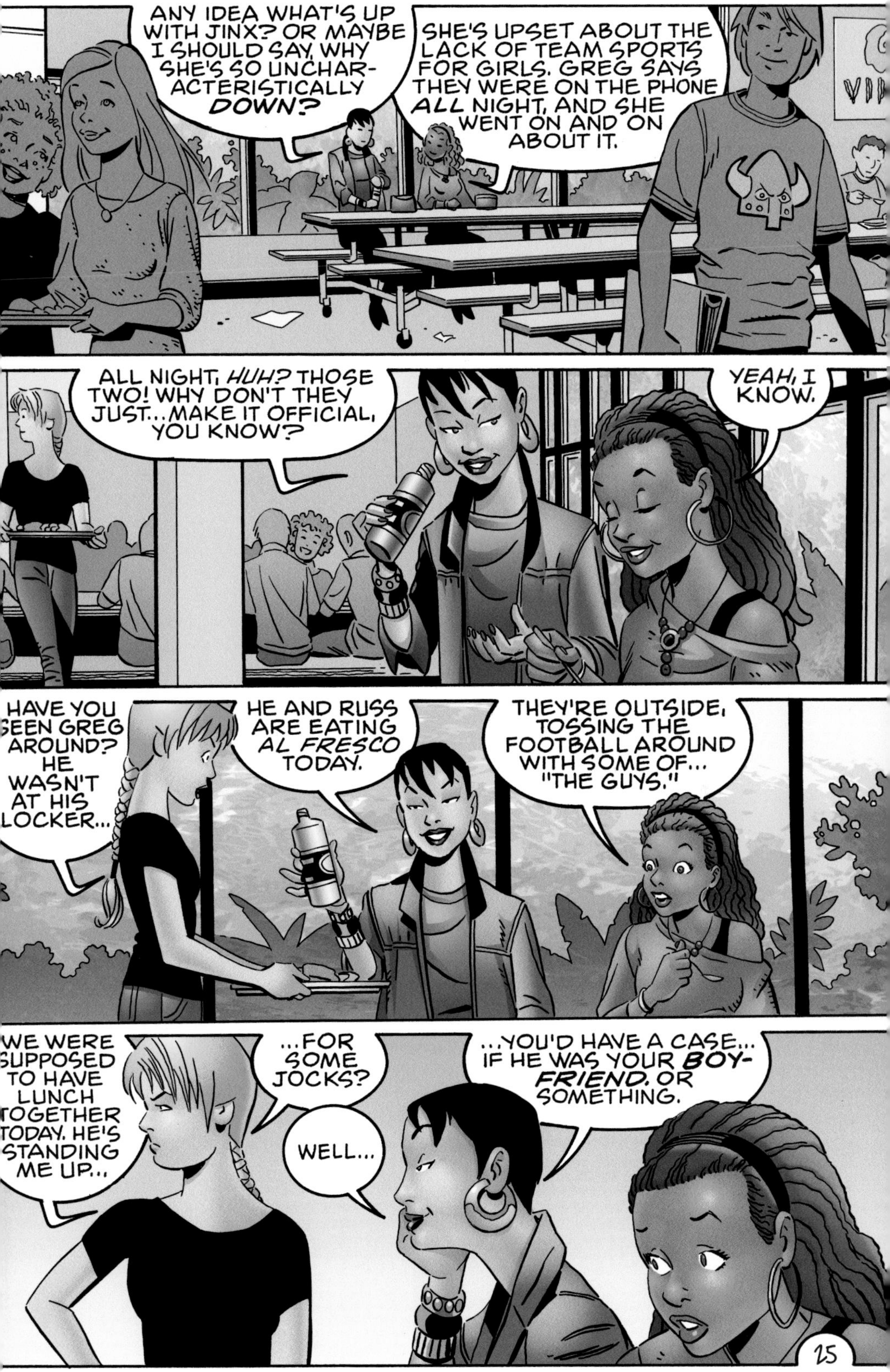

ANY IDEA WHAT'S UP WITH JINX? OR MAYBE I SHOULD SAY, WHY SHE'S SO UNCHARACTERISTICALLY DOWN?
SHE'S UPSET ABOUT THE LACK OF TEAM SPORTS FOR GIRLS. GREG SAYS THEY WERE ON THE PHONE ALL NIGHT, AND SHE WENT ON AND ON ABOUT IT.
ALL NIGHT, HUH? THOSE TWO! WHY DON'T THEY JUST...MAKE IT OFFICIAL, YOU KNOW?
YEAH, I KNOW.
HAVE YOU SEEN GREG AROUND? HE WASN'T AT HIS LOCKER...
HE AND RUSS ARE EATING AL FRESCO TODAY.
THEY'RE OUTSIDE, TOSSING THE FOOTBALL AROUND WITH SOME OF... "THE GUYS."
WE WERE SUPPOSED TO HAVE LUNCH TOGETHER TODAY. HE'S STANDING ME UP...
...FOR SOME JOCKS?
WELL...
...YOU'D HAVE A CASE... IF HE WAS YOUR BOYFRIEND. OR SOMETHING.

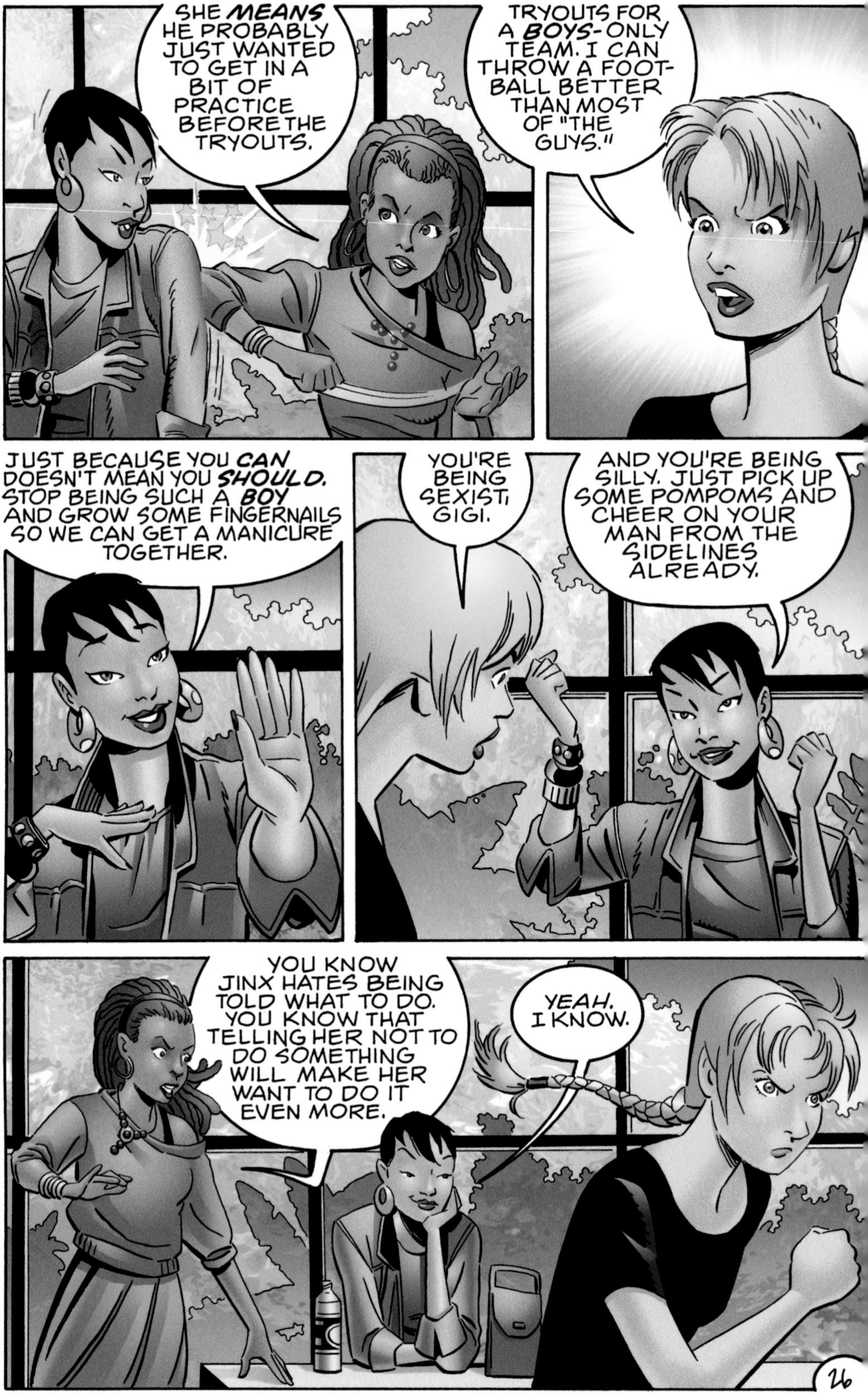
SHE *MEANS* HE PROBABLY JUST WANTED TO GET IN A BIT OF PRACTICE BEFORE THE TRYOUTS.
TRYOUTS FOR A *BOYS*-ONLY TEAM. I CAN THROW A FOOTBALL BETTER THAN MOST OF "THE GUYS."
JUST BECAUSE YOU *CAN* DOESN'T MEAN YOU *SHOULD.* STOP BEING SUCH A *BOY* AND GROW SOME FINGERNAILS SO WE CAN GET A MANICURE TOGETHER.
YOU'RE BEING SEXIST, GIGI.
AND YOU'RE BEING SILLY. JUST PICK UP SOME POMPOMS AND CHEER ON YOUR MAN FROM THE SIDELINES ALREADY.
YOU KNOW JINX HATES BEING TOLD WHAT TO DO. YOU KNOW THAT TELLING HER NOT TO DO SOMETHING WILL MAKE HER WANT TO DO IT EVEN MORE.
YEAH. I KNOW.

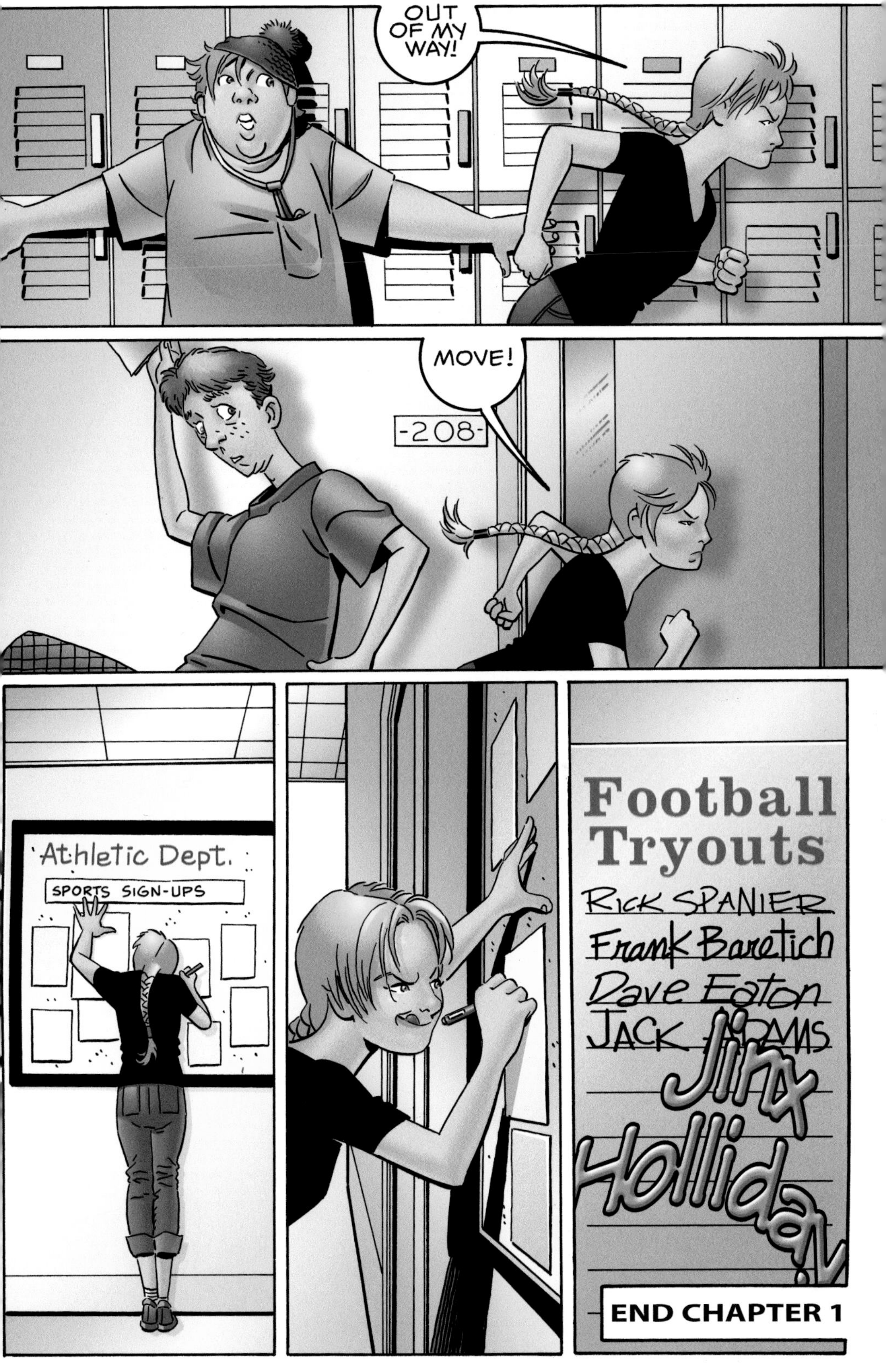
OUT OF MY WAY!
MOVE!
-208-
Athletic Dept.
SPORTS SIGN-UPS
Football Tryouts
RICK SPANIER
Frank Baretich
Dave Eaton
JACK ADAMS
Jinx Holliday
END CHAPTER 1

JINX™

CHAPTER 2

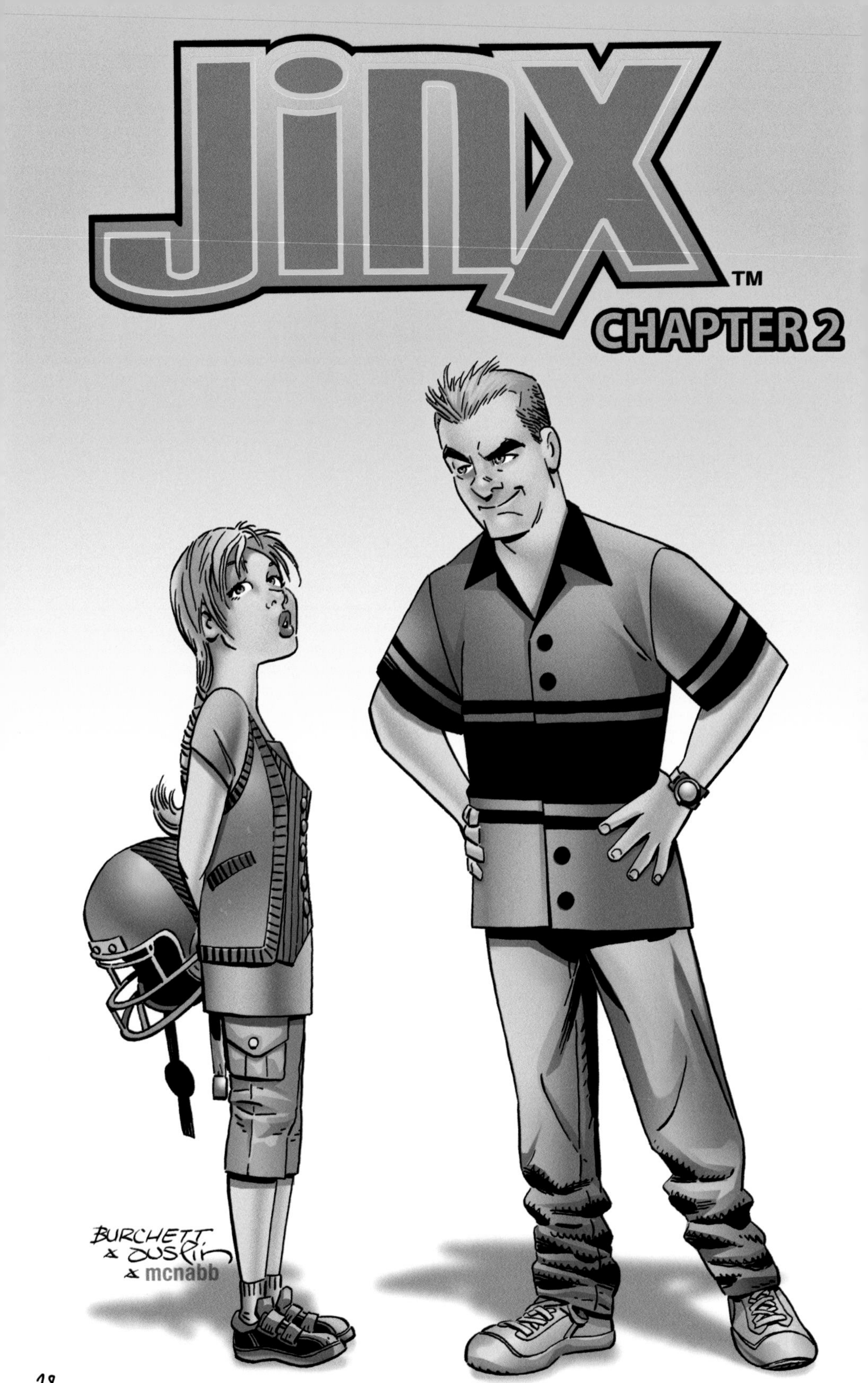
BURCHETT
& AUSTIN
& mcnabb

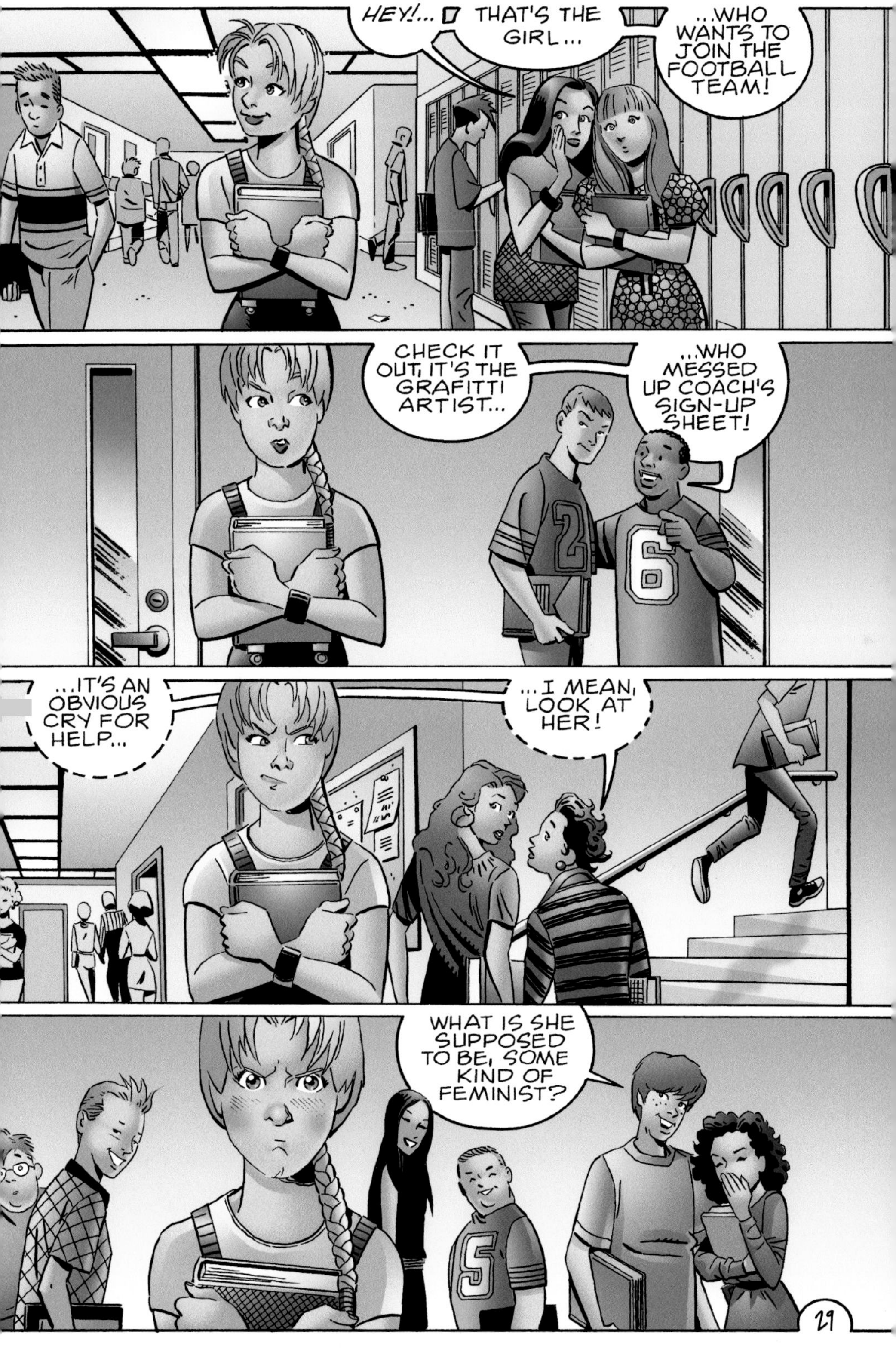
HEY!...
THAT'S THE GIRL...
...WHO WANTS TO JOIN THE FOOTBALL TEAM!
CHECK IT OUT, IT'S THE GRAFITTI ARTIST...
...WHO MESSED UP COACH'S SIGN-UP SHEET!
...IT'S AN OBVIOUS CRY FOR HELP...
...I MEAN, LOOK AT HER!
WHAT IS SHE SUPPOSED TO BE, SOME KIND OF FEMINIST?

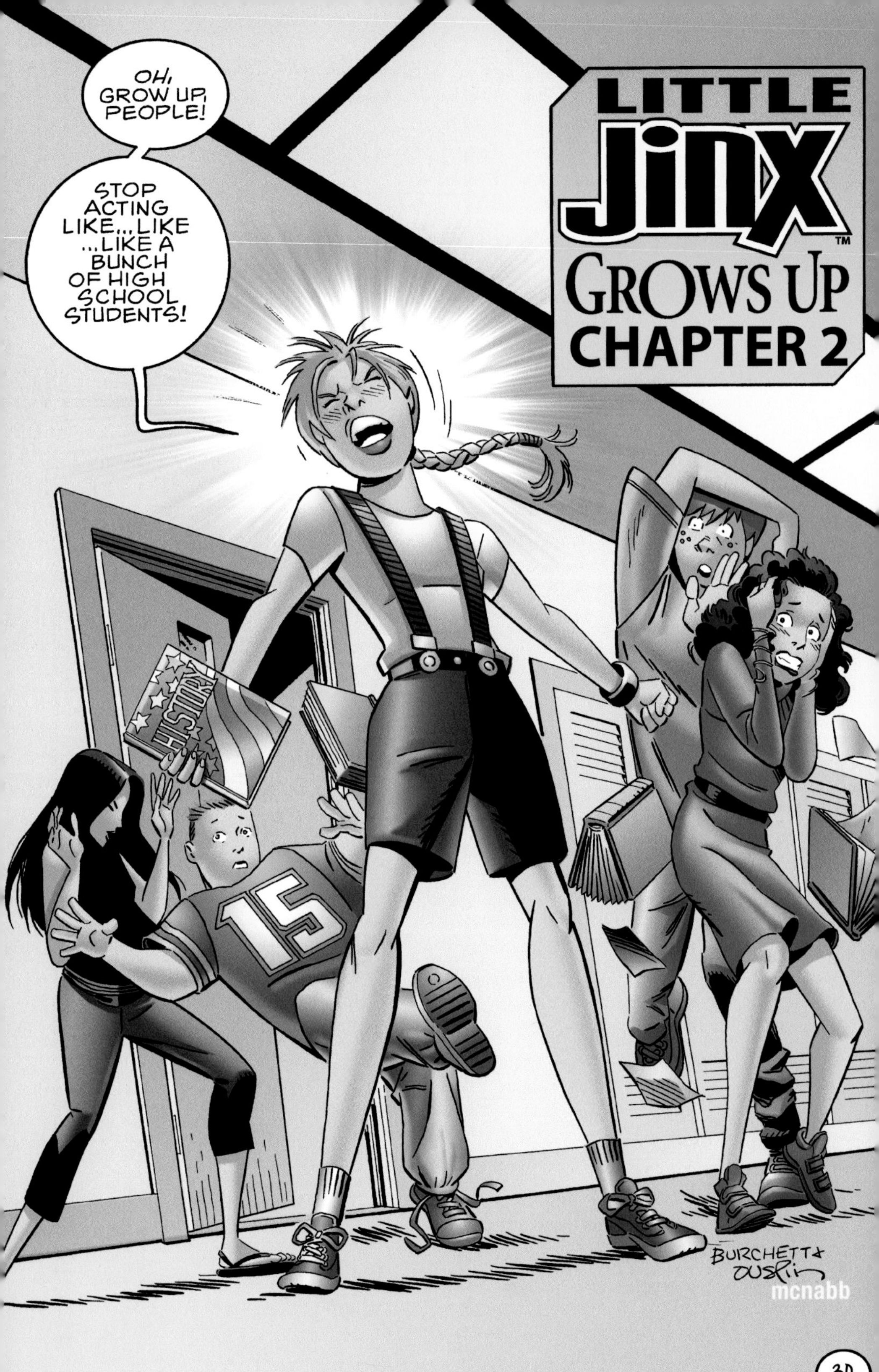

OH, GROW UP, PEOPLE!
STOP ACTING LIKE... LIKE ...LIKE A BUNCH OF HIGH SCHOOL STUDENTS!
LITTLE JINX™
GROWS UP
CHAPTER 2
BURCHETT & AUSTIN
mcnabb

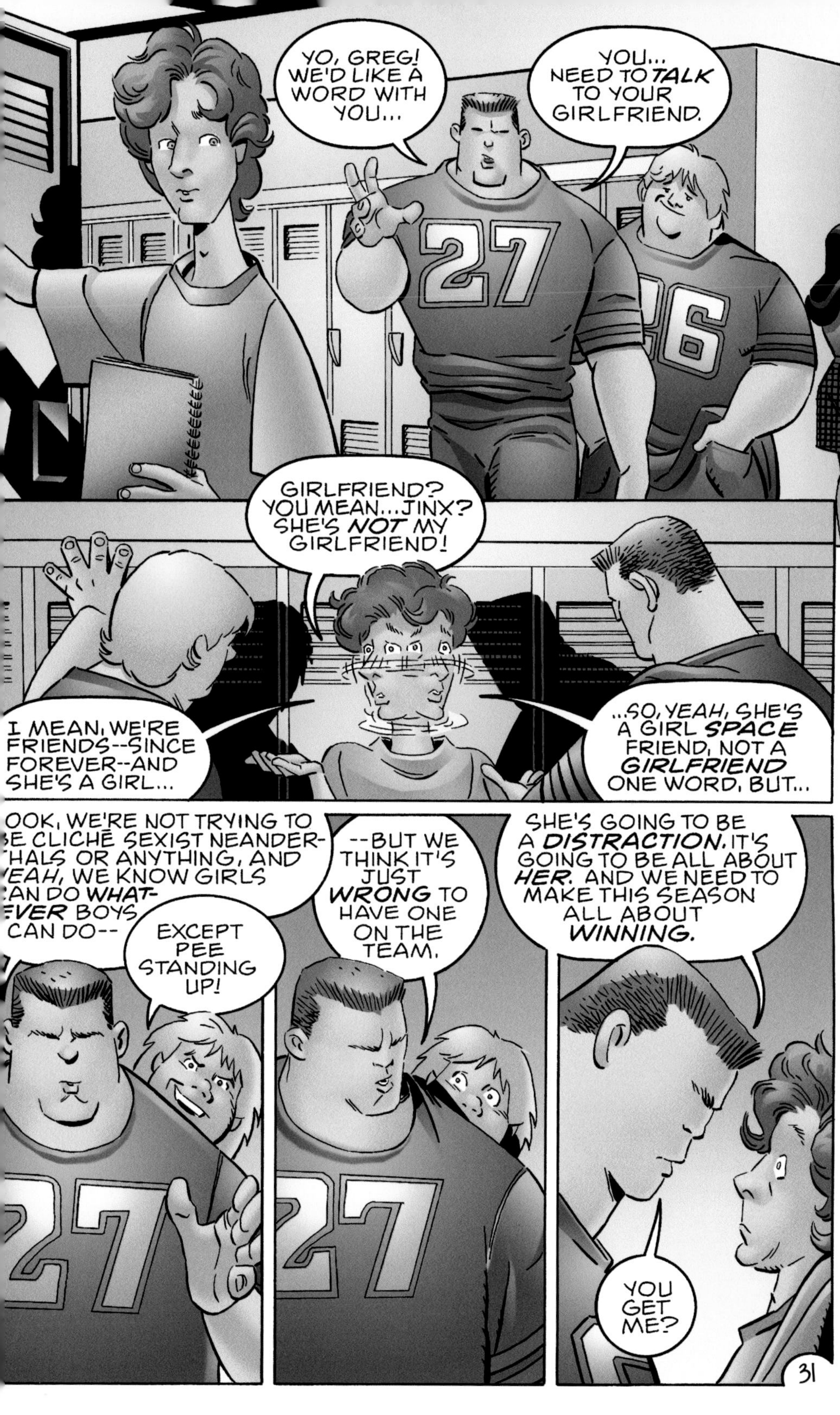
YO, GREG! WE'D LIKE A WORD WITH YOU...
YOU... NEED TO *TALK* TO YOUR GIRLFRIEND.
GIRLFRIEND? YOU MEAN...JINX? SHE'S *NOT* MY GIRLFRIEND!
I MEAN, WE'RE FRIENDS--SINCE FOREVER--AND SHE'S A GIRL...
...SO, YEAH, SHE'S A GIRL *SPACE* FRIEND, NOT A *GIRLFRIEND* ONE WORD, BUT...
OOK, WE'RE NOT TRYING TO E CLICHÉ SEXIST NEANDER-THALS OR ANYTHING, AND *EAH*, WE KNOW GIRLS AN DO *WHAT-EVER* BOYS CAN DO--
EXCEPT PEE STANDING UP!
--BUT WE THINK IT'S JUST *WRONG* TO HAVE ONE ON THE TEAM.
SHE'S GOING TO BE A *DISTRACTION*. IT'S GOING TO BE ALL ABOUT *HER*. AND WE NEED TO MAKE THIS SEASON ALL ABOUT *WINNING*.
YOU GET ME?

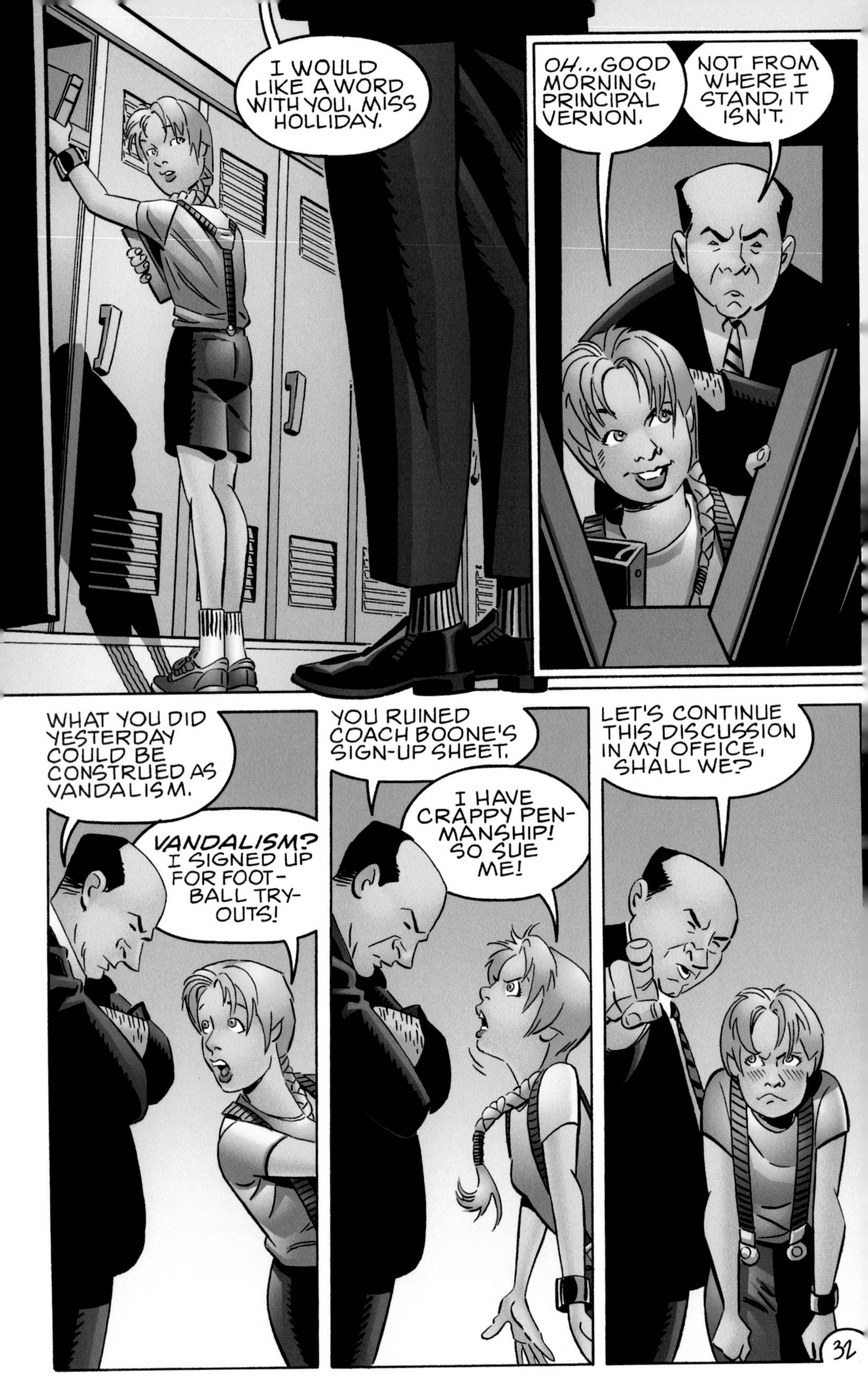
I WOULD LIKE A WORD WITH YOU, MISS HOLLIDAY.
OH...GOOD MORNING, PRINCIPAL VERNON.
NOT FROM WHERE I STAND, IT ISN'T.
WHAT YOU DID YESTERDAY COULD BE CONSTRUED AS VANDALISM.
VANDALISM? I SIGNED UP FOR FOOT-BALL TRY-OUTS!
YOU RUINED COACH BOONE'S SIGN-UP SHEET.
I HAVE CRAPPY PEN-MANSHIP! SO SUE ME!
LET'S CONTINUE THIS DISCUSSION IN MY OFFICE, SHALL WE?

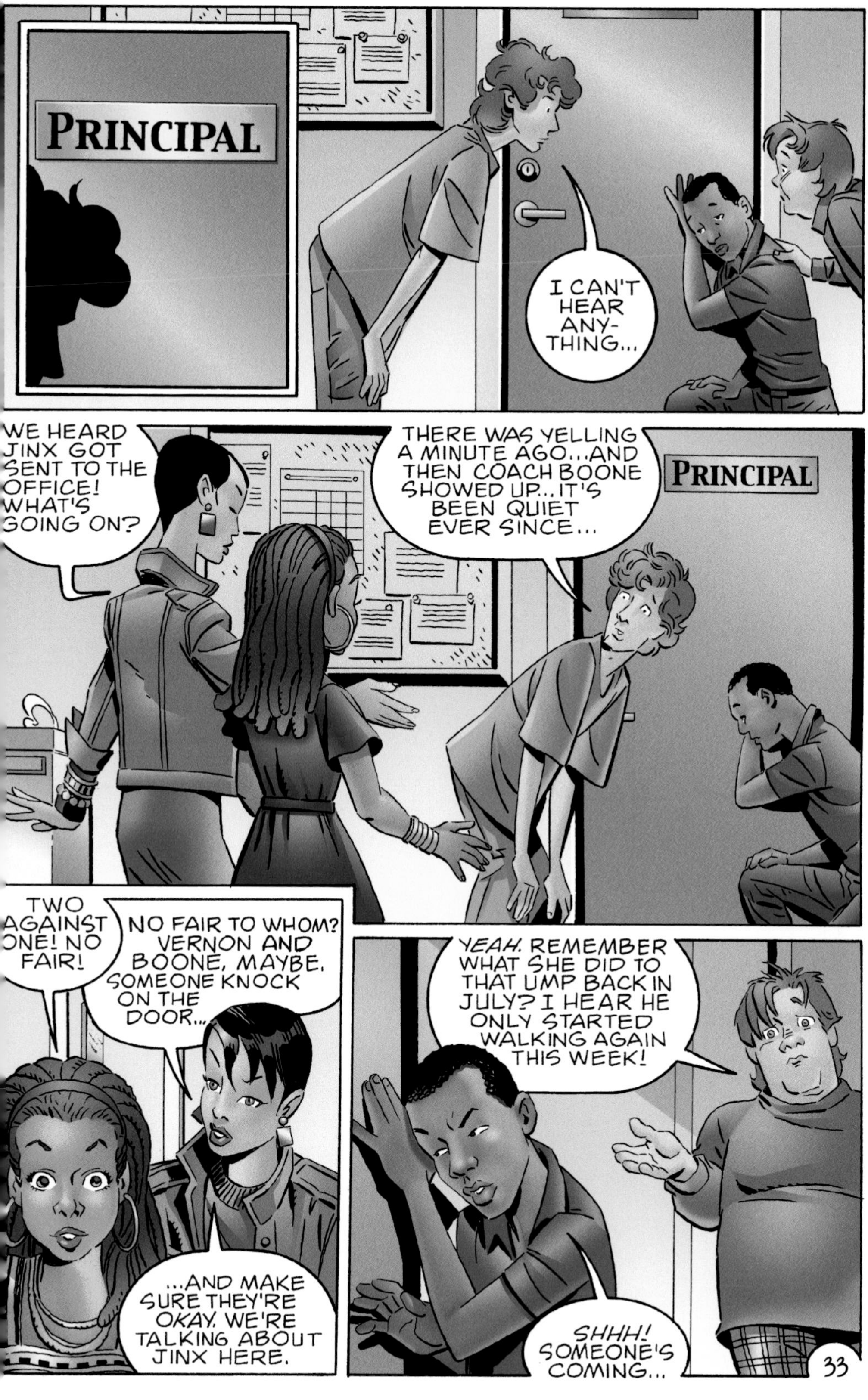
PRINCIPAL
I CAN'T HEAR ANY-THING...
WE HEARD JINX GOT SENT TO THE OFFICE! WHAT'S GOING ON?
THERE WAS YELLING A MINUTE AGO...AND THEN COACH BOONE SHOWED UP...IT'S BEEN QUIET EVER SINCE...
PRINCIPAL
TWO AGAINST ONE! NO FAIR!
NO FAIR TO WHOM? VERNON AND BOONE, MAYBE. SOMEONE KNOCK ON THE DOOR...
...AND MAKE SURE THEY'RE OKAY. WE'RE TALKING ABOUT JINX HERE.
YEAH. REMEMBER WHAT SHE DID TO THAT UMP BACK IN JULY? I HEAR HE ONLY STARTED WALKING AGAIN THIS WEEK!
SHHH! SOMEONE'S COMING...

PRINCIPAL

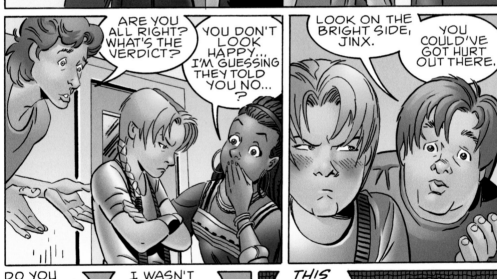

ARE YOU ALL RIGHT? WHAT'S THE VERDICT?

YOU DON'T LOOK HAPPY... I'M GUESSING THEY TOLD YOU NO...?

LOOK ON THE BRIGHT SIDE, JINX.

YOU COULD'VE GOT HURT OUT THERE.

DO YOU SERIOUSLY THINK I WAS SCARED OF GETTING INJURED ON THE FIELD, CHARLEY?

I WASN'T THE LEAST BIT AFRAID OF THAT.

THIS ON THE OTHER HAND...

Permission to Participate in Sports

X

34

THAT'S SO
UNFAIR,
DAD!

LIFE
ISN'T
FAIR,
JINX!

THAT
RESPONSE
ISN'T
FAIR!

WE CAN HEAR
EVERYTHING!
I HOPE THE
NEIGHBORS
DON'T CALL
THE COPS!

WAIT,
THEY'RE
NOT
YELLING
ANY-
MORE...

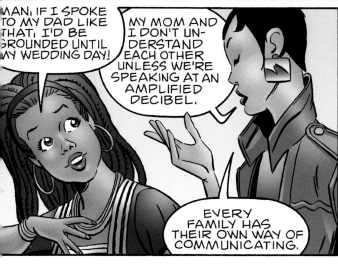

MAN, IF I SPOKE
TO MY DAD LIKE
THAT, I'D BE
GROUNDED UNTIL
MY WEDDING DAY!

MY MOM AND
I DON'T UN-
DERSTAND
EACH OTHER
UNLESS WE'RE
SPEAKING AT AN
AMPLIFIED
DECIBEL.

EVERY
FAMILY HAS
THEIR OWN WAY OF
COMMUNICATING.

SHH!
SOMEONE'S
COMING...

35

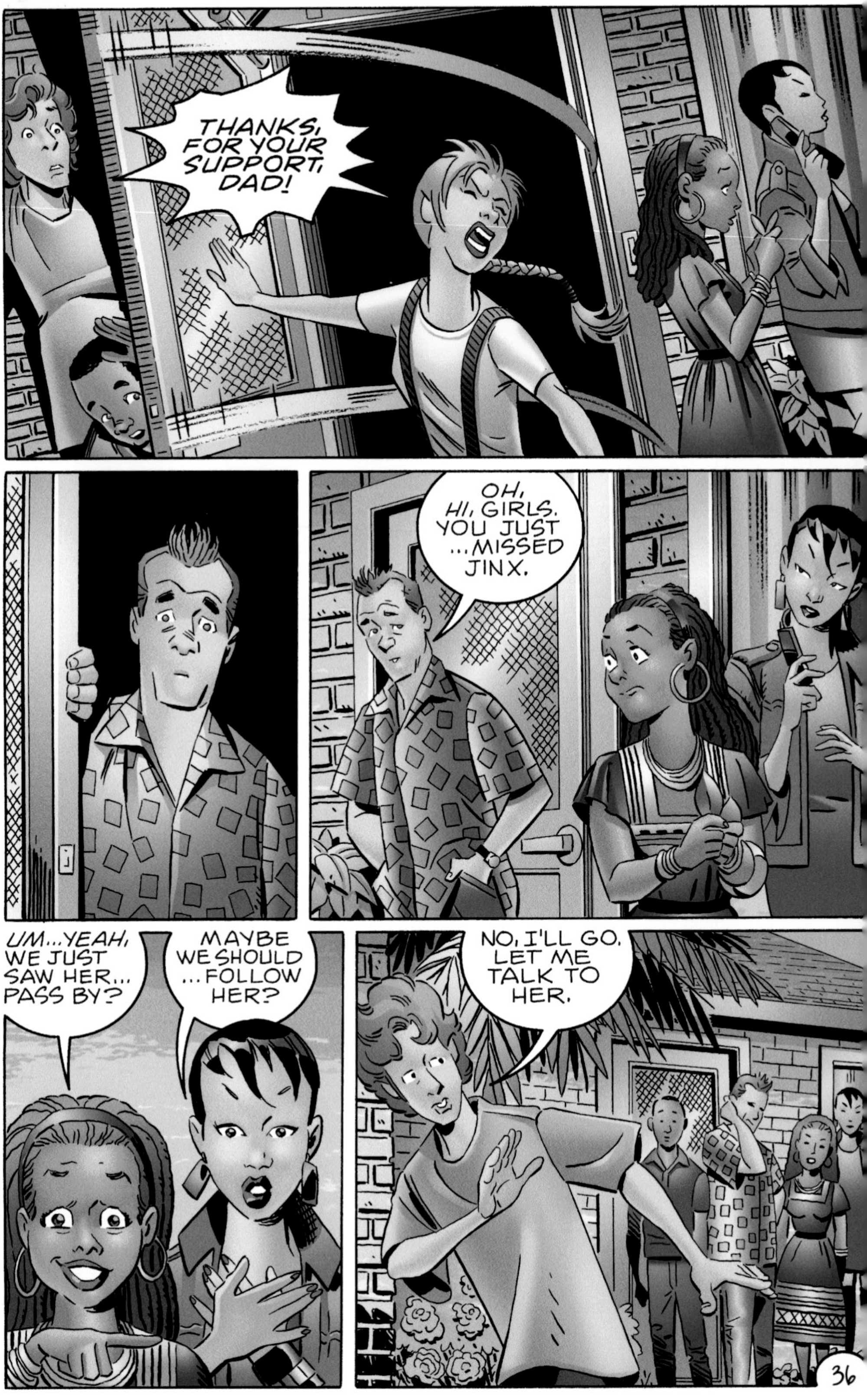
THANKS, FOR YOUR SUPPORT, DAD!
OH, HI, GIRLS. YOU JUST ...MISSED JINX.
UM...YEAH, WE JUST SAW HER... PASS BY?
MAYBE WE SHOULD ...FOLLOW HER?
NO, I'LL GO. LET ME TALK TO HER.

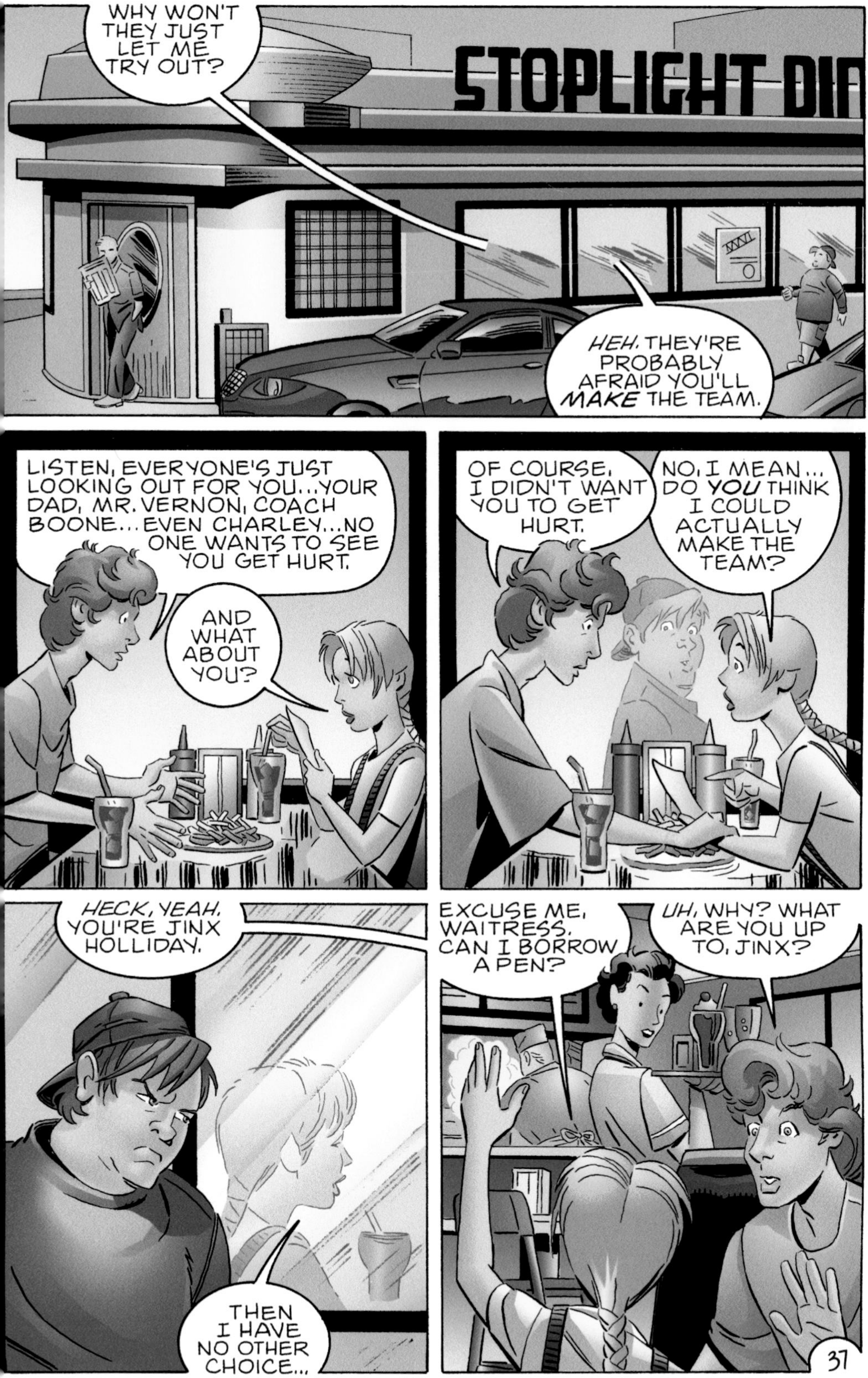
STOPLIGHT DI
WHY WON'T THEY JUST LET ME TRY OUT?
HEH. THEY'RE PROBABLY AFRAID YOU'LL ***MAKE*** THE TEAM.
LISTEN, EVERYONE'S JUST LOOKING OUT FOR YOU...YOUR DAD, MR. VERNON, COACH BOONE... EVEN CHARLEY...NO ONE WANTS TO SEE YOU GET HURT.
AND WHAT ABOUT YOU?
OF COURSE, I DIDN'T WANT YOU TO GET HURT.
NO, I MEAN... DO ***YOU*** THINK I COULD ACTUALLY MAKE THE TEAM?
HECK, YEAH. YOU'RE JINX HOLLIDAY.
THEN I HAVE NO OTHER CHOICE...
EXCUSE ME, WAITRESS. CAN I BORROW A PEN?
UH, WHY? WHAT ARE YOU UP TO, JINX?

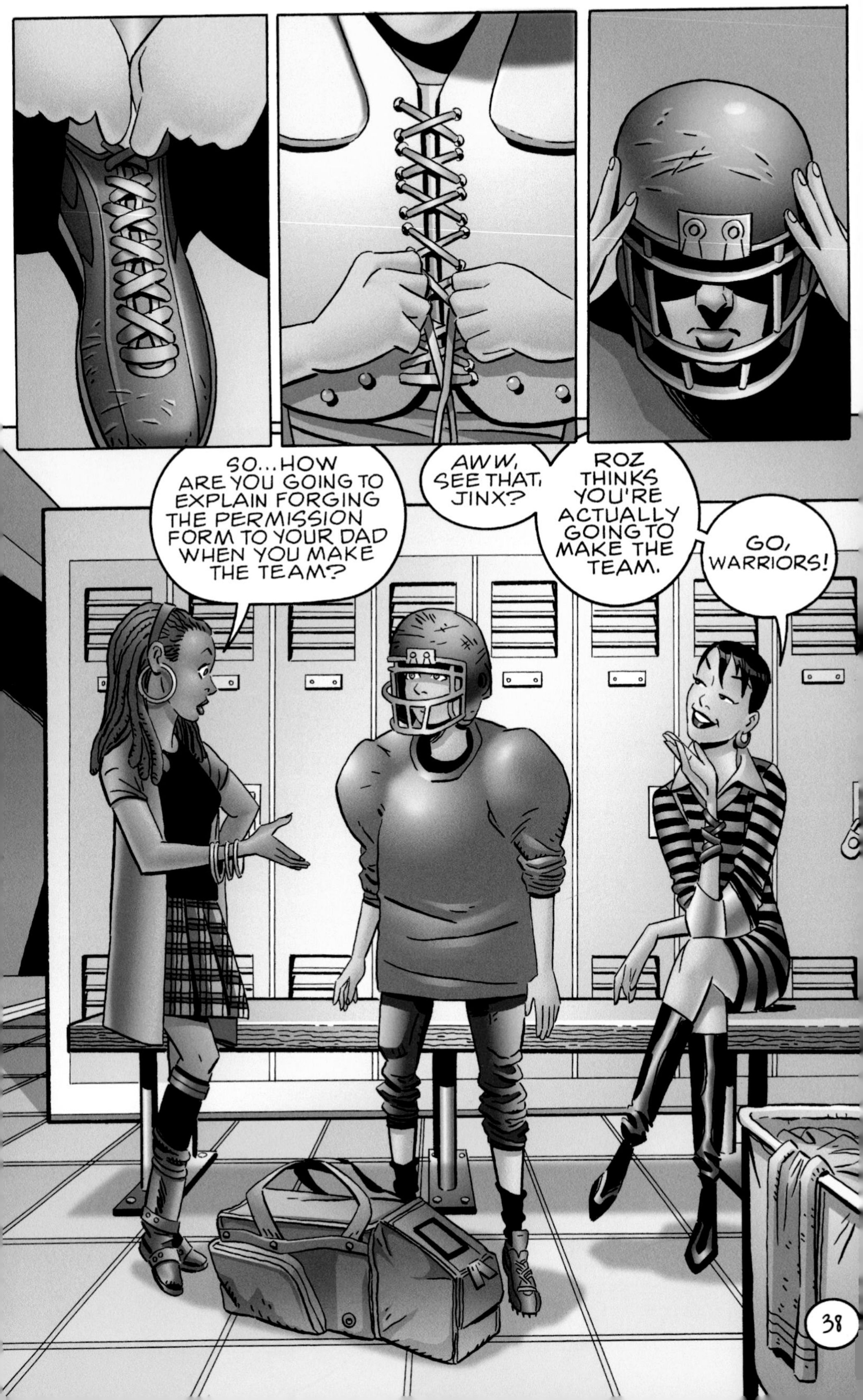
SO...HOW ARE YOU GOING TO EXPLAIN FORGING THE PERMISSION FORM TO YOUR DAD WHEN YOU MAKE THE TEAM?
AWW, SEE THAT, JINX?
ROZ THINKS YOU'RE ACTUALLY GOING TO MAKE THE TEAM.
GO, WARRIORS!

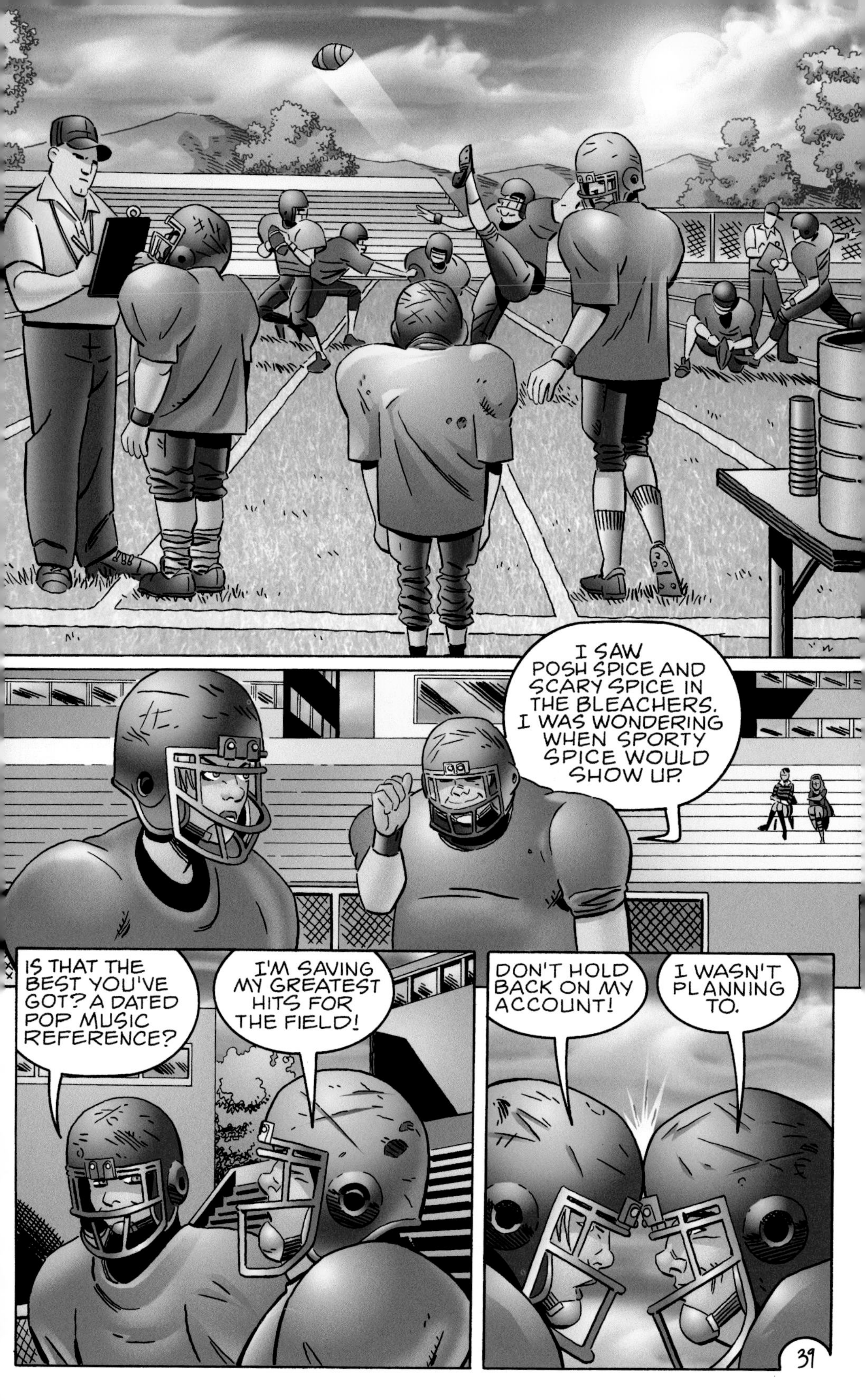

I SAW POSH SPICE AND SCARY SPICE IN THE BLEACHERS. I WAS WONDERING WHEN SPORTY SPICE WOULD SHOW UP.
IS THAT THE BEST YOU'VE GOT? A DATED POP MUSIC REFERENCE?
I'M SAVING MY GREATEST HITS FOR THE FIELD!
DON'T HOLD BACK ON MY ACCOUNT!
I WASN'T PLANNING TO.

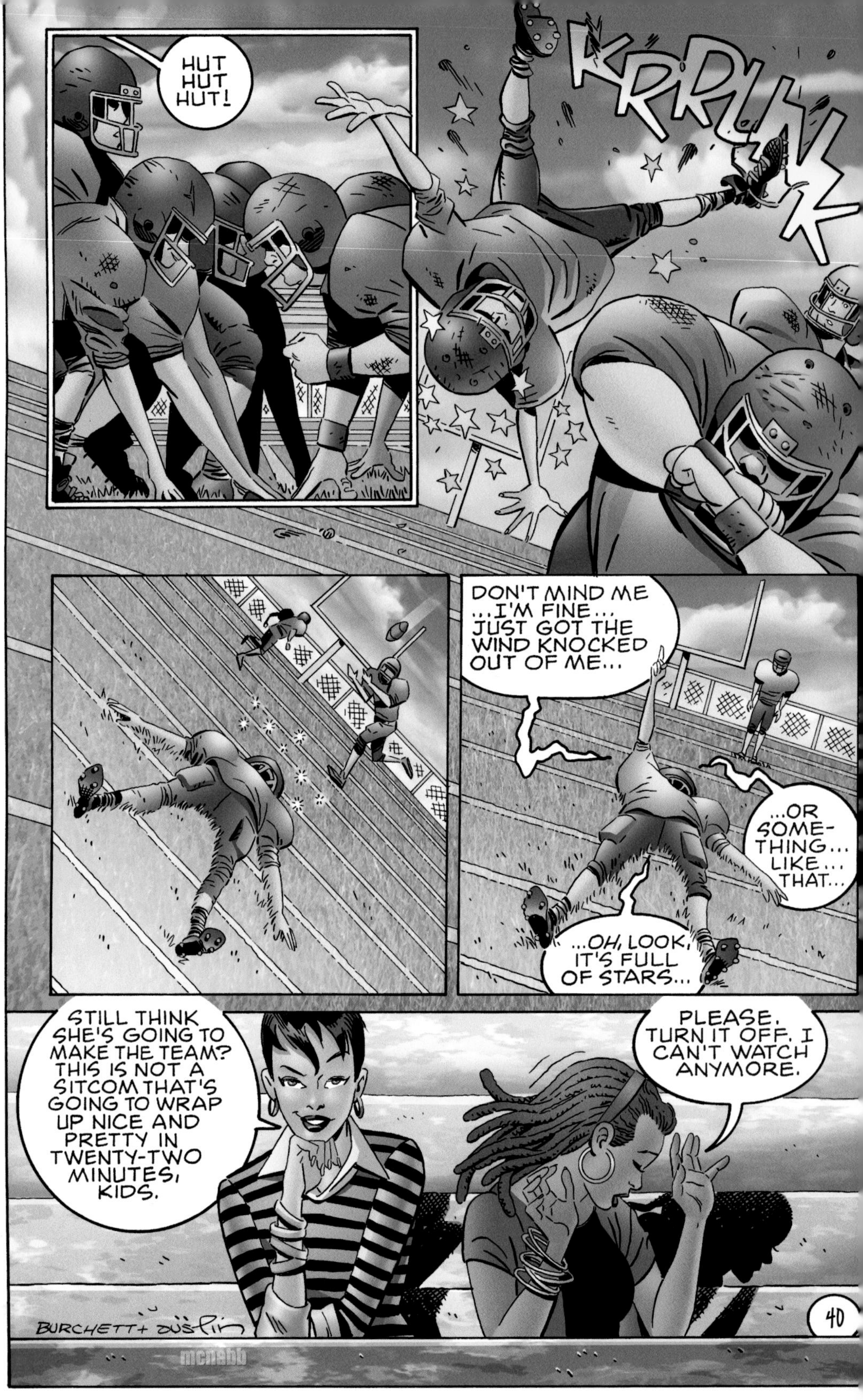
HUT HUT HUT!
KRRUNK
DON'T MIND ME ...I'M FINE... JUST GOT THE WIND KNOCKED OUT OF ME...
...OH, LOOK, IT'S FULL OF STARS...
...OR SOME-THING... LIKE... THAT...
STILL THINK SHE'S GOING TO MAKE THE TEAM? THIS IS NOT A SITCOM THAT'S GOING TO WRAP UP NICE AND PRETTY IN TWENTY-TWO MINUTES, KIDS.
PLEASE. TURN IT OFF. I CAN'T WATCH ANYMORE.
BURCHETT+ AUSPIN
40

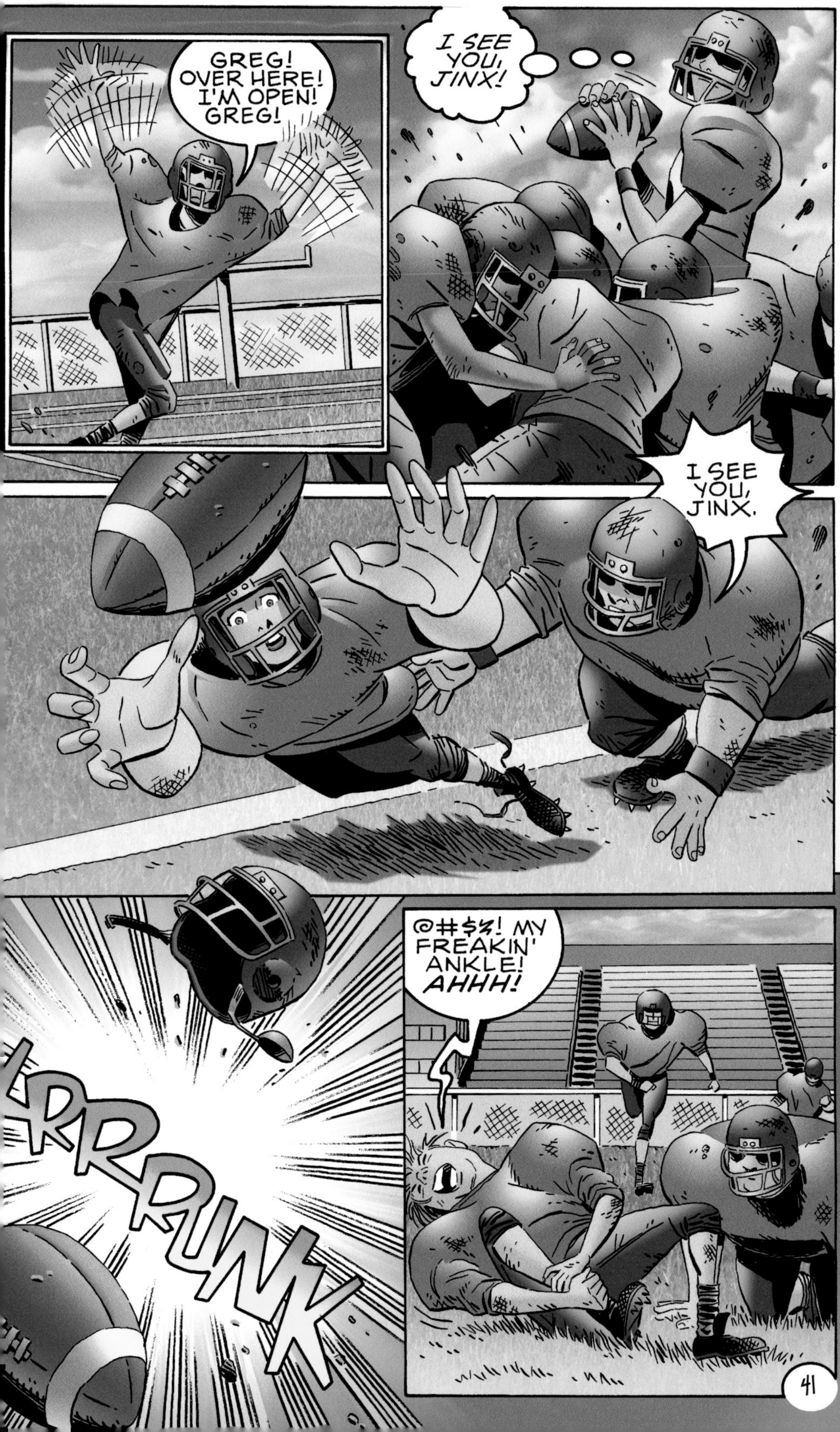
GREG! OVER HERE! I'M OPEN! GREG!
I SEE YOU, JINX!
I SEE YOU, JINX.
@#$%! MY FREAKIN' ANKLE! AHHH!

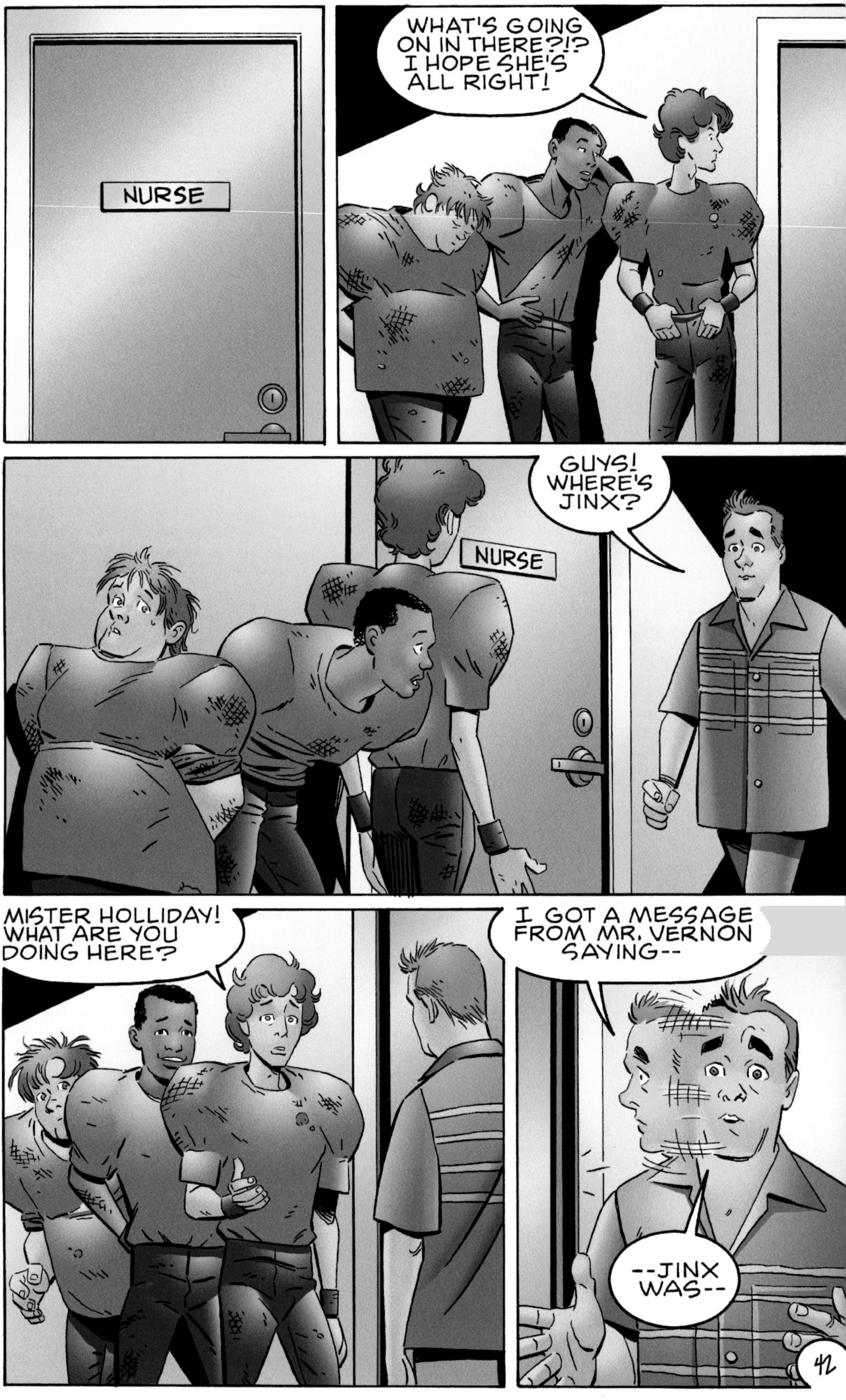
NURSE
WHAT'S GOING ON IN THERE?!? I HOPE SHE'S ALL RIGHT!
NURSE
GUYS! WHERE'S JINX?
MISTER HOLLIDAY! WHAT ARE YOU DOING HERE?
I GOT A MESSAGE FROM MR. VERNON SAYING--
--JINX WAS--

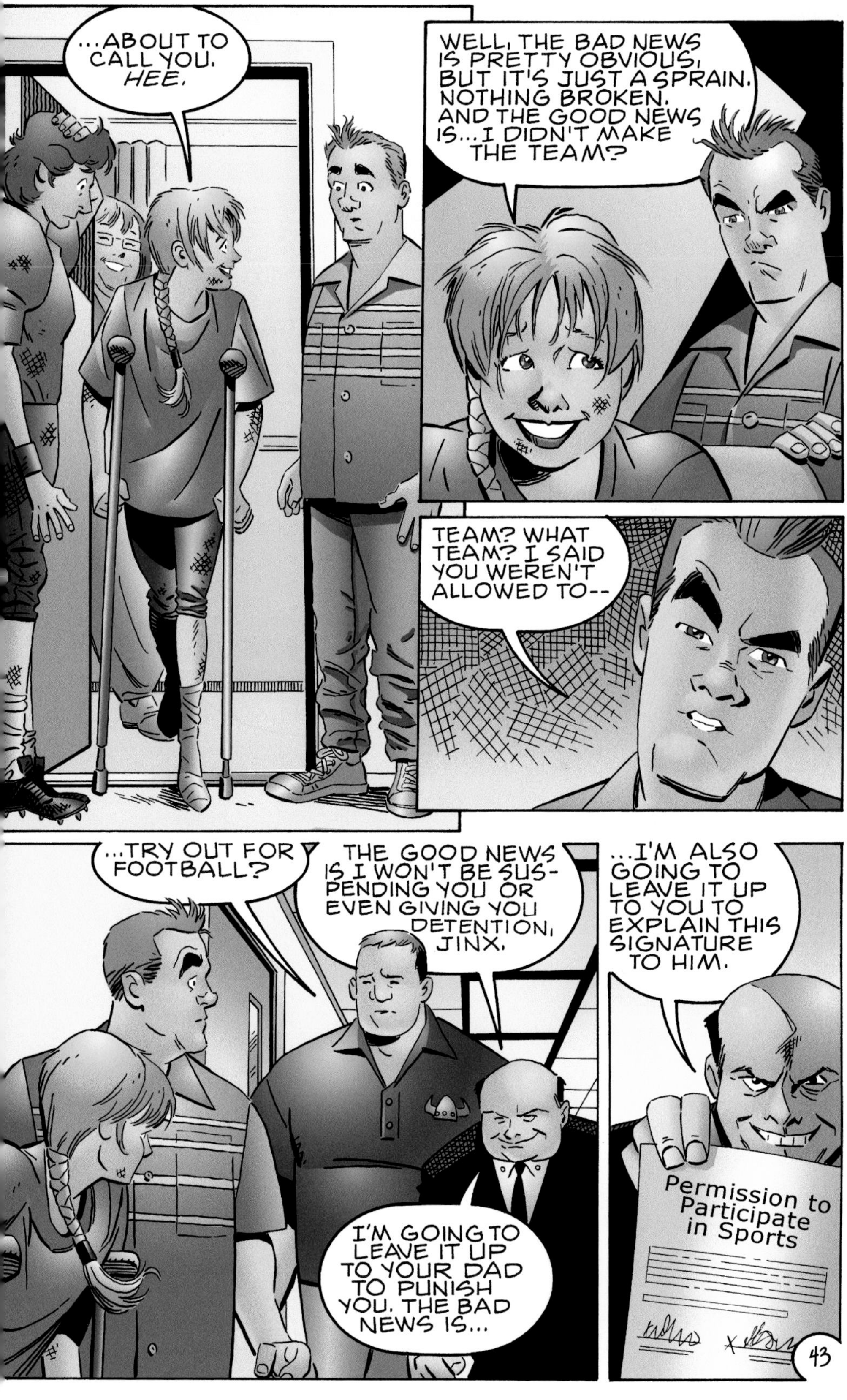
...ABOUT TO CALL YOU. HEE.
WELL, THE BAD NEWS IS PRETTY OBVIOUS, BUT IT'S JUST A SPRAIN. NOTHING BROKEN. AND THE GOOD NEWS IS... I DIDN'T MAKE THE TEAM?
TEAM? WHAT TEAM? I SAID YOU WEREN'T ALLOWED TO--
...TRY OUT FOR FOOTBALL?
THE GOOD NEWS IS I WON'T BE SUSPENDING YOU OR EVEN GIVING YOU DETENTION, JINX.
I'M GOING TO LEAVE IT UP TO YOUR DAD TO PUNISH YOU. THE BAD NEWS IS...
...I'M ALSO GOING TO LEAVE IT UP TO YOU TO EXPLAIN THIS SIGNATURE TO HIM.
Permission to Participate in Sports

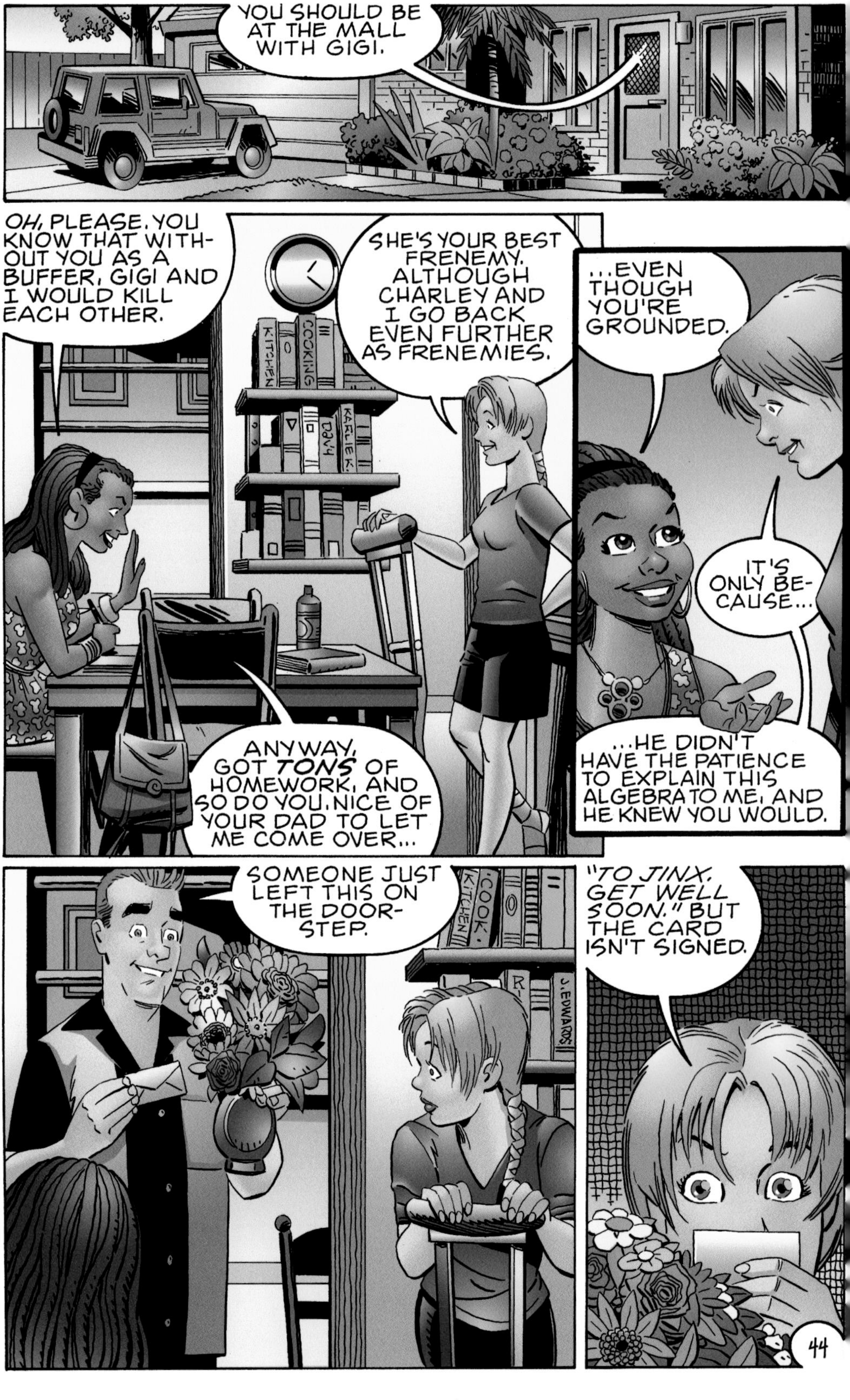
YOU SHOULD BE AT THE MALL WITH GIGI.
OH, PLEASE. YOU KNOW THAT WITH-OUT YOU AS A BUFFER, GIGI AND I WOULD KILL EACH OTHER.
SHE'S YOUR BEST FRENEMY. ALTHOUGH CHARLEY AND I GO BACK EVEN FURTHER AS FRENEMIES.
KITCHEN
COOKING
KARLIE K.
ANYWAY, GOT *TONS* OF HOMEWORK, AND SO DO YOU. NICE OF YOUR DAD TO LET ME COME OVER...
...EVEN THOUGH YOU'RE GROUNDED.
IT'S ONLY BE-CAUSE...
...HE DIDN'T HAVE THE PATIENCE TO EXPLAIN THIS ALGEBRA TO ME, AND HE KNEW YOU WOULD.
SOMEONE JUST LEFT THIS ON THE DOOR-STEP.
KITCHEN
COOK
J. EDWARDS
"TO JINX, GET WELL SOON." BUT THE CARD ISN'T SIGNED.

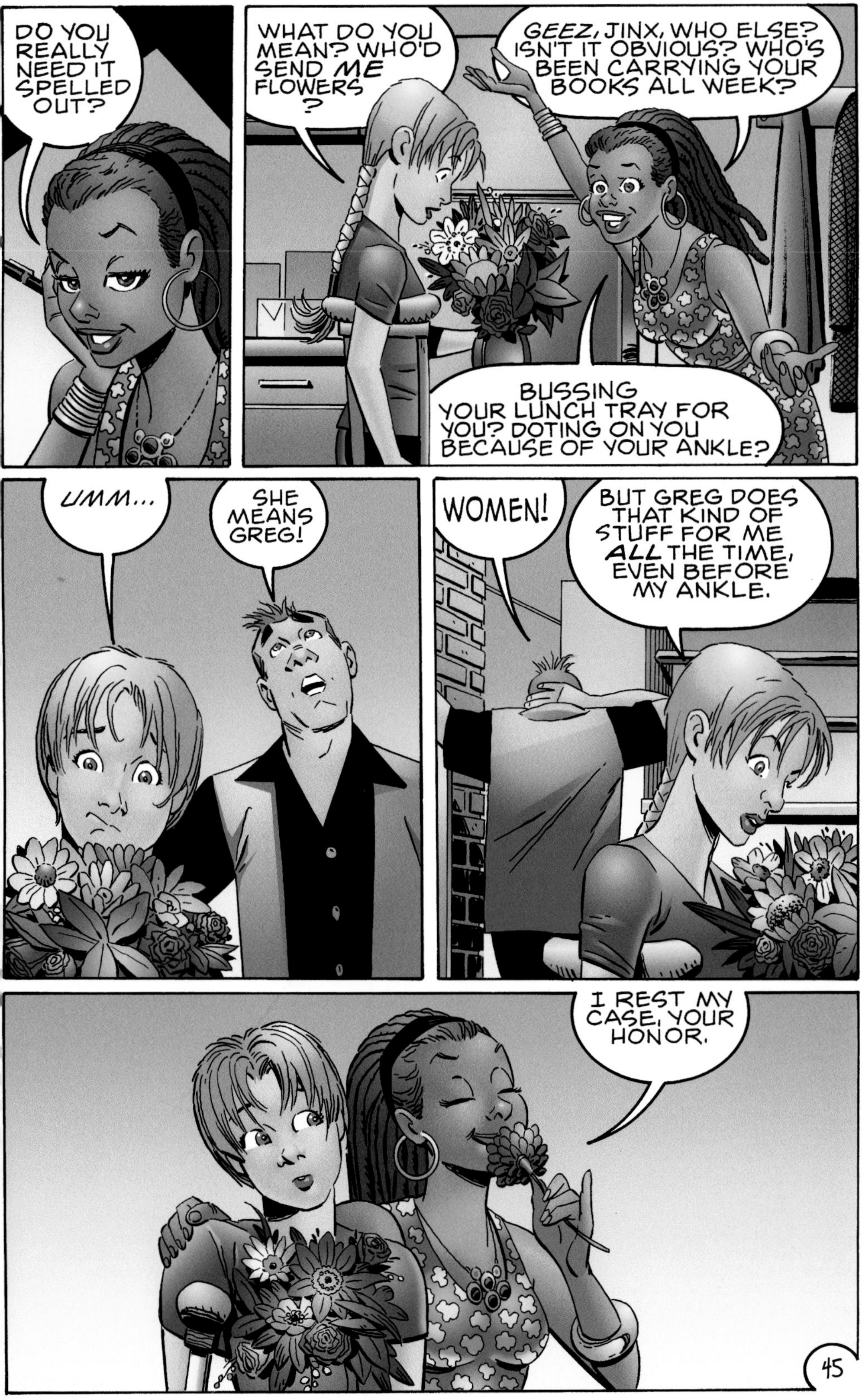
DO YOU REALLY NEED IT SPELLED OUT?
WHAT DO YOU MEAN? WHO'D SEND ME FLOWERS ?
GEEZ, JINX, WHO ELSE? ISN'T IT OBVIOUS? WHO'S BEEN CARRYING YOUR BOOKS ALL WEEK?
BUSSING YOUR LUNCH TRAY FOR YOU? DOTING ON YOU BECAUSE OF YOUR ANKLE?
UMM...
SHE MEANS GREG!
WOMEN!
BUT GREG DOES THAT KIND OF STUFF FOR ME ALL THE TIME, EVEN BEFORE MY ANKLE.
I REST MY CASE, YOUR HONOR.

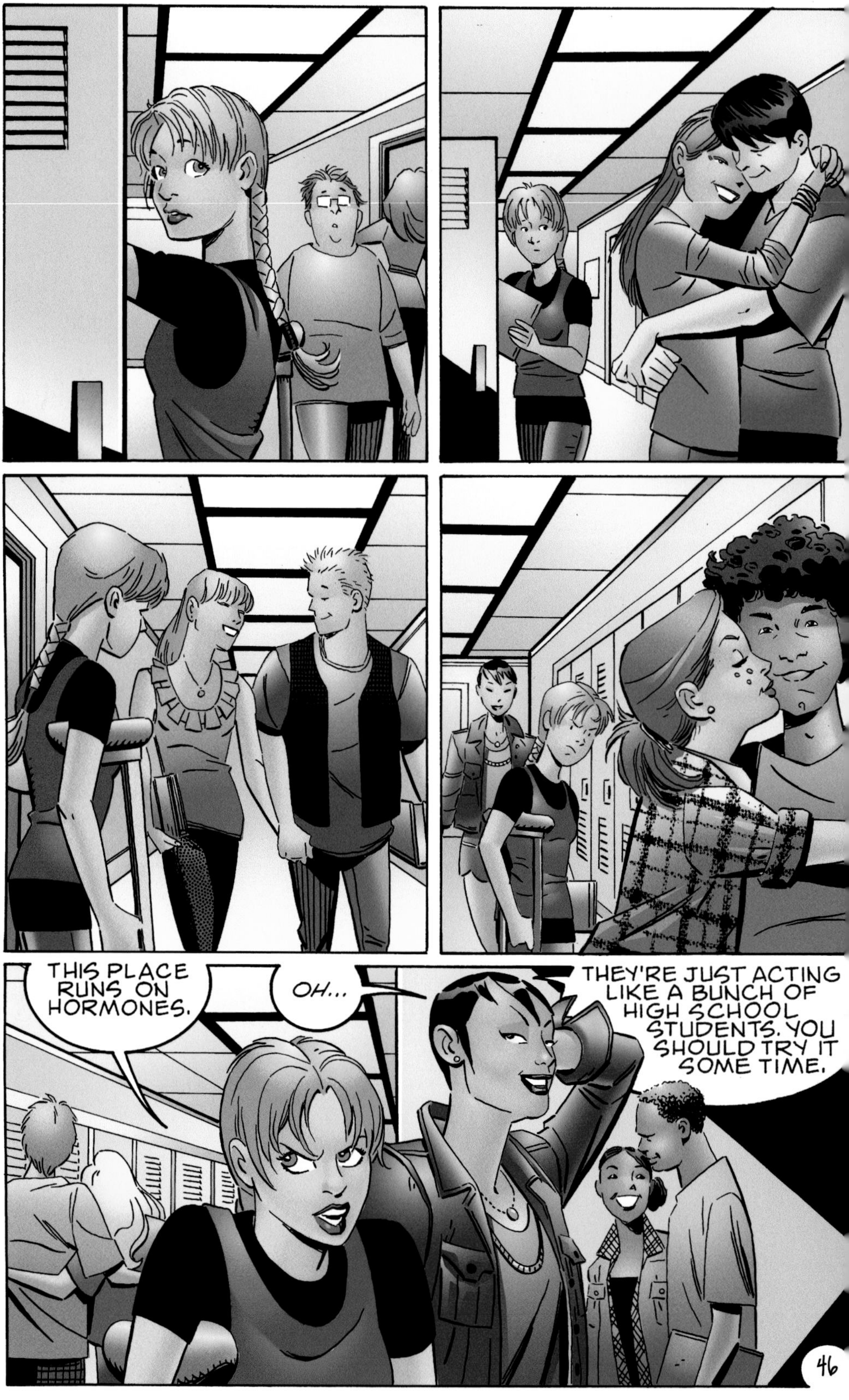
THIS PLACE RUNS ON HORMONES.
OH...
THEY'RE JUST ACTING LIKE A BUNCH OF HIGH SCHOOL STUDENTS. YOU SHOULD TRY IT SOME TIME.

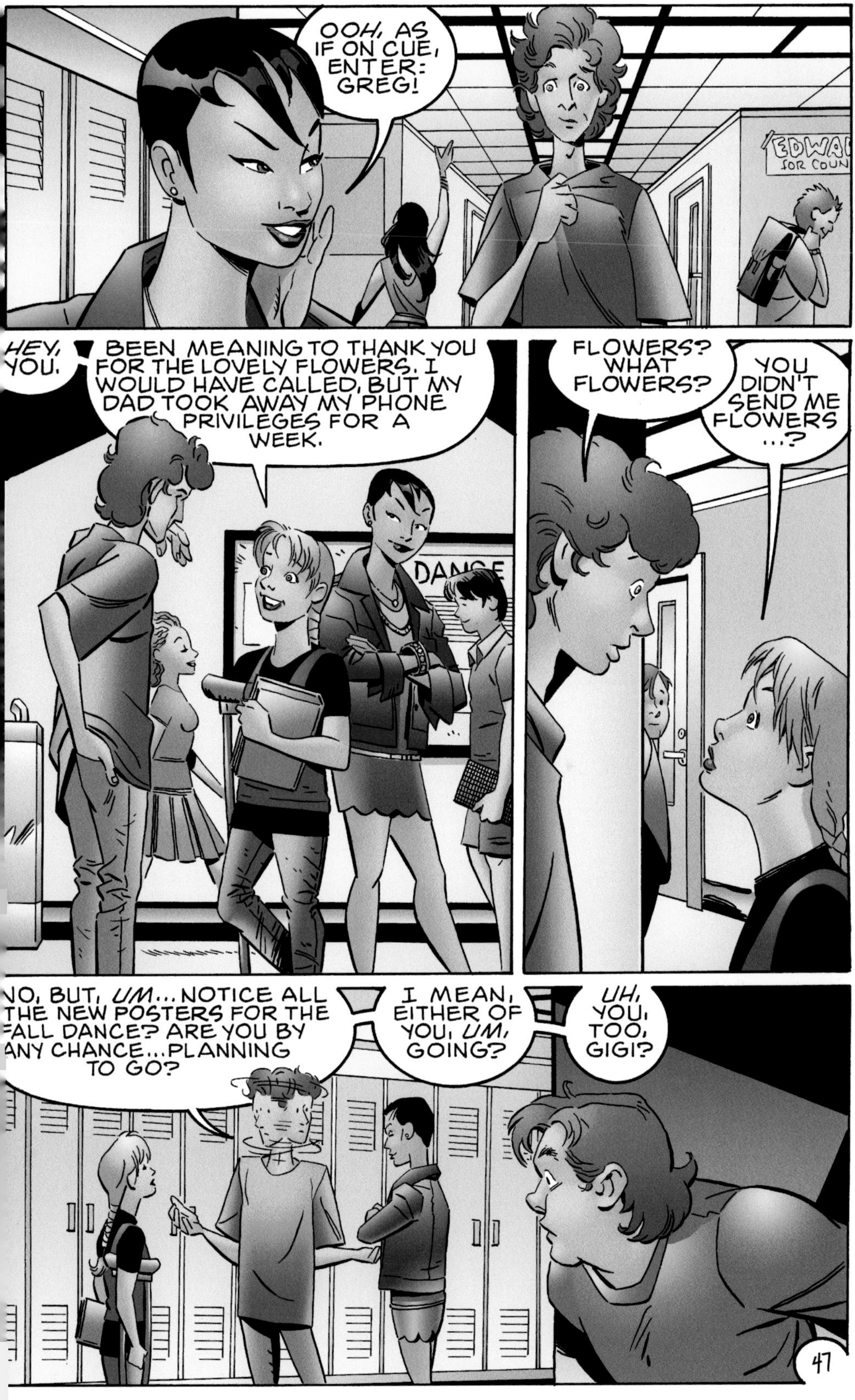
OOH, AS IF ON CUE, ENTER: GREG!
EDWA
FOR COUN
HEY, YOU.
BEEN MEANING TO THANK YOU FOR THE LOVELY FLOWERS. I WOULD HAVE CALLED, BUT MY DAD TOOK AWAY MY PHONE PRIVILEGES FOR A WEEK.
DANCE
FLOWERS? WHAT FLOWERS?
YOU DIDN'T SEND ME FLOWERS ...?
NO, BUT, UM... NOTICE ALL THE NEW POSTERS FOR THE FALL DANCE? ARE YOU BY ANY CHANCE...PLANNING TO GO?
I MEAN, EITHER OF YOU, UM, GOING?
UH, YOU, TOO, GIGI?

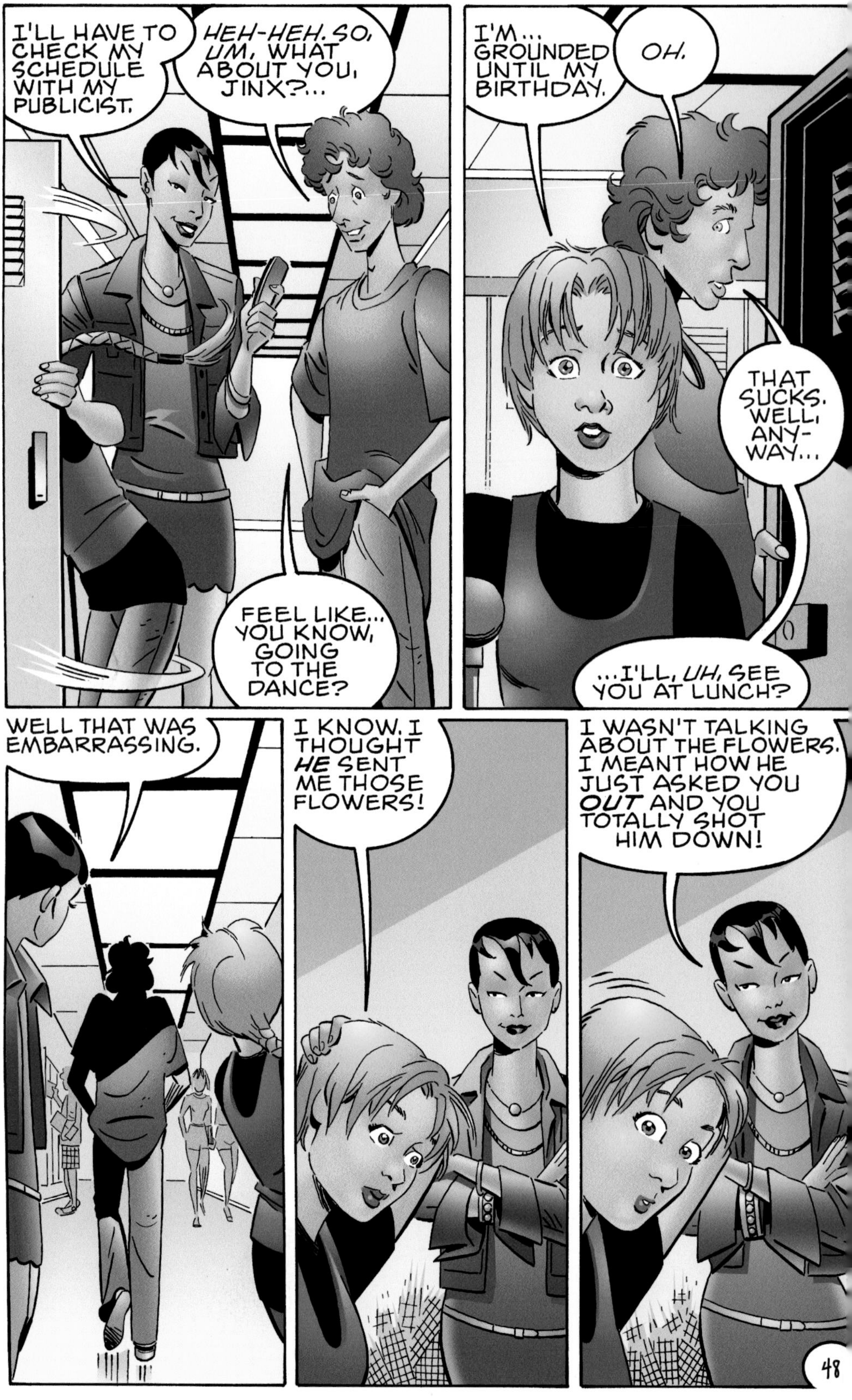
I'LL HAVE TO CHECK MY SCHEDULE WITH MY PUBLICIST.
HEH-HEH. SO, UM, WHAT ABOUT YOU, JINX?...
FEEL LIKE... YOU KNOW, GOING TO THE DANCE?
I'M... GROUNDED UNTIL MY BIRTHDAY.
OH.
THAT SUCKS. WELL, ANY-WAY...
...I'LL, UH, SEE YOU AT LUNCH?
WELL THAT WAS EMBARRASSING.
I KNOW. I THOUGHT HE SENT ME THOSE FLOWERS!
I WASN'T TALKING ABOUT THE FLOWERS. I MEANT HOW HE JUST ASKED YOU OUT AND YOU TOTALLY SHOT HIM DOWN!

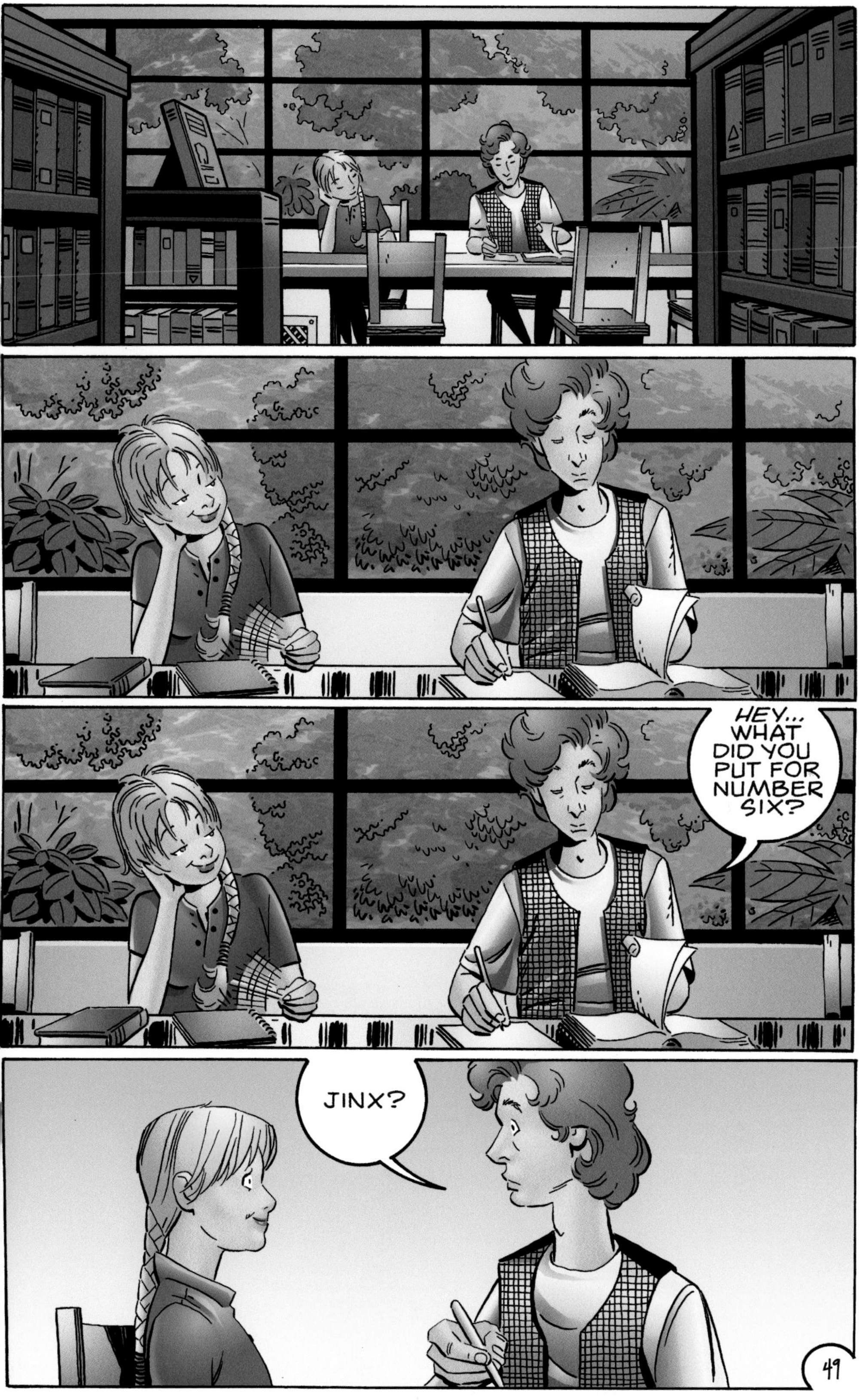
HEY... WHAT DID YOU PUT FOR NUMBER SIX?
JINX?
49

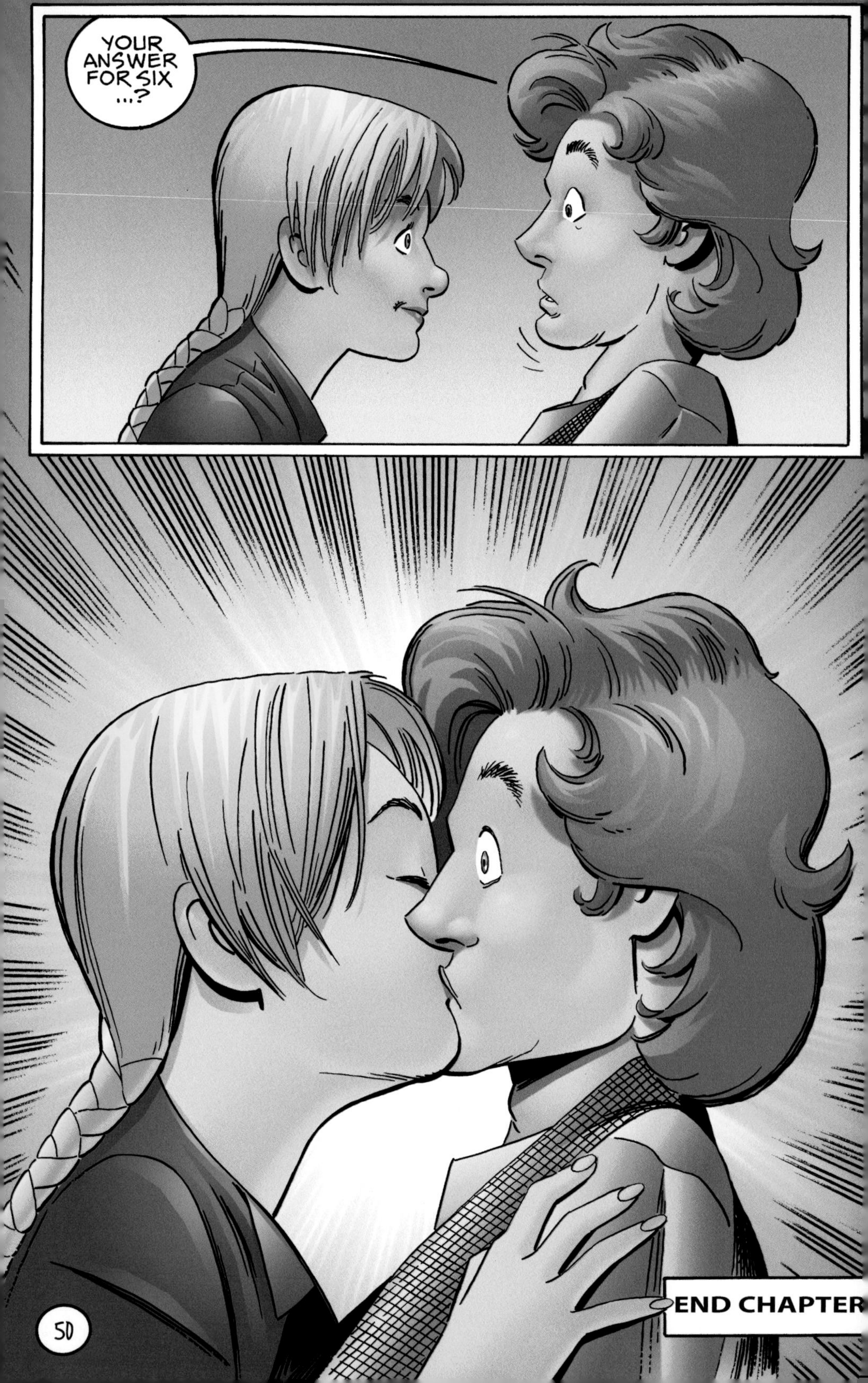
YOUR ANSWER FOR SIX ...?
END CHAPTER

JINX™

CHAPTER 3

BURCHETT & AUSTIN
mcnabb

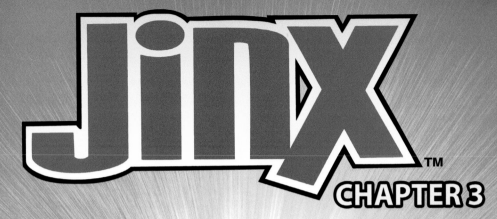

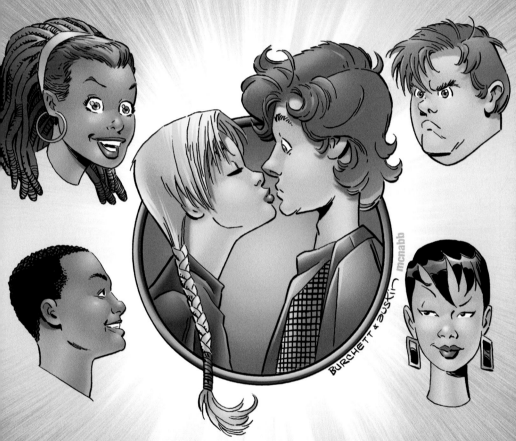

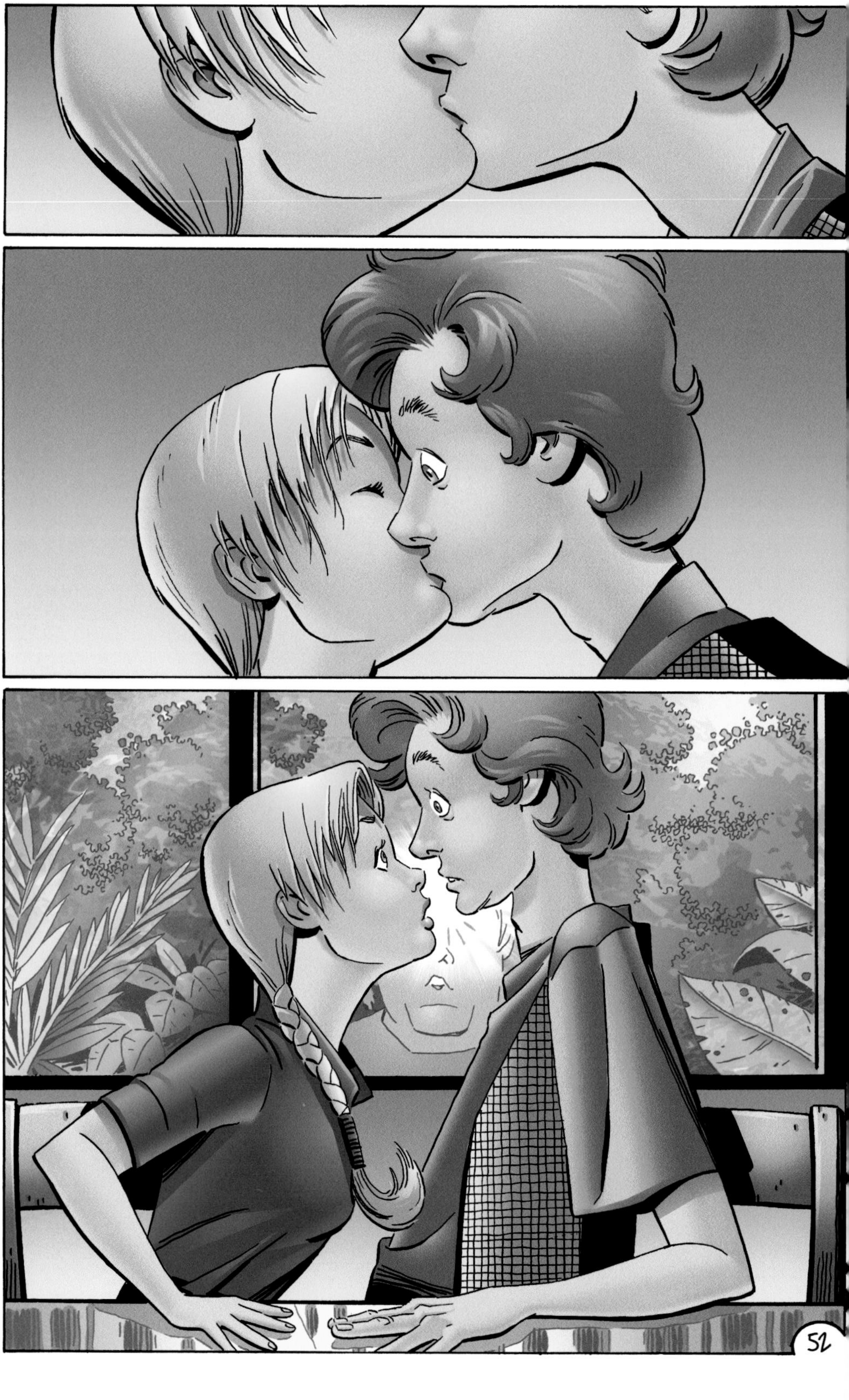

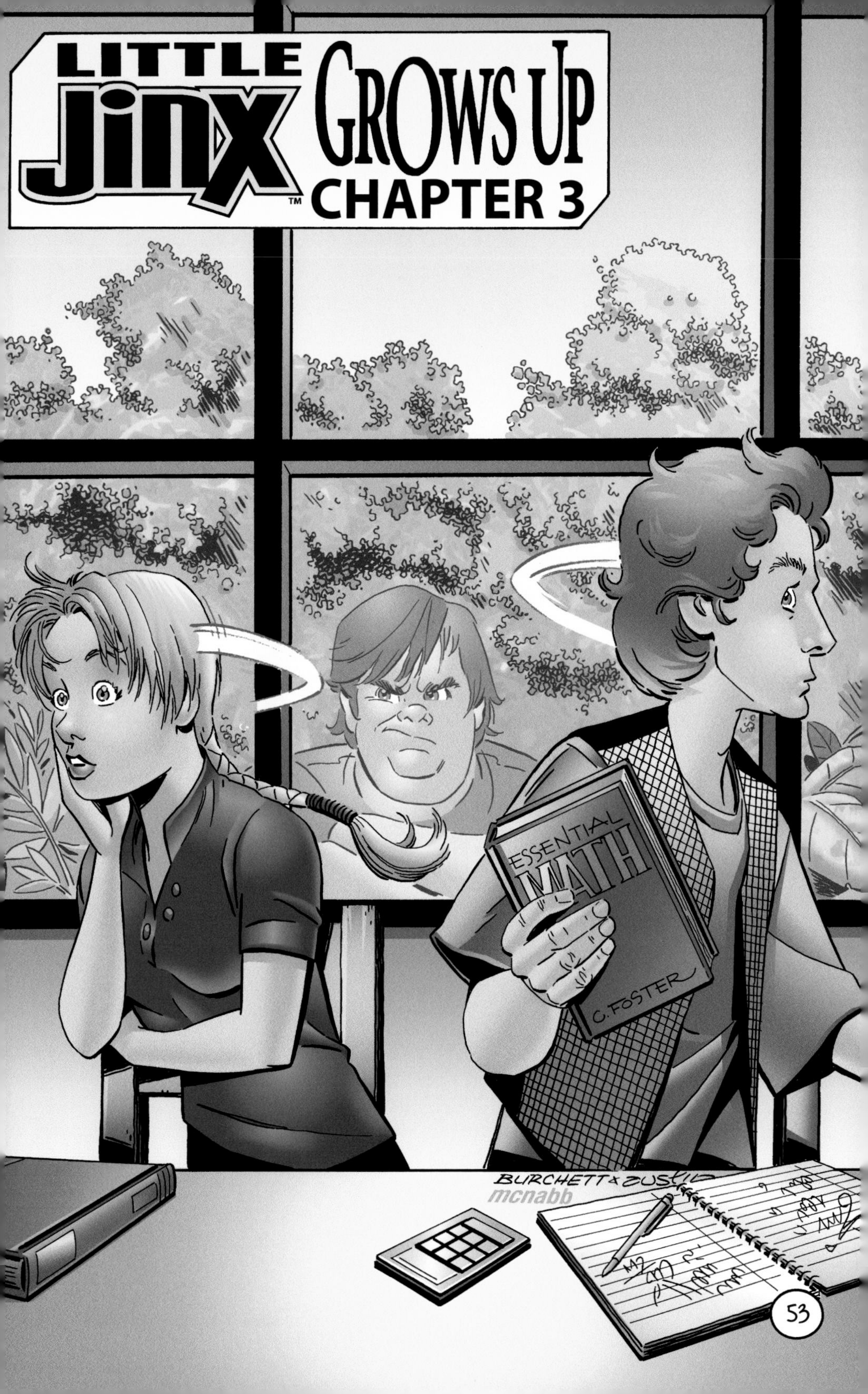
LITTLE JINX™
GROWS UP
CHAPTER 3
ESSENTIAL MATH
C. FOSTER
BURCHETT & ZUSKID
mcnabb
53

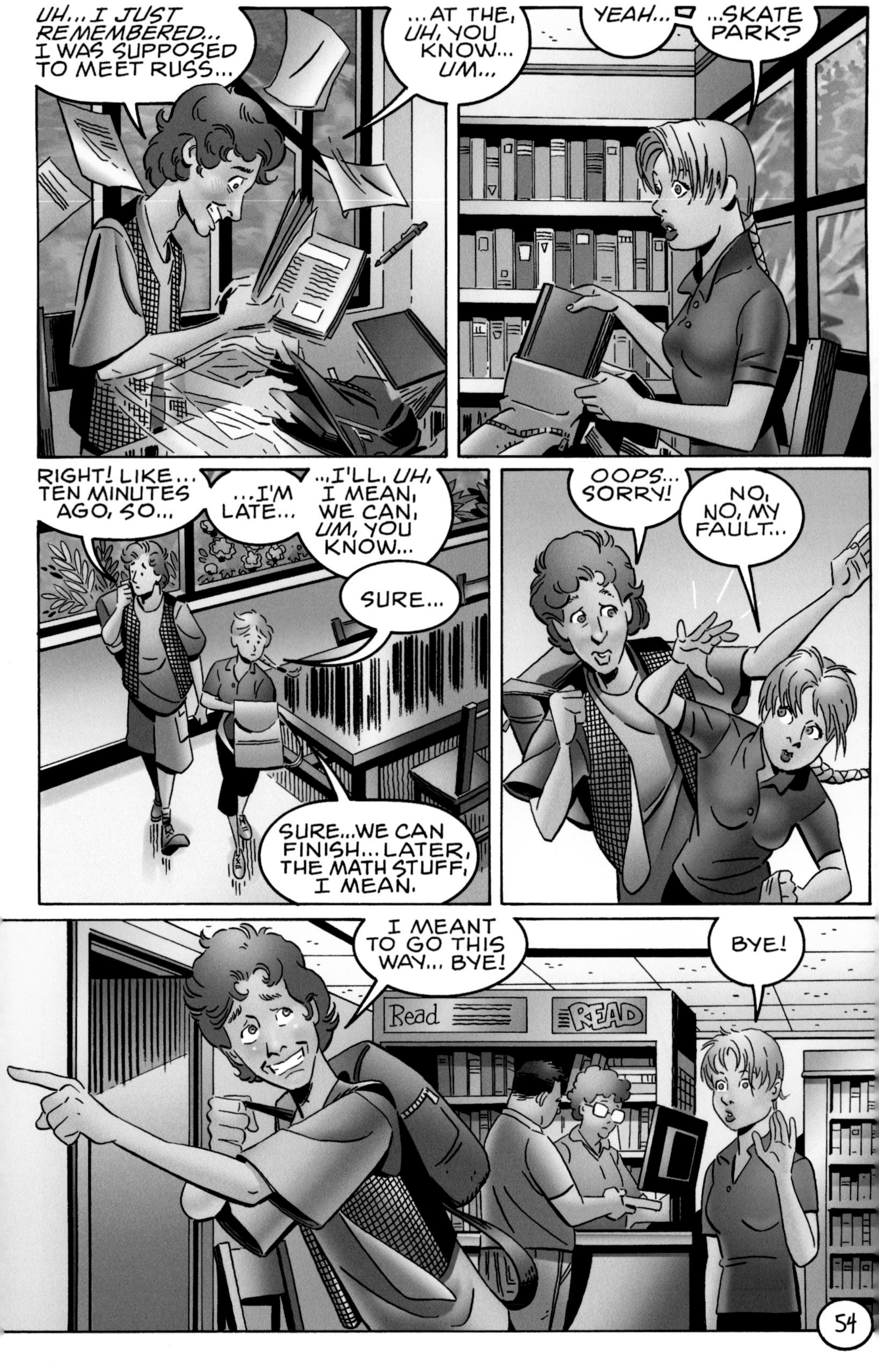
UH... I JUST REMEMBERED... I WAS SUPPOSED TO MEET RUSS...
...AT THE, UH, YOU KNOW... UM...
YEAH...
...SKATE PARK?
RIGHT! LIKE... TEN MINUTES AGO, SO...
...I'M LATE...
...I'LL, UH, I MEAN, WE CAN, UM, YOU KNOW...
SURE...
SURE...WE CAN FINISH... LATER, THE MATH STUFF, I MEAN.
OOPS... SORRY!
NO, NO, MY FAULT...
I MEANT TO GO THIS WAY... BYE!
BYE!
Read
READ

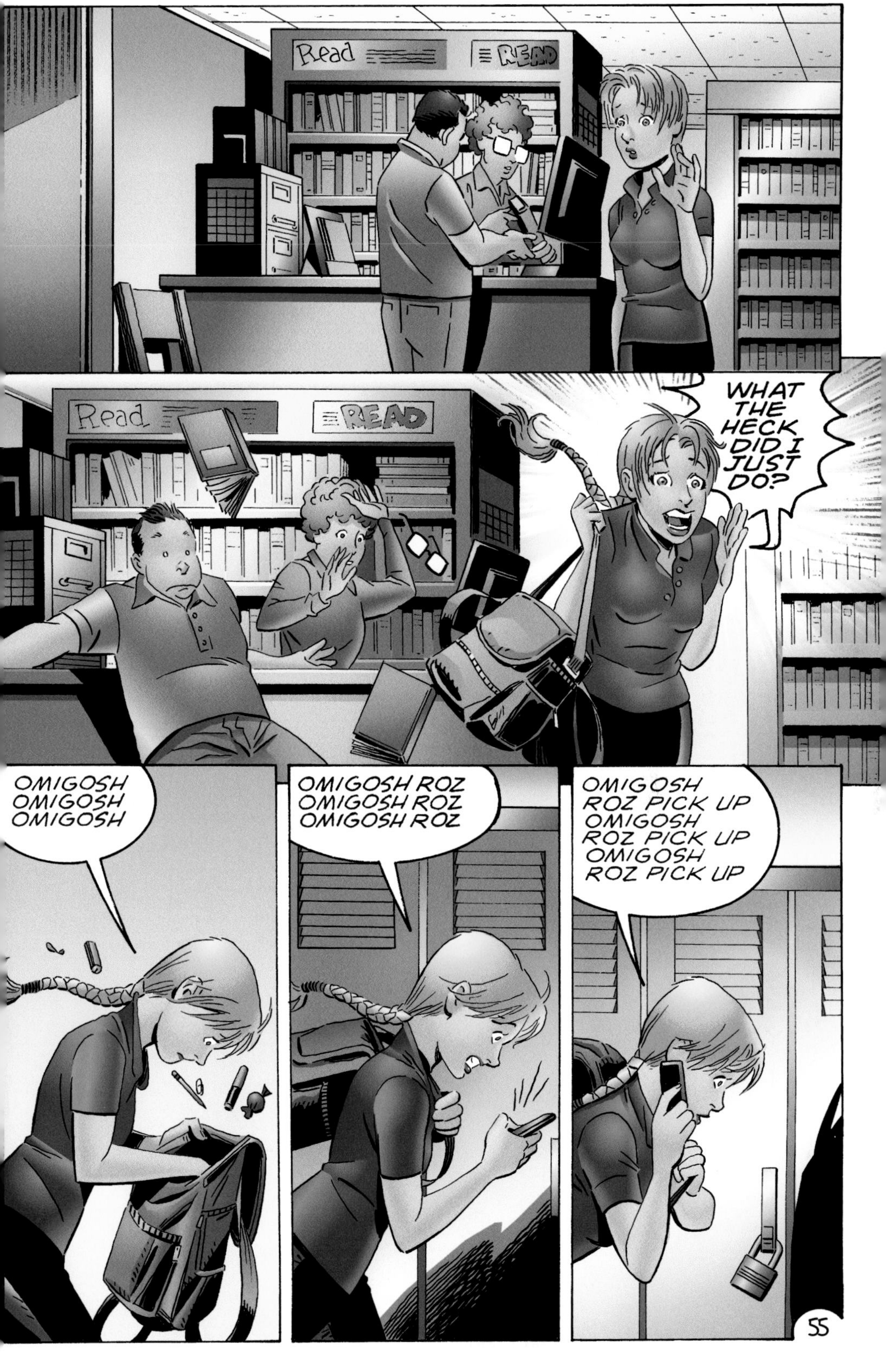
Read
READ
WHAT THE HECK DID I JUST DO?
OMIGOSH OMIGOSH OMIGOSH
OMIGOSH ROZ OMIGOSH ROZ OMIGOSH ROZ
OMIGOSH ROZ PICK UP OMIGOSH ROZ PICK UP OMIGOSH ROZ PICK UP

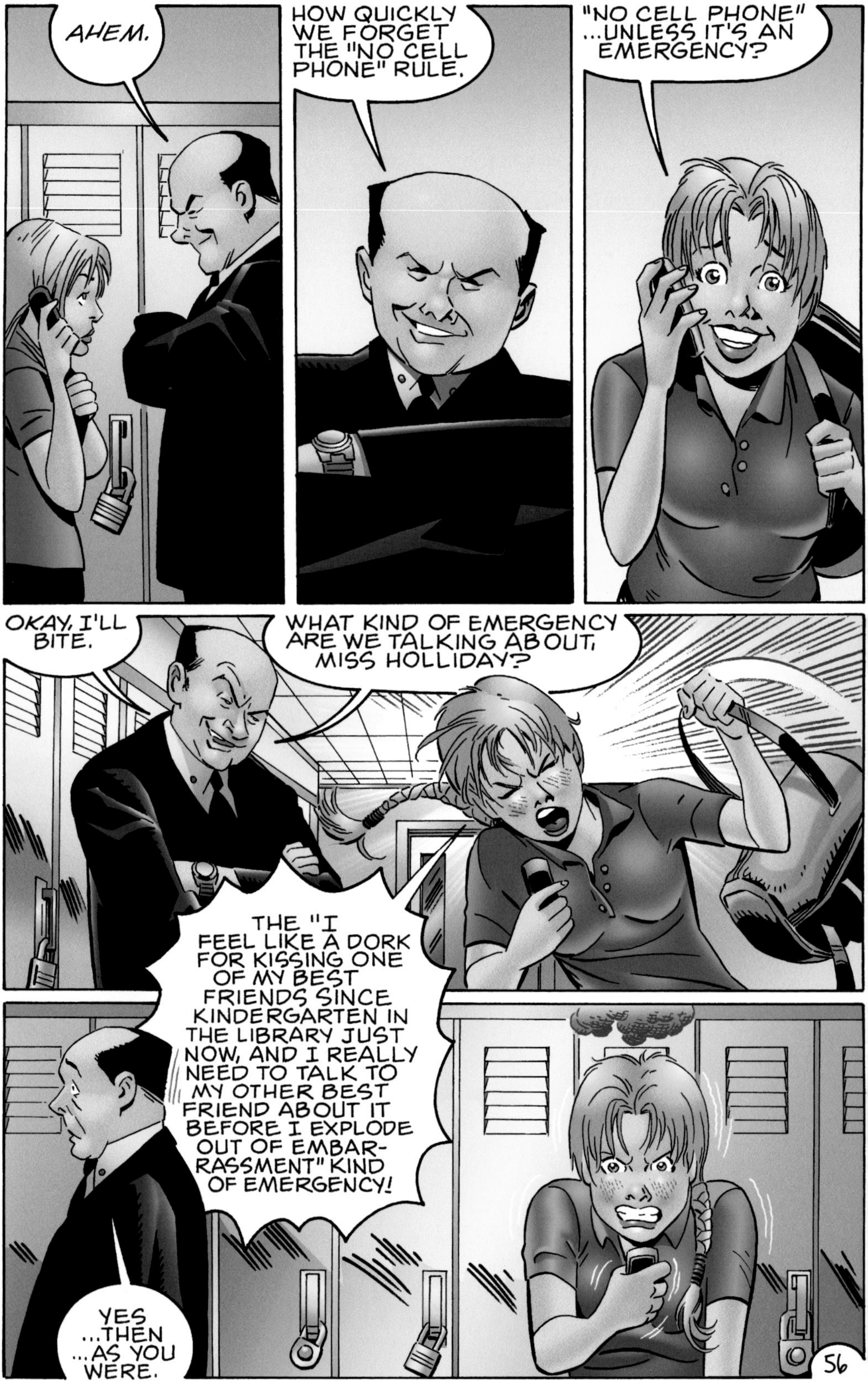
AHEM.
HOW QUICKLY WE FORGET THE "NO CELL PHONE" RULE.
"NO CELL PHONE" ...UNLESS IT'S AN EMERGENCY?
OKAY, I'LL BITE.
WHAT KIND OF EMERGENCY ARE WE TALKING ABOUT, MISS HOLLIDAY?
THE "I FEEL LIKE A DORK FOR KISSING ONE OF MY BEST FRIENDS SINCE KINDERGARTEN IN THE LIBRARY JUST NOW, AND I REALLY NEED TO TALK TO MY OTHER BEST FRIEND ABOUT IT BEFORE I EXPLODE OUT OF EMBAR-RASSMENT" KIND OF EMERGENCY!
YES ...THEN ...AS YOU WERE.

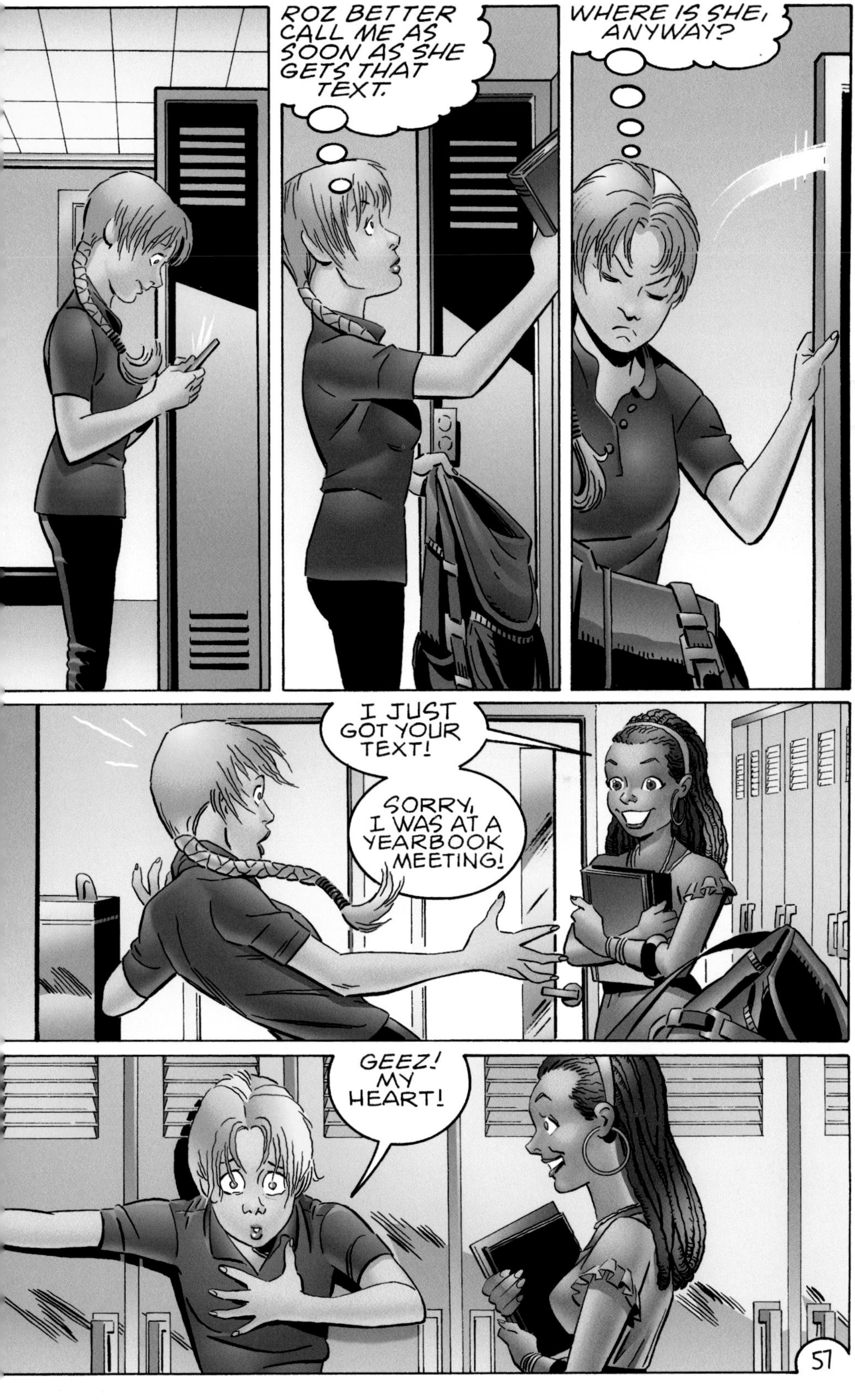
ROZ BETTER CALL ME AS SOON AS SHE GETS THAT TEXT.
WHERE IS SHE, ANYWAY?
I JUST GOT YOUR TEXT!
SORRY, I WAS AT A YEARBOOK MEETING!
GEEZ! MY HEART!

...IS BEATING A MILE A MINUTE *BECAUSE YOU KISSED GREG!*

JINX...WHAT'S THE MATTER? WHY DO YOU LOOK SO...SAD?

OH.

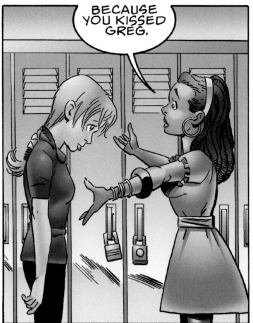

BECAUSE YOU KISSED GREG.

WHAT WAS I THINKING, ROZ?

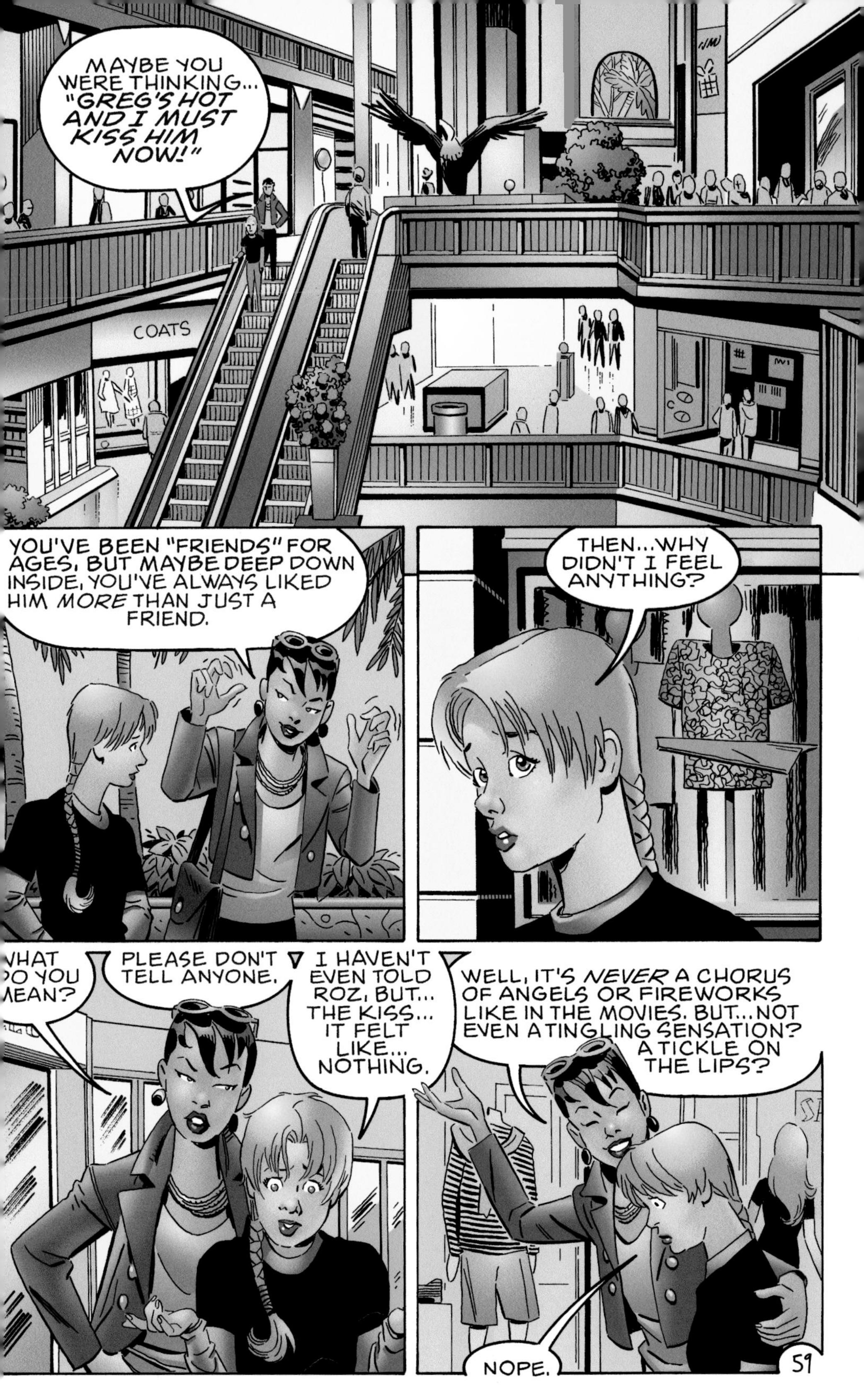

MAYBE YOU WERE THINKING... "*GREG'S HOT AND I MUST KISS HIM NOW!*"
COATS
YOU'VE BEEN "FRIENDS" FOR AGES, BUT MAYBE DEEP DOWN INSIDE, YOU'VE ALWAYS LIKED HIM *MORE* THAN JUST A FRIEND.
THEN...WHY DIDN'T I FEEL ANYTHING?
WHAT DO YOU MEAN?
PLEASE DON'T TELL ANYONE.
I HAVEN'T EVEN TOLD ROZ, BUT... THE KISS... IT FELT LIKE... NOTHING.
WELL, IT'S *NEVER* A CHORUS OF ANGELS OR FIREWORKS LIKE IN THE MOVIES. BUT...NOT EVEN A TINGLING SENSATION? A TICKLE ON THE LIPS?
NOPE.

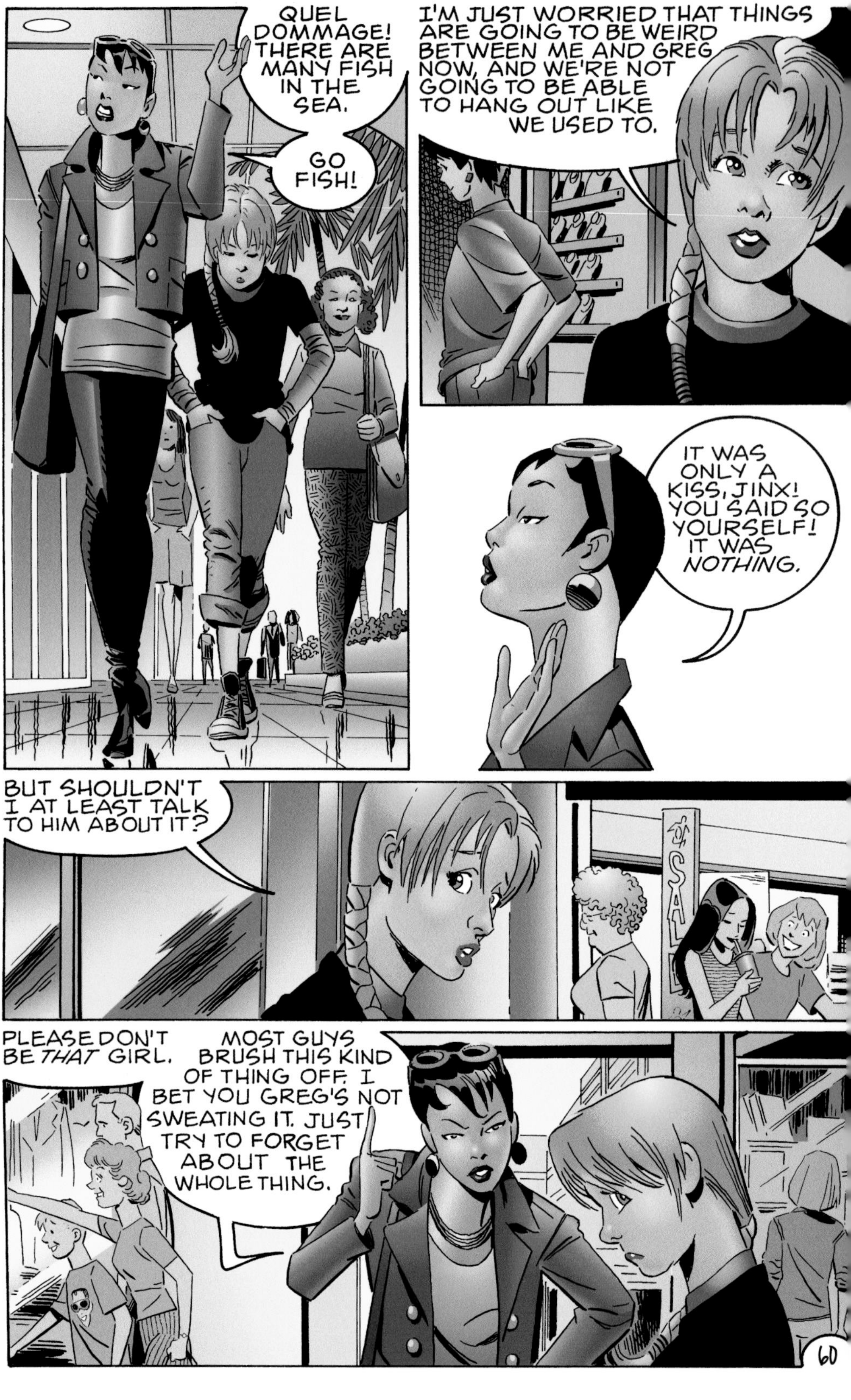
QUEL DOMMAGE! THERE ARE MANY FISH IN THE SEA.
GO FISH!
I'M JUST WORRIED THAT THINGS ARE GOING TO BE WEIRD BETWEEN ME AND GREG NOW, AND WE'RE NOT GOING TO BE ABLE TO HANG OUT LIKE WE USED TO.
IT WAS ONLY A KISS, JINX! YOU SAID SO YOURSELF! IT WAS *NOTHING.*
BUT SHOULDN'T I AT LEAST TALK TO HIM ABOUT IT?
PLEASE DON'T BE *THAT* GIRL.
MOST GUYS BRUSH THIS KIND OF THING OFF. I BET YOU GREG'S NOT SWEATING IT. JUST TRY TO FORGET ABOUT THE WHOLE THING.

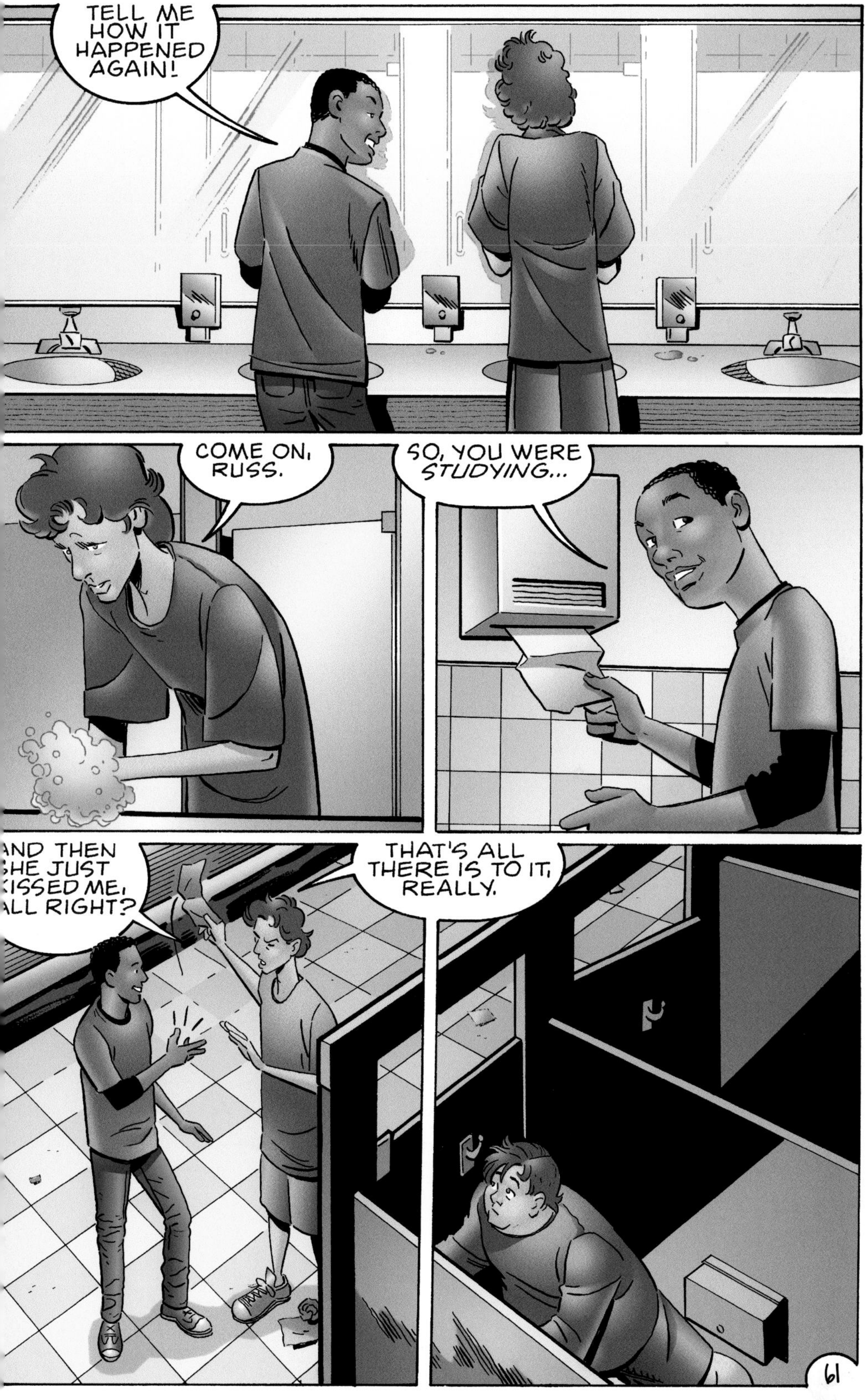
TELL ME HOW IT HAPPENED AGAIN!
COME ON, RUSS.
SO, YOU WERE *STUDYING*...
AND THEN SHE JUST KISSED ME, ALL RIGHT?
THAT'S ALL THERE IS TO IT, REALLY.

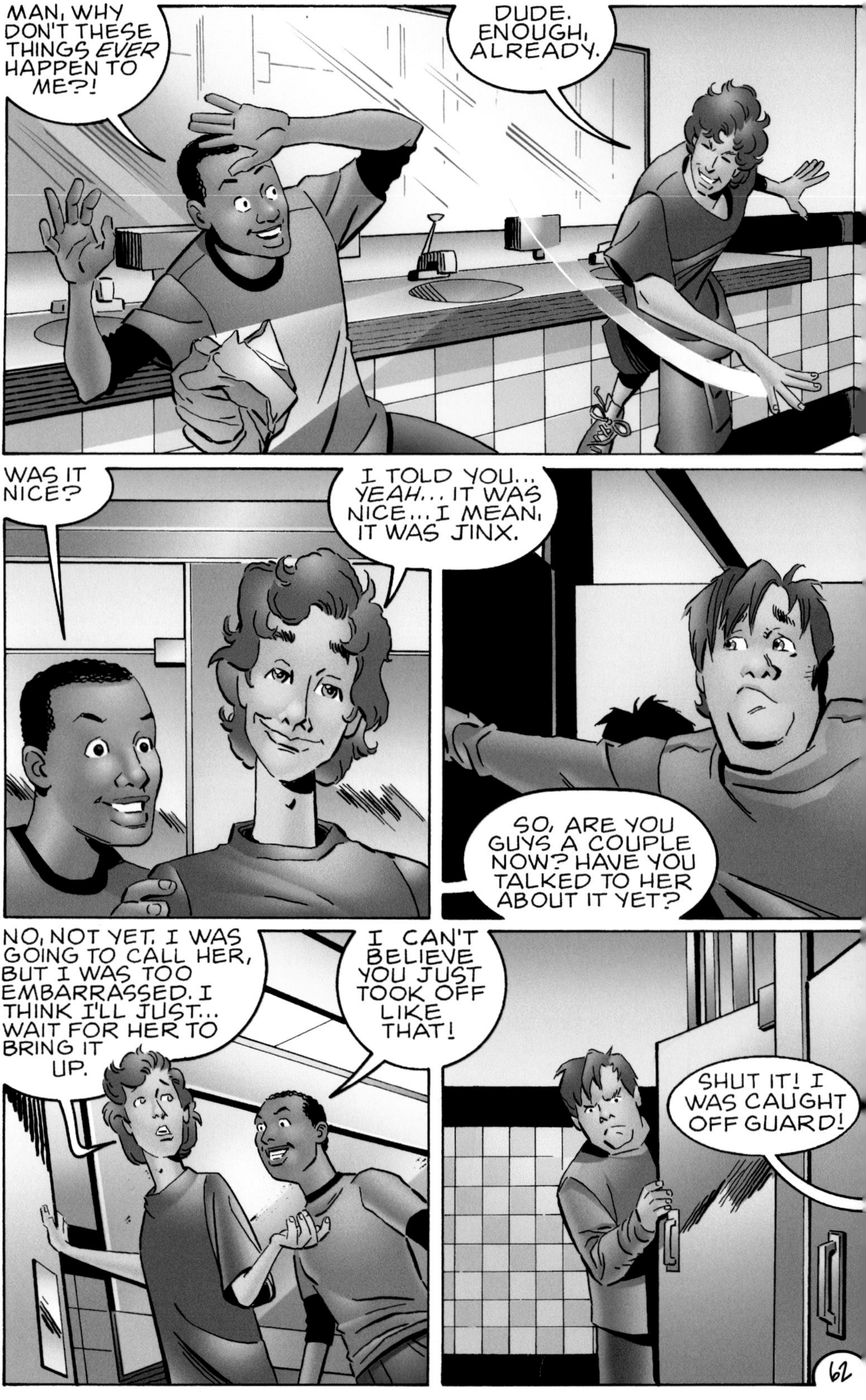
MAN, WHY DON'T THESE THINGS *EVER* HAPPEN TO ME?!
DUDE. ENOUGH, ALREADY.
WAS IT NICE?
I TOLD YOU... *YEAH*... IT WAS NICE... I MEAN, IT WAS JINX.
SO, ARE YOU GUYS A COUPLE NOW? HAVE YOU TALKED TO HER ABOUT IT YET?
NO, NOT YET. I WAS GOING TO CALL HER, BUT I WAS TOO EMBARRASSED. I THINK I'LL JUST... WAIT FOR HER TO BRING IT UP.
I CAN'T BELIEVE YOU JUST TOOK OFF LIKE THAT!
SHUT IT! I WAS CAUGHT OFF GUARD!

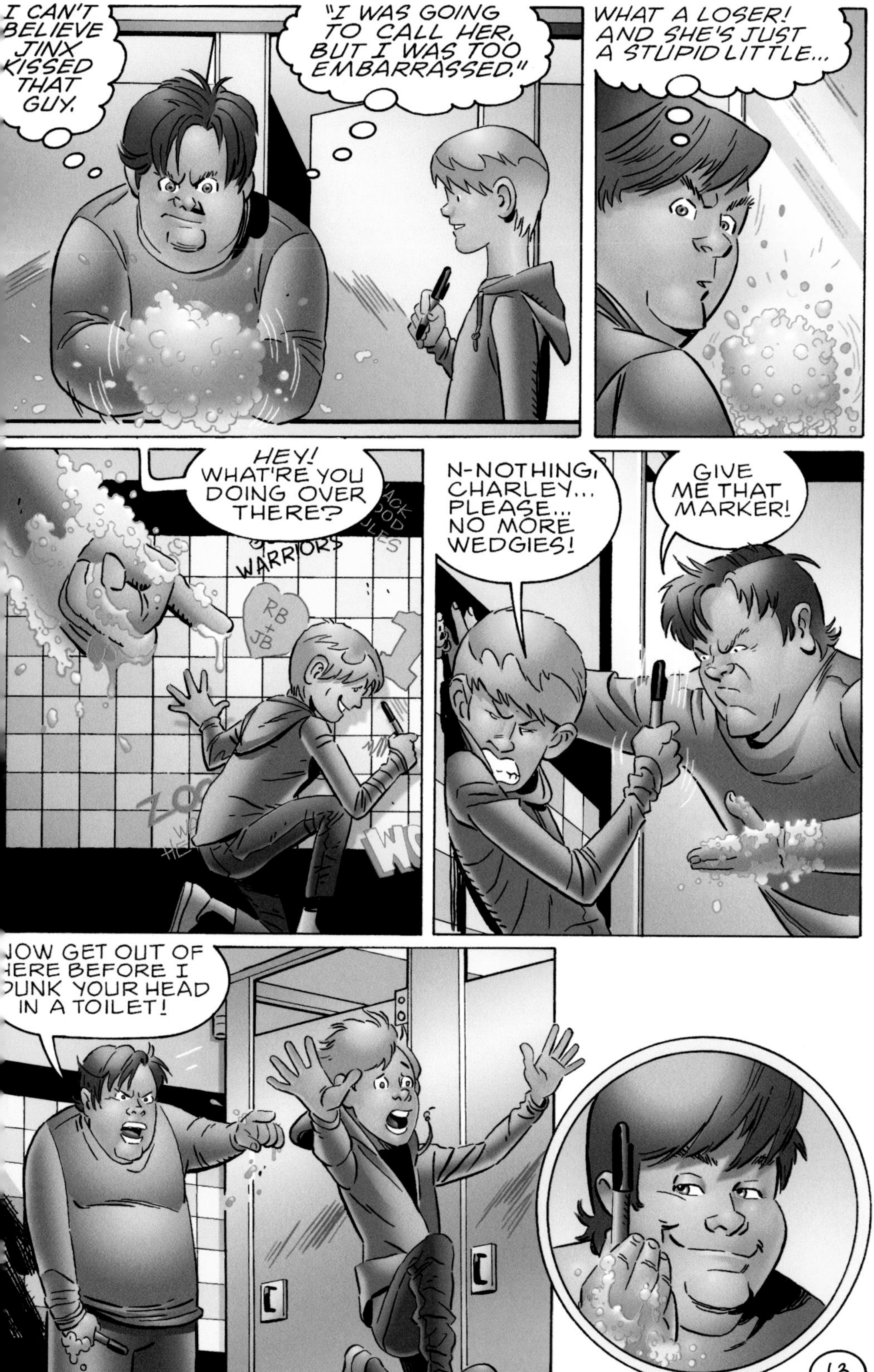
I CAN'T BELIEVE JINX KISSED THAT GUY.
"I WAS GOING TO CALL HER, BUT I WAS TOO EMBARRASSED."
WHAT A LOSER! AND SHE'S JUST A STUPID LITTLE...
HEY! WHAT'RE YOU DOING OVER THERE?
WARRIORS
RB + JB
N-NOTHING, CHARLEY... PLEASE... NO MORE WEDGIES!
GIVE ME THAT MARKER!
OW GET OUT OF
ERE BEFORE I
UNK YOUR HEAD
IN A TOILET!

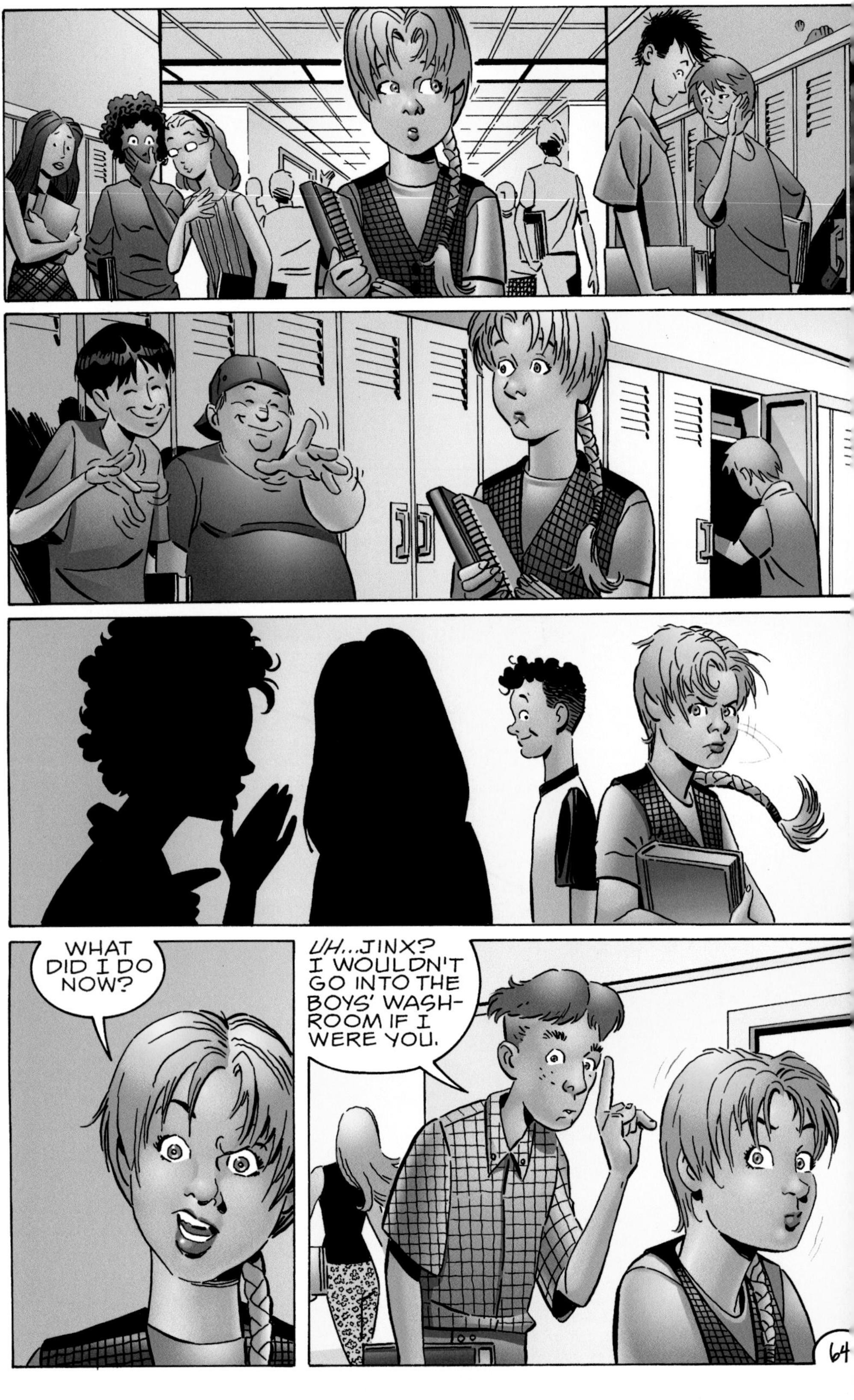
WHAT DID I DO NOW?
UH...JINX? I WOULDN'T GO INTO THE BOYS' WASH-ROOM IF I WERE YOU.

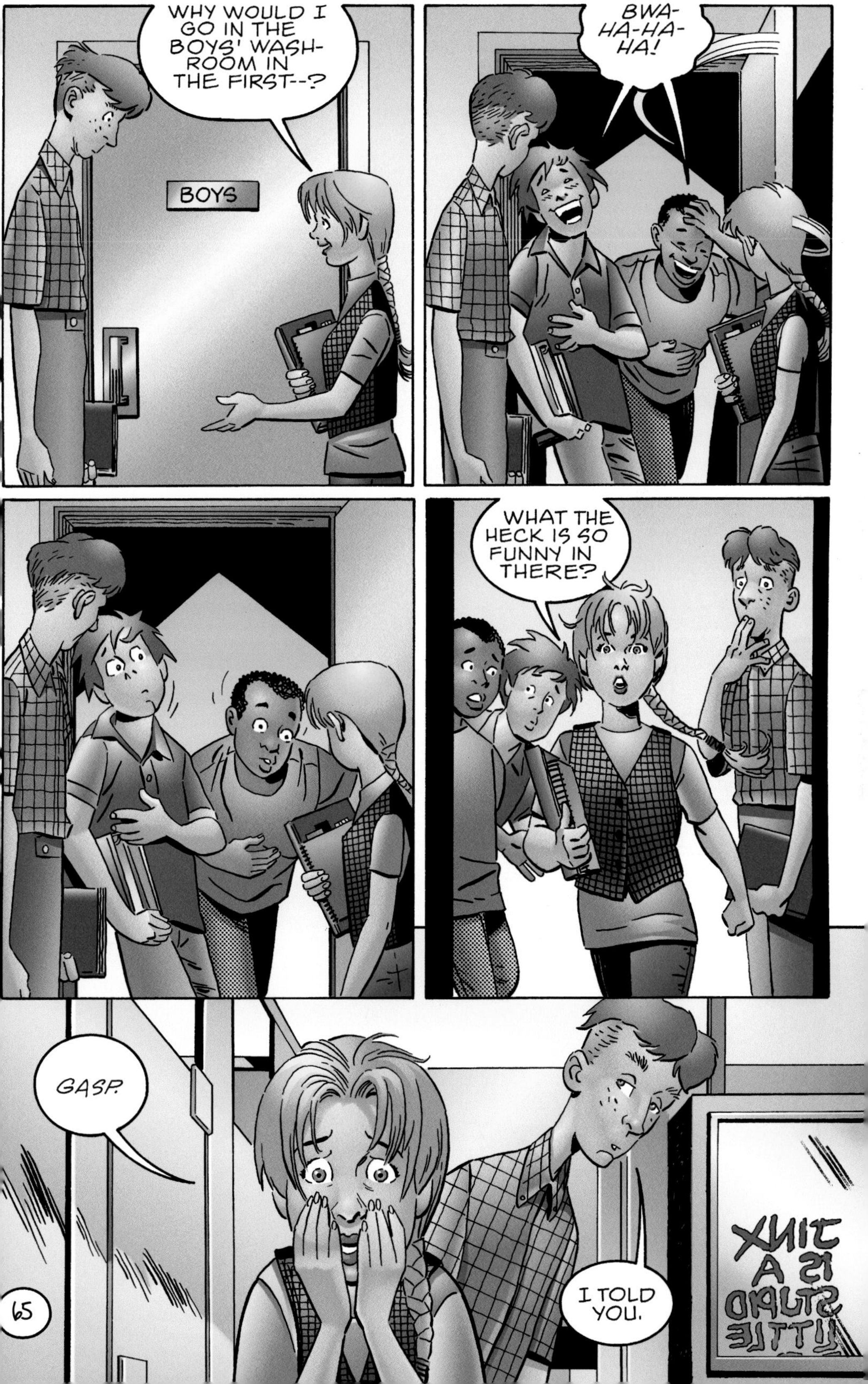
WHY WOULD I GO IN THE BOYS' WASH-ROOM IN THE FIRST--?
BOYS
BWA-HA-HA-HA!
WHAT THE HECK IS SO FUNNY IN THERE?
GASP!
JINX IS A STUPID LITTLE
I TOLD YOU.

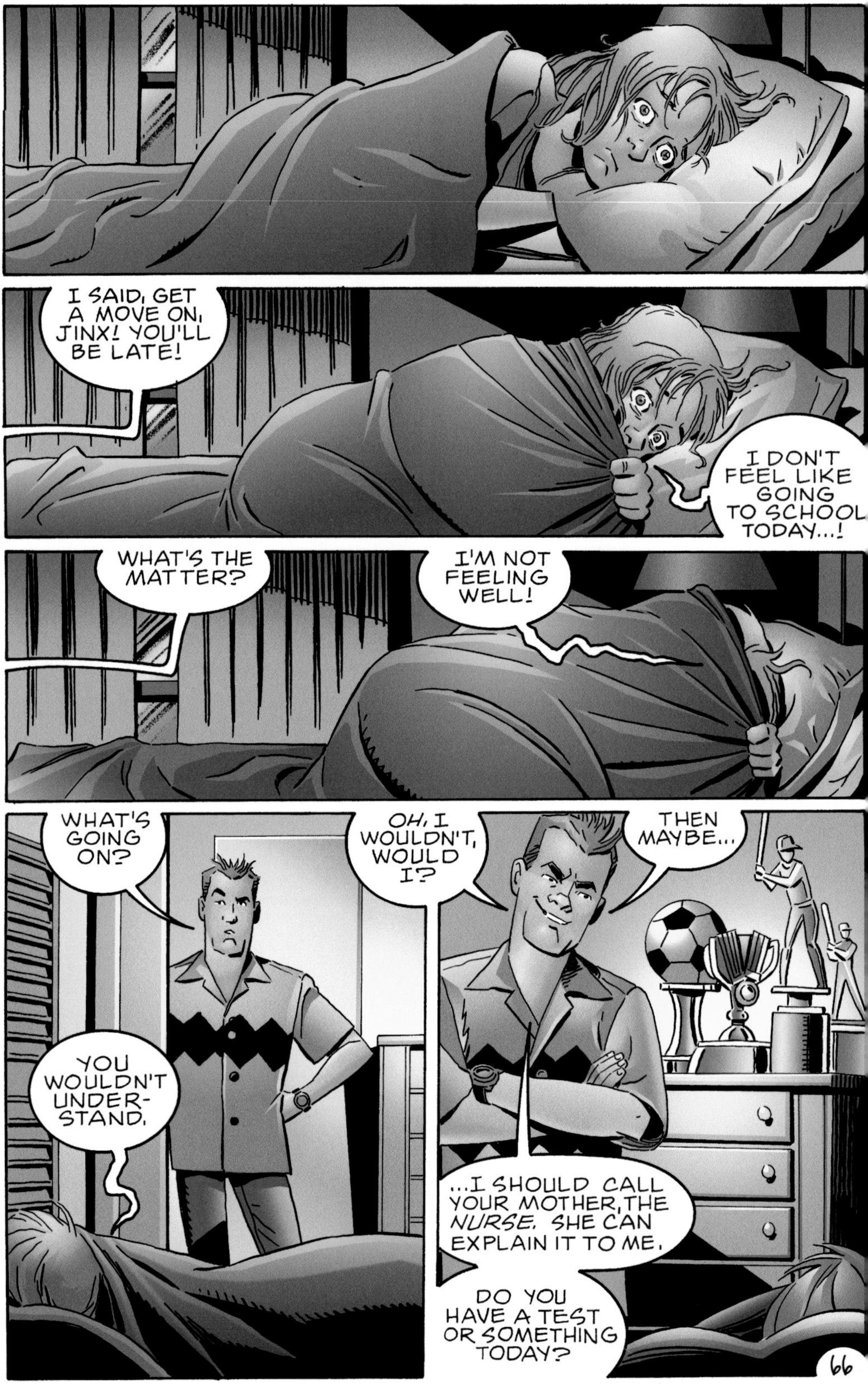
I SAID, GET A MOVE ON, JINX! YOU'LL BE LATE!
I DON'T FEEL LIKE GOING TO SCHOOL TODAY...!
WHAT'S THE MATTER?
I'M NOT FEELING WELL!
WHAT'S GOING ON?
YOU WOULDN'T UNDER-STAND.
OH, I WOULDN'T, WOULD I?
THEN MAYBE...
...I SHOULD CALL YOUR MOTHER, THE NURSE. SHE CAN EXPLAIN IT TO ME.
DO YOU HAVE A TEST OR SOMETHING TODAY?

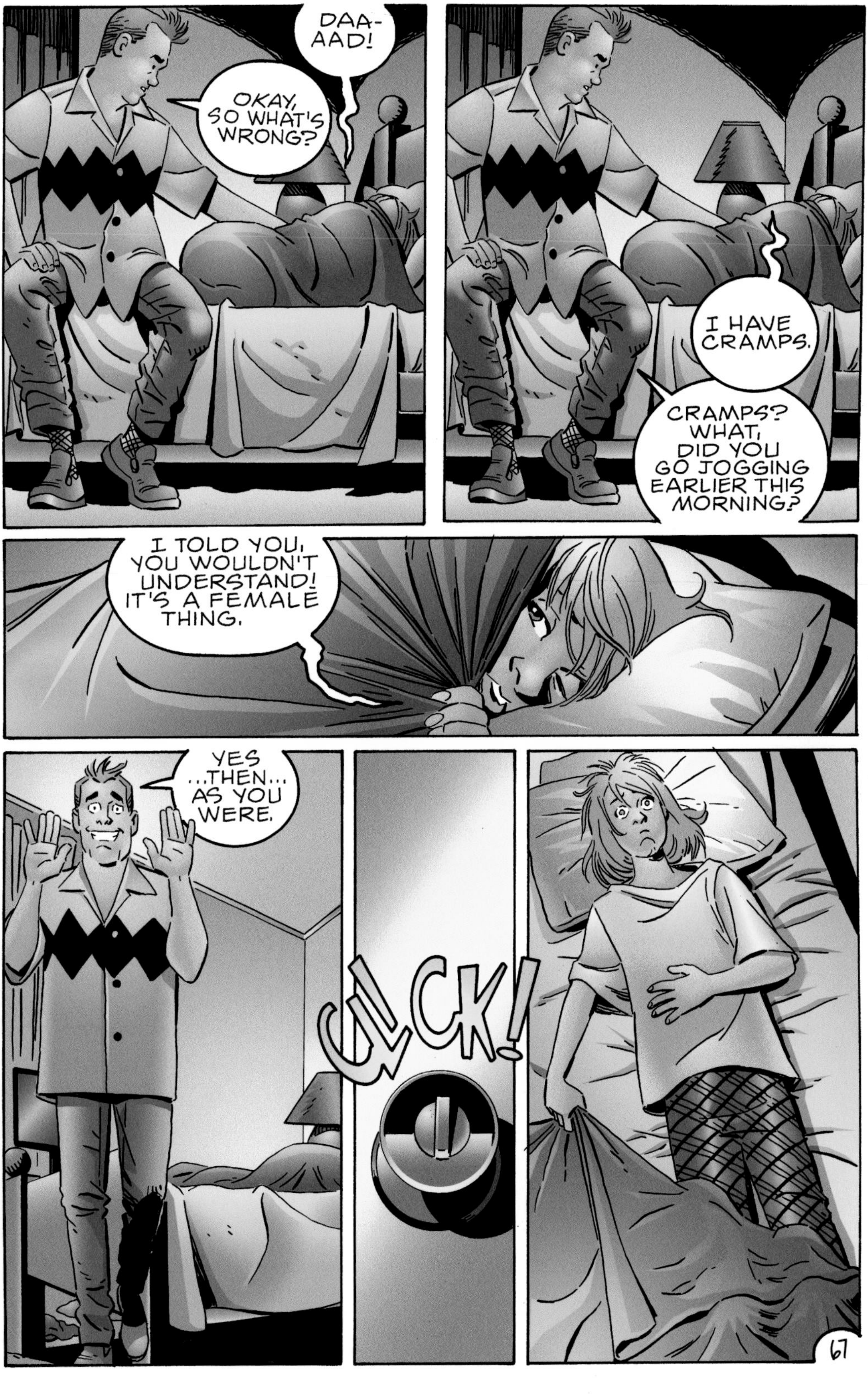
DAA-AAD!
OKAY, SO WHAT'S WRONG?
I HAVE CRAMPS.
CRAMPS? WHAT, DID YOU GO JOGGING EARLIER THIS MORNING?
I TOLD YOU, YOU WOULDN'T UNDERSTAND! IT'S A FEMALE THING.
YES ...THEN... AS YOU WERE.
CLICK!

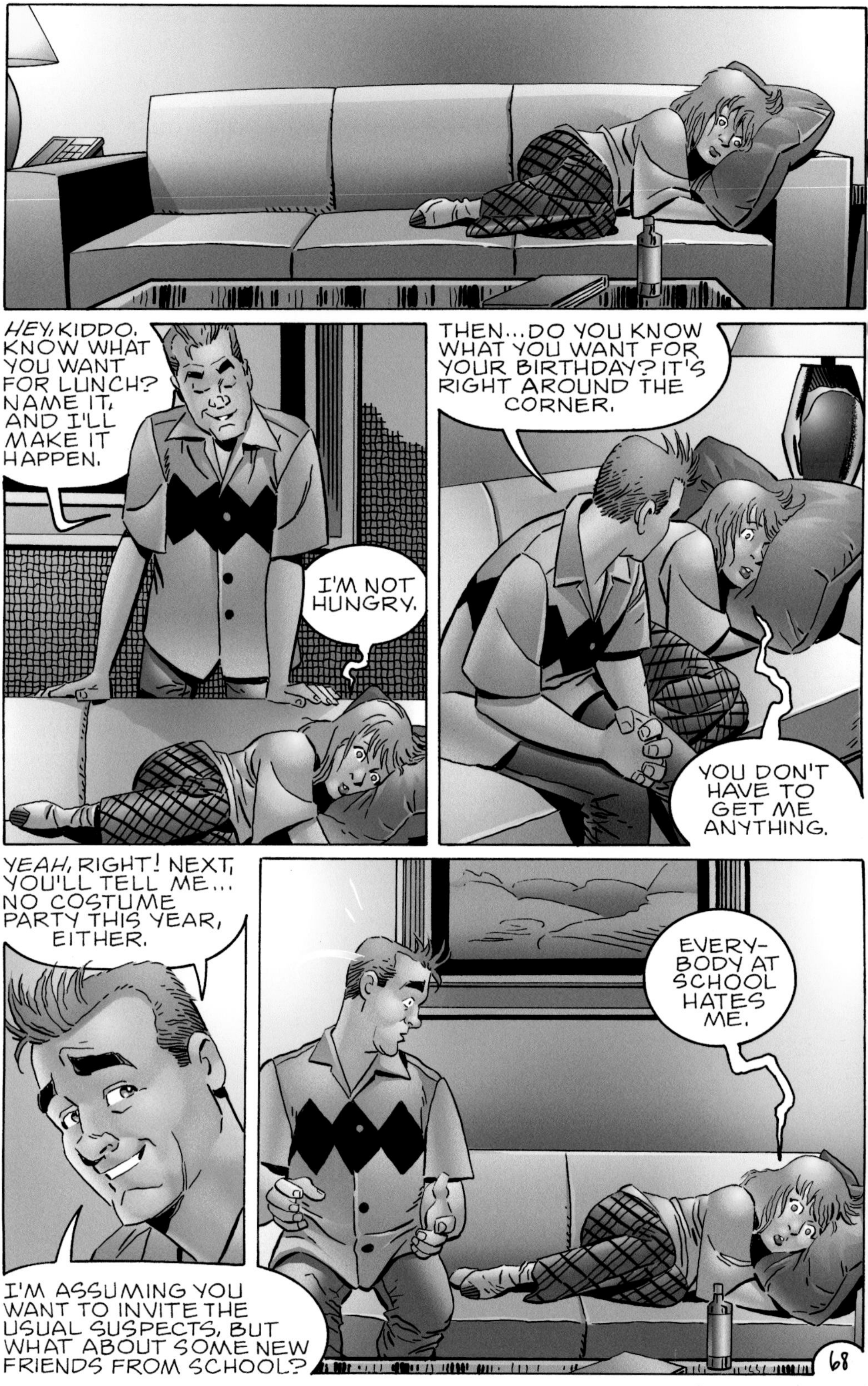
HEY, KIDDO. KNOW WHAT YOU WANT FOR LUNCH? NAME IT, AND I'LL MAKE IT HAPPEN.
I'M NOT HUNGRY.
THEN...DO YOU KNOW WHAT YOU WANT FOR YOUR BIRTHDAY? IT'S RIGHT AROUND THE CORNER.
YOU DON'T HAVE TO GET ME ANYTHING.
YEAH, RIGHT! NEXT, YOU'LL TELL ME... NO COSTUME PARTY THIS YEAR, EITHER.
I'M ASSUMING YOU WANT TO INVITE THE USUAL SUSPECTS, BUT WHAT ABOUT SOME NEW FRIENDS FROM SCHOOL?
EVERY-BODY AT SCHOOL HATES ME.

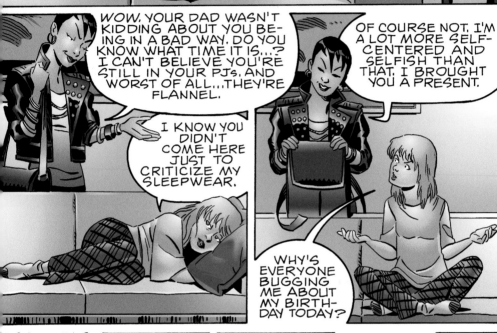

WOW, YOUR DAD WASN'T KIDDING ABOUT YOU BEING IN A BAD WAY. DO YOU KNOW WHAT TIME IT IS...? I CAN'T BELIEVE YOU'RE STILL IN YOUR PJs, AND WORST OF ALL...THEY'RE FLANNEL.

I KNOW YOU DIDN'T COME HERE JUST TO CRITICIZE MY SLEEPWEAR.

OF COURSE NOT. I'M A LOT MORE SELF-CENTERED AND SELFISH THAN THAT. I BROUGHT YOU A PRESENT.

WHY'S EVERYONE BUGGING ME ABOUT MY BIRTH-DAY TODAY?

I SAID THIS WASN'T ABOUT YOU. PAY ATTENTION.

YOU AREN'T KIDDING! THIS IS A SCRAP-BOOK ALL ABOUT YOU.

69

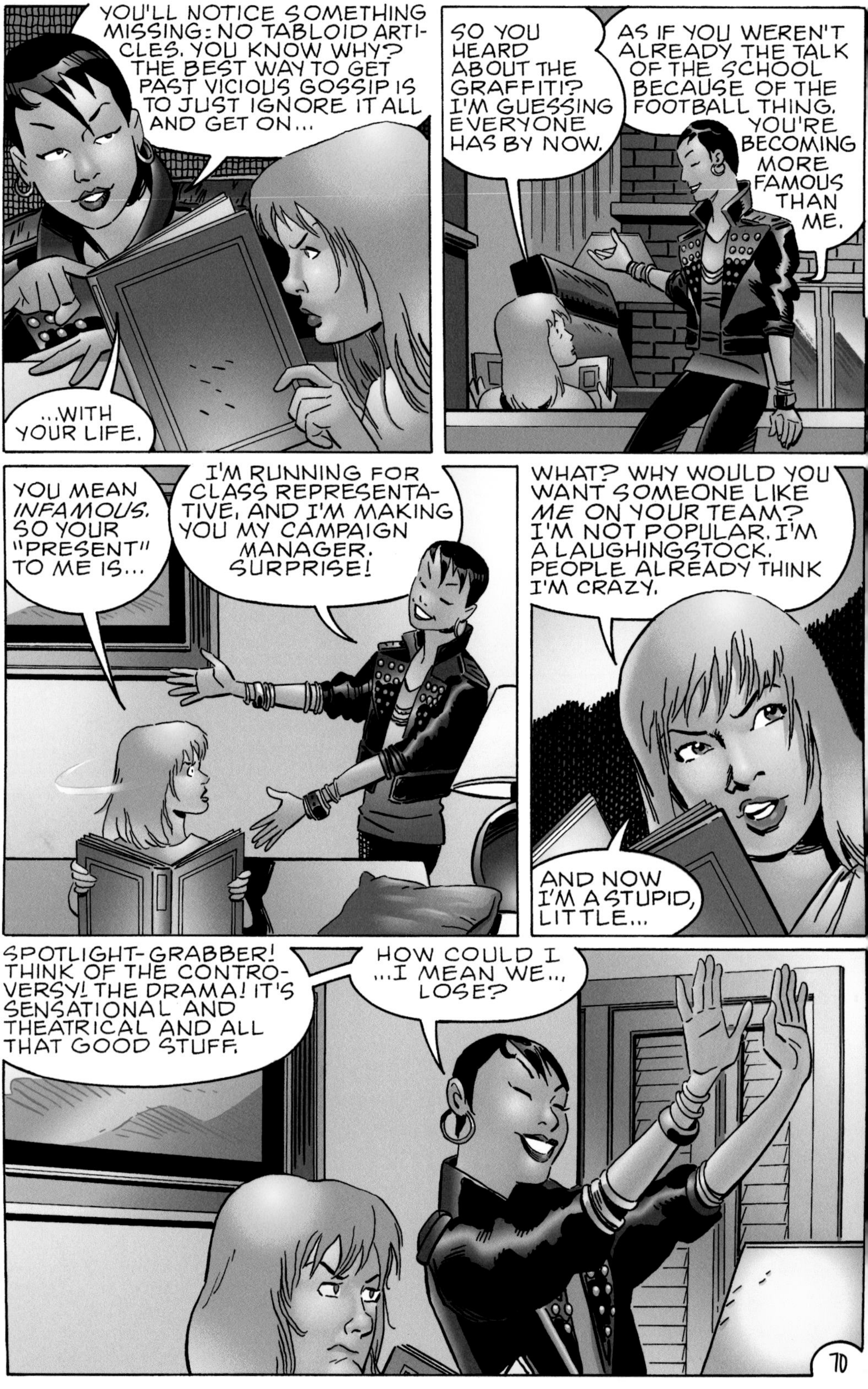

YOU'LL NOTICE SOMETHING MISSING: NO TABLOID ARTICLES. YOU KNOW WHY? THE BEST WAY TO GET PAST VICIOUS GOSSIP IS TO JUST IGNORE IT ALL AND GET ON...
...WITH YOUR LIFE.
SO YOU HEARD ABOUT THE GRAFFITI? I'M GUESSING EVERYONE HAS BY NOW.
AS IF YOU WEREN'T ALREADY THE TALK OF THE SCHOOL BECAUSE OF THE FOOTBALL THING. YOU'RE BECOMING MORE FAMOUS THAN ME.
YOU MEAN *INFAMOUS.* SO YOUR "PRESENT" TO ME IS...
I'M RUNNING FOR CLASS REPRESENTATIVE, AND I'M MAKING YOU MY CAMPAIGN MANAGER. SURPRISE!
WHAT? WHY WOULD YOU WANT SOMEONE LIKE *ME* ON YOUR TEAM? I'M NOT POPULAR. I'M A LAUGHINGSTOCK. PEOPLE ALREADY THINK I'M CRAZY.
AND NOW I'M A STUPID, LITTLE...
SPOTLIGHT-GRABBER! THINK OF THE CONTROVERSY! THE DRAMA! IT'S SENSATIONAL AND THEATRICAL AND ALL THAT GOOD STUFF.
HOW COULD I ...I MEAN WE..., LOSE?

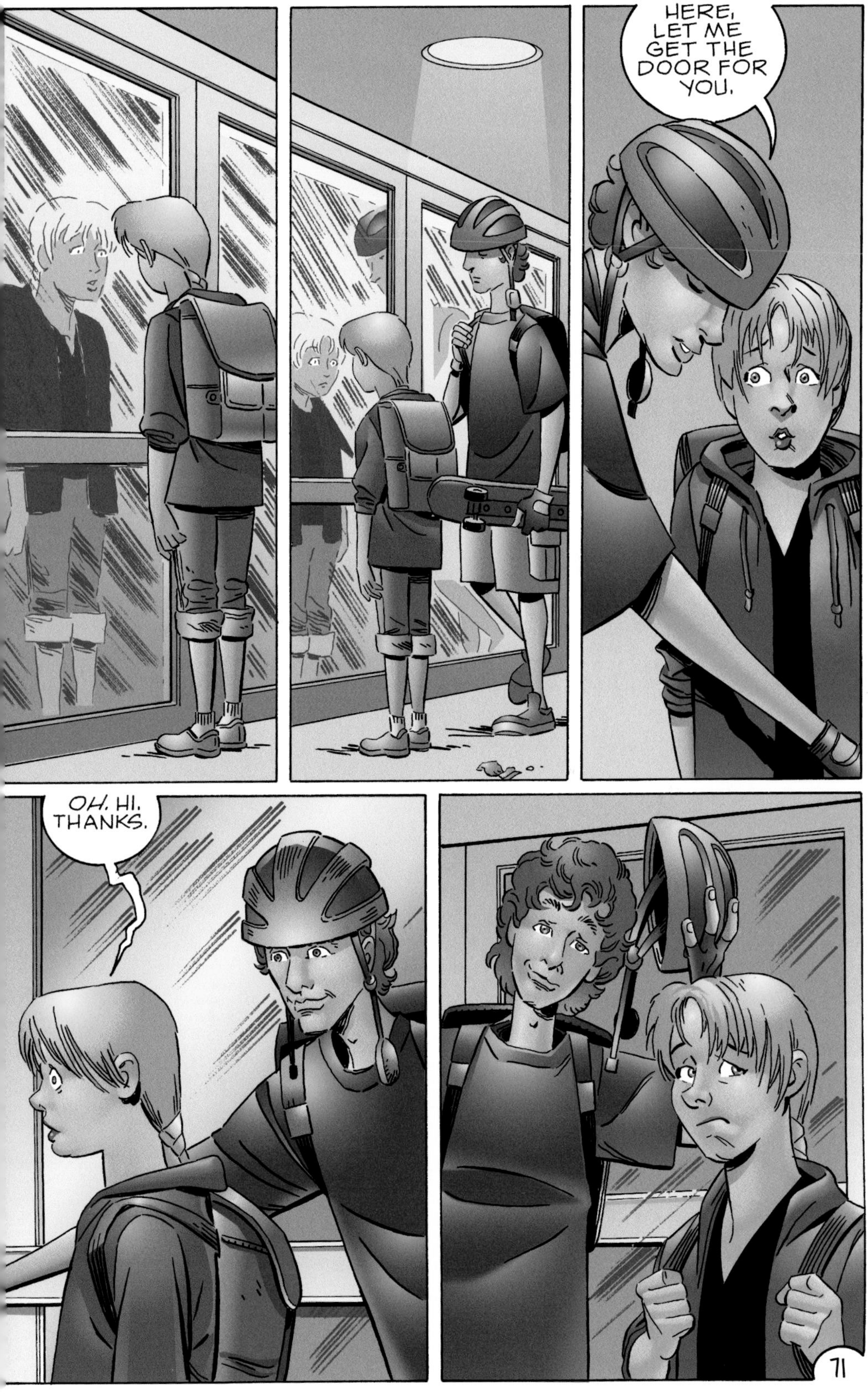
HERE, LET ME GET THE DOOR FOR YOU.
OH. HI. THANKS.

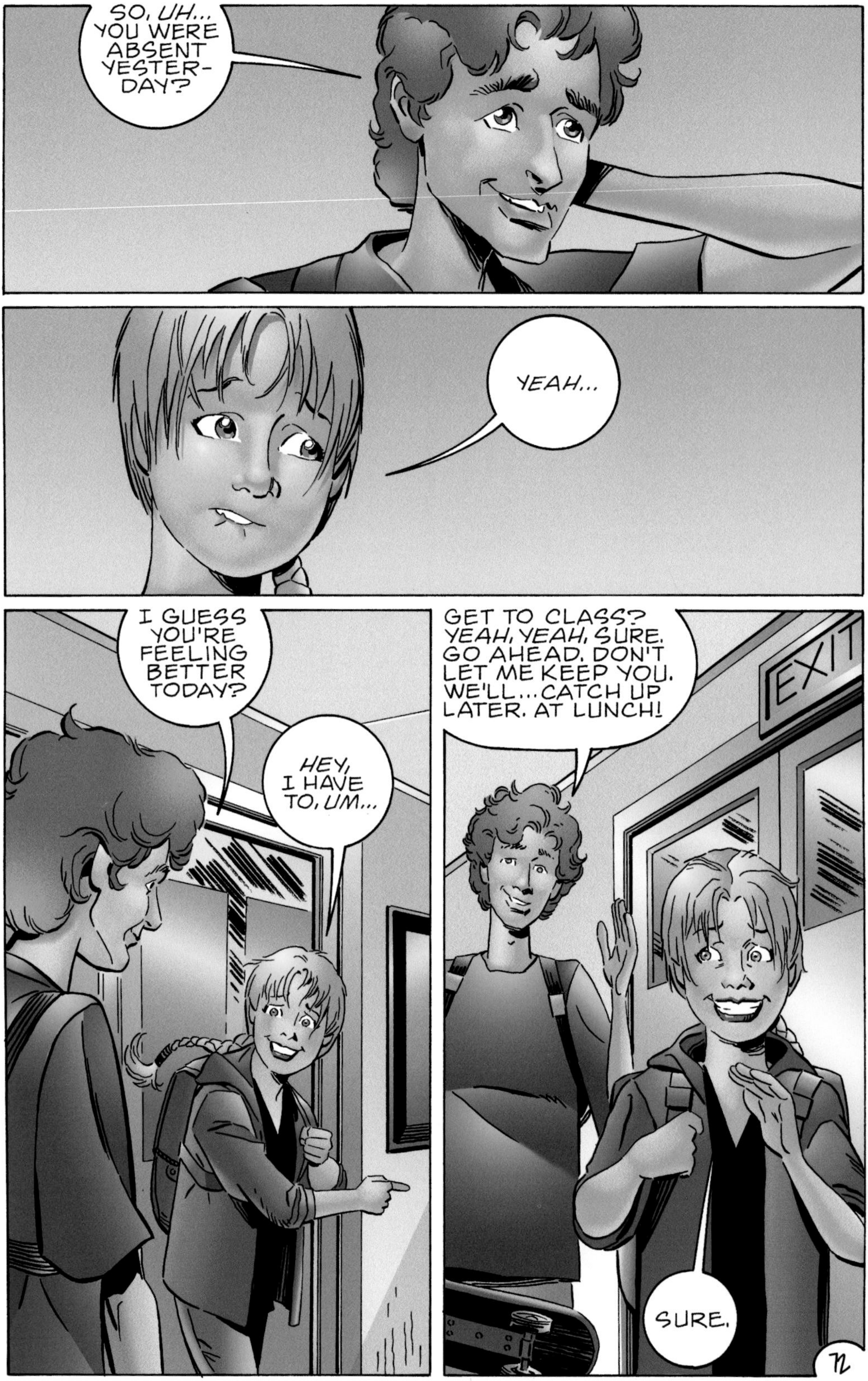
SO, UH... YOU WERE ABSENT YESTER-DAY?
YEAH...
I GUESS YOU'RE FEELING BETTER TODAY?
HEY, I HAVE TO, UM...
GET TO CLASS? YEAH, YEAH, SURE. GO AHEAD. DON'T LET ME KEEP YOU. WE'LL...CATCH UP LATER. AT LUNCH!
EXIT
SURE.

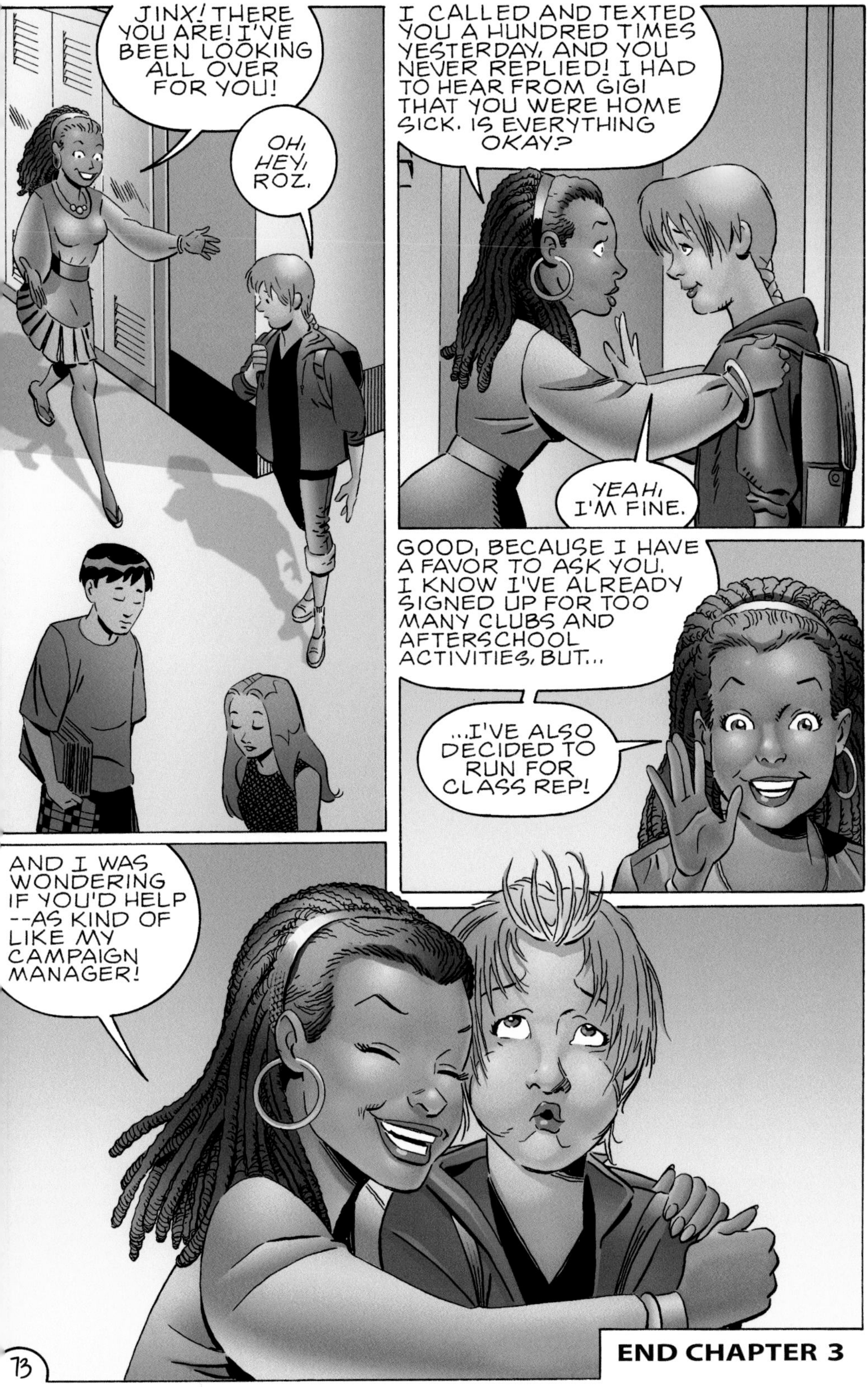
JINX! THERE YOU ARE! I'VE BEEN LOOKING ALL OVER FOR YOU!
OH, HEY, ROZ.
I CALLED AND TEXTED YOU A HUNDRED TIMES YESTERDAY, AND YOU NEVER REPLIED! I HAD TO HEAR FROM GIGI THAT YOU WERE HOME SICK. IS EVERYTHING OKAY?
YEAH, I'M FINE.
GOOD, BECAUSE I HAVE A FAVOR TO ASK YOU. I KNOW I'VE ALREADY SIGNED UP FOR TOO MANY CLUBS AND AFTERSCHOOL ACTIVITIES, BUT...
...I'VE ALSO DECIDED TO RUN FOR CLASS REP!
AND I WAS WONDERING IF YOU'D HELP --AS KIND OF LIKE MY CAMPAIGN MANAGER!
END CHAPTER 3

Lil' JINX ™

CHAPTER 4

BURCHETT
& DUSTIN
★ mcnabb

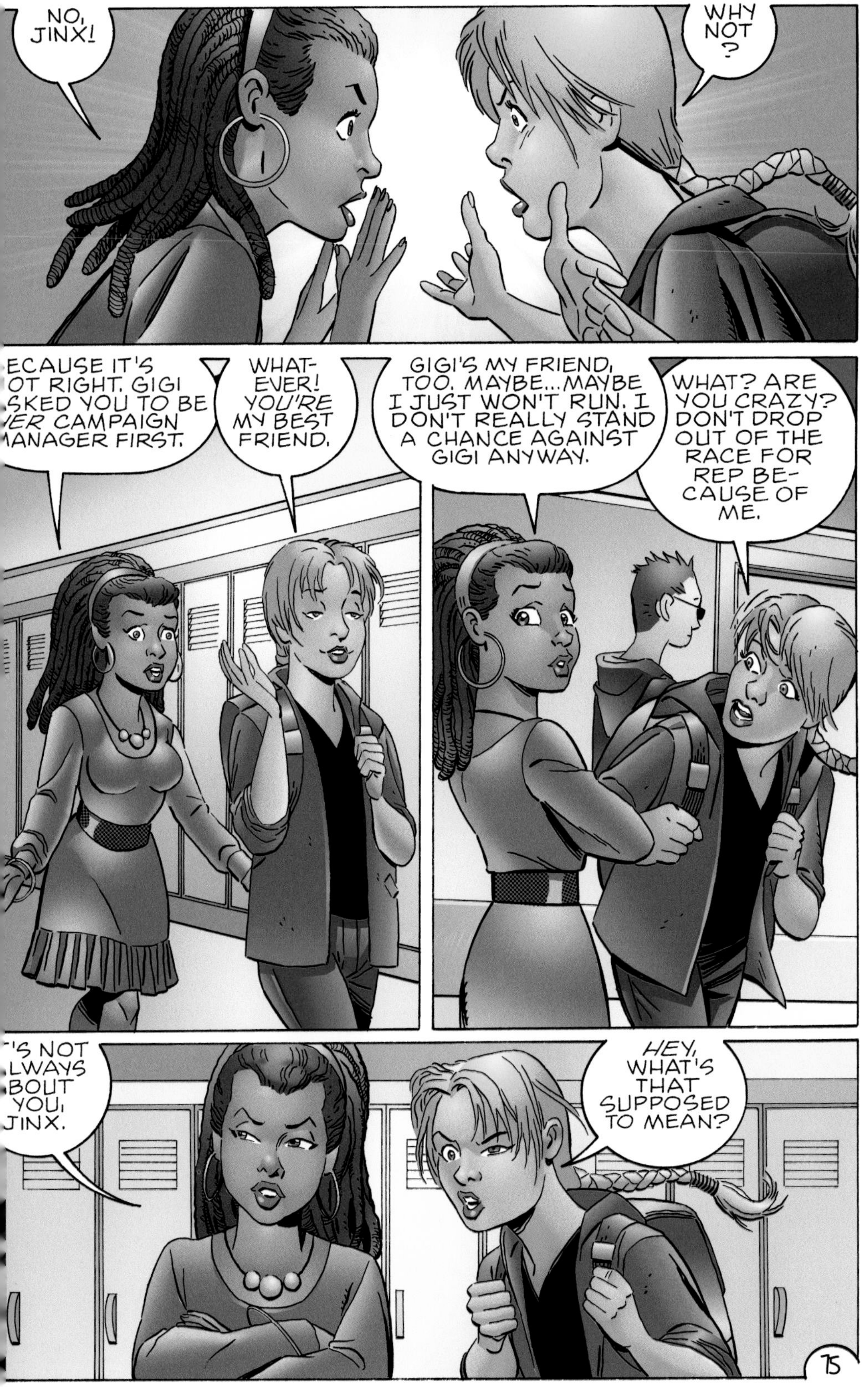
NO, JINX!
WHY NOT?
ECAUSE IT'S OT RIGHT. GIGI SKED YOU TO BE *ER* CAMPAIGN ANAGER FIRST.
WHAT-EVER! *YOU'RE* MY BEST FRIEND.
GIGI'S MY FRIEND, TOO. MAYBE...MAYBE I JUST WON'T RUN. I DON'T REALLY STAND A CHANCE AGAINST GIGI ANYWAY.
WHAT? ARE YOU *CRAZY*? DON'T DROP OUT OF THE RACE FOR REP BE-CAUSE OF ME.
'S NOT LWAYS BOUT YOU, JINX.
HEY, WHAT'S THAT SUPPOSED TO MEAN?

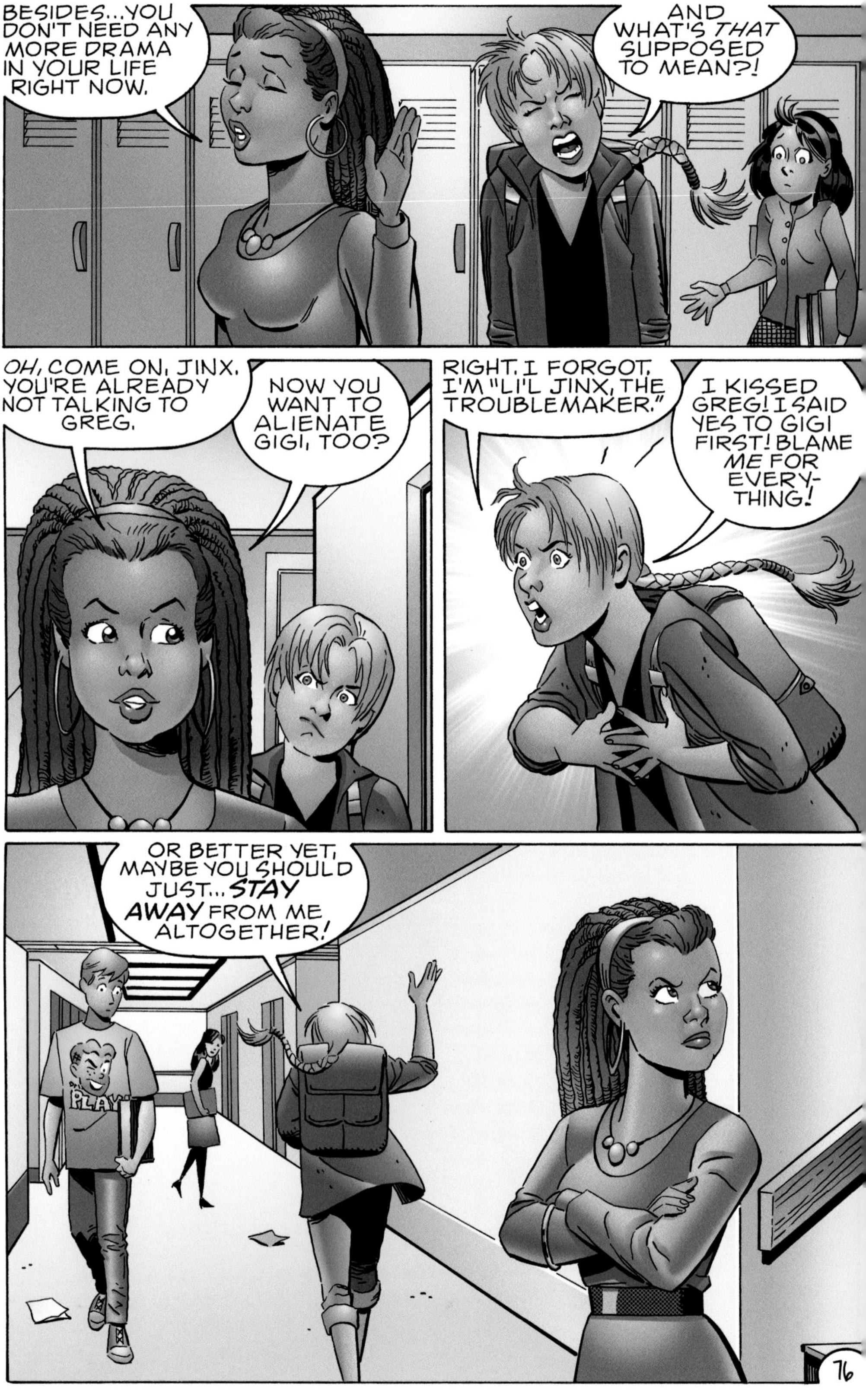
BESIDES...YOU DON'T NEED ANY MORE DRAMA IN YOUR LIFE RIGHT NOW.
AND WHAT'S *THAT* SUPPOSED TO MEAN?!
OH, COME ON, JINX. YOU'RE ALREADY NOT TALKING TO GREG.
NOW YOU WANT TO ALIENATE GIGI, TOO?
RIGHT. I FORGOT. I'M "LI'L JINX, THE TROUBLEMAKER."
I KISSED GREG! I SAID YES TO GIGI FIRST! BLAME *ME* FOR EVERY-THING!
OR BETTER YET, MAYBE YOU SHOULD JUST... **STAY AWAY** FROM ME ALTOGETHER!
PLAY

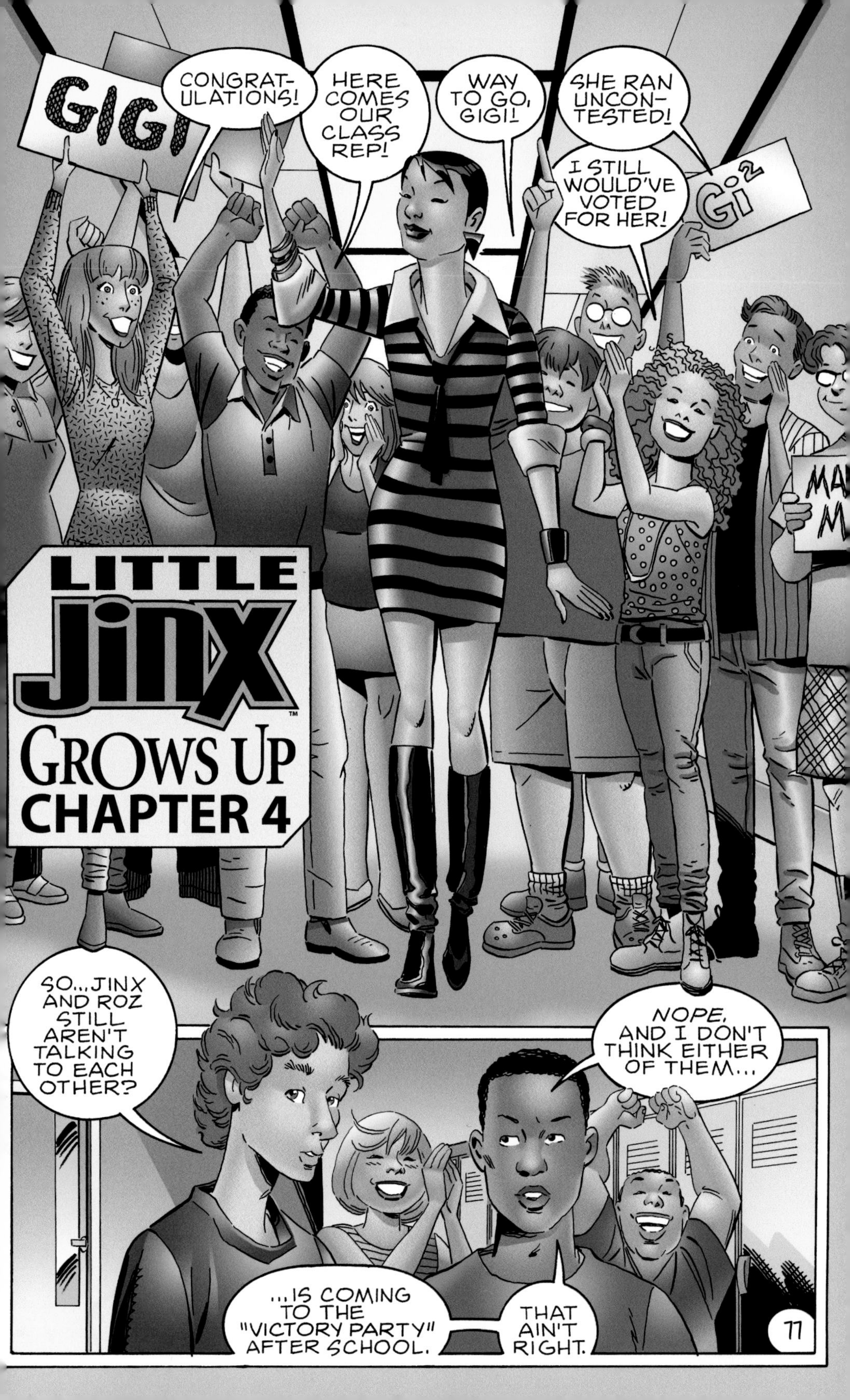
GIGI
CONGRAT-ULATIONS!
HERE COMES OUR CLASS REP!
WAY TO GO, GIGI!
SHE RAN UNCON-TESTED!
I STILL WOULD'VE VOTED FOR HER!
Gi²
LITTLE JINX™
GROWS UP
CHAPTER 4
SO...JINX AND ROZ STILL AREN'T TALKING TO EACH OTHER?
NOPE, AND I DON'T THINK EITHER OF THEM...
...IS COMING TO THE "VICTORY PARTY" AFTER SCHOOL.
THAT AIN'T RIGHT.

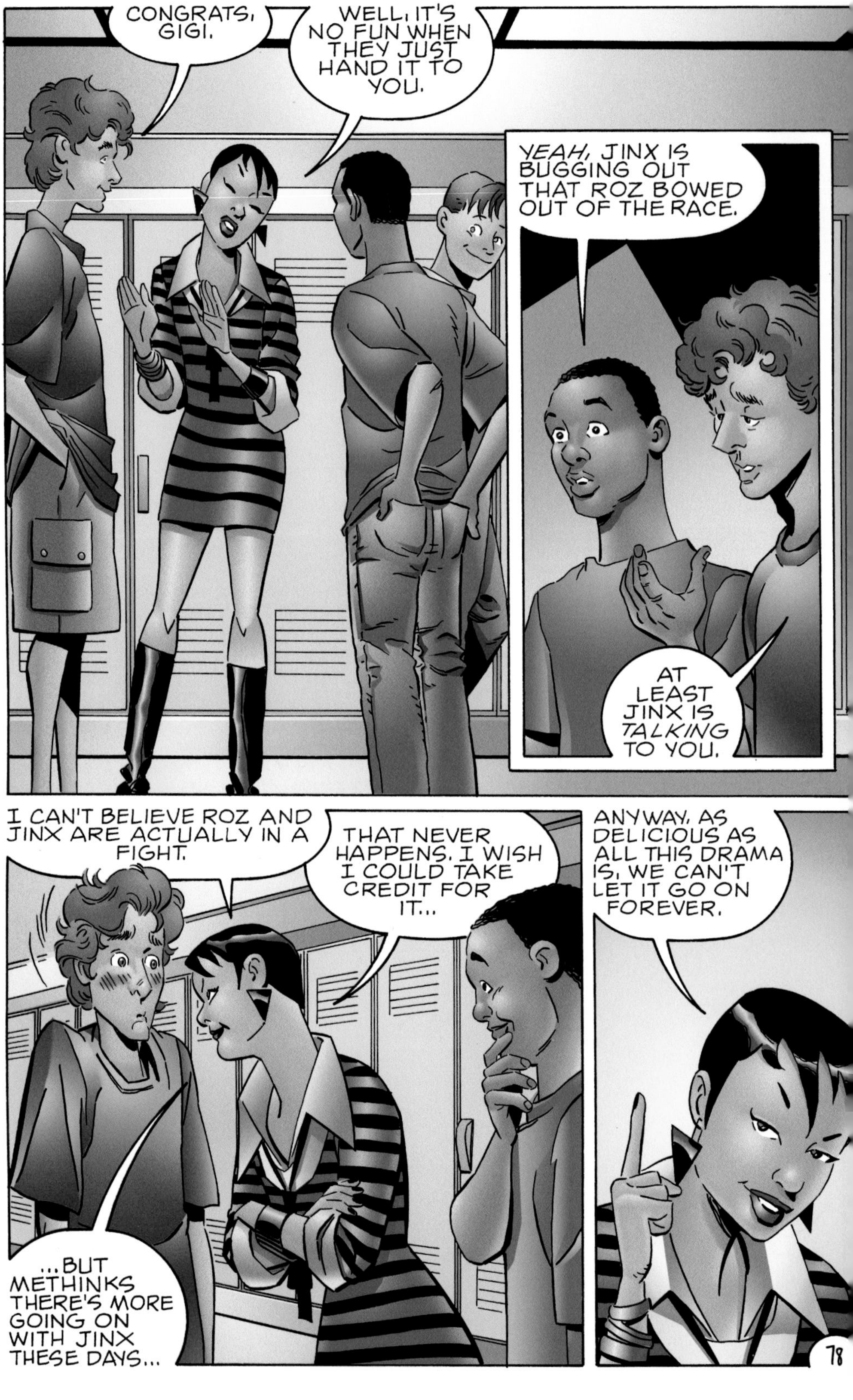
CONGRATS, GIGI.
WELL, IT'S NO FUN WHEN THEY JUST HAND IT TO YOU.
YEAH, JINX IS BUGGING OUT THAT ROZ BOWED OUT OF THE RACE.
AT LEAST JINX IS TALKING TO YOU.
I CAN'T BELIEVE ROZ AND JINX ARE ACTUALLY IN A FIGHT.
THAT NEVER HAPPENS. I WISH I COULD TAKE CREDIT FOR IT...
...BUT METHINKS THERE'S MORE GOING ON WITH JINX THESE DAYS...
ANYWAY, AS DELICIOUS AS ALL THIS DRAMA IS, WE CAN'T LET IT GO ON FOREVER.

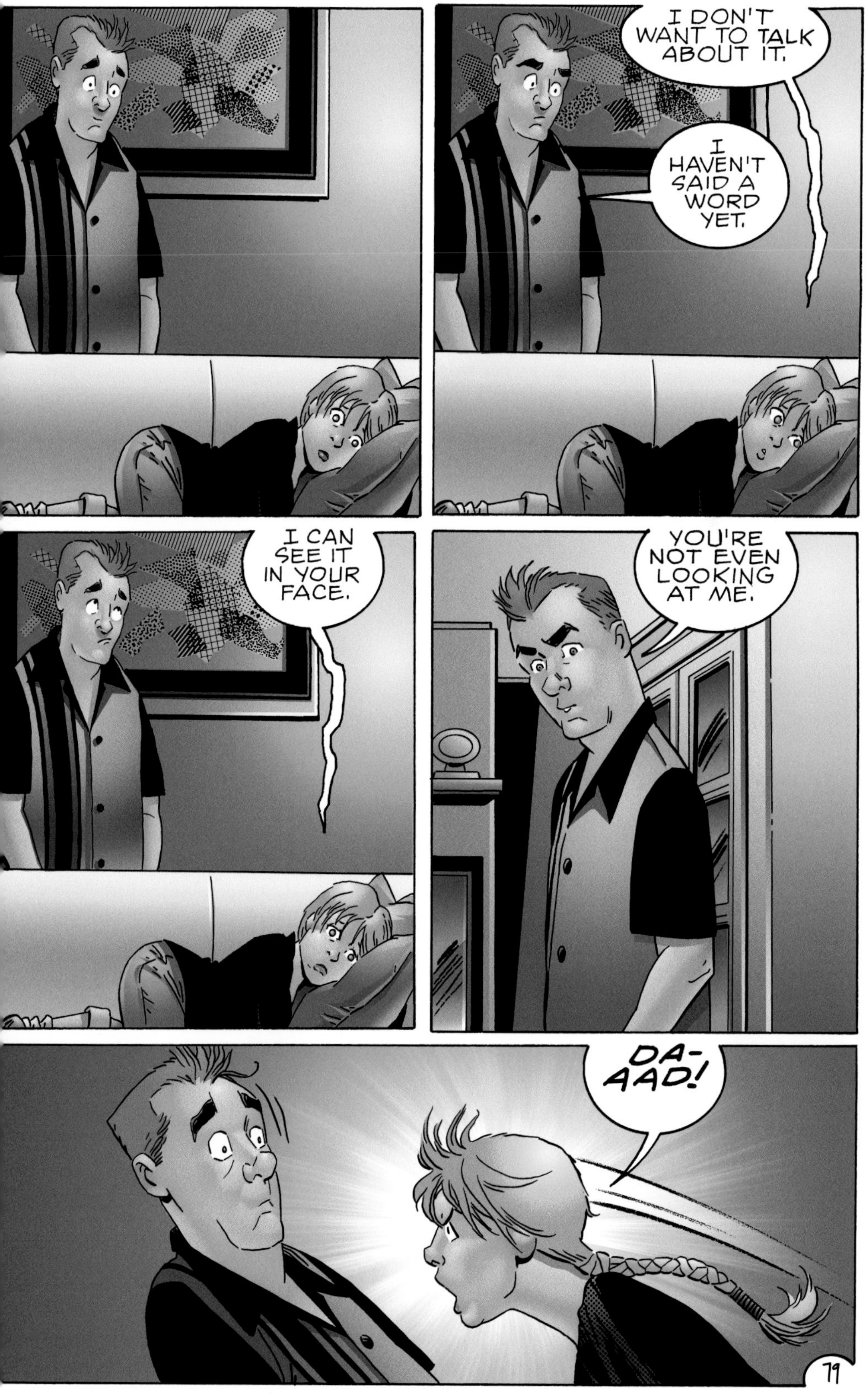
I DON'T WANT TO TALK ABOUT IT.
I HAVEN'T SAID A WORD YET.
I CAN SEE IT IN YOUR FACE.
YOU'RE NOT EVEN LOOKING AT ME.
DA-AAD!

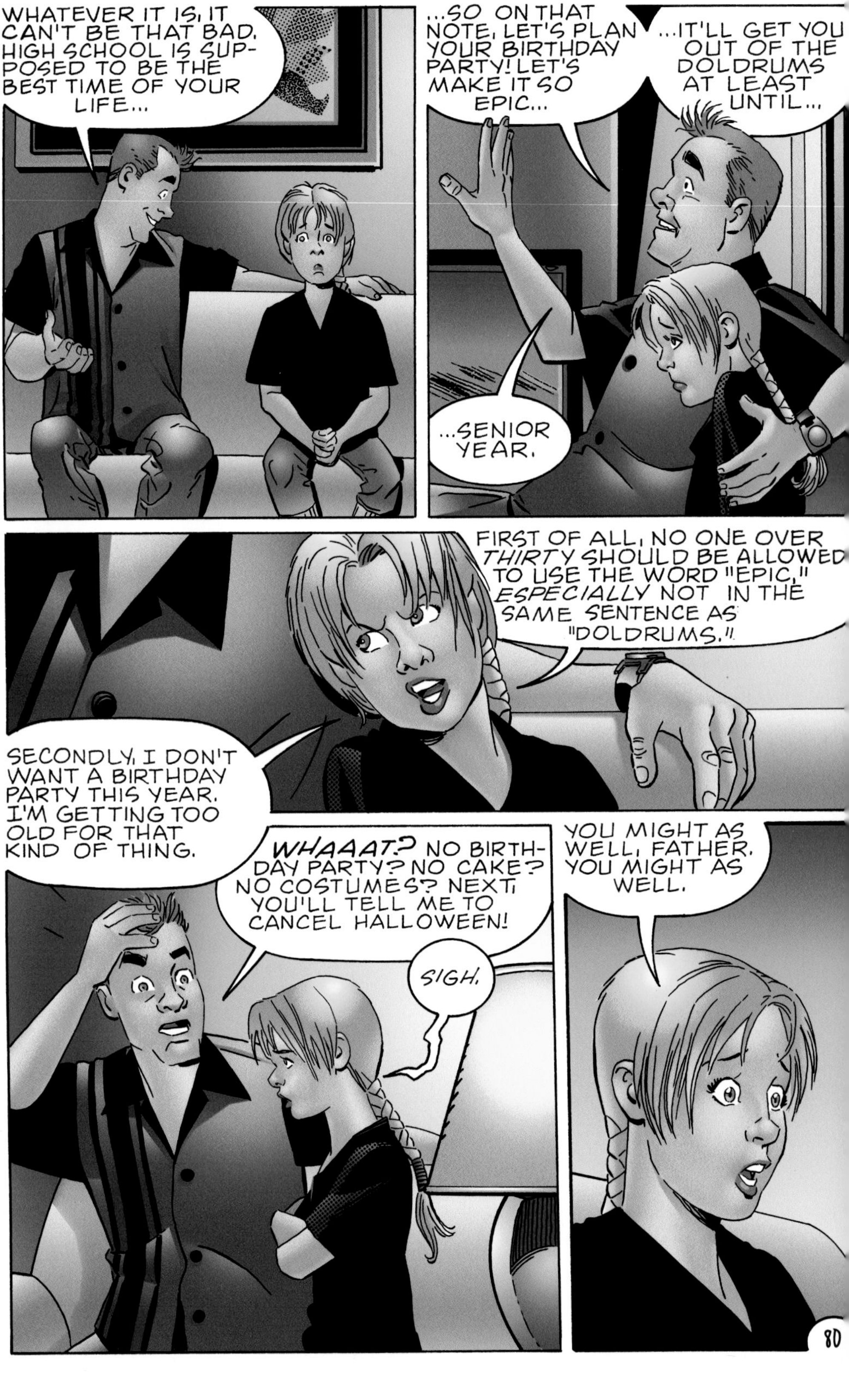
WHATEVER IT IS, IT CAN'T BE THAT BAD. HIGH SCHOOL IS SUPPOSED TO BE THE BEST TIME OF YOUR LIFE...
...SO ON THAT NOTE, LET'S PLAN YOUR BIRTHDAY PARTY! LET'S MAKE IT SO EPIC...
...IT'LL GET YOU OUT OF THE DOLDRUMS AT LEAST UNTIL...
...SENIOR YEAR.
FIRST OF ALL, NO ONE OVER THIRTY SHOULD BE ALLOWED TO USE THE WORD "EPIC," ESPECIALLY NOT IN THE SAME SENTENCE AS "DOLDRUMS."
SECONDLY, I DON'T WANT A BIRTHDAY PARTY THIS YEAR. I'M GETTING TOO OLD FOR THAT KIND OF THING.
WHAAAT? NO BIRTHDAY PARTY? NO CAKE? NO COSTUMES? NEXT, YOU'LL TELL ME TO CANCEL HALLOWEEN!
SIGH.
YOU MIGHT AS WELL, FATHER. YOU MIGHT AS WELL.

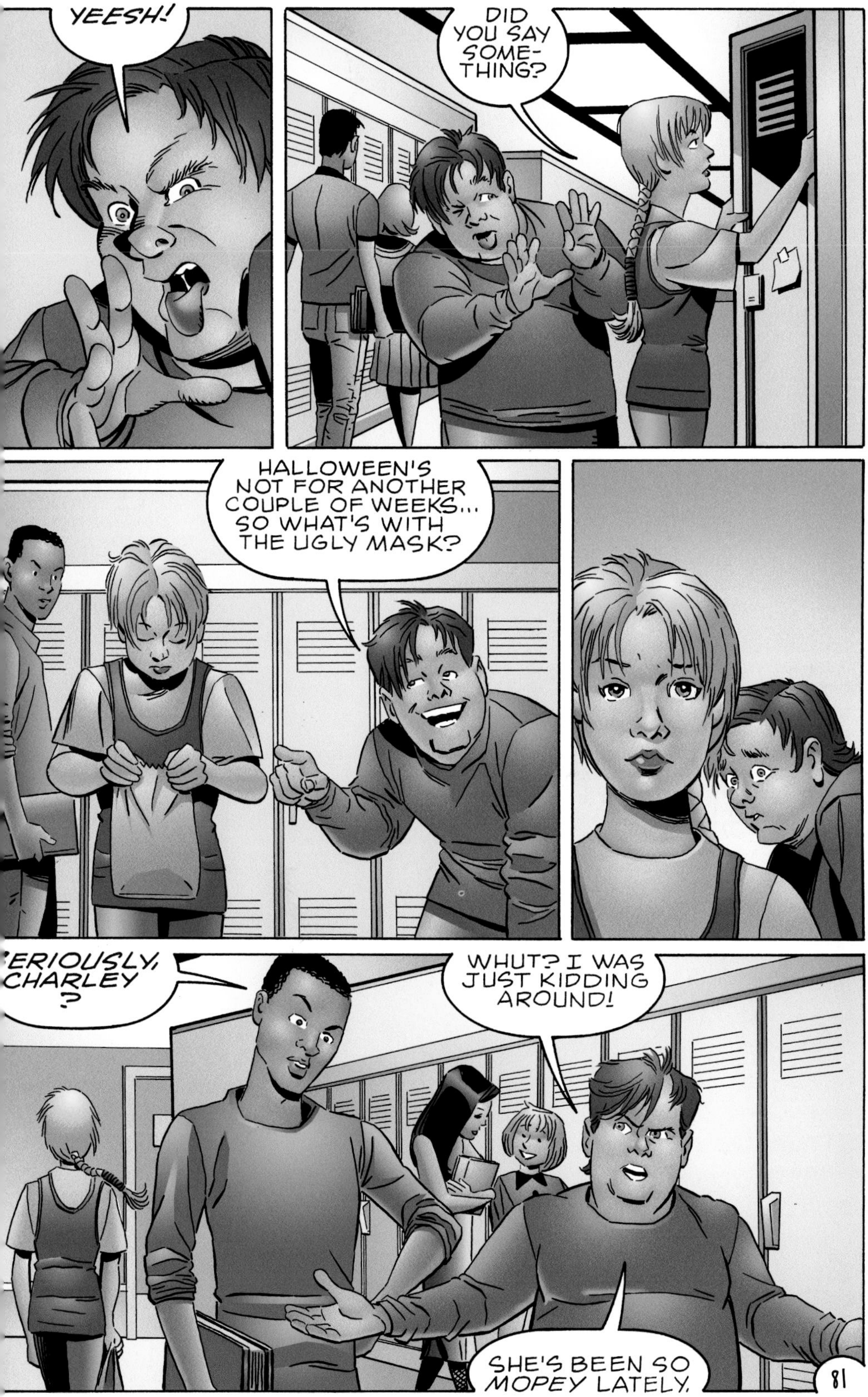
YEESH!
DID YOU SAY SOME-THING?
HALLOWEEN'S NOT FOR ANOTHER COUPLE OF WEEKS... SO WHAT'S WITH THE UGLY MASK?
ERIOUSLY, CHARLEY ?
WHUT? I WAS JUST KIDDING AROUND!
SHE'S BEEN SO MOPEY LATELY.

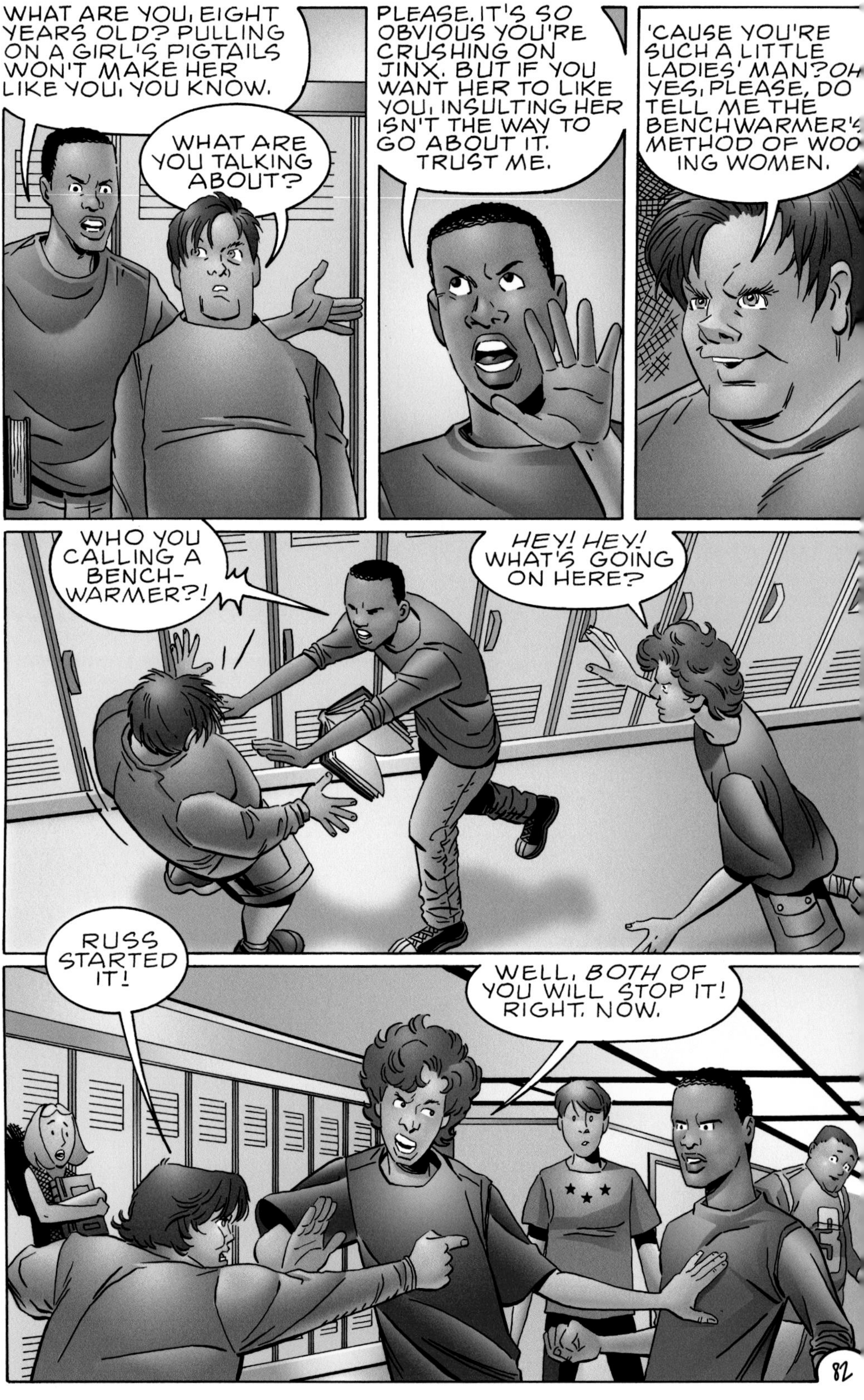
WHAT ARE YOU, EIGHT YEARS OLD? PULLING ON A GIRL'S PIGTAILS WON'T MAKE HER LIKE YOU, YOU KNOW.
WHAT ARE YOU TALKING ABOUT?
PLEASE. IT'S SO OBVIOUS YOU'RE CRUSHING ON JINX. BUT IF YOU WANT HER TO LIKE YOU, INSULTING HER ISN'T THE WAY TO GO ABOUT IT. TRUST ME.
'CAUSE YOU'RE SUCH A LITTLE LADIES' MAN? OH YES, PLEASE, DO TELL ME THE BENCHWARMER'S METHOD OF WOOING WOMEN.
WHO YOU CALLING A BENCH-WARMER?!
HEY! HEY! WHAT'S GOING ON HERE?
RUSS STARTED IT!
WELL, BOTH OF YOU WILL STOP IT! RIGHT. NOW.

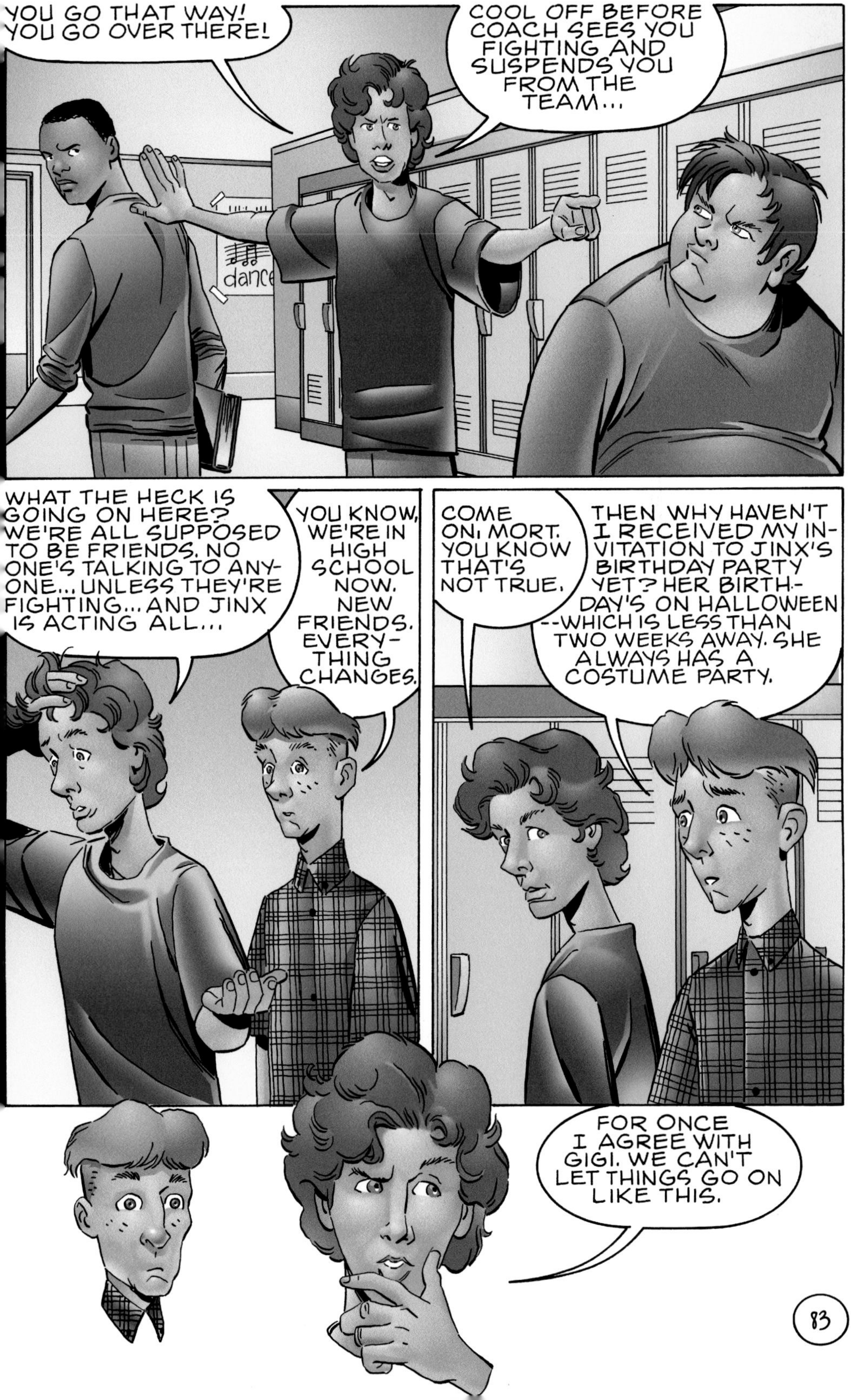
YOU GO THAT WAY! YOU GO OVER THERE!
COOL OFF BEFORE COACH SEES YOU FIGHTING AND SUSPENDS YOU FROM THE TEAM...
dance
WHAT THE HECK IS GOING ON HERE? WE'RE ALL SUPPOSED TO BE FRIENDS. NO ONE'S TALKING TO ANYONE... UNLESS THEY'RE FIGHTING... AND JINX IS ACTING ALL...
YOU KNOW, WE'RE IN HIGH SCHOOL NOW. NEW FRIENDS. EVERYTHING CHANGES.
COME ON, MORT. YOU KNOW THAT'S NOT TRUE.
THEN WHY HAVEN'T I RECEIVED MY INVITATION TO JINX'S BIRTHDAY PARTY YET? HER BIRTHDAY'S ON HALLOWEEN --WHICH IS LESS THAN TWO WEEKS AWAY. SHE ALWAYS HAS A COSTUME PARTY.
FOR ONCE I AGREE WITH GIGI. WE CAN'T LET THINGS GO ON LIKE THIS.

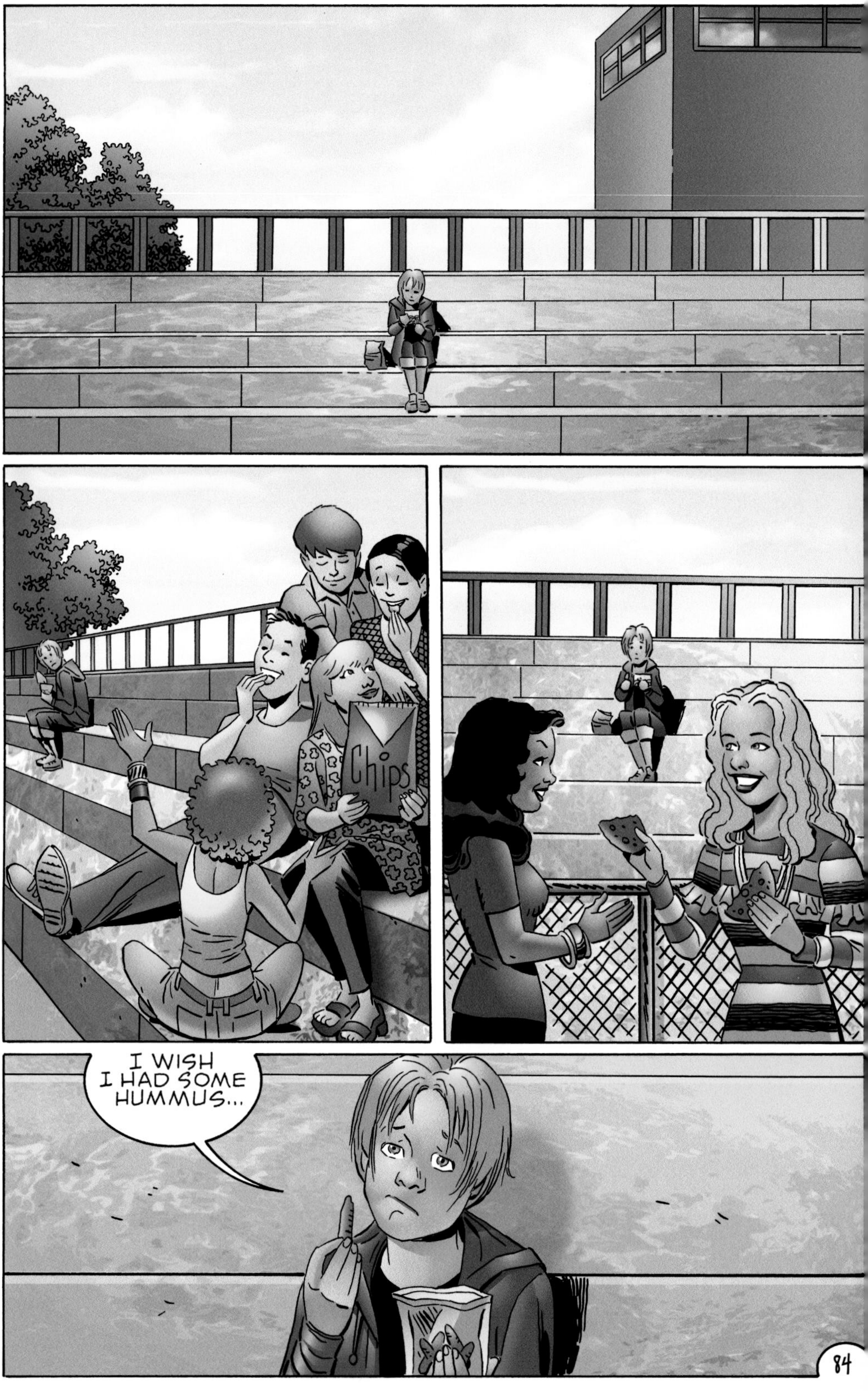
Chips
I WISH I HAD SOME HUMMUS...

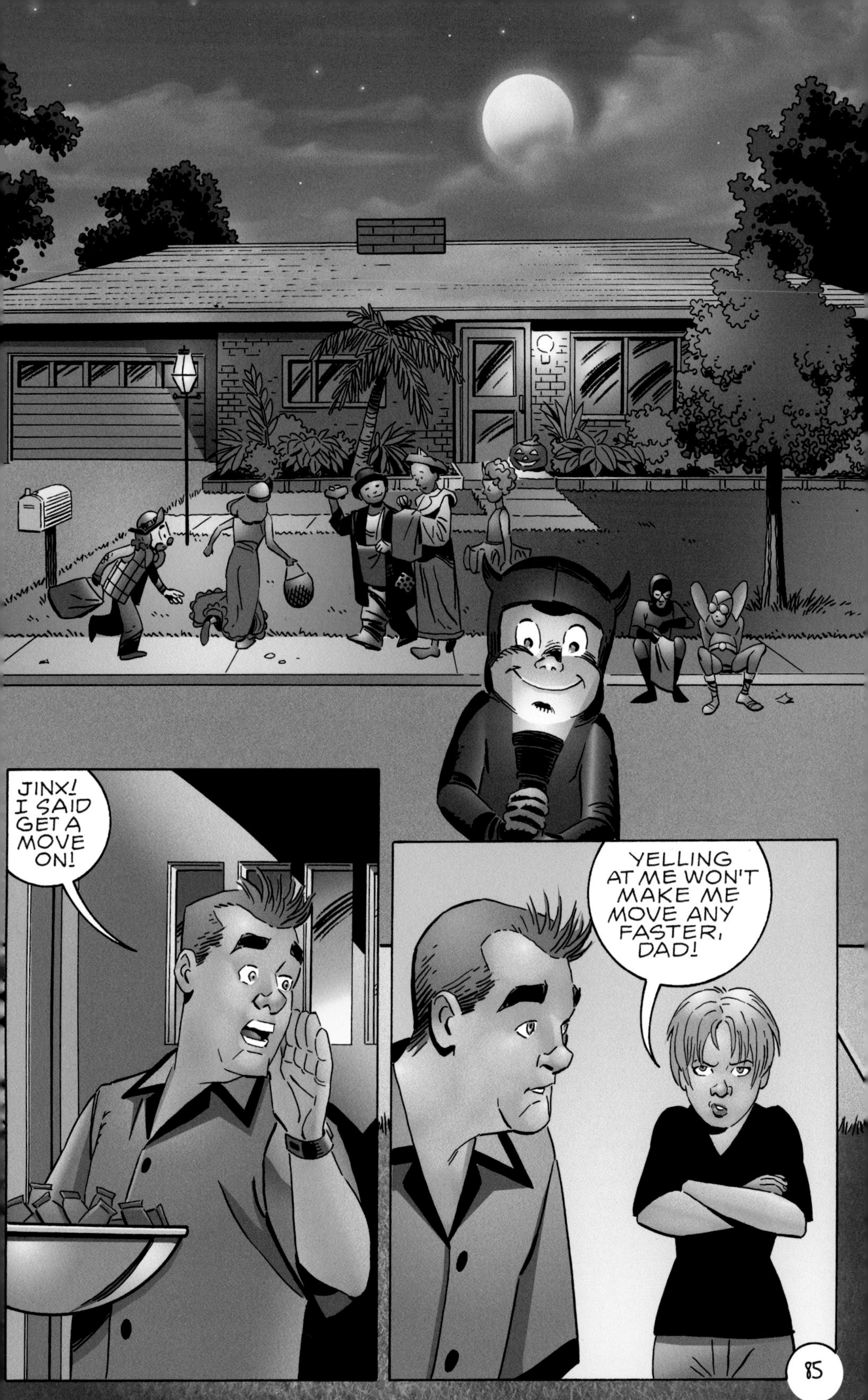
JINX! I SAID GET A MOVE ON!
YELLING AT ME WON'T MAKE ME MOVE ANY FASTER, DAD!

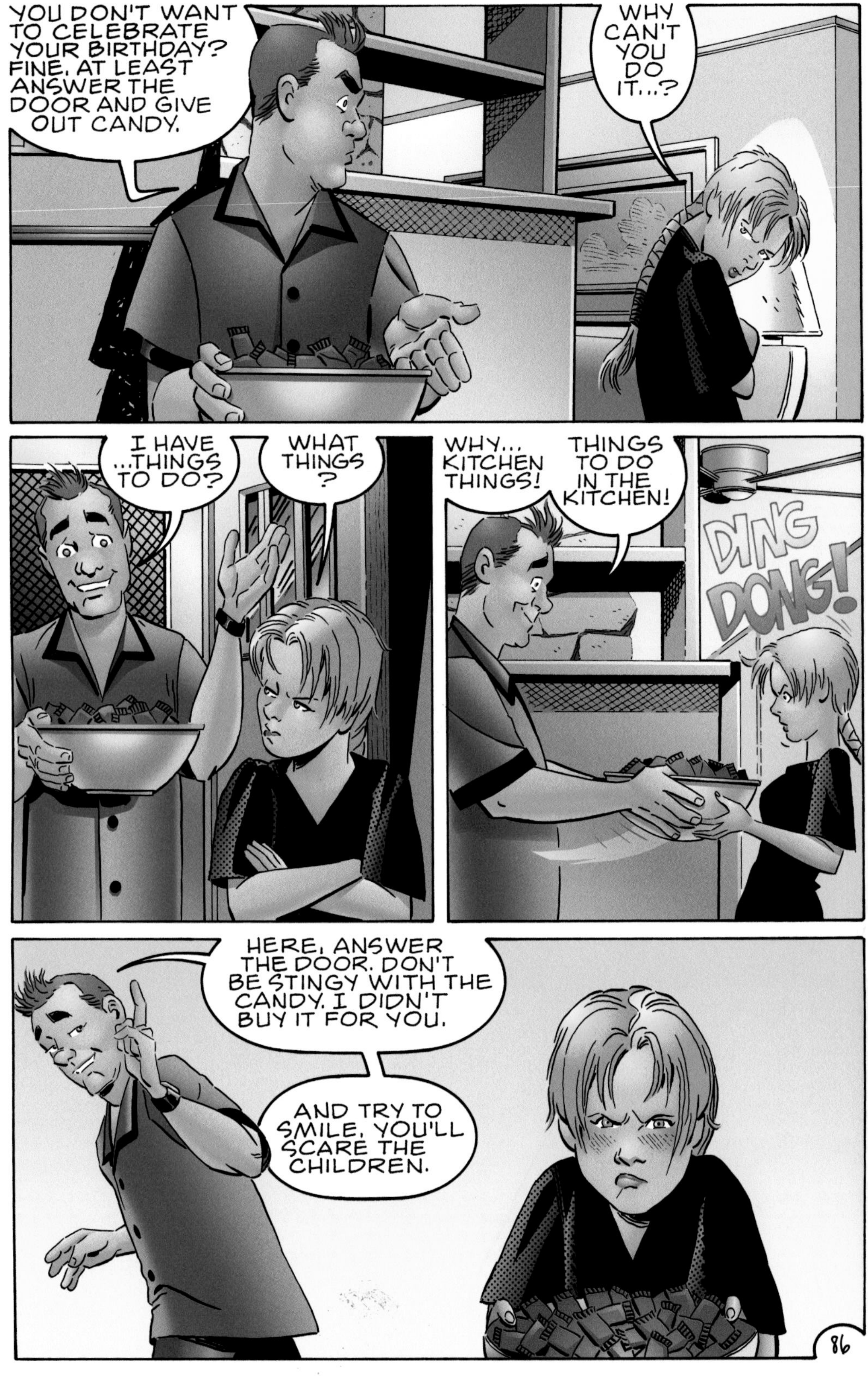
YOU DON'T WANT TO CELEBRATE YOUR BIRTHDAY? FINE. AT LEAST ANSWER THE DOOR AND GIVE OUT CANDY.
WHY CAN'T YOU DO IT...?
I HAVE ...THINGS TO DO?
WHAT THINGS ?
WHY... KITCHEN THINGS!
THINGS TO DO IN THE KITCHEN!
DING DONG!
HERE, ANSWER THE DOOR. DON'T BE STINGY WITH THE CANDY. I DIDN'T BUY IT FOR YOU.
AND TRY TO SMILE, YOU'LL SCARE THE CHILDREN.

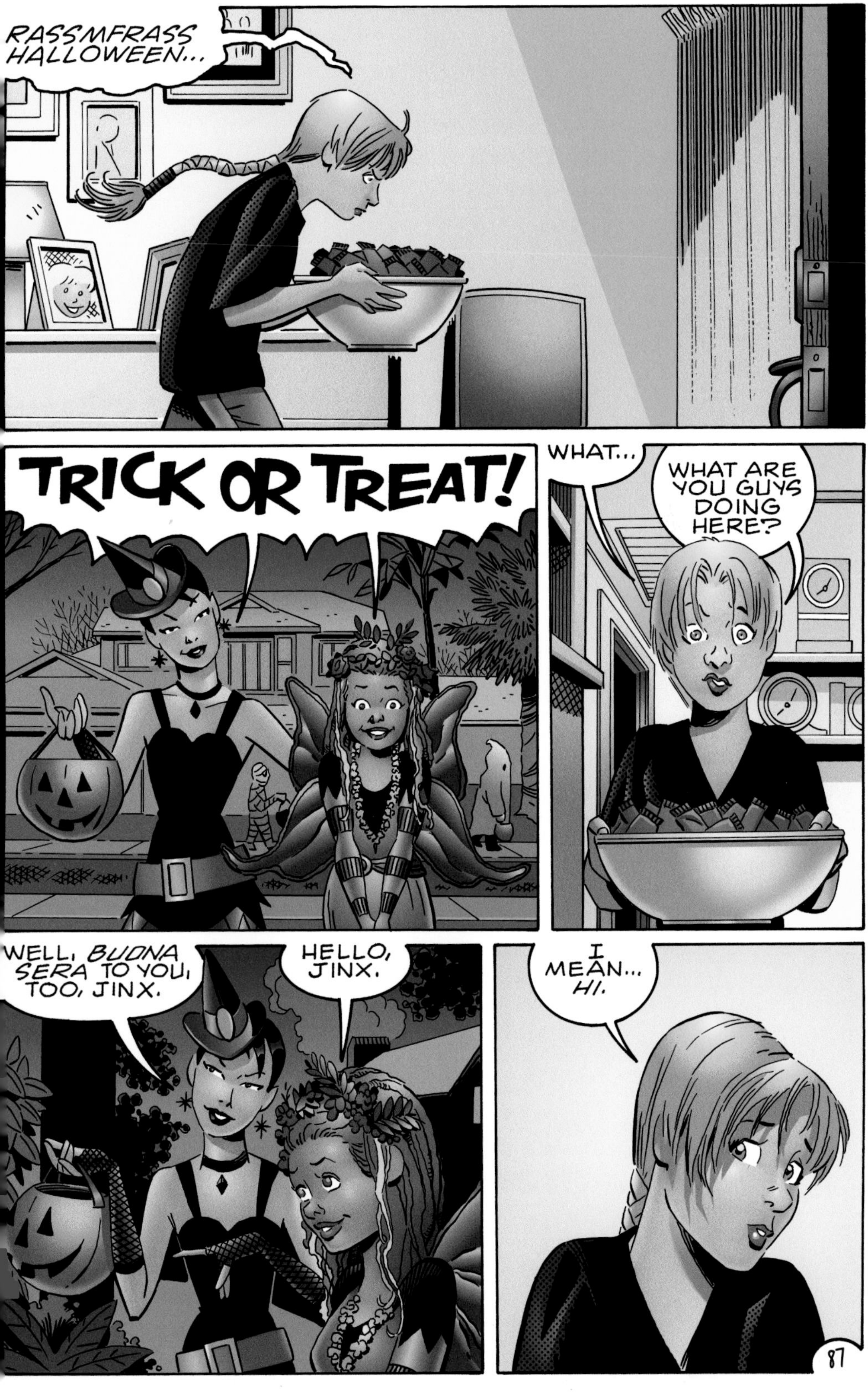
RASSMFRASS HALLOWEEN...
TRICK OR TREAT!
WHAT...
WHAT ARE YOU GUYS DOING HERE?
WELL, *BUONA SERA* TO YOU, TOO, JINX.
HELLO, JINX.
I MEAN... *HI*.

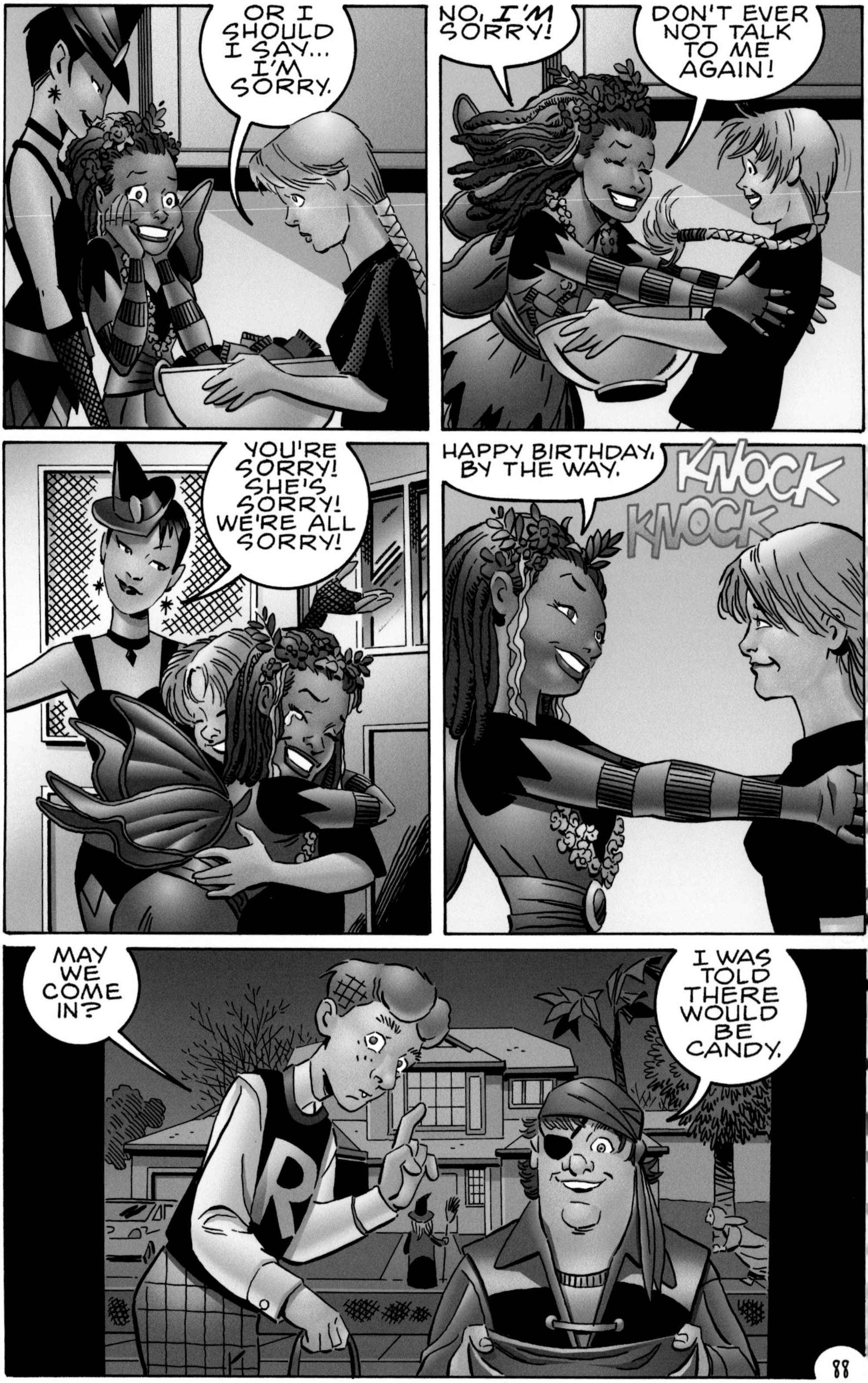
OR I SHOULD I SAY... I'M SORRY.
NO, I'M SORRY!
DON'T EVER NOT TALK TO ME AGAIN!
YOU'RE SORRY! SHE'S SORRY! WE'RE ALL SORRY!
HAPPY BIRTHDAY, BY THE WAY.
KNOCK
KNOCK
MAY WE COME IN?
I WAS TOLD THERE WOULD BE CANDY.

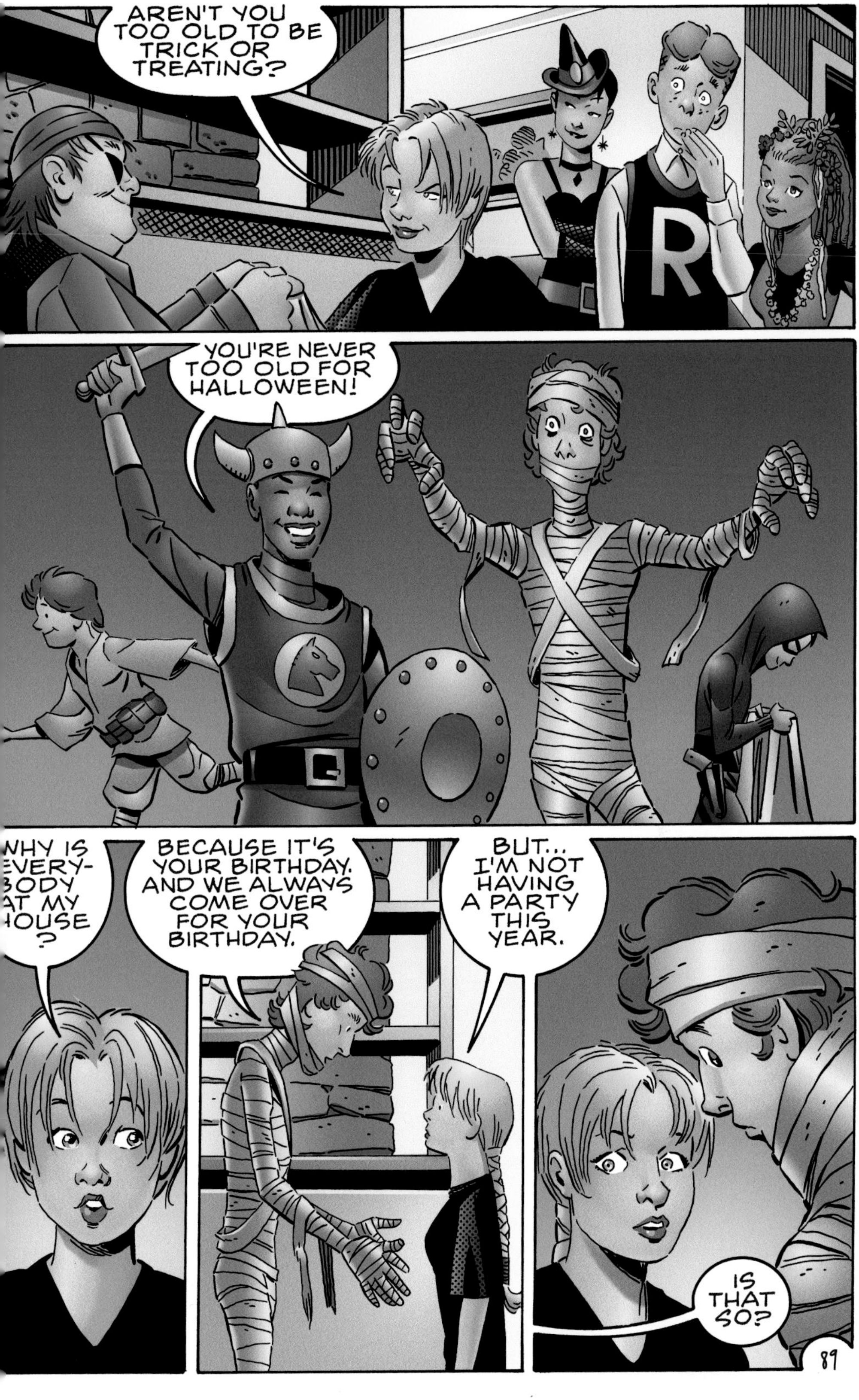

AREN'T YOU TOO OLD TO BE TRICK OR TREATING?
YOU'RE NEVER TOO OLD FOR HALLOWEEN!
WHY IS EVERYBODY AT MY HOUSE?
BECAUSE IT'S YOUR BIRTHDAY. AND WE ALWAYS COME OVER FOR YOUR BIRTHDAY.
BUT... I'M NOT HAVING A PARTY THIS YEAR.
IS THAT SO?

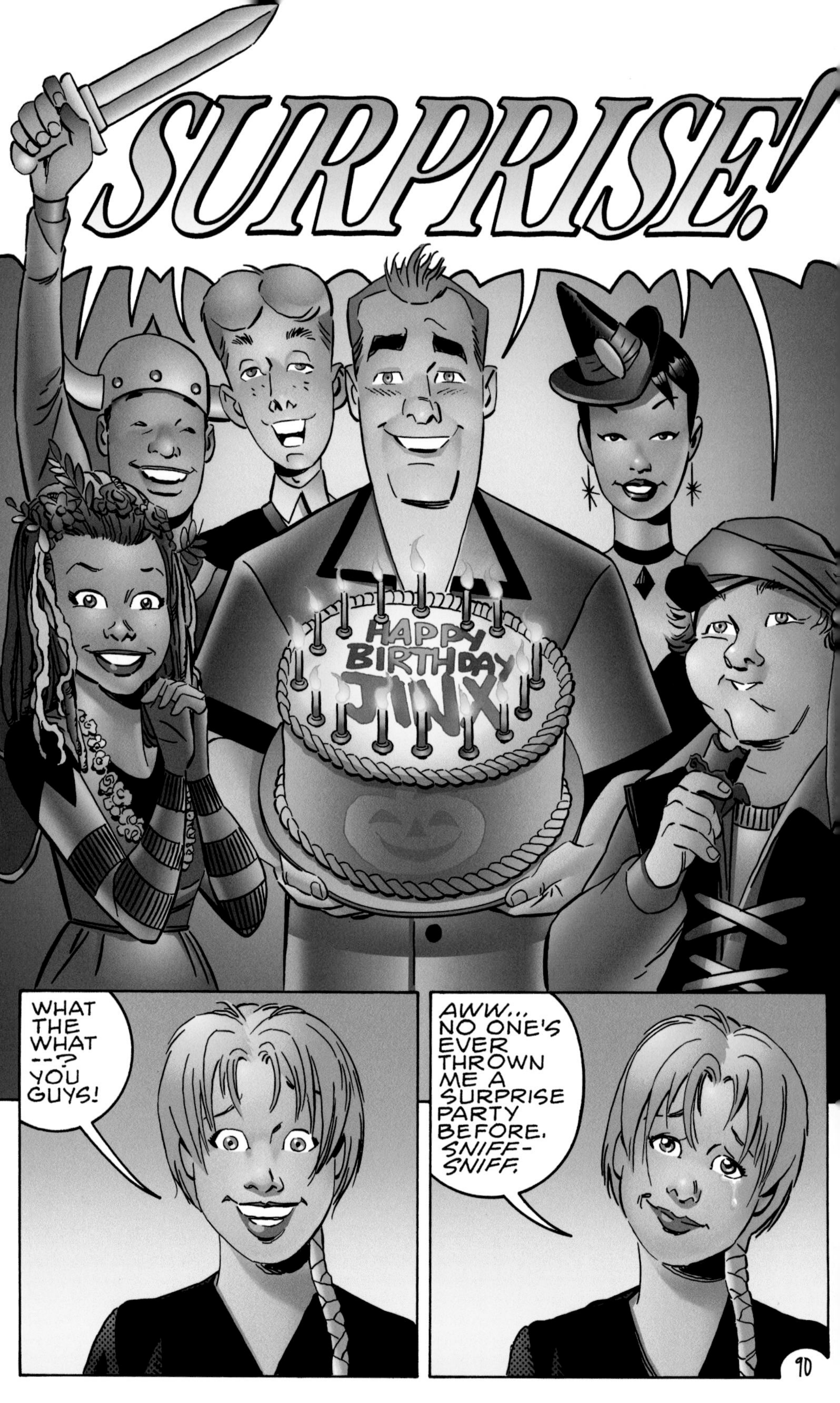
SURPRISE!
HAPPY BIRTHDAY JINX
WHAT THE WHAT --? YOU GUYS!
AWW... NO ONE'S EVER THROWN ME A SURPRISE PARTY BEFORE. SNIFF-SNIFF.

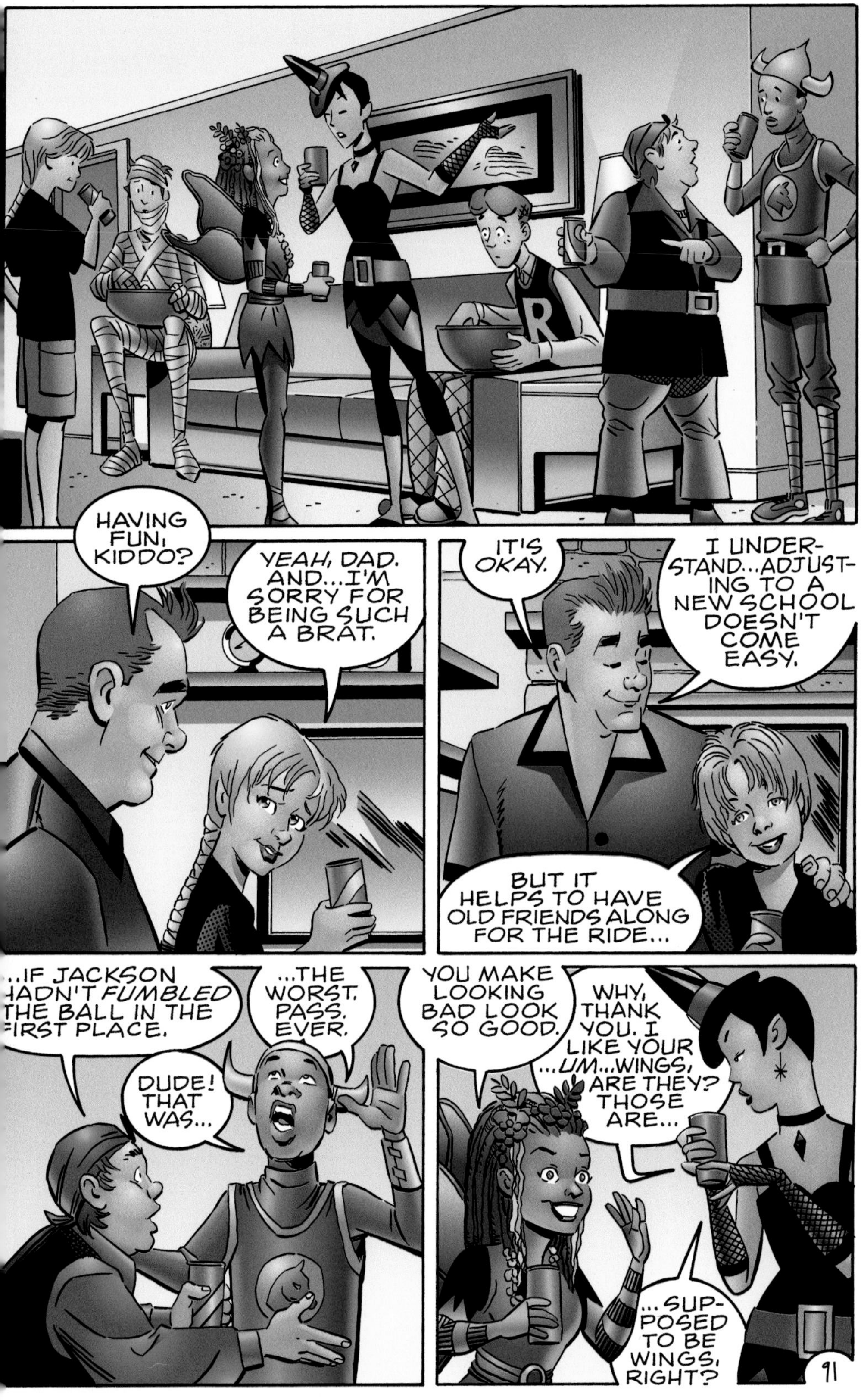
HAVING FUN, KIDDO?
YEAH, DAD. AND...I'M SORRY FOR BEING SUCH A BRAT.
IT'S OKAY.
I UNDERSTAND...ADJUSTING TO A NEW SCHOOL DOESN'T COME EASY.
BUT IT HELPS TO HAVE OLD FRIENDS ALONG FOR THE RIDE...
...IF JACKSON HADN'T *FUMBLED* THE BALL IN THE FIRST PLACE.
DUDE! THAT WAS...
...THE WORST. PASS. EVER.
YOU MAKE LOOKING BAD LOOK SO GOOD.
WHY, THANK YOU. I LIKE YOUR ...*UM*...WINGS, ARE THEY? THOSE ARE...
...SUPPOSED TO BE WINGS, RIGHT?

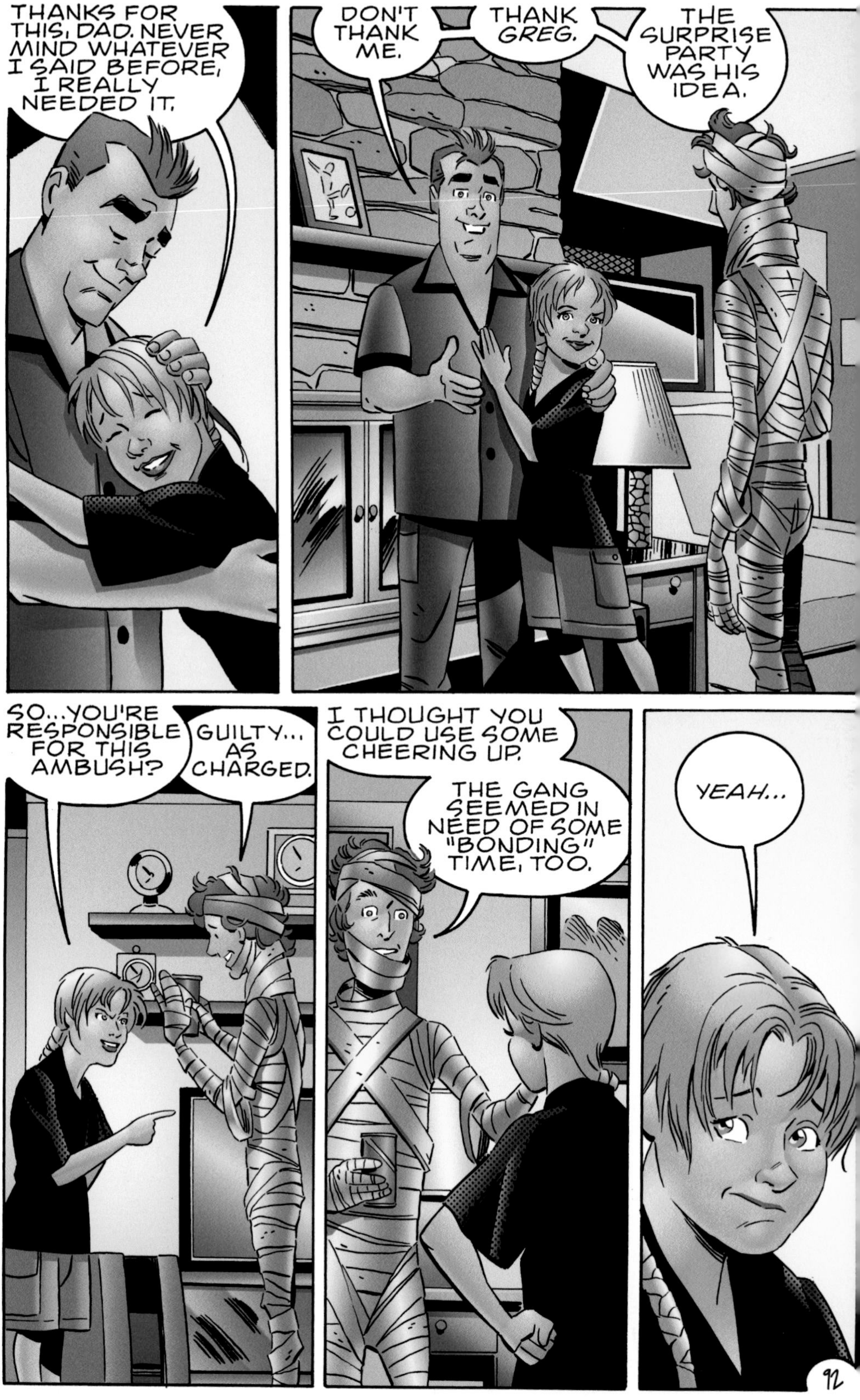
THANKS FOR THIS, DAD. NEVER MIND WHATEVER I SAID BEFORE, I REALLY NEEDED IT.
DON'T THANK ME.
THANK GREG.
THE SURPRISE PARTY WAS HIS IDEA.
SO...YOU'RE RESPONSIBLE FOR THIS AMBUSH?
GUILTY... AS CHARGED.
I THOUGHT YOU COULD USE SOME CHEERING UP.
THE GANG SEEMED IN NEED OF SOME "BONDING" TIME, TOO.
YEAH...

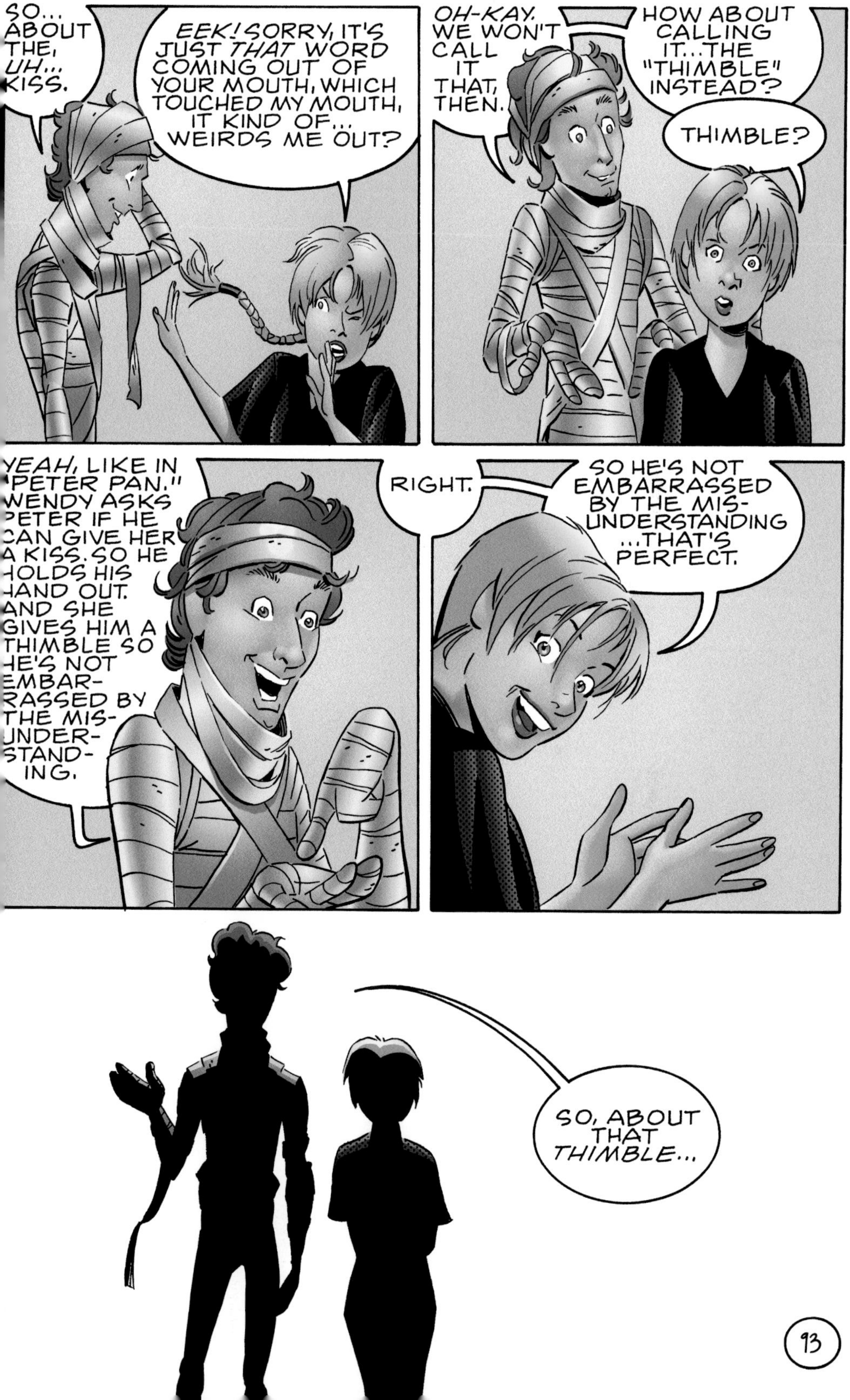
SO... ABOUT THE, UH... KISS.
EEK! SORRY, IT'S JUST THAT WORD COMING OUT OF YOUR MOUTH, WHICH TOUCHED MY MOUTH, IT KIND OF... WEIRDS ME OUT?
OH-KAY. WE WON'T CALL IT THAT, THEN.
HOW ABOUT CALLING IT...THE "THIMBLE" INSTEAD?
THIMBLE?
YEAH, LIKE IN "PETER PAN." WENDY ASKS PETER IF HE CAN GIVE HER A KISS. SO HE HOLDS HIS HAND OUT. AND SHE GIVES HIM A THIMBLE SO HE'S NOT EMBARRASSED BY THE MISUNDERSTANDING.
RIGHT.
SO HE'S NOT EMBARRASSED BY THE MISUNDERSTANDING ...THAT'S PERFECT.
SO, ABOUT THAT THIMBLE...

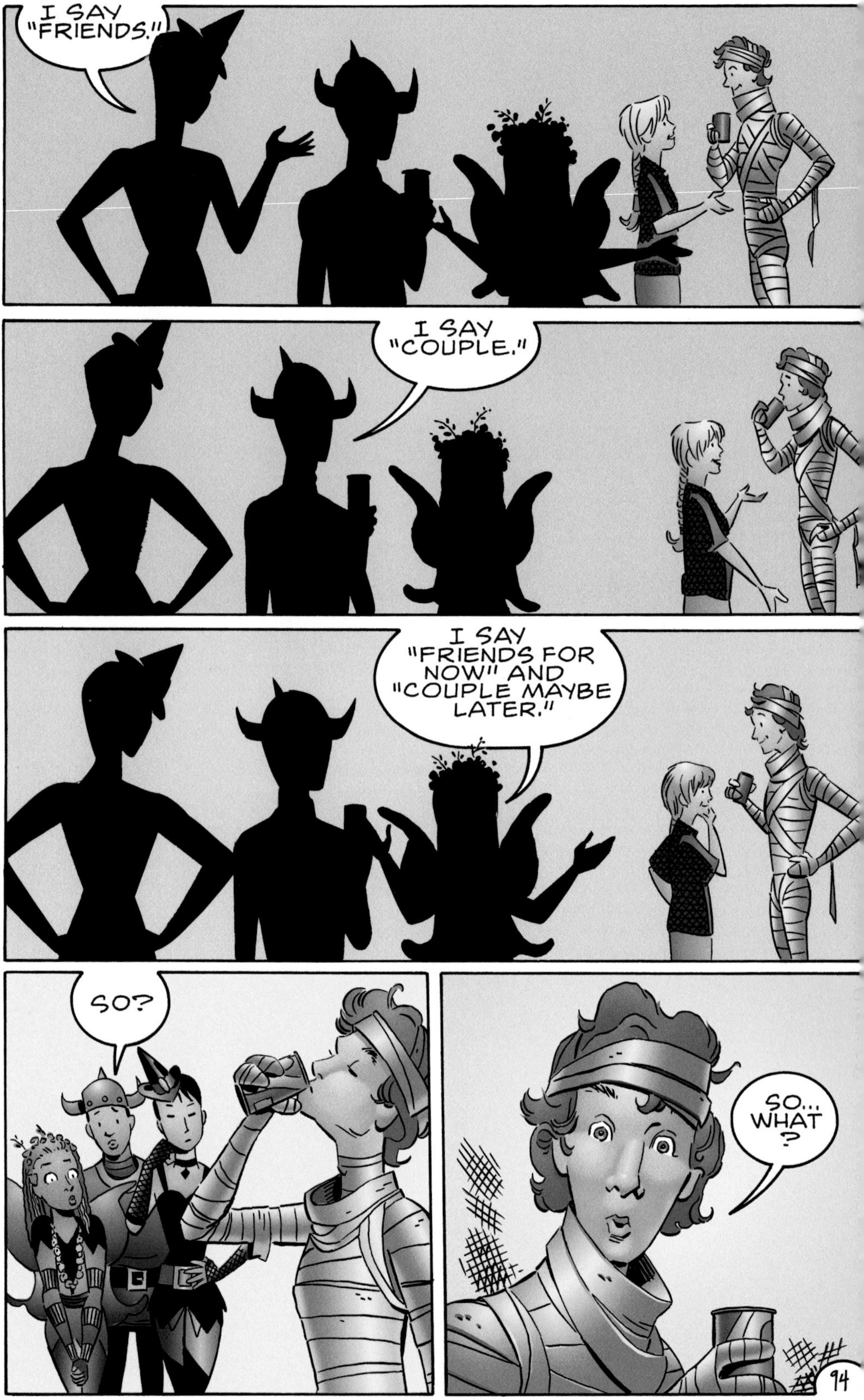
I SAY "FRIENDS."
I SAY "COUPLE."
I SAY "FRIENDS FOR NOW" AND "COUPLE MAYBE LATER."
SO?
SO... WHAT?

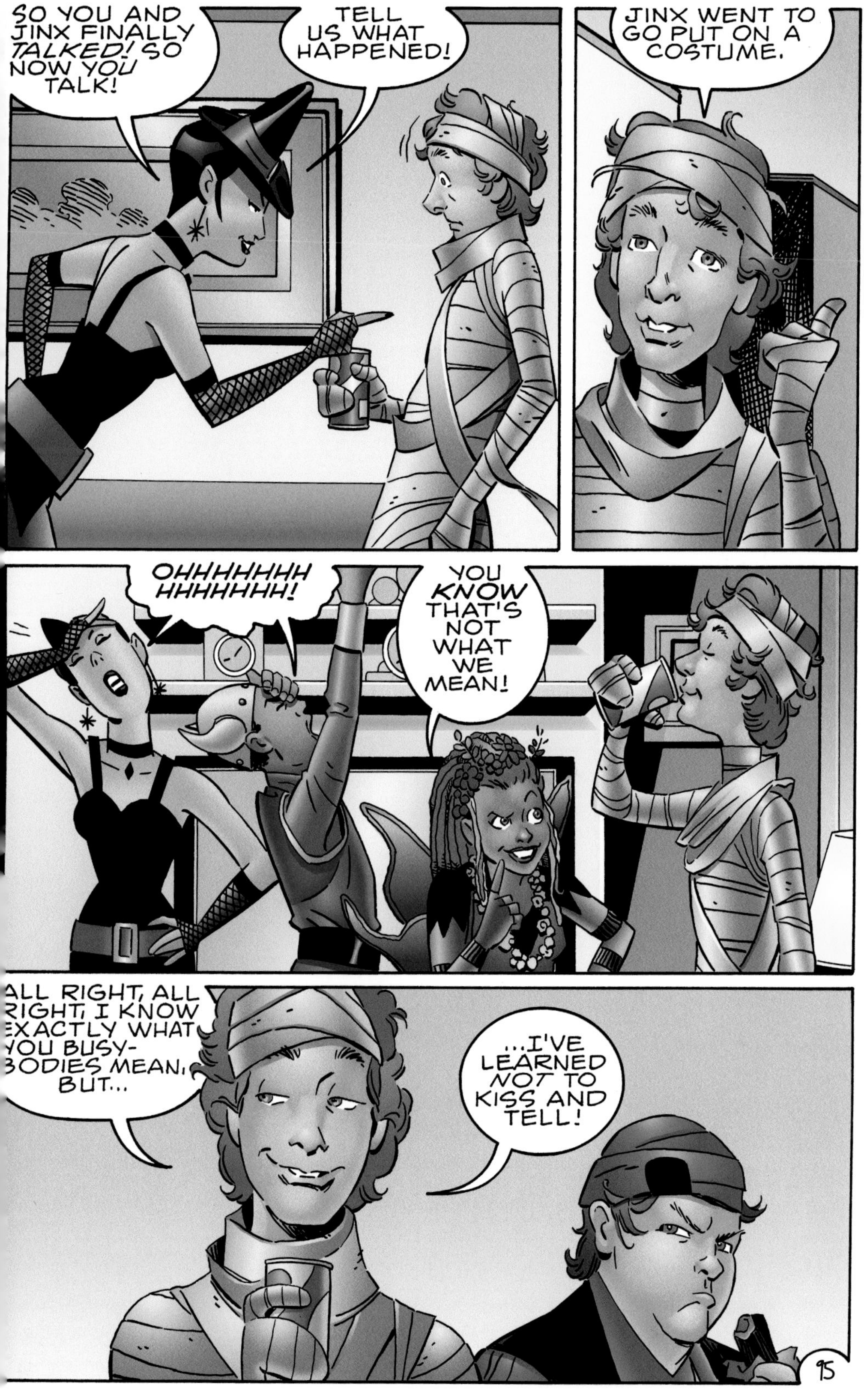
SO YOU AND JINX FINALLY *TALKED!* SO NOW *YOU* TALK!
TELL US WHAT HAPPENED!
JINX WENT TO GO PUT ON A COSTUME.
OHHHHHHH HHHHHHH!
YOU *KNOW* THAT'S NOT WHAT WE MEAN!
ALL RIGHT, ALL RIGHT, I KNOW EXACTLY WHAT YOU BUSY-BODIES MEAN, BUT...
...I'VE LEARNED *NOT* TO KISS AND TELL!

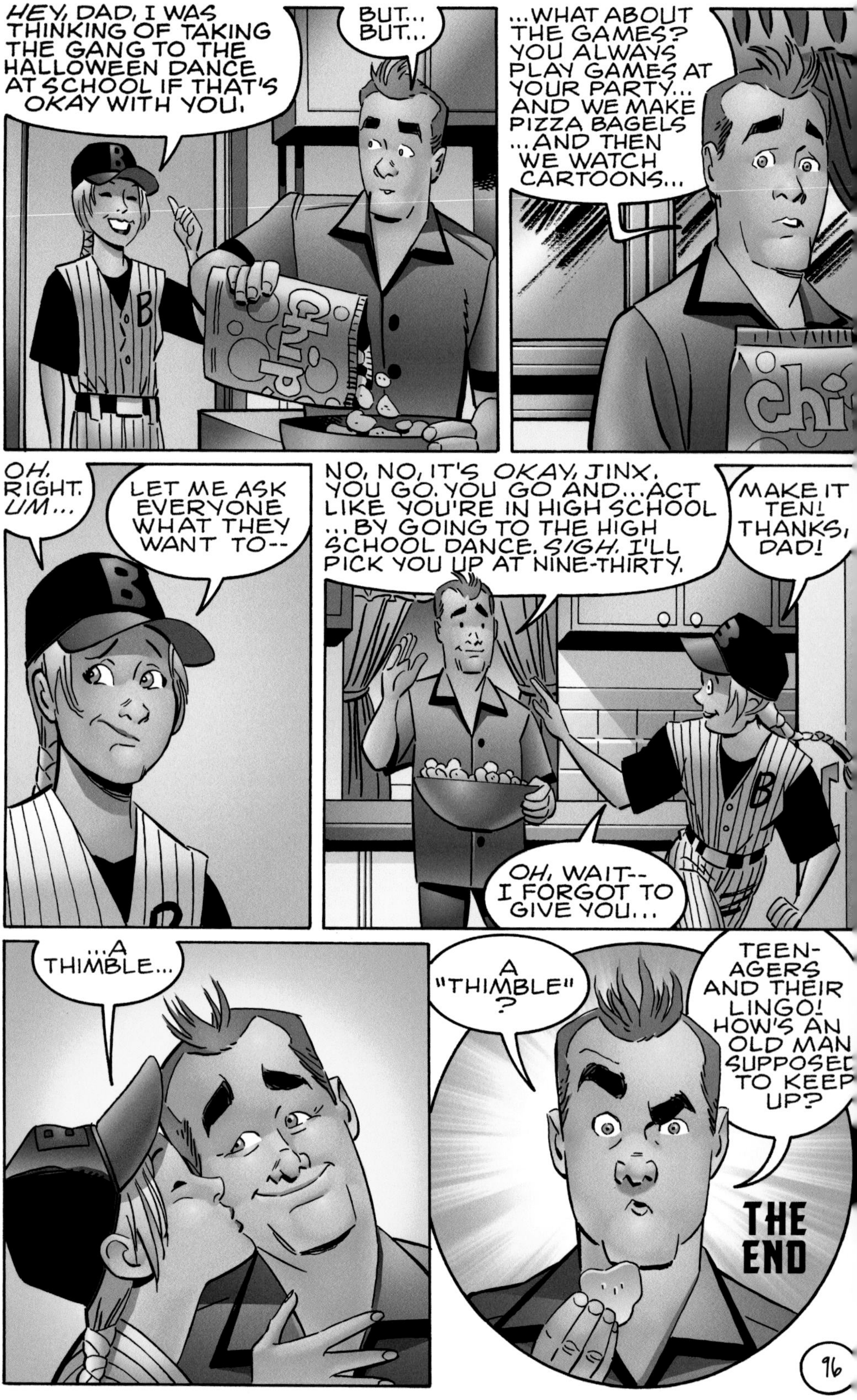
HEY, DAD, I WAS THINKING OF TAKING THE GANG TO THE HALLOWEEN DANCE AT SCHOOL IF THAT'S OKAY WITH YOU.
BUT... BUT...
...WHAT ABOUT THE GAMES? YOU ALWAYS PLAY GAMES AT YOUR PARTY... AND WE MAKE PIZZA BAGELS ...AND THEN WE WATCH CARTOONS...
OH. RIGHT. UM...
LET ME ASK EVERYONE WHAT THEY WANT TO--
NO, NO, IT'S OKAY, JINX. YOU GO. YOU GO AND...ACT LIKE YOU'RE IN HIGH SCHOOL ...BY GOING TO THE HIGH SCHOOL DANCE. SIGH. I'LL PICK YOU UP AT NINE-THIRTY.
MAKE IT TEN! THANKS, DAD!
OH, WAIT-- I FORGOT TO GIVE YOU...
...A THIMBLE...
A "THIMBLE"?
TEEN-AGERS AND THEIR LINGO! HOW'S AN OLD MAN SUPPOSED TO KEEP UP?
THE END

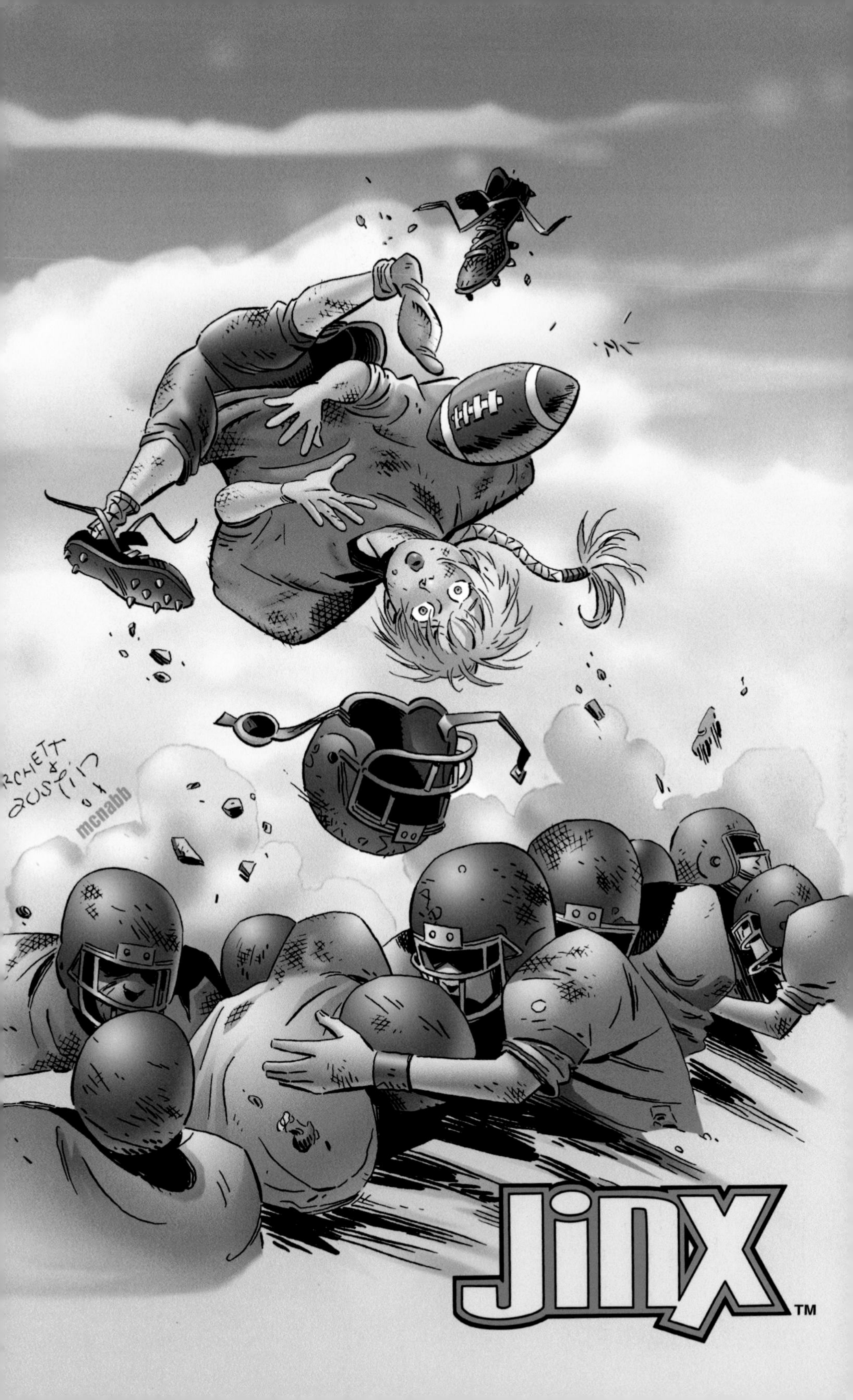

mcnabb
JINX™

the voice of jinx

by j. torres

I'm not a teenage girl but I write one in a comic book.

I've written a few different teenage girl characters in different comic book genres: Starfire and Raven in *Teen Titans Go*, Ellie, Emma, Liberty, and Paige in the *Degrassi: Extra Credit* graphic novels, and Katara in *Avatar: The Last Airbender* comics. Some of my creator-owned titles (e.g. *Days Like This*, *Sidekicks*) have also had teenage girl characters in the lead roles.

So, how does some married guy with two sons write stories about the experiences of a teenage girl?

I remember asking a similar question about author S.E. Hinton when, as a young boy, I discovered that the person writing my favorite books at the time, books about boys coming of age (*The Outsiders*, *Rumble Fish*) ... was actually girl!

Back when I was a teenager, Jinx (the character) was still in Li'l Jinx (the comic strip). She was a precocious little girl in a red dress and pigtails who was determined to take on the world. Li'l Jinx (the character) was started by legendary cartoonist Joe Edwards for Archie Comics. She first appeared in Pep Comics #62 (July, 1947). The Li'l Jinx comic strip ran for over thirty years, and reprints of these stories continue to appear in various Archie digests to this day. That was the Jinx that I got to know: a baseball-playing, mischief-making, headstrong little girl.

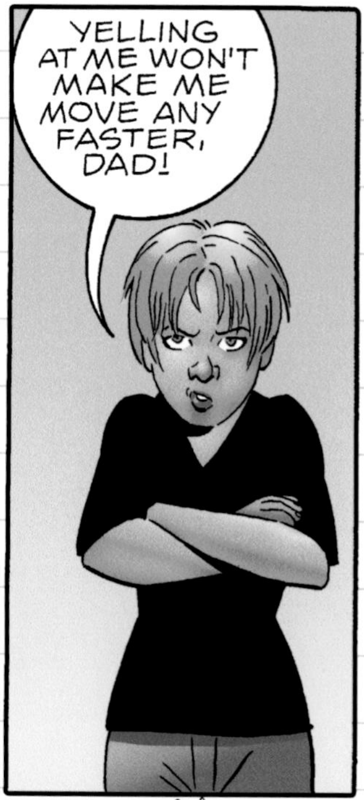
YELLING AT ME WON'T MAKE ME MOVE ANY FASTER, DAD!
j. torres dialogue

Now, as far as I know, Mr. Edwards was never a little girl in pigtails, yet he found the inspiration to write and draw one. So, while they say that you should write what you know, I am clearly in fine company.

Mr. Edwards was a father (of two sons and a daughter) and he based some of Jinx's stories on his own experiences as a dad. Many of my favorite classic Li'l Jinx comics are the ones focused on Jinx and her long-suffering father, Hap Holliday, butting heads. As the writer of Jinx's new adventures, I wanted to keep with the tradition of telling stories grounded in this father/daughter relationship. I don't have the experience of raising a daughter to draw from as Mr. Edwards did, but I did grow up with a father and younger sister; and boy, did they butt heads!

Besides, high school experiences are universal. While I was mapping out Jinx's life as she grows from little kid to young adult, starts high school, and maneuvers her way through puberty, I thought: "Been there, done that." As a teenager, I had to deal with schoolwork and zits, curfews and crushes, fitting in and sticking out. We all grow up.

Yes, some of my own personal teenage experiences can be found within these pages too but for the most part, well, I just made stuff up -- that's what writers do, right? But I've had a lot of help in that department, of course. Suzannah Rowntree isn't "only" my editor, she's responsible for initially developing the idea of "Jinx as a high school student" as tasked to her by Jon Goldwater himself. Suzannah wanted the series to be about teenagers who were "real, not ideal." So Jinx isn't exactly the glamorous, fashionable and flawless beauty Veronica Lodge is; nor is she the straight-A student, girl-next-door type that Betty Cooper is.

The interesting thing is, two of her closest friends in the series kind of stand in for Betty and Veronica: there's Roz who is as down-to-earth, kind and studious as Betty; and then there's Gigi -- who's quite possibly as rich, stylish and popular as Veronica. But neither of them are perfect, we try to portray them as "real, not ideal" as best we can in a comic book that, of course, has sometimes unreal, comical situations.

Comical situations that involve boys! Jinx's best friend Greg isn't exactly smooth with the ladies. He's athletic, but also awkward. He's popular, but unsure of himself. He's a good friend but doesn't know the first thing about being a boyfriend. Like a lot of teenage boys. Like I was. "Real, not ideal."

All of this was in the original pitch. I just had to flesh it all out and build a story around it. Suzannah also included illustrations and photographic reference for what the cast could look like, what they could wear, etc. Our amazing art team of Rick Burchett and Terry Austin worked all of that out, designed our characters, and built a very familiar, realistic yet wonderfully stylized world for us to visit each issue.

I still can't believe I'm sharing a credit box with these two artists! They've worked on some of my favorite comics of all-time!

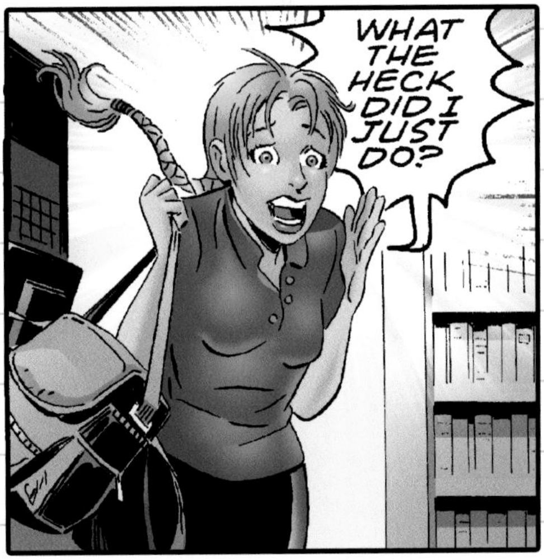
WHAT THE HECK DID I JUST DO?

j. torres dialogue

So that's how a married man with two sons but no daughter (yet?) wrote these stories about the trials and tribulations of a spunky, sporty, sometimes spoiled teenage girl named Jinx, who was named so because she was born on Halloween.

Whether you're a teenage girl, a fellow old fogey, someone's daughter, or someone's dad -- I hope you consider what you're about to read a treat.

torres

the concept art of jinx

jinx

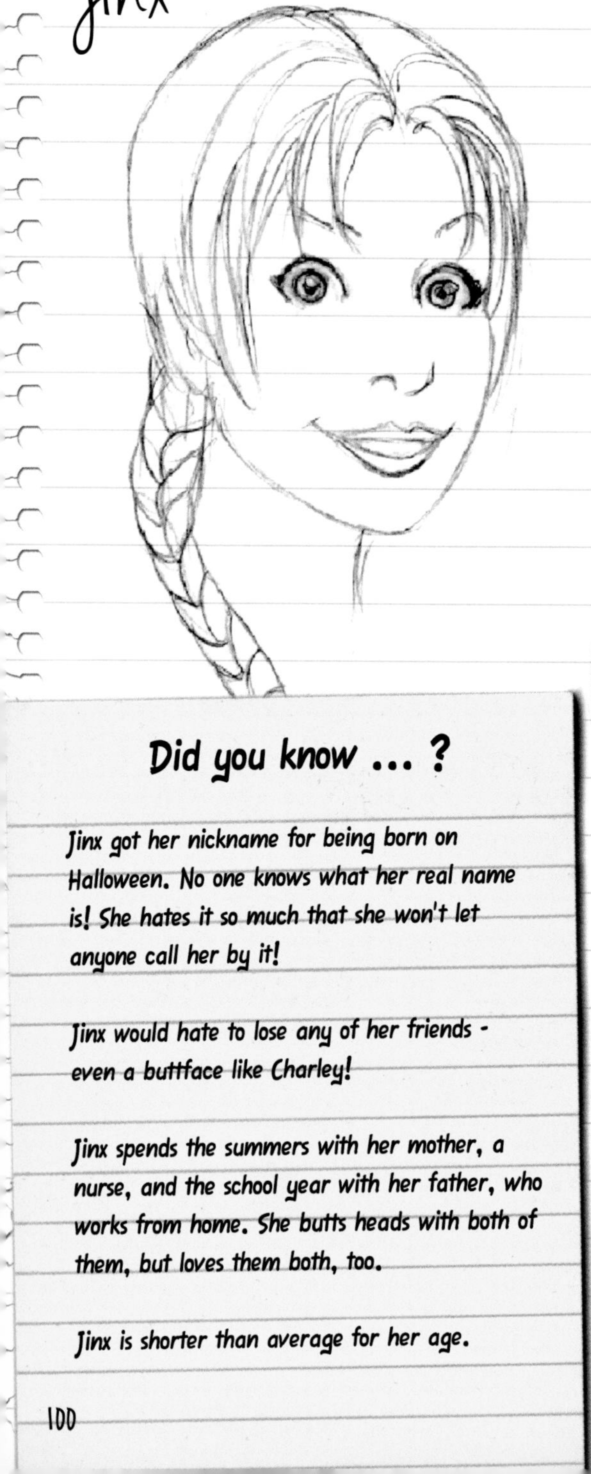

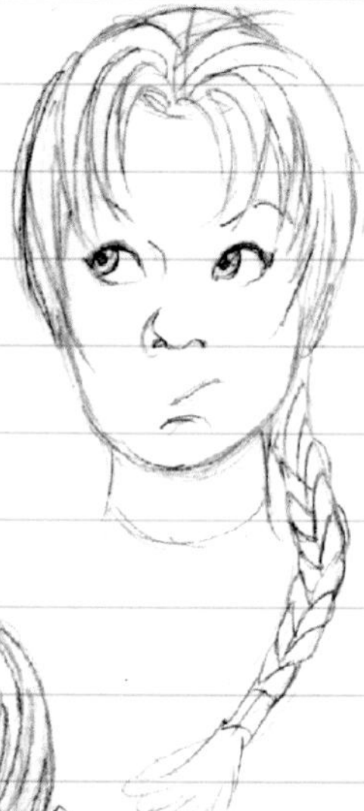

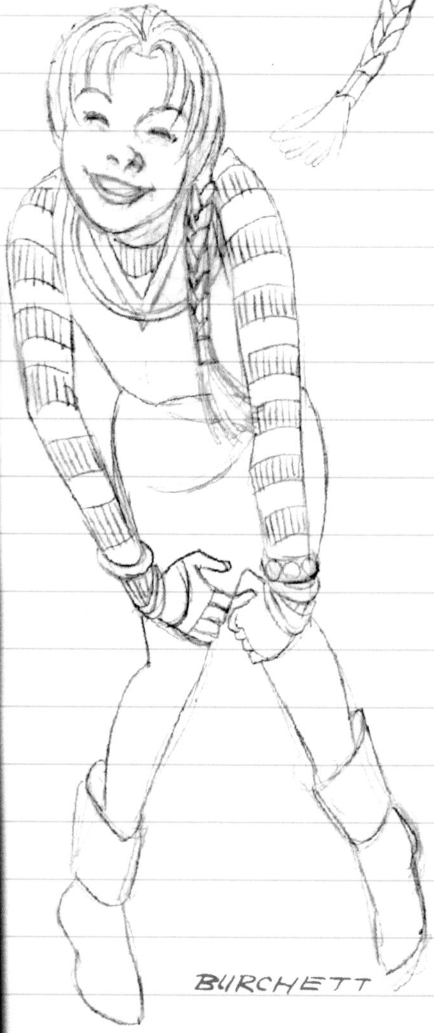
BURCHETT

Did you know ... ?

Jinx got her nickname for being born on Halloween. No one knows what her real name is! She hates it so much that she won't let anyone call her by it!

Jinx would hate to lose any of her friends - even a buttface like Charley!

Jinx spends the summers with her mother, a nurse, and the school year with her father, who works from home. She butts heads with both of them, but loves them both, too.

Jinx is shorter than average for her age.

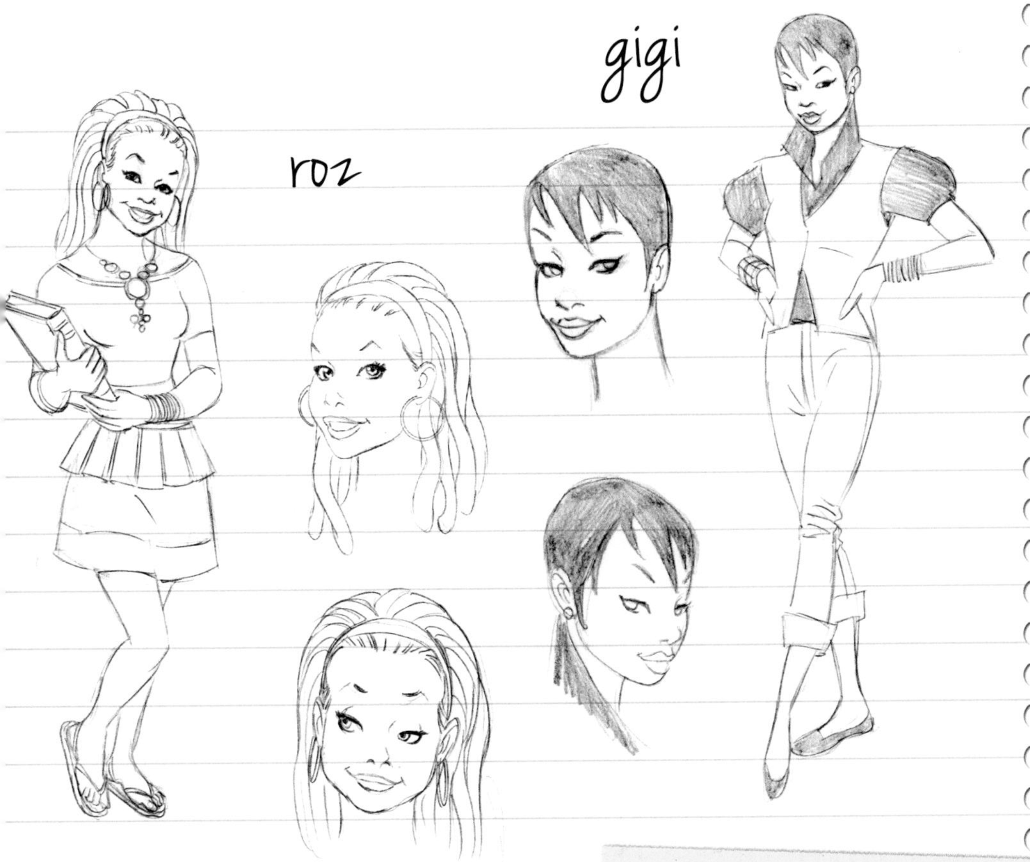
gigi
roz

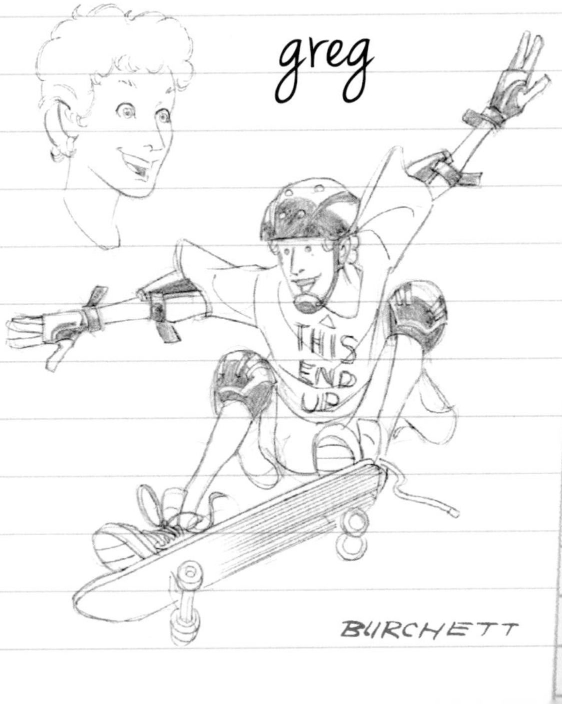
greg
THIS
END
UP
BURCHETT

Did you know ... ?

Gigi and Roz don't like each other as much as they both like Jinx. Their common friendship brings them together, but if it weren't for Jinx they wouldn't hang out at all.

Gigi was sometimes called "Gaga" in early Li'l Jinx strips.

Greg loves hackey sack. Whether he's playing baseball, football or video games, he gives all of his attention to what he's doing. What's going on with other people often goes over his head!

charley

mort

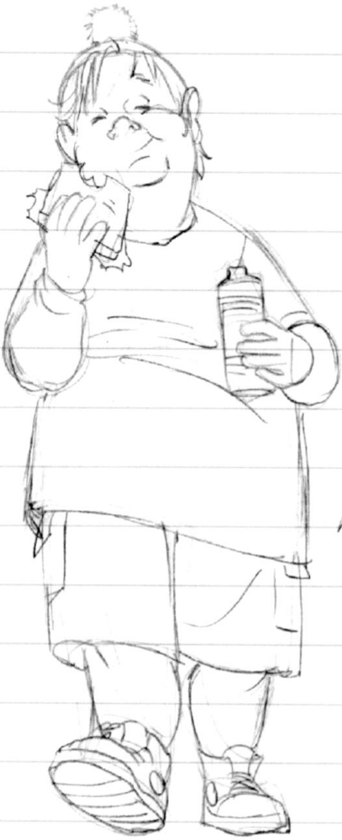

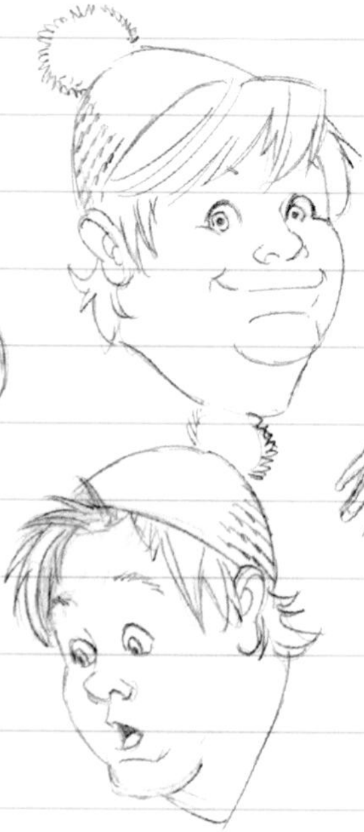

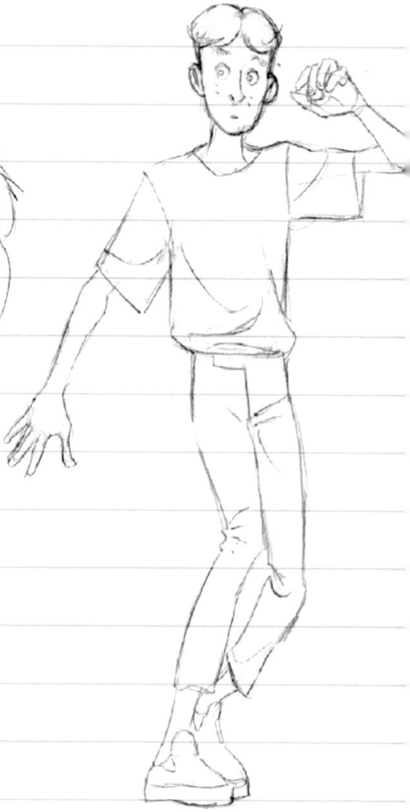

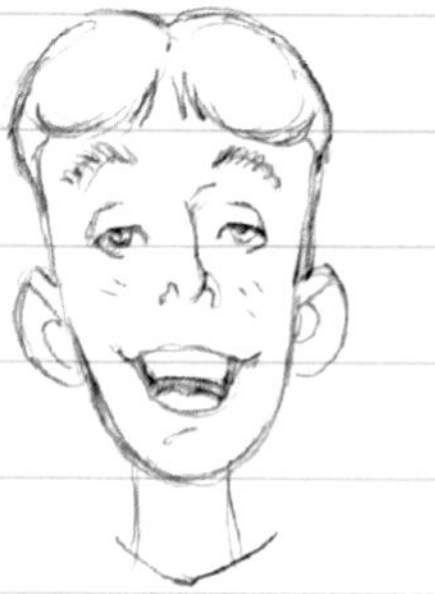

Did you know ... ?

Charley was once the tallest of the group. When everyone was eight years old, Charley was taller and bigger than everyone else. He hasn't grown any taller in quite a few years!

Mort has **ALWAYS** been a pessimist! Even as a little kid, he always acted like he thought the world was out to get him.

Charley and Mort got along really well when they were little kids.

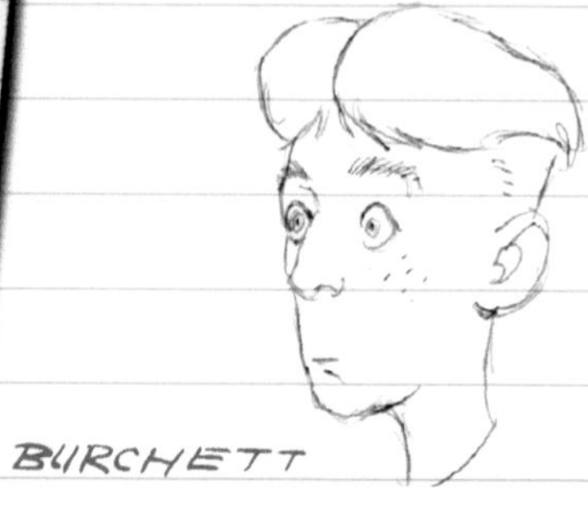
BURCHETT

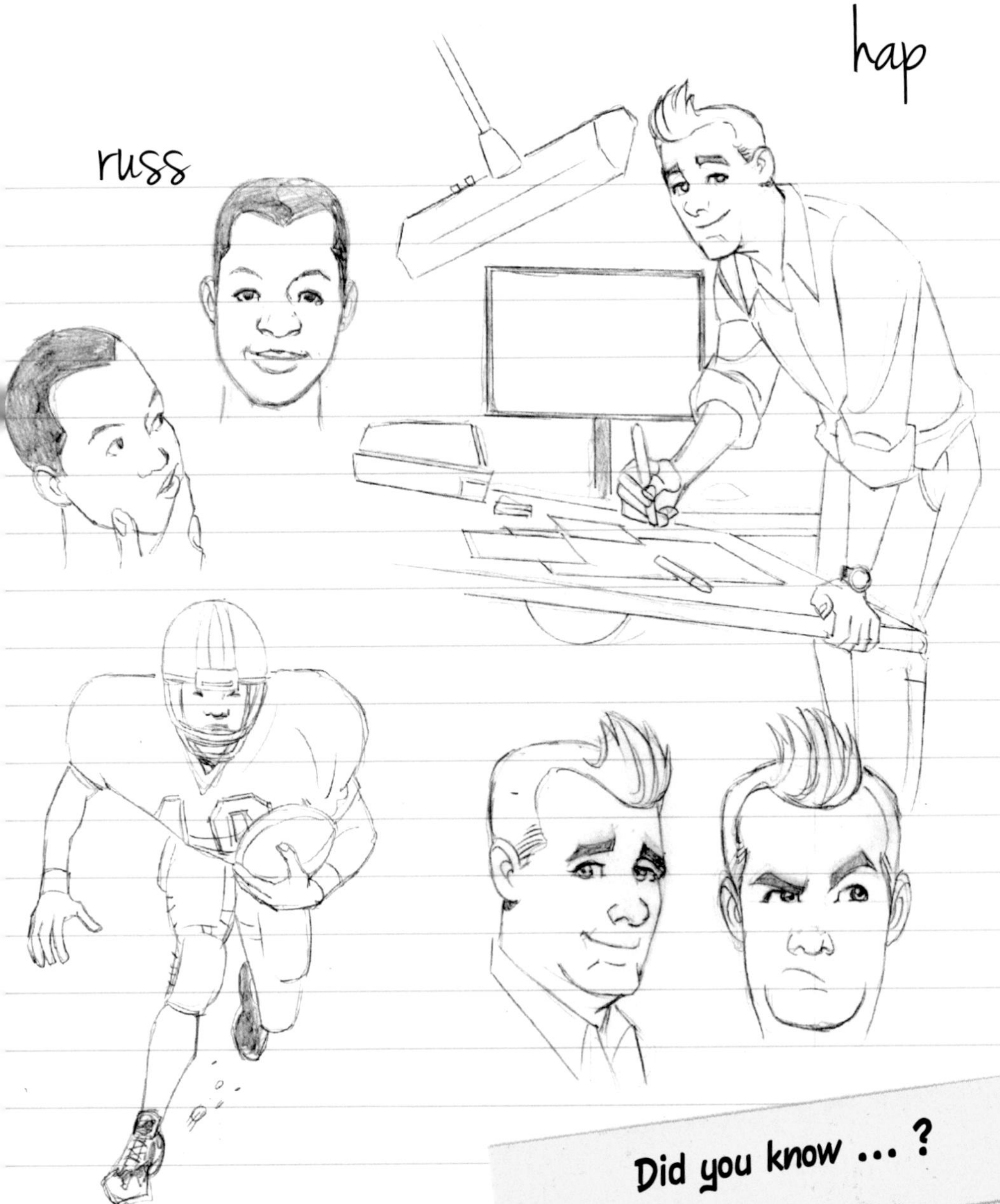
hap
russ

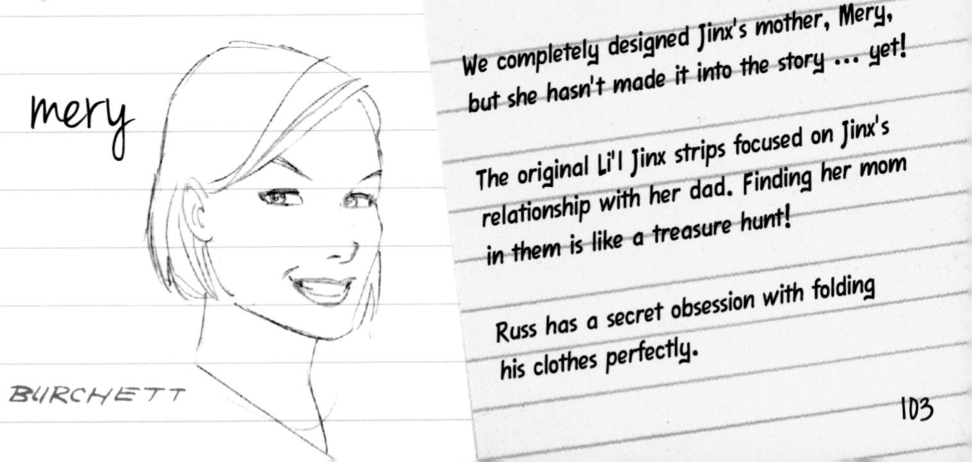
mery
BURCHETT

Did you know … ?

We completely designed Jinx's mother, Mery, but she hasn't made it into the story … yet!

The original Li'l Jinx strips focused on Jinx's relationship with her dad. Finding her mom in them is like a treasure hunt!

Russ has a secret obsession with folding his clothes perfectly.

the story of teen jinx

by suzannah rowntree

It all began when Jon Goldwater, Co-CEO of Archie Comics, was chatting in the art department one afternoon about the classic ACP character Li'l Jinx. "How great would that be," he said, "if Jinx was a trendy, fun teenager?" (Li'l Jinx, for those not in the know, is a stubborn eight-year-old tomboy with a very close-knit group of friends, many of whom you see grow up with Jinx in this book. Stories about Li'l Jinx, her friends, and her almost-always patient father have been published by Archie since the 40's.)

As they say, "Ask and you shall receive!" I presented Jon with character designs, story outlines, style guides and sketches. Jinx, I decided, would be a little bit different from anything we had tried so far. She would be real, not ideal, and experience the emotional highs and lows of high school life -- thrilling romance, cringe-worthy humiliations -- the real growing pains that we all go through as teenagers.

Writer J. Torres was the first talent to join the team working to bring Jinx to life; we couldn't have chosen better! J. somehow knew things about Jinx and her friends that no one had ever told him. Industry great Rick Burchett perfectly captured the concentrated emotions of high school. From Jinx to Mort, his characters jump off of the page. Inking legend Terry Austin, with his vast portfolio and years of working

the first ever drawing of jinx ⟶

with the best of the best, took on Jinx like it was the most exciting project he'd seen in years. John Workman, another industry legend, lettered Jinx's story. John's lettering is among the most admired in the industry and perfectly complimented the art to help readers glide through the story. The team was rounded out by colorist Mark McNabb, an expert at setting the mood of a scene.

Under the leadership of Co-CEO Jon Goldwater, Archie Comics has become one of the best outlets in the comic book industry for new, innovative, and ground-breaking creativity. President Mike Pellerito and Co-President/Editor-in-Chief Victor Gorelick have been a crucial element in this evolution. Jinx's success -- and this book -- could not have happened without their editorial guidance and unwavering support.

li'l jinx was a happy kid

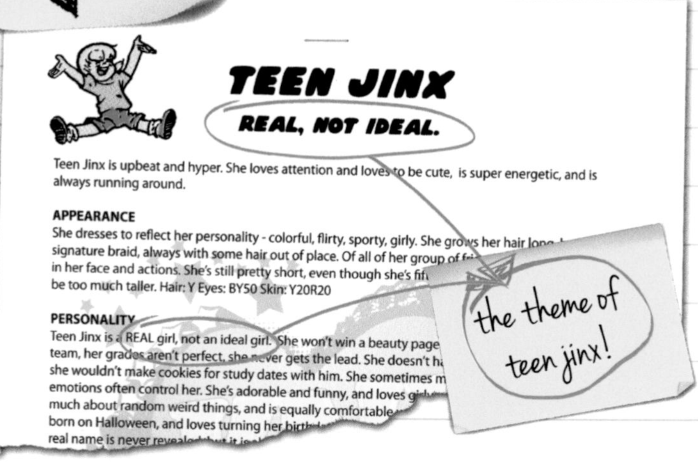

TEEN JINX

REAL, NOT IDEAL.

Teen Jinx is upbeat and hyper. She loves attention and loves to be cute, is super energetic, and is always running around.

APPEARANCE
She dresses to reflect her personality - colorful, flirty, sporty, girly. She grows her hair long signature braid, always with some hair out of place. Of all of her group of f... in her face and actions. She's still pretty short, even though she's fi... be too much taller. Hair: Y Eyes: BY50 Skin: Y20R20

PERSONALITY
Teen Jinx is a REAL girl, not an ideal girl. She won't win a beauty page... team, her grades aren't perfect, she never gets the lead. She doesn't h... she wouldn't make cookies for study dates with him. She sometimes m... emotions often control her. She's adorable and funny, and loves gi... much about random weird things, and is equally comfortable... born on Halloween, and loves turning her birth... real name is never revealed...

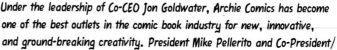

the theme of teen jinx!

104

gigi was a glam princess for years!

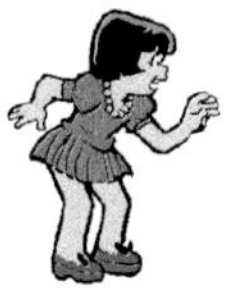

GIGI

SLEEK AND CHIC

APPEARANCE
Gigi is very slim and always catches the latest trends. She usually wears monochrome outfits, mostly black, white and grey. She's constantly being taken for older than she really is. She looks like a model. Her face is narrow and delicate. She has short-cut black hair - a hair style that most people can't pull off and black hair, perhaps with a few chunky streaks that change color every issue. She looks like a supermodel. She is of Vietnamese heritage. Eyes: YR80B50, Hair: Flat Black, Skin: Y10R10, Lips: R30

PERSONALITY
She's quiet, calm and confident. She has zero interest in pursuing the acting career she had as a child, not liking what she sees in the lifestyle of the entertainment industry. She comes off as very laid back and sometimes smug. She works well as Jinx's antithesis - Jinx wants to be the coolest, most rich, most beautiful - as many teen girls do. Gigi has all of those things, but thinks that they are not important. She balances out Jinx's hotheaded side. She and Roz have a quietly friendly relationship.

STORY
Gigi was a child star, mostly in advertising. Her parents pulled her out of the industry when she was ten, in order to give her a normal teen life. Of all of the Teen Jinx characters, she is the most wealthy. She comes off as snobby and cold, but in reality, she simply doesn't feel interested in impressing anyone. Gigi's parents are both American, but were born to freshly immigrated families - her mother's from France, and her father's from Vietnam.

STYLE REFERENCES
Rihanna, Posh Spice/ Victoria Beckham

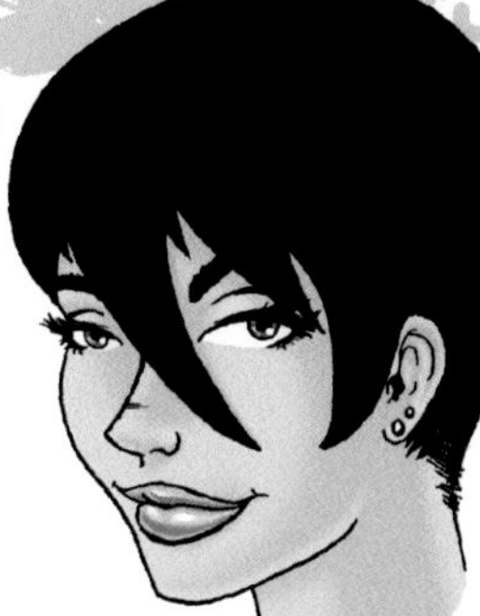

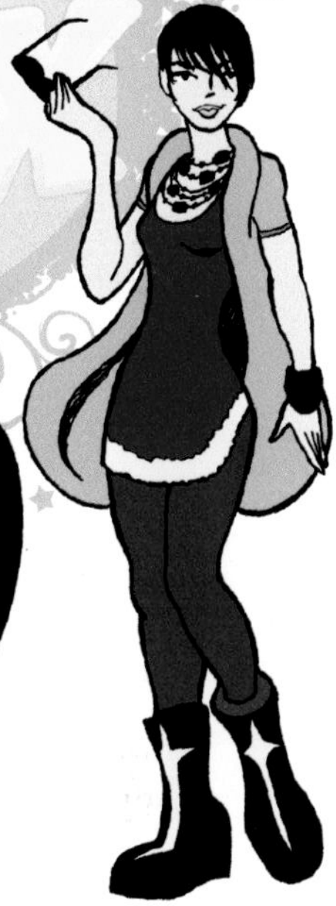

a Gigi page from the original pitch

The more people I speak to about their high school experiences, the more stories come out about people wanting to watch and read stories that represented their actual high school experiences. We wanted to tell the stories that showed the real, not ideal tales of high school life. With Jinx, we've been able to give readers these stories.

You might be reading this book in middle school, nervous and excited for your upcoming freshman year. You might be reading it in the thick of high school, surrounded by your own Charley's and Gigi's. Or, you might be taking a trip down memory lane when reading Jinx's stories. Whichever one you are, we hope it's been as fun to read as it has been for all of us to make!

Suzannah Rowntree

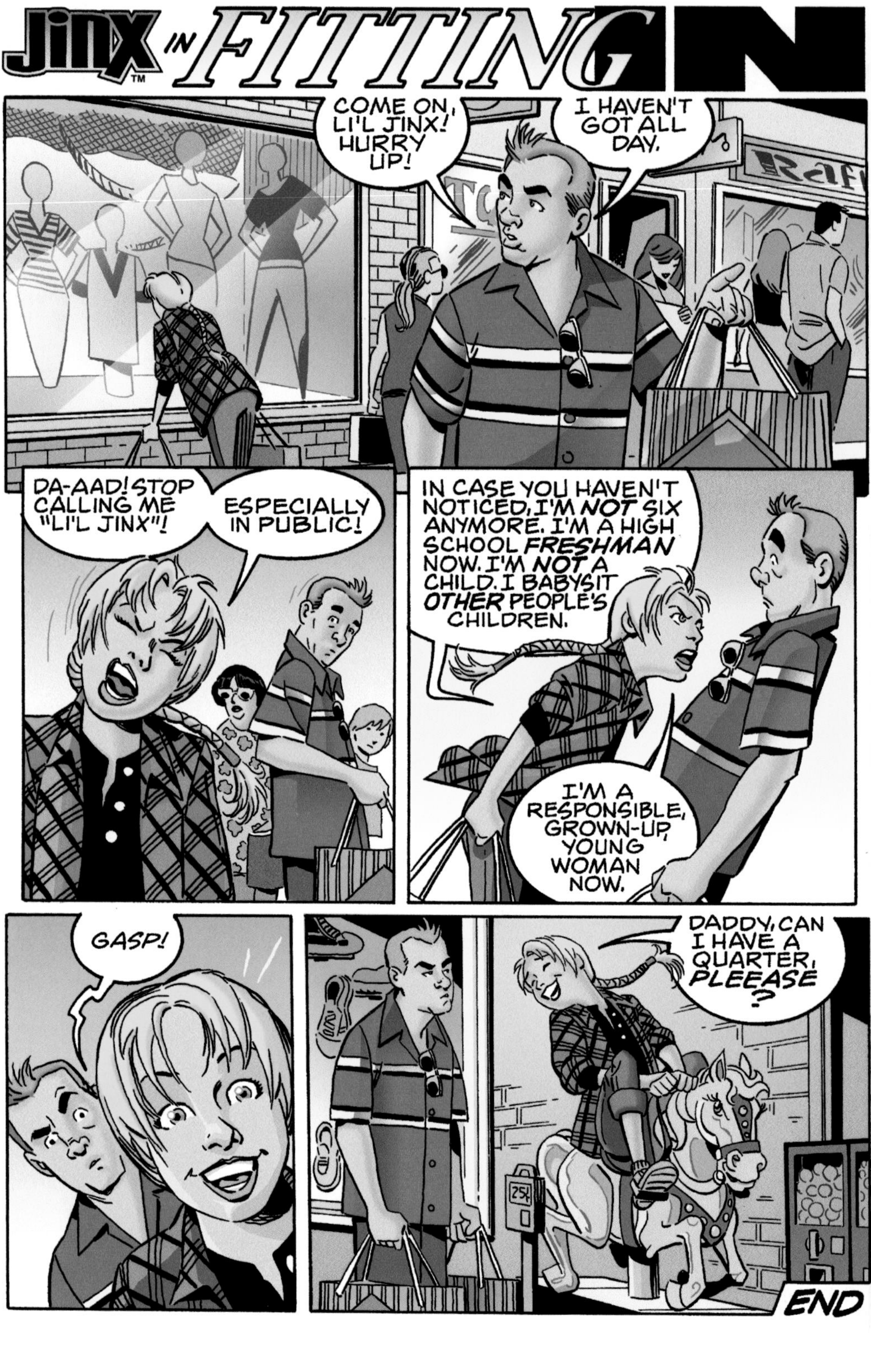
JINX™ IN FITTING IN
COME ON, LI'L JINX! HURRY UP!
I HAVEN'T GOT ALL DAY.
DA-AAD! STOP CALLING ME "LI'L JINX"!
ESPECIALLY IN PUBLIC!
IN CASE YOU HAVEN'T NOTICED, I'M NOT SIX ANYMORE. I'M A HIGH SCHOOL FRESHMAN NOW. I'M NOT A CHILD. I BABYSIT OTHER PEOPLE'S CHILDREN.
I'M A RESPONSIBLE, GROWN-UP, YOUNG WOMAN NOW.
GASP!
DADDY, CAN I HAVE A QUARTER, PLEEASE?
25¢
END

JINX™ in IT'S COMPLICATED

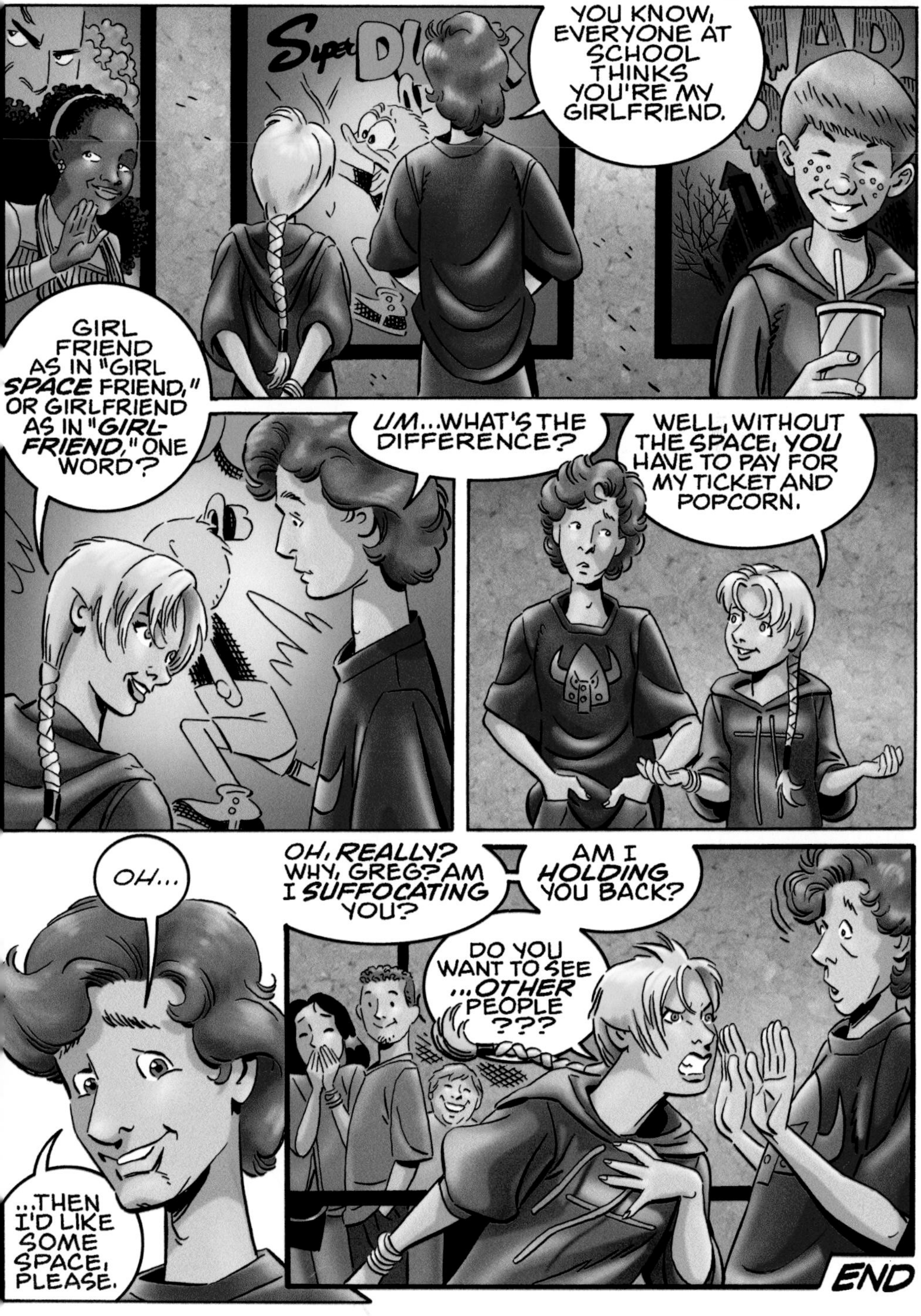
YOU KNOW, EVERYONE AT SCHOOL THINKS YOU'RE MY GIRLFRIEND.
GIRL FRIEND AS IN "GIRL *SPACE* FRIEND," OR GIRLFRIEND AS IN "*GIRLFRIEND*," ONE WORD?
UM...WHAT'S THE DIFFERENCE?
WELL, WITHOUT THE SPACE, *YOU* HAVE TO PAY FOR MY TICKET AND POPCORN.
OH...
...THEN I'D LIKE SOME SPACE, PLEASE.
OH, *REALLY*? WHY, GREG? AM I *SUFFOCATING* YOU?
AM I *HOLDING* YOU BACK?
DO YOU WANT TO SEE ...*OTHER* PEOPLE???
END

JINX™ in FRENEMY OF THE STATE

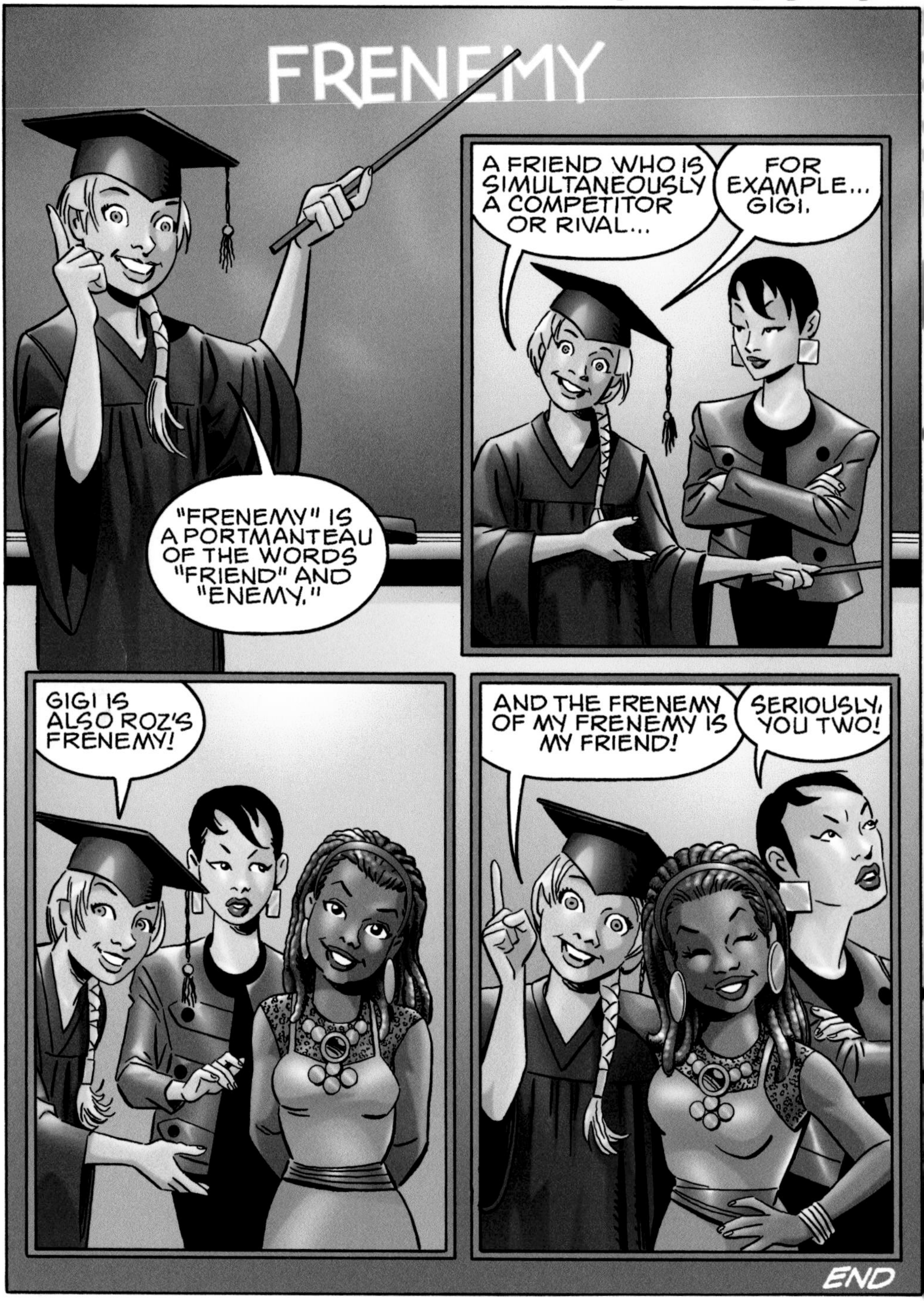
FRENEMY
"FRENEMY" IS A PORTMANTEAU OF THE WORDS "FRIEND" AND "ENEMY."
A FRIEND WHO IS SIMULTANEOUSLY A COMPETITOR OR RIVAL...
FOR EXAMPLE... GIGI.
GIGI IS ALSO ROZ'S FRENEMY!
AND THE FRENEMY OF MY FRENEMY IS MY FRIEND!
SERIOUSLY, YOU TWO!
END

JINX in THE Dating GAME

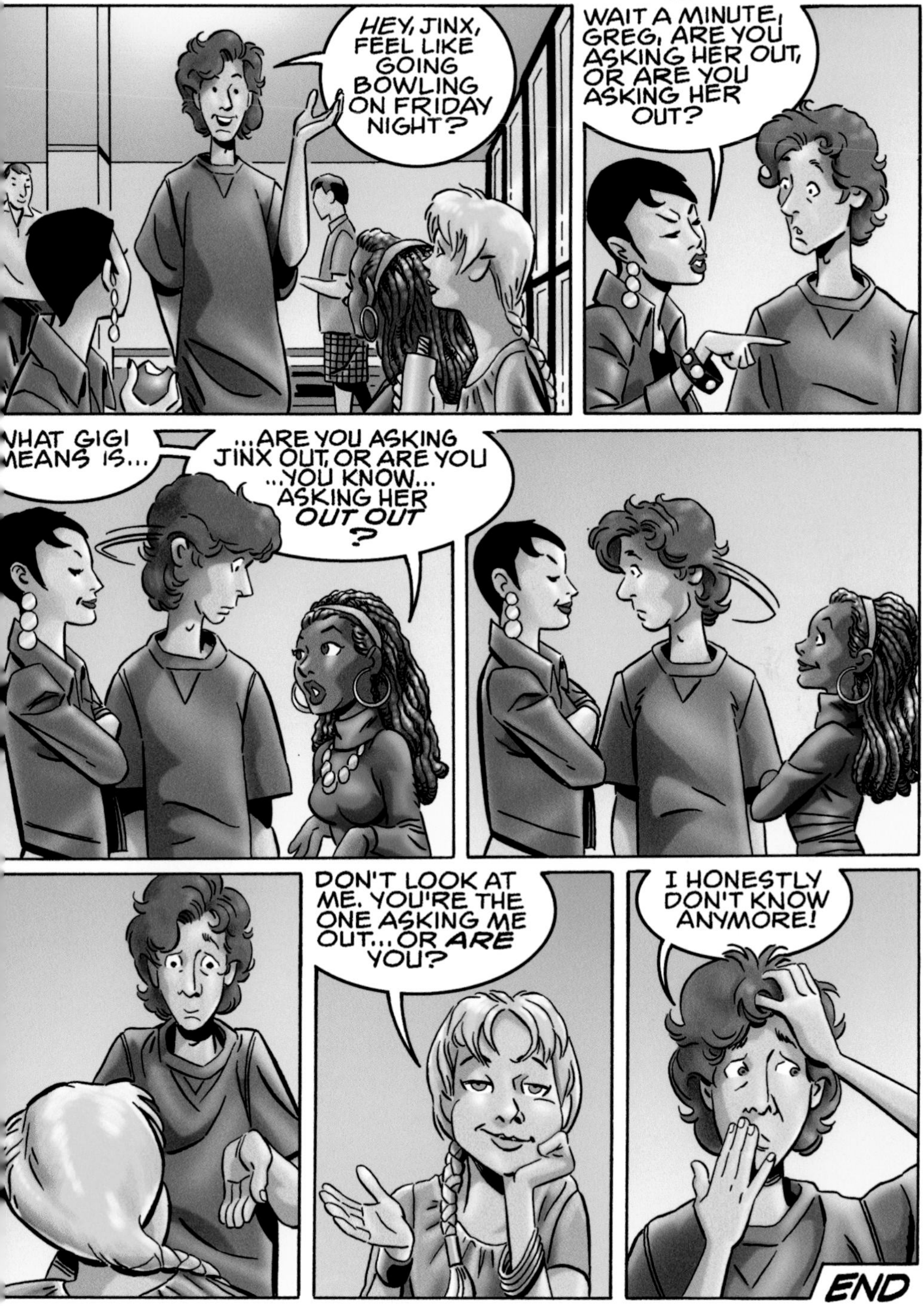
HEY, JINX, FEEL LIKE GOING BOWLING ON FRIDAY NIGHT?
WAIT A MINUTE, GREG, ARE YOU ASKING HER OUT, OR ARE YOU ASKING HER OUT?
WHAT GIGI MEANS IS...
...ARE YOU ASKING JINX OUT, OR ARE YOU ...YOU KNOW... ASKING HER OUT OUT?
DON'T LOOK AT ME. YOU'RE THE ONE ASKING ME OUT... OR ARE YOU?
I HONESTLY DON'T KNOW ANYMORE!
END

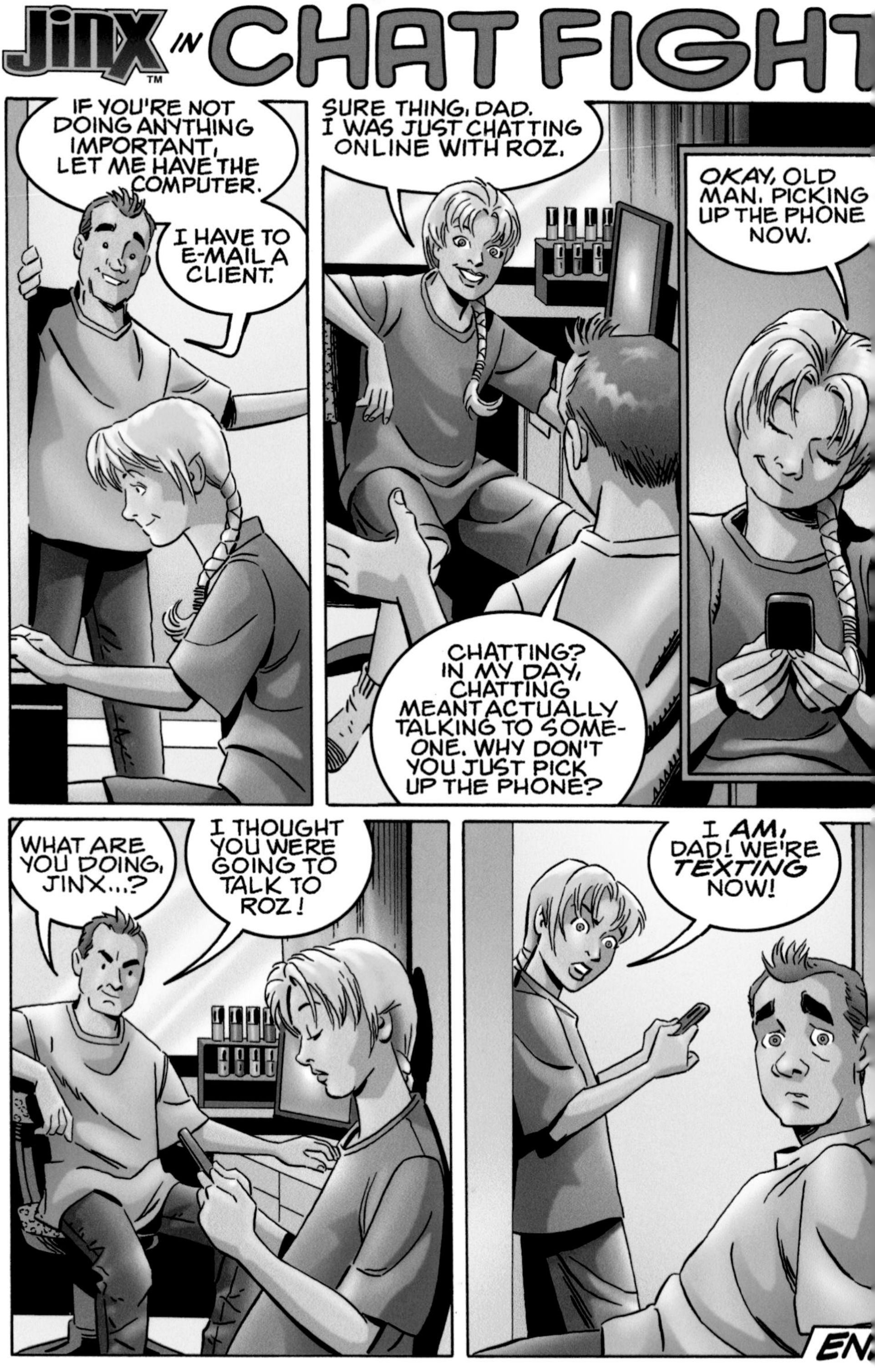

JINX IN CHAT FIGHT
IF YOU'RE NOT DOING ANYTHING IMPORTANT, LET ME HAVE THE COMPUTER.
I HAVE TO E-MAIL A CLIENT.
SURE THING, DAD. I WAS JUST CHATTING ONLINE WITH ROZ.
CHATTING? IN MY DAY, CHATTING MEANT ACTUALLY TALKING TO SOME-ONE. WHY DON'T YOU JUST PICK UP THE PHONE?
OKAY, OLD MAN. PICKING UP THE PHONE NOW.
WHAT ARE YOU DOING, JINX...?
I THOUGHT YOU WERE GOING TO TALK TO ROZ!
I AM, DAD! WE'RE TEXTING NOW!

the end

... for now!

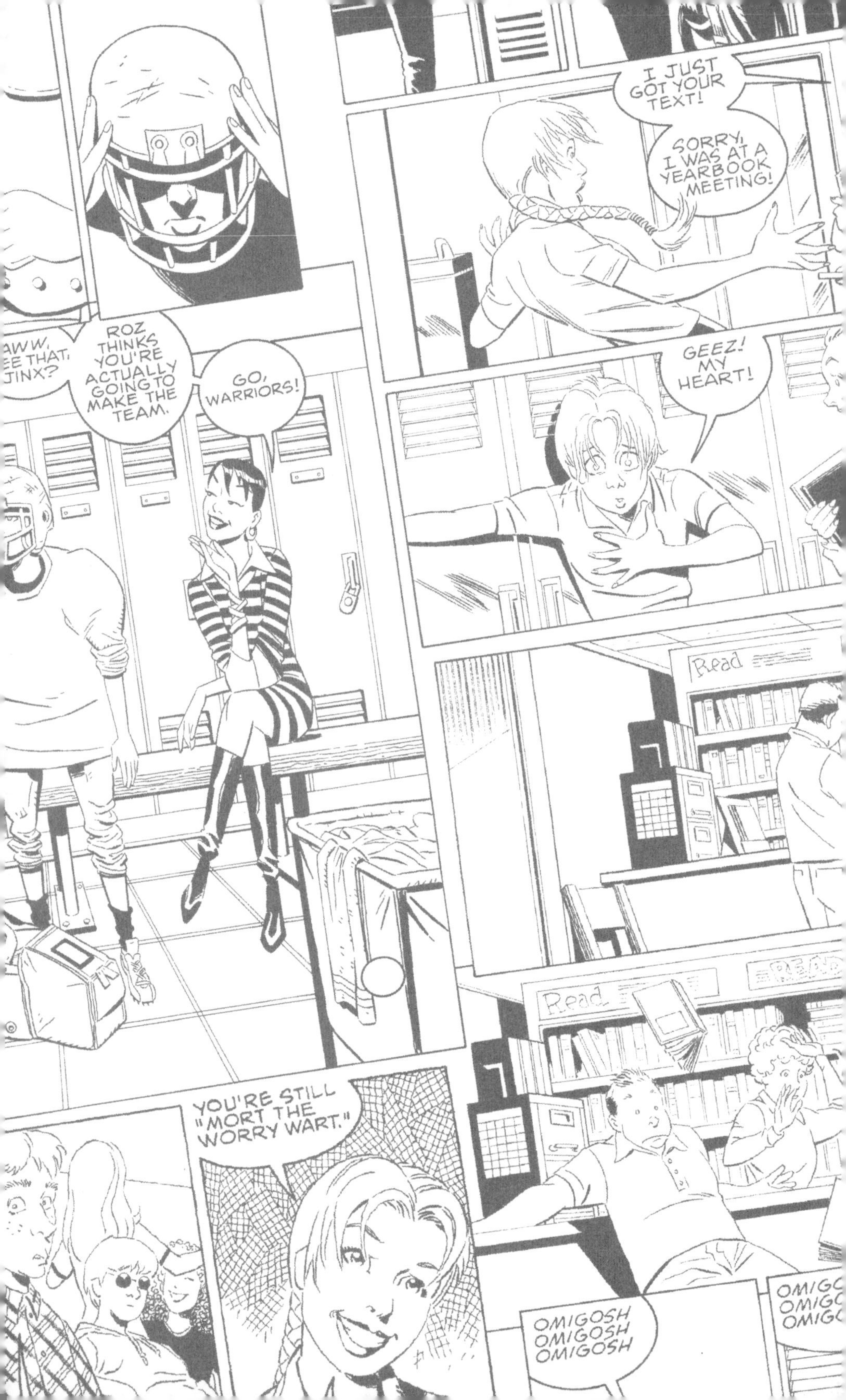
I JUST GOT YOUR TEXT!
SORRY, I WAS AT A YEARBOOK MEETING!
AWW, SEE THAT, JINX?
ROZ THINKS YOU'RE ACTUALLY GOING TO MAKE THE TEAM.
GO, WARRIORS!
GEEZ! MY HEART!
Read
Read
YOU'RE STILL "MORT THE WORRY WART."
OMIGOSH OMIGOSH OMIGOSH